Orchards *of* Almonds

DONALD JUNKINS

iUniverse, Inc.
Bloomington

Orchards of Almonds

iUniverse books may be ordered through booksellers or by contacting:

iUniverse
1663 Liberty Drive
Bloomington, IN 47403
www.iuniverse.com
1-800-Authors (1-800-288-4677)

Because of the dynamic nature of the Internet, any Web addresses or links contained in
this book may have changed since publication and may no longer be valid. The views
expressed in this work are solely those of the author and do not necessarily reflect the
views of the publisher, and the publisher hereby disclaims any responsibility for them.

Any people depicted in stock imagery provided by Thinkstock are models,
and such images are being used for illustrative purposes only.

Certain stock imagery © Thinkstock.

Cover by Kaimei Zheng

Cover quotation by Allen Josephs, author of *White Wall of Spain* and
Ritual and Sacrifice in the Corrida: The Saga of Cesar Rincon

ISBN: 978-1-4502-9925-1 (pbk)
ISBN: 978-1-4620-0652-6 (cloth)
ISBN: 978-1-4502-9926-8 (ebk)

Printed in the United States of America

iUniverse rev. date: 3/25/2011

For Gerry Hardesty
—and in memory of Ben Franklin, John and Ruth Jaeckel, and Bob Nedry

Orchards *of* Almonds

Book One

Chapter I

I DROVE TO CALIFORNIA at the beginning of July in the early sixties and settled temporarily, I thought, in the northern valley town of Chico. I was taking a vacation from an unpleasantness in Detroit in order to settle a small inheritance from a great aunt who left me a dilapidated old house on the outskirts of Chico. On the way I visited an old friend in Wallace, Idaho whom I knew from a summer job in Coeur d'Alene ten years earlier, and whose daughter had lived in Chico. He said that there are other places in northern California to live but Chico is as good as any, hot in the summer but nice in the fall. It's also a lively town known mostly for the college, but bristling with businessmen on the make and a lot of socially active young married types who take politics seriously. He said that Chico had two other things that described but didn't necessarily distinguish it, the largest oak tree in the world and California's most conservative newspaper, the *Valley Advocate*. This sounded good to me because I had drawn occasional political cartoons for a Detroit weekly, and written a few unsigned editorials for three small western chain papers after getting out of college. I thought my friend was finished describing my anticipated temporary residence, but then he said, "And it's close enough to the Sacramento River for a couple hours steelhead fishing in the early evening, and Paradise is only a half hour into the Sierras a few miles to the east."

"Paradise?" I said.

"That's it," he said, breaking the last Hamms' beer from our sixpack, "It was called Pair of Dice after the gold rush days but the respectables changed the pronunciation when the town got old enough to have a senior citizenry. When they light the smudge pots in the almond orchards in February, the soot hangs over the valley like black wool. I looked down on it once from one of those scenic lookouts—it was eerie, impressive in a strange way. The next day I had to drive down into it on my way north and had to put on my windshield wipers for the soot. Without those smudge pots and the windmills blowing the air around, the almond blossoms would freeze."

"I guess I'll miss it, I won't be there that long," I said.

A few days later I found myself sitting in my car about forty miles east of the atomic proving grounds in Washington state, listening to a Bob Newhart record on the radio with my engine hood up. My Nash motor had overheated and the engine block cracked and I had no water or radiator fluid. An old man in overalls pulled up beside me in a '53 Chevy and offered me a ride. He took me to a filling station where the owner sent a one-armed teenage mechanic in an old pickup and a piece of tow chain to get another friend and retrieve my car. The overalls man said his dinner was waiting and I thanked him as he eased away toward some nearby hills.

About an hour later the teenager drove in, pulling my car behind. His girl friend was driving my car. The teenager puzzled over my problem for fifteen or twenty minutes and asked me a few spaced questions while he poured sealing cement into the radiator. His girl friend poked around under my hood, touching things with her fingers.

"You say you were running hot before it blew and you had plenty of water?" he said.

"Couldn't calm her down," I said. "She boiled over the first time and I filled her up and then she ran just below the red line for four or five hours."

"Nash automobiles aint no damn good anyway," he said. "I don't mean nuthin personal by it, that's just my assessment."

"No offense," I said.

I walked around the side of the station and found the men's room. When I came back he and his girlfriend both had their heads under the hood. They were talking, then they both lifted their heads and looked at each other. The boy looked at me.

"You know what, mister? I know your problem."

He unscrewed the radiator cap and put it on the battery, then walked into the open mechanic's area and got a tool from a drawer on the back side of the oil pit.

"Thermostats!" he said, working over the radiator.

He held up the thermostat. "You know what this is good for?"

"I haven't a clue," I said as he turned to face an expansive sunburnt field cluttered with an old axle and several used tires. He threw the thermostat about seventy yards.

"Well, he'd have been out at second base," I said.

"Damn right," he said, grinning.

"Lapith's arm's just fine," his girl friend said with conviction, and Lapith twirled her long blonde pigtail around one of his fingers.

My overalls friend eased back into the station and asked if we'd solved the problem. He had pulled up to the pumps and left his motor running. I noted the black exhaust puffing from his tailpipe.

"The first part anyway," I said.

"My wife sent me back to bring you home for dinner. There's no eatin place for some miles. Can you drive that ashcan yet?"

"Yeah, he can drive to your house, Uncle Bobby, if he keeps it down, but I don't have one of them Nash thermostats, and if he goes much further tomorra he'll blow out that block sealer sure as gas burns." Looking at me, he said, "I can call now and get one sent over in the morning, but it'll cost you a dollar or two."

"You mean like twenty bucks? I said.

"On one side or t'other of it. Probably less. The bugger don't cost much but my friend's got to drive it here's the problem," he said.

"Well," I said to Uncle Bobby, "looks like you've got a supper guest."

"OK, foller me," he said. "It's only beans and some side ham, but we got plenty, and fresh biscuits up the gooch."

I turned to tell the mechanic to make the call, but he already had the phone propped between his shoulder and his left ear, and he was dialing with the middle finger of his good right hand.

I followed Uncle Bobby for six or seven miles before we turned off on a dirt road toward some low rising hills and another ten minutes to a small farm with a water windmill turning slowly and a small house under a stand of cottonwood trees. Several steers grazed in the fields. We parked and a woman met us at the screen door, drying her hands in her apron.

"He doesn't have a lick of sense sometimes," she said, laughing, "you should a been here forty-five minutes ago, the first time." She was small, with narrow shoulders, and her hair was done in a pug in the back. She wore a white apron embroidered with blue and yellow daisies. She offered her hand.

"Thank you. I'm much obliged. I'm sure glad to be here."

"He might's well stay over, Sadie, Lapith can't get a part till tomorra."

"Come on in, my name's Sarah. You'll stay over, then. We're ready to eat but you can freshen yourself in the bathroom right off'n that hallway there, if you're a mind to."

I ate the baked beans with Bobby and Sarah, and later stayed the night. It was too warm to eat in the kitchen where Sarah had been baking, and she had set up a card table on the screened-in porch, but it was almost as warm out there. The yellow hills nearby were soft in the early evening sunshine, and an imperceptible breeze barely ruffled the leaves of the cottonwood trees. Petunias of several colors grew in a small flower garden beside the steps, and hollyhocks brushed against the bottoms of the screens next to where we ate.

Bobby and Sarah didn't talk during the meal, and it was pleasant to be in a quiet place with the wisps of cotton dropping out of the green overarching tree. They didn't know who I was or where I came from or what I'd done and left undone somewhere else, and they didn't care.

Halfway through the meal, Bobby dished himself a second helping of the hot baked beans, and cut off another piece of salt pork. Then he took out his handkerchief and wiped his forehead and the back of his neck.

"Eatin sure is hot work," he said.

Around noon the next day I drove away from the filling station with a new thermostat, and the teenage mechanic waved his ball player's arm at me as I left.

In Oregon I followed the watershed of the Columbia River for a while and kept my eye on the temperature gauge on the dashboard. It held steady between normal and the red zone, and I left the Columbia and drove south through the Willamette Valley and crossed the mountains into California. Mt. Lassen stayed off to my left for a long time.

I slept that night in a small motel in Happy Camp. My room was wainscotted with thin, shellacked strips of pine, and a calendar with a Vermont farm scene was thumbtacked to the wall beside a window. Outside the window there was a dropoff and I could see a body of water in the distance. I went for a walk along the road and stopped in a railroad car diner for a coffee and a piece of strawberry rhubarb pie.

In the morning I went back to the diner and ate one of those western breakfasts with fried potatoes and pancakes and what the menu called "the works." By eleven I was driving through Red Bluff, Senator Clare Engel's hometown. An article on the front page of yesterday's morning paper said he was dying, but I wasn't interested in politics and that fact didn't mean anything to me. I remembered it though, as I drove through town because my Idaho friend told me that I should forget my troubles and lose myself in California politics.

In mid afternoon of July 4th, I drove through a long stand of eucalyptus trees on route 99 South, and entered Chico. The temperature, I found out later, was 104 degrees.

Chapter Two

ACROSS FROM THE SQUARE town park shaded by giant elms and rimmed with orange trees whose dropped oranges dotted the edges of the four streets, the real estate office displayed window photos of ranch houses festooned with oleander, rice-paper trees, wisteria arbors and gardenia and camellia bushes. I had stopped on the edge of the college campus and asked a co-ed where the real estate office was. She had braided red hair and blue eyes and she bent toward my open passenger car window when I pulled up next to her.

"This is the Esplanade. Keep going for about three blocks. It's right down there, you can't miss it. If you get thirsty before you get there, stop in at the Brazen Onager, they've got great draft beer. Get the dark"

"Thanks. Maybe I will."

"Do it." She was walking again. "Only live once, you know," she called.

I waved and headed straight down the Esplanade. She had pronounced it like "lemon*ade*."

In my rear view mirror I could see that she was wearing a light blue cotton dress several inches above the knees and I thought of a story that my wife had given me to read the first year we were married, called "The Girls in Their Summer Dresses." A voice in my head warned me not to go there, and I concentrated on finding the real estate office.

Four people got up from their desks simultaneously when I entered. I held out my hand to the man and smiled at the three disappointed women behind him as democratically as I could. Two of them were knockouts, but I didn't need any knockouts. The man said, "Whatever it is, we can help," blinked, and by sucking air into the corner of his mouth made a little popping noise. He blinked and popped several more times as we began to talk and I thought he had something in his eyes and the corner of his mouth, but they were only his personal ticks. By the time I later signed a rental lease, I had to check myself to keep from imitating him. Tics do that to me. I had an older neighbor who came back from the Solomon Islands after the war who kept sucking air into the right corner of his mouth by making the same kind of popping noise, and after a weekend fishing trip to Maine with him I was doing it too.

I told the real estate agent that I was looking for a house rental in a quiet neighborhood.

"And we've got it." Blink. Pop pop. "Furnished, I presume." Pop pop. Blink blink.

"Right."

Blink. Pop pop. "My car's parked right out in front." Blink. Pop pop.

It went like that.

Out in the street I asked if it was always this hot.

"Yup, sometimes hotter, sometimes not so hot. That's what I tell the newcomers, sometimes hotter, sometimes not so hot. Better to kid than commiserate. When you see the house I've got for you, you'll feel cool in a second."

Three hours and several hundred blinks later I signed a three month lease. We had looked at seven houses, and for the first six I never got out of the car. I liked the seventh and walked around and then checked inside. It would cost me $117 a month, all three in advance, and another $117 for the people my man worked for who had given him the blinks. The house was on Violet Lane, and it had all the California landscaping specials, including the camellias, gardenias, grape arbor, bamboo, giant roses, and Japanese rice paper trees. It even had an orange tree, lemon tree, and grapefruit tree in the back yard with a high, redwood fence, and on the north side of the house, a lonely looking, scrawny olive tree that I couldn't see unless I looked out the bathroom window.

The backyard grass was dichondra, and Blinky warned me that by August 15th it would turn brown from lack of rain unless I kept my hose running all the time. If I didn't mind the snails hidden in the rice paper that squiggled over the grass at night, leaving a silvery trail, I could have escargot at my pleasure.

"Most people sprinkle arsenic pellets around to shrivel up the snails, but then you have to pick 'em up anyway. Blink blink. Pop. "Right?" Blink.

"Right. Where do I sign?"

Back in his office for the paper work, he directed me to the Hotel Oaks where I could stay the night. It would take them a day to get the house cleaned. I told him I didn't mind a little dust, it looked fine to me when we walked through it, and if it was all the same to him, I'd just go over and move in.

"House rules. We have to hire a cleaning lady on the rentals. Same's the termite-spraying for sales, it's in the contract. State laws and all that. We can get it done tomorrow and you can move in the next day. Shall I call the Oaks and reserve a room for tonight?" I'm leaving out the blinks and the little air pops at the corner of his mouth, but they were there.

"Sure."

I circled the town square with its freshly dropped oranges, drove two blocks north and turned left. Another two blocks and the hotel was right where he said it would be.

One block over, the campus of Chico State College began. From my room I could see the brick buildings with the curved tile roofs, and huge trees everywhere, looming over the deep green, watered grass. Between two gigantic pines I could see athletic fields in the distance. Ivy covered parts of the old, Spanish style buildings. Back east, my Detroit friend told me that Chico State was a party school, and I remembered my blue-eyed red headed guide on the lemonade Esplanade.

I changed out of my sweaty jersey and put on a short-sleeved cotton shirt and walked several blocks to the Brazen Onager pub. Outside the entrance, overhead, a large brass donkey looked pleased with himself. Well, I thought, I might as well have the first brew of my California period in the Brass Ass, and went in.

Inside, it was dark and cool. The bar extended along the whole right side of the room, and heavy wooden tables were spaced solidly around the shiny, shellacked oak pillars that reached to the twelve-foot ceiling.

I sat at the bar. "A friend recommended your draft beer," I said to the blonde, wavy-haired bartender wearing a sleeveless football jersey. I was thinking of the redhead.

"You got a driver's license?" he said, looking at his hands.

I thought he might be kidding. I hadn't been carded for fifteen years.

"You're flattering me," I said.

"Maybe so. You got an I.D.?"

"I'm thirty-five years old," I said, with an obvious edge in my voice, knowing I was being stupid.

"Mac, you could be sixty-five for all I know. You want a brew, flash your card."

He looked at me and I looked at him. I knew I had lost. I took out my wallet and gave him my driver's license. He took it and looked at it. He nodded his head and dropped the driver's license on the bar in front of him where I had to reach for it. Standing in front of several long wooden draft handles he tilted one of them and drew a dark beer until the foam hit the top, then left it to settle, moving to the sink to lift wet glasses and place them on the wooden knobbed drying-rack.

I was thinking how I would like to ruffle his wavy blonde hair and start something, when I remembered a story I once read about western town jails. The warrant was right in front of me, and all I had to do was start something. The kid in the sleeveless football jersey had pretty good biceps. I could see that he enjoyed profiling his upper arm as he lowered the wooden draft beer handle. Three times he topped off the beer, letting the foam settle, and placed the tall mug of beer with its inch of pure white head in front of me. "One seventy-five," he said, looking away from me toward the group of college kids entering through the door.

I sipped the beer and then took a large swallow. I was watching the wavy blonde kid, waiting to nod my head in approval of the taste of the beer, but he had looked away from the new arrivals, as if the person he was looking for wasn't among them, and he ignored me.

I was still unnerved by the carding incident, and looked at the TV above the bar at the other end. Kennedy was having a press conference. He was coming to the Whiskeytown dam in two weeks.

I remembered the night before Kennedy was elected. I was in Boston on business and I called an old friend from graduate school. He was still a graduate student and his wife restored paintings at the Gardner Museum where they lived in the old carriage house. He met me in the Eliot Lounge and we were having a drink when he reminded me that Kennedy was in town to motorcade from Cambridge to Back Bay and then to Faneuil Hall near Quincy Market where he would make his last TV speech of the campaign. My friend said the motorcade would go down Boylston and turn up Tremont. We looked at our watches and my friend said we could still make it. We were going to take the subway from Copley but the station was jammed with people so we walked over to the entrance of the Tremont MTA station and stood in the cold, slapping our gloved hands together like everyone else.

It was like a crowd at Fenway Park. Everyone was excited and friendly. We waited a long time and then the black cars were coming up Boylston Street and everyone was on tiptoes and jumping up to see if they could see Kennedy coming. Several big Cadillacs and Lincolns went by and someone yelled "Here he comes." The cars were moving very fast. I was on tiptoes and people were yelling "Jack, Jack!" And then he passed us, sitting up on the back of an open-air Lincoln in his blue navy topcoat, smiling and waving his hand slightly, the way he did. I jumped in the air and yelled "Kennedy!" And then he was gone, around the corner and up Tremont Street.

But I was in Chico, California. I couldn't hear the TV at the end of the bar, and new arrivals were laughing and smoking cigars and ordering food. I asked my bartender friend if he could turn up the volume on the TV, just a bit.

He shrugged and walked down the bar and did something on the back counter that switched the picture that rolled vertically for awhile and fixed on a Roadrunner cartoon. The slapstick voices were loud and clear. The kid bartender came back and said, "When the crowd starts coming in, the sound goes down again when it gets too noisy." He ran his hand over the top and back of his hair, primping it to make sure it was setting just right.

"I was watching Kennedy's press conference," I said.

He shrugged and walked back to the counter and did something that changed the station. Pierre Salinger was talking. I listened for a while.

I asked the kid how far the Whiskeytown dam is from Chico.

"Too far to go to see Kennedy," he said.

I heard that California is Kennedy country," I said. I felt like baiting him.

"California went Nixon. We count absentee ballots out here." The kid walked away.

"When does the crowd arrive?" I called to him. He was at the other end of the bar, pinching the skin on one of his thumbs.

"When it gets here," he said without turning his head or looking up.

"I wasn't planning to come back when they got here," I said, "just curious."

"Curiosity killed the cat," he said, concentrating on his thumb.

I debated whether to push it any further. Part of me still wanted to pick a fight with him. I drained my beer, slid off my stool, and left. After the first swallow, I hadn't enjoyed the beer.

Chapter Three

TWO WEEKS LATER I drove to Whiskeytown with a new friend I heard about later that first night in the Oaks bar. I originally decided not to go to Whiskeytown after my encounter with the young bartender in the Brass Ass because young conservative punks bring out the worst in me and I didn't want to give in to the part of me that felt the urge to prove something. Better save it, I might get a cartoon out of it, I thought as I left the bar.

I ate dinner alone in the Hotel Oaks then walked around the campus of Chico State for an hour. It had cooled down to about 95 degrees and there were a couple small groups of summer students sitting on the grass.

Summer school students have a different look about them, I thought. They seem older, I decided, but knew after I thought about it that it wasn't it. I was thinking of my own summer students when I taught once, for the money, at Clark University in Massachusetts as I rounded the back corner of the old Spanish style administration building and saw several modernist sculptures in a park-like terrace outside a glass-fronted structure that had to be the art building. Inside one of the spun glass doors two students were molding clay. One of them was a co-ed in white shorts with her head down. I thought it might be my redhead, but it wasn't, and I realized suddenly that my checking out the campus had an ulterior motive. I decided to reverse that gear, and walked back to the Oaks.

Later in the bar I met a local almond rancher who bought me a drink when he found out I was originally from Boston and had drawn a few political cartoons for money. He was thick-necked and burly, somewhere between husky and fat. He had little blue eyes that twinkled when he was amused, and once when he laughed I saw the space between his front teeth. When I got to know him better I realized that the twinkling was always ironic. When something genuinely pleased him that wasn't ironic, the twinkle wasn't there.

This night he was wearing an open-necked rainbow colored silk sport shirt, the bottom two buttons of which were missing, exposing the lower part of his belly. He didn't seem to care about his belly or its exposure. He reminded me of the big-bellied cartoon character in Smiling Jack who was always popping buttons off his too tight shirt, but before we parted I knew he was no cartoon character. His name was John Jaeckel, and the thing he cared the most about after almonds was Democratic politics. I told him that it was refreshing to meet a Democrat who was neither an Irishman nor an academic liberal.

"We got 'em," he said.

"Irish Democrats?"

"College liberals. They're crawling all over the place."

I told him I was looking for an inheritance tax appraiser.

"We got them too. One lives in Paradise and the other in Marysville. They'll both be in town on Thursday night for the Democratic Club meeting."

Then I got an unsolicited twenty-minute lecture on the inheritance tax system in California, and how it was part of state politics.

"Did you ever hear of Alan Cranston?" he asked.

"Never."

"You will, unless you don't read the newspaper or watch the news on TV. He's the next Democratic senator from California, unless Clare Engel dies in office. That could happen."

"I don't know much about California politics."

"Cranston's the state controller. He appoints all the state's inheritance tax appraisers, and they all owe him. He's building his campaign for senator around them. We've got a grass roots system out here that works. Democratic clubs all over the state, state nominating conventions."

"But not the Republicans?"

"They're not organized."

"I heard you've got an interesting local paper."

"That fucking rag?"

"Which appraiser should I get?"

"Bob Camion. He lives in Paradise, but he's in here all the time. I'm surprised he's not here tonight. He's an old timer from Minnesota who grew up with the Farmer-Labor Party of Bob LaFollette. Grass roots Democratic politics from the beginning. If you like believers, you might like him. The other guy is Will Curling, not a bad guy but he's always in trouble because of his dick. He comes to club meeting to show his face around.

We closed the bar at one a.m., and John said he'd see me around.

Chapter Four

THE NEXT DAY I found the house I inherited. Blinkey from the real estate office drove me out there in mid morning. It wasn't much. Nineteenth century Spanish wooden. The lawyer who got in touch with me in Detroit was right. It was actually a wreck. He said that my aunt hadn't lived in it for the last five years before she died, and the termites had found it.

We got out of the car and Blinkey lit a cigarette, took one puff and when I walked around the house he got back into the car. I walked up onto the porch, stepped on several termites and gave it up. They were on the posts that held up the second balcony, going up and down in two lines, busy as miners.

I unlatched the screen door and opened it and it fell away from the doorjamb. The screws had rotted out of the hinges.

I used the key the lawyer had given me and went inside, took one look and left.

The house was spitting distance from the north side of the college campus. I remembered that my aunt's second husband taught chemistry there before he died of pneumonia, that northern California greeting for easterners. He was from Ohio Northern University and went west to get his full professorship. He got it all right, within three years. My aunt stayed on and never re-married.

I dropped off Blinkey, checked out of the Oaks, and walked around the back yard of my new house while the vacuum cleaner purred inside. I counted 138 snails up inside the curled rotten leaves of one of my rice paper trees. I was peeling a grapefruit when the cleaning lady came out on the patio pushing back a wisp of hair from her face, and told me it was OK, I could go in now, she was finished.

"Thank you."

"I checked the air-conditioner. It works. You can turn it off if you don't want it on."

"Thanks."

"You need some kitchen stuff. I'll go get it if you want; otherwise, I'll call in."

"I can get it. Thanks a lot. Is there a food store around here?"

"There's a Safeway about five blocks over, across First and down Manzanita. Go right at the corner and take a left at the lights. You'll come right to it."

"Do you know where the famous oak tree is?"

"Every soul in California knows the Hooker Oak. They made the picture Robin Hood there with Errol Flynn. It's ten minutes from here, in Bidwell Park."

"Maybe I'll drive over later."

"You know how to get to the park?"

"I think so."

"Just keep on Manzanita, it goes right by the park after the new houses. Go left on the first road and you'll bump right into it."

I tipped her ten dollars and she left. She was driving an old Borgward.

I turned off the air-conditioner and checked the brick fireplace. Air conditioners make going outside worse. I wondered if I'd ever use the fireplace. I went out in the yard and looked at the redwood fence. It went three quarters of the way around the house. I wished I had gotten Jaeckel's telephone number.

In the front yard I lifted a red camellia blossom and smelled it, to no avail. I leaned close to a gardenia on the bush next to it and that smell brought back the Rainbow Girls dance in the seventh grade, as always. Only the water lilies in the cove at the lake can beat that smell, I thought. I saw the mistletoe hanging from the middle limbs of the ash tree in the middle of the front lawn. I walked over and reached up and touched it.

Later that afternoon I parked my car at the end of a dirt road on a bluff overlooking a bend in the Sacramento River and edged down the bank with a spinning rod I had bought in town. Three fishermen were coming up. I asked them how the steelhead were biting, and they said they hadn't had a hit in three hours.

"Good luck to you," the tall one said as we passed. He was wearing sunglasses and an army fatigue jacket with large trout streamers on a piece of purple flannel sewed to his breast pocket. The other two were short and wore orange and black baseball caps.

I waded out into the river about twenty yards and the water got shallower over a pebbly shoal, just above my knees. It was cold, and sucked at my dungarees. I cast my aluminum lure downstream and held it in the current. My friend in Idaho had given it to me and said it would get me a steelhead. "It's got the action of a flatfish," he said, but it sinks if you don't keep it moving."

The three fishermen had stopped at the top of the bluff and were watching me fish the spot they had been fishing.

I could feel the action of my lure, wriggling against the current, the tip of my pole answering the pressure, nodding. I liked the feeling of the flashing lure far downstream where the steelhead coming up would see it long before they saw me. I could see the outline of the Coastal Range thirty miles off in the distance. This is far enough west, I thought. There are mountains on both sides of this valley and a beautiful river right down the middle, and I'm standing in the river in high summer. I reeled slowly, feeling the pull of the flat face of the lure against the rush of the downstream water, wobbling side-to-side, faster if I reeled faster. I slowed it down. I was in no hurry. I felt the pebbly bottom underneath my old sneakers and moved my feet to test the bottom, getting a good footing. I caught sight of my silvery lure flashing six inches beneath the surface ten yards downstream. I reeled slower.

Six feet in front of me I lost sight of the lure and immediately felt the weight of the hit. I raised my spinning rod high in the air, holding it with both hands. At the back of my head I could feel the eyes of the three fishermen standing on the bluff watchng me and I held my pole steady as the line poured off the spool. I turned my head to see if they were still there. They were there, and I felt foolish. The look was only bragging and I knew I didn't deserve this fish. I didn't look again, but I remembered that one of the short men had taken his cap off, and he was bald.

I stopped the first run about a hundred yards downstream, and worked him back halfway where he took off downstream again. He made two more runs and forty minutes later I had worked him toward the shore where he lay in the water, almost floating. I reached down, squeezed my thumb and first two fingers behind his head and walked the few feet to the banking.

The three fishermen had gone and I sat down in the brush on the bank with my steelhead and rested. I was alone with the river and the distant Coastal Range. The sun was afternoon silvery on the riffling water in front of me. After a while I waded out in the river, the water cold again against my legs. I fished for two hours without a strike.

That night, after returning to Safeway to buy a small jar of mayonnaise, peppercorns, rosemary, and olive oil, I ate half of one of the filets and covered the rest with wax paper for the refrigerator. I wanted to get Jaeckel's number from information but my phone wasn't connected yet. I drove to the Hotel Oaks and smiled at my luck when I saw him sitting at the bar next to a man with thinning gray hair and steel-rimmed glasses. Their drinks were on the bar in front of them and the gray haired man was laughing. Jaeckel was smiling, and his small beady eyes were flashing.

"I'm in luck," I said, sitting on the stool next to Jaeckel.

"This is Patrick Henry," he said. "It's not a joke."

"Yes, it's my real name, "the man said, offering his hand, still laughing.

"Bill Armature," I said, and we shook hands.

Patrick Henry taught political science at the college, and I learned later that although he was as rabid a Democrat as Jaeckel, he was soft sell. He liked the game of politics and accepted winning and losing with an air of resigned gamesmanship. At the bar that day, Jaeckel said that some of Pat's best friends were Reagan and Goldwater people, and when he said it, his eyes twinkled. Pat looked at Jaeckel and said, "Hell John, how do you know I'm not a mole?"

Jaeckel was slightly suspicious of Pat because Pat taught at the college, and Pat thought Jaeckel's style was a little too cursory and dismissive, but he trusted Jaeckel, and he liked him.

When Jaeckel went to the men's room, I asked Pat if he knew Bob Camion.

"The Robert LaFollett of Butte County," Pat said. "Every Democrat in Butte County knows Bob Camion."

"I inherited a ramshackle mansion on the edge of the college campus and I need to get it appraised," I said.

"Not that old Spanish house near the new engineering building?"

"That's it. That's the one."

"You just had a windfall, boy. Willard Mooney has been trying to buy that property for four years."

"Who's he?"

"It's the one lot the trustees don't own and they want to put up a social science building over there to complete the building plan for the north perimeter of the campus. Mooney's the president of the college."

Jaeckel came back from the men's room and said he had to shove off.

"Me too," Pat said. "My wife thinks I'm somewhere else."

Jaeckel said, "Don't forget the Democratic Club meeting at Veterans' Memorial Hall, Thursday at eight o'clock, 220 Shasta."

After they left I had another Maker's Mark and then drove around town for awhile, down Broadway, around the central town park and the courthouse, back up Broadway, and up the Esplanade to Third where I turned right and followed it to Violet Lane, turning at the Hooker Oak School. I turned into my driveway wondering why people didn't pick up the fallen oranges on Broadway and around the city square.

Inside the house, I took a soft chair from the living room and put it out on the patio. Sitting under the grape arbor, I wasn't sleepy, and began mulling over what Pat Henry said about the old house being a windfall. After a while my eyes adjusted to the dark and I could distinguish the grapefruit and the lemons hanging in the trees across the lawn.

Chapter Five

AT THE DEMOCRATIC CLUB meeting I found Bob Camion. Two days later we looked at the old house together and he appraised it and did the paperwork. I told him what Pat said about the college wanting the property and he roared an expletive that came out somewhere between "Hah!" and "Oho!" It tickled him that he could save me some money on the appraisal if we acted before any negotiations with the college raised the property value of the house. We had a drink at the Oaks bar and he invited me to ride with him to Whiskeytown to see Kennedy dedicate the dam.

Northern California in early fall is hot and dry, and the blue cloudless sky repeats itself day after day. We drove by yellow fields with low flying hawks, and the low rounded foothills of the Sierras on our right were dotted with black spidery live oaks. Some of the rolling hills were laced with symmetrical stonewalls built in the nineteenth century by coolie labor. There were patches of orange California poppies on the sides of the road. People grew ice plants in small front yard gardens.

Camion didn't talk much, but I could tell he was excited. When he mentioned Jack Kennedy there was honest affection in his voice and he looked straight ahead and drove the car, seemingly oblivious of the conversation in the back seat. He was wearing a white shirt and tie and his thinning red hair was slicked back with a pomade that glistened as if he had just combed his hair with water. He drove with both hands on the wheel and grinned when something was said that amused him. If his amusement reached the higher plane of political passion, he would grunt "Hah!" and dip his head and swallow. He referred to the Democratic Party as "our party," and he called Kennedy "our young president." Camion chewed gum constantly, sometimes holding it in his front teeth and nibbling at it. I liked him from the very beginning. He was punctual, efficient, loyal, and distracted. In the three years that I would know him, he was a close friend, though I never got to know anything personal about him.

The other two in the car were club members who needed rides to Whiskeytown. Pearl Kennealy was honored to be in Camion's comfortable new car. She was a fiercely partisan Democrat, jolly, overweight, and tireless, and she wore a new, darkly colored dress. She sat in the back seat with a writer named Luke from the college, absorbing the landscape as we passed through Red Bluff and Redding. She relished every word that was said during the trip. Her husband Joe had stayed at home with two grandchildren so that she could see Kennedy. Pearl's married daughter had left the children and gone off with a plumber from Oroville. When Camion spontaneously erupted with

"This is a great day for Democrats!" Pearl purred, "I wouldn't miss it," and was embarrassed that she had nothing else to say.

Camion pointed out Mt. Lassen off to the right, and after passing the Whiskeytown city limits, turned off left toward the dam.

Four months later when Kennedy was shot in Dallas, I remembered the crowds this day in Whiskeytown, and the way the massive dam looked, curved and sculptured and new under the sun, and the president small on the platform, his voice clear over the loudspeakers, the road across the top of the dam with the elevated grandstand at one end, and the power station seven stories below looking like a miniature toy built by a giant with an Electra set, deep in the canyon with the water roaring through the lower invisible portals at twelve thousand gallons a minute.

We couldn't get any closer to the grandstand because of the mass of people, and the country seemed big that late morning as we looked at the dam with the red, white, and blue bunting draped along its top edge. Kennedy looked small, but the presidency seemed grand. Screw Nixon and all those people, I thought.

Kennedy was enjoying himself, reeling off the places in America with colorful names, Muskogee, Tippecanoe, Bird in Hand, Monongahela, and he gave the crowd their money's worth that day when all those who were there were Whiskeytowners for a couple hours.

We had met six more Chico Democrats at the historic marker approaching the dam site, and watched the ceremonies with them. Pat and Jaeckel were there with a tall, portly lawyer, a fat, jolly fellow named Jancey who ran the Chico art gallery; and Jaeckel's wife Ruth. Joan Jay Henry, Pat's wife, found us later at the buses going back to town. Pearl said, "Joan Jay, you beat all. You're always late."

Joan Jay was a tall, gangly brunette with a huge smile and a nervous, overcompensating laugh. When she found us she looked carefully at the group before glancing at Pat, as if she expected to see someone else. She said, "I was going to bring two of my students, but they never showed up and I couldn't find them. I thought I'd never get here." Joan Jay taught civics at Chico High School. She was laughing. When Joan Jay laughed, spit sometimes appeared at the corners of her mouth. Camion told me later that Pat was having an affair.

Jaeckel suggested that because of the crowd we ought to split up for lunch and meet later. The Redding Democratic Club was hosting a big clambake starting at four-thirty in the field across from the Elks' Club and we agreed to meet there.

Camion pulled my arm and said, "I want to show you something." I followed him through the crowd to the VIP bus lot where he showed a security guard a small yellow card he took from his tan seersucker suit coat.

The guard said, "There are two of you." Camion reached into his pocket again and found another card. The guard said "OK" and we went to a large, double decker bus with shade windows and a caption above the front windshield that said, "Alan Cranston."

When I met Cranston for the first time, I misjudged him. I liked him but bald politicians didn't impress me and Alan was bald. He was also friendly and compelling and open. He wanted to be a U.S Senator and he didn't pretend to hide that ambition. Outside the bus, he was surrounded by inheritance tax appraisers who knew Camion, and friends and Sacramento politicos who were already on the bandwagon. When Camion told Cranston that I was a newcomer from the East who played football in college, he said, "California politics needs people like you. I'd appreciate any help you could give me, we've got a huge job to do." Later I found out that he had been an English major at Stanford and he still held the over-fifty record for the 100-yard dash.

On the way to Camion's car I told him he needn't build me up, I had no political ambitions.

"I wasn't building you up, our party needs people like you."

"I only rented my house for three months."

"You never know."

"You got that extra VIP pass for me, didn't you?"

"Yup. Called Alan after that first Democratic Club meeting. Told him you are his next Butte County campaign manager."

"I don't even belong to the Democratic Party. The closest I could get to it would be in a cartoon. Hired pencils don't join political parties."

"What's a hired pencil?"

"I ghosted a few editorials back east when I got low on cash."

"Nobody belongs officially to the Democratic Party. You register as a Democrat and you vote the Democratic ticket. I knew you were a speech writer."

"I'm not a speech writer. I wrote editorials on the Chicopee water district and the Pittsfield town reservoir in Massachusetts."

"Water's the biggest political football in California right now. You're perfect. Think about it. I want you to meet someone else. Come on."

Thirty minutes later we found the car and drove through Whiskeytown a couple miles northeast where we turned off through a stand of walnut trees to a large sprawling ranch house shaded by tall ranging oaks and locust trees. The air was clear and the mountains seemed very close. I looked at the tops of the oak trees and they were absolutely still. Everything was quiet. Fifteen or twenty cars were parked along the post fence of a long corral. There was a barn and a yellow field stretching off to low brown hills. Reddish Hereford steers grazed in the field.

"I hope you like books and writers," Camion said as we approached the front door of the ranch house.

"I like some books," I said. "I don't know any writers."

The ranch belonged to Shirley Custerfield and her husband. They ran the Whiskeytown Democratic Club. Shirley was the president and her husband Wally was the treasurer. Wally bought and sold cattle and Shirley went to political conventions, according to Camion, and tried to stay out of trouble. She was best friends with Joan Jay Henry and they had shared hotel rooms in Sacramento and San Francisco and Los Angeles. Shirley knew all the gossip about Chico. She was a substitute teacher in Whiskeytown where she also taught civics. Shirley wasn't made to teach high school every day, but sometimes she took a few students to conventions where Joan Jay brought students. They had already made plans to take students to the Democratic state convention in San Diego in the spring.

I heard all this after I got inside the ranch, and also that Shirley and Wally were hosting a reception for Eugene Burdick, a novelist who had written *The Ninth Wave*, a brawling political novel about a young, ambitious over-reacher in California politics, which I read a couple months later. I dipped into California Democratic politics in that book, and got Burdick's view of Jesse Unruh who walked barefoot into California from Oklahoma and was now the Speaker of the California Assembly.

At the door, Shirley said "Hi Bob Camion!" and hugged him as she gave me the smiling once-over. Bob introduced me and she said, "It's great you came," leading us into the kitchen and out into the patio where Burdick was talking. I chose a place to stand behind others also standing behind rows of occupied chairs, almost within reach of a long table spread with food and beer. I pondered whether to reach for a Hamms sitting in a bowl of ice, but Shirley was standing behind me, handing me a tall clear drink with ice and a red cherry on top.

"I hope you like gin and tonic," she said, "It's Tanqueray." The glass was ice cold and the frost melted on my fingers as I took it.

"You're very intuitive," I said. "Much obliged."

"On me. Enjoy," she said, and came back a minute later with what looked like a scotch or bourbon and water for Camion. He nodded as he took it, concentrating on the speaker.

I watched Burdick as he talked, but I was thinking how nice it was to be in a group of people who didn't know or care who I was, drinking a Tom Collins in a ranch house on a fall afternoon in northern California. Someone had asked Burdick to read a passage from his book, and he was thumbing through pages, looking for something appropriate. Authors reading their own work bored me almost as much as actors reading poetry, and I didn't listen. Outside, the long corral was visible through the wide glass doors that led to a patio made of round sunken slabs of tree trunks beveled with crushed white granite. Three shiny black Arabian horses stood unmoving in the shade of a cottonwood tree.

I was feeling objective and disengaged. Burdick seemed straightforward as he read. He didn't play to the audience. When several women laughed out loud to show how with it they were, he never looked up. He looked the athletic type, solidly built, in good shape. I began studying him as a way of not getting caught up in his story. His hair was dark blonde, almost light brown, and he had brown eyes. He seemed to eschew the role of star guest, unlike the poets I'd heard read in the east who always seemed to accept their stardom easily. *Don't go there*, I thought.

Outside, one of the black shiny horses suddenly reared and whinnied, then settled down and nuzzled up to one of the other two, who stepped away.

I could see the darker outline of the Sierras beyond the rolling foothills. Soon it would snow in the high mountains. I thought of the Donner Party trying to reach the southern part of this valley before winter, more than a hundred years ago. In September they were still in the Utah desert.

I wonder what my daughter is doing. September is a nice month in Detroit.

As I was watching Burdick, Shirley took my empty glass and brought me another. She was a very good hostess.

Two years later, Burdick died of a heart attack on a tennis court. He collapsed, racing to the net, and died immediately.

Chapter Six

A COUPLE DAYS LATER I drove route 99 South to Sacramento to visit an old friend, now a senior editor at the *Sacramento Bee*. On the way I stopped at Marysville to meet Will Curling who had the inheritance tax papers for my aunt's house. He had seen them in Cranston's office and called me to ask if I wanted him to bring them to Chico rather than mail them. I said I was coming to Sacramento but he said he was coming north anyway. We agreed to meet in Marysville for lunch at a small bar called Delaney's on the northern outskirts of town and I found him waiting in his car in the parking lot. We drove out to the Sutter Buttes, a mountain formation in the center of the valley. He wanted to show me a new restaurant that featured happy hours starting at ten in the morning. It was eleven when I found him, and I didn't want to start the late afternoon that early, but I agreed to go with him.

The Buttes are a strange geological formation that rises in the middle of the Sacramento Valley, with its own population of wild animals, according to Curling, and its own set of local admirers. The restaurant was within several hundred feet of its almost vertical foothills. A long bar stretched the length of the pool and at one end three caddy-corner tables had been designed for swimmers who could sit on submerged stools and set their drinks on pastel blue and green fiberglass tables just above the water. There was a rounded glassed-in view of the nearby buttes, and overhead a glass roof lined with redwood timbers. The leaves of two massive walnut trees checkered the sun on the glass roof.

We sat down two tables from two blondes in two-piece bathing suits at one of the submerged stools. They were drinking something yellow over ice.

"What do you think?" Curling said. His half gray, half black hair needed a trim, and his face was pasty white. I decided that he ought to get some sun. Before I could answer, he said, "Classy, huh?"

"Nice place," I said.

"You mean it?" he asked. He was childlike and friendly. He really wanted me to like it, and I wanted to like it for his sake.

"Mermaids and happy hours, it's like the Caribbean," I said, lying.

"Yeah, it is, sort of, though I've never been to Bermuda."

I let it go, and ordered a bloody Mary. Curling ordered an onion gimlet.

"The god damndest thing happened to me in here last week," he said.

I knew he wanted to tell me a story, so I chewed the long piece of celery in my bloody Mary and waited.

"You want to hear about it?" he asked.

I wasn't sure whether I wanted to hear about it or not, but I heard myself saying, "Sure, what happened?"

Curling was looking at the mermaids as he started his story. They had ordered more yellow on ice and the waiter had brought it.

"It was the god damndest thing," he said, looking back at me, "right out of a novel. That guy Burdick could have written it."

"You read *The Ninth Wave?*" I asked.

"A girl read me some parts," he said. "It's all crap about the ninth ninth wave. I was at the beach where surfers hang out, something Del Rey, and we spent a whole morning counting real waves. We were looking out the window of a beach house on a water-bed. There's nothing to it."

"I've never surfed," I said.

He finished his gimlet and raised it at the waiter.

"This thing last week you wouldn't believe," he said.

I looked at him and waited.

"I'm sitting right here where you're sitting, and there's a dame sitting next to me and she's sipping a coke. She's young, but not too young, not a co-ed or anything. She's about your age, maybe a couple years younger. I wasn't staring or anything but I knew she was there and she knew I was there. She wasn't a knockout, but she wasn't a dog either. Appealing, you could say. It was the god damndest thing. You know what she did?"

I don't enjoy conversations where the other person forces you to make an obvious reply but I didn't want to hurt his feelings. "What?" I said.

"Well, she just turned, casual like, and looked at me and said, as calm as anything, "I'm in trouble, will you help me?""

Curling looked at me and I looked at him. He said, "What do you think she wanted?"

I thought for a minute but nothing came to my mind. I said, "I don't know.

"Take a guess, just for the hell of it."

I looked at the buttes and wondered what caused the glacier to dump them there. I looked back at Curling and said, "She wanted a loan."

"That's what I thought exactly. Good guess. Nope, that's not what she wanted. She eased over onto that stool there, next to me. She wasn't coming on to me, I didn't think, but she says, very calmly, 'I took a pill a half hour ago, and it's starting to work.' It's like we're talking about the rent or something, and she says, 'Do you know what LSD is?' I told her I'd heard of it. She says, 'It's starting to work.'"

Curling waited and looked at me. "Do you know anything about LSD?"

"I've heard of it," I said.

Curling laughed. "Can you believe it?"

I nodded.

"She says, smiling at me, 'I'm sexually in trouble. Can we go to my room?' I said 'Sure.' She opened her pocketbook and held up a key for me to see, then put it back, got up from the stool you're sitting on and I followed her upstairs to her room."

He looked at me and I nodded. It was an interesting story but the interesting part was over. Every apple has a core in the middle.

"Well you can imagine the next two hours. It wasn't the same old thing I can tell you. Wow! All I can say is Wow! Whatever was in that pill turned her into some hungry lady."

I didn't know how to turn him off. "You don't think we have to worry about those two mermaids over there, do you?"

"We could check it out."

"Hey whoa, I'm on my way to Sacramento. We'd be interrupting their party. You didn't bring those tax papers, did you?"

"You bet I got them, they're right here. I didn't mean to bend your ear, but it was the god damndest thing. Being here just remended me of it. LSD must be some stuff."

"I never tried it."

"Me neither. How about one more Mary before you shove off?"

"No thanks, I've got a mid-afternoon lunch to make. Next time."

Curling took an envelope out of his patent leather briefcase and handed it to me. He motioned to the bartender for another drink and the bartender held up two fingers. Curling shook his head and held up one finger and pointed to himself. Then he held up one finger again.

I looked at the papers briefly and told him to tell Camion if he saw him that I had the papers. "I'll be going," I said. "This is an interesting place. I enjoyed it." I put a ten on the table.

He picked up the ten and stuffed it delicately in my shirt pocket. "Nope, this is mine. Business lunch, you know how it works. I'm going to stick around for a while, and the tab may get bigger. Might take a swim."

"So long," I said and left.

I drove down the valley with the car windows open. It was very hot.

Chapter Seven

I HAD NEVER BEEN to Sacramento before, and I drove around the capitol building twice. I had brought a lot of unfinished things with me to California and they were not falling into place. I kept my eyes peeled for a parking space as I remembered my fourth grade geography book with a picture of this same Sacramento capitol building and the small thrill I got by showing the open page to the girl across the aisle and mis-pronouncing "Scaramento" in a whisper that elicited her feigned fright.

A space opened at an expired meter and I pulled into it.

Her name was Dorothy, and I had made her a ring by stringing colored glass beads on a wire, and rode my bike to her neighborhood after school and it was June and she kept saying that her mother would kill her if she saw me, and she didn't like my ring of old glass beads and she didn't want it, but she took it and ran back to her house.

I thought of my daughter now in the fourth grade, walking home from school somewhere, and the distance between me and things I cared about. I remembered my dead thermostat flying through the air into the field with the discarded junk, and I daydreamed as I sat there inside my car. Vertical lines of termites passed up and down the doorjamb of the old house in Chico. Downstream I could feel the heavy pull of the steelhead as the cold river sucked my dungarees against my thighs.

A policewoman was writing out a parking ticket because my meter had expired.

"Hey officer, right here, I got it. I just pulled in and was daydreaming."

The meter maid looked at me with my head out the window and stopped writing. She was wearing brown pants and a white shirt with a necktie portraying the seal of the state of California. She flipped the page over and put the book in her back pocket and kept walking. I called "Thank you" and she kept walking.

I put a dime in the meter and walked two blocks to the offices of the *Sacramento Bee.* My friend sat in a large alcove office on the third floor. "Ribald Reed," I said, as he started up from his chair, grinning. "Anal Armature," he said, and we grasped hands and hugged. He had played right end for Amherst College when I played defensive back for Worcester Tech, thirty miles down the road. We had gone to high school together and scrimmaged against each other every spring and fall during pre-season for four years. His older brother was a famous literary critic who had gone to Amherst College and his father made him go also to Amherst even though we had made a vow to go to the same college together. I didn't have the money to go to Amherst College.

Jack had been editor of the Amherst College newspaper, was carefree in his grooming, and practical. He had a bull neck and a tendency to take well-calculated risks. He was also defensive about Hemingway and Faulkner, and made fun of me because I thought Dreiser's *American Tragedy* was a great novel.

"So you got yourself out here, finally," he said, grinning at me.

"Probably a mistake," I said, sitting down in the chair he was pointing toward, "I left some unfinished business."

"I'll miss her if it's permanent. I've seen your cartoons here and there. Not bad, Arm."

"Very selected short subjects. At the last count, the published list numbered seven."

"The one we ran was damn good.

"I only remember the check."

"This town needs a sense of humor, especially our esteemed speaker of the assembly. Why don't you stick around?"

"Make me an offer."

"I thought you jousted free lance. You're condescending to security?" He had swung his chair around so he could reach the lower drawer in a filing cabinet.

"I inherited a house in Chico."

"That journalistic dead end?"

"The paper is bad. I hear that they pay well, though, for acidic cartoons featuring fat presidential press secretaries."

"What's your poison, Jack or a gill of Glenfiddich?"

"Jack. You think I turned into a literary type who drinks Scotch?"

"I only keep it to put down the Dewars drinkers who wander in from the state house."

"Chico doesn't seem a bad town to live in. Ceil wants to come out. She says that Puss needs a father."

"And you're thinking about it?"

"It's not much of a reason."

"Reasons. What are reasons? Reasons are never *the* reason, boy. What the hell? Even if it was a reason, it's a good reason. I heard you named that little girl Puss and Boots. You actually did that?"

"Nickname. Ceil's grandmother's name was Boutelia. When Puss was born, Ceil called her Boo-Boo. I couldn't stand it."

"I heard you punched out a guy."

"Jesus, sometimes I think the United States is made up of three small towns connected by trolley cars."

"That's because you picked a newspaperman. If you hit a jockey or a lawyer, no one would have cared."

"Yeah, a jockey. Thanks. Actually he was a lawyer. He was an editor only by accident. A week after I got out here, the D.A. dropped the charge because he had a record. He had also fooled around with the D.A.'s wife."

"Do you want any job or a real job? We got jobs but nothing real right now, maybe in six months. What we got is a great bar around the corner, if you can stand the senators from places like Butte and Placer counties who carry water canteens on their hips and nibble garlic almonds all day. They get the almonds in five pound cans from the growers at Christmas."

"They sell food there?"

"What do you want to eat food for? It's afternoon. Food is for early morning and late at night. This is the West, man. Yeah, you can get food, no problem. They cater to skinny types from the east. We can go after the hour, they don't need my wizardry here for awhile."

"OK, just so's I don't have to meet your chick on the side. I've had one bad experience today already."

"I could be so lucky. My neck's too thick for chicks." He handed me a glass from his filing cabinet. "I hate paper cups. No ice, though." He poured us both two fingers of Jack Daniels. "I actually hate Scotch. It's a funny thing. Bourbon drinkers say Scotch is too sweet and Scotch drinkers say bourbon is too sweet. There's a story in that somewhere."

"My pleasure," I said, taking a swallow of the Jack.

"Here's to the single wing," he said.

"And the arm lift," I said.

"Screw face masks," he said.

"Screw low cut cleats," I said.

We did a lot more damage on the bottle of Jack and walked to a restaurant with bear and elk heads on the wall. The tables and chairs were made of black mahogany from Indonesia. The waitresses wore black shorts and white shirts with red bow ties.

"You were obviously kidding about the food," I said, looking at the menu. "Everything looks great."

"If you like Caesar salad, it's the best in town. Salmon or chicken, both great. If you like political studs, the big man just came in."

"I hear Burdick wrote the book on him," I said, not looking up. How will I know him?"

"More jowls than face. Burdick got him in the wave book. The ninety-ninth wave or something."

"That's the one," I said. "Only know by friends, though. Don't read anymore. Just listen to writers reading their own writings at political fund raisers."

"Burdick gets around the Democratic circuit," Jack said.

"He must be an Indian."

"Burdick?"

"No, Unruh."

"Heap big Chief. Much wampum. Probably is an Indian. The son of a bitch actually walked into California barefoot from Oklahoma just like he says."

"I heard. It's impressive." I glanced quickly and saw a group of men sitting at a far wall table in the corner. "Looks like he's wearing shoes."

"Count on it. Made in Italy. He knows where to get the good stuff and how to get it. You can't see it because it's in his pockets. Once you get near him you can feel it."

I ordered a jumbo shrimp cocktail and a cup of French onion soup, and

Jack ordered rare lamb chops and a Caesar salad. A tall waitress with thin hips and a full white shirt brought them in twenty-five minutes.

"They tell me in Chico that the Democratic Clubs around the state are taking him on."

"God love 'em, they're trying. It'll be fun to watch. Cranston's army."

"I should think it's Pat Brown's army."

"Brown's solid right now."

"But it's Cranston's army?"

"Right."

"We don't have state comptrollers in the east."

"You don't have city limits signs either, but the courthouses are county courthouses. The state comptroller out here is big. It's not like being treasurer of the state of Massachusetts or even Michigan. There are fifty-eight million people out here, and cash is the game. Cash and organization. Cranston's got all his inheritance tax appraisers and they're all tied in with the Democratic clubs."

"How many are there."

"Enough to start a grass fire in every town, city, and county in the state."

"Do you know Don Way?" I asked.

"Sure, he fronts for that prick Sandhill at the Chico newspaper. I like Don, though, he's an old fashioned gentleman. I believe in legalized prostitution."

"I might go see him."

"Say hello for me. I've met him around at conventions."

"If I do, I will."

"But you might not."

"I've only got a three month lease. If I tell Ceil to come out with Puss, I'll probably hit up Way for some kind of pickup job."

"If I know Ceil, she'll come if she decides to."

"You remember well."

"I ought to, I dated her before you did."

"We never actually talked about that."

"What's to talk about? It was the old days."

"How's Helen?"

"Democratic Club of Walnut Creek. Never home. I guess I don't mind, she's pretty good at it."

After we ate, I was restless with the domestic talk. Jack must have sensed it.

"You're not going are you? What's your hurry? We don't go to press until midnight. I have another place to show you."

"Rain check if it's OK. This is a big day for me. I've got to meet one of

Cranston's inheritance tax appraisers at nine tonight at some seafood place on the outskirts of Chico."

"I know the place. It's called "Mothers," famous for fried oysters in the middle of nowhere called Dayton Four Corners."

"That's it all right. This guy did the inheritance tax forms on my ramshackle house in Chico."

"I know Bob Camion. He's a knight of the Democratic Garters. Strange guy, but can't be had. I've eaten at that restaurant twice. If you drive out there after dark, you'll kill half a dozen jackrabbits on the road. You know what else is good there? Sweetbreads."

"I can never remember whether sweetbreads are kidneys or gonads."

"I'd tell you, but either way it would disappoint you."

"I'll find out sooner or later, I guess."

When I got to my car, the meter had expired, and there was a ticket on my windshield.

Chapter Eight

DRIVING BACK TO CHICO from Mother's late that night, Camion hit three jackrabbits that never had a chance. He kept the car speed at an easy sixty-five on the straightway, both hands on the wheel, and when the long white jacks loomed in the headlights and thunked under the car, he said, "There he was" and held steady at the easy sixty-five.

"I make a good rabbit stew," I said.

"Hah!" Camion ejaculated, and smiled his split-second smile, his blue eyes locked on the pitch-black northern valley road.

I was pretty sure the rabbit stew was the part of the offer that set off Camion's "hah!" button, so I dropped the idea. In the silence, it occurred to me that eating wild jackrabbit couldn't set well on a full stomach, and Camion had just eaten a New York sirloin steak and a large piece of home made custard pie.

I started thinking of other diversions to keep me busy if I stayed in Chico for a while. I remembered the steelhead and the afternoon at the river.

"How's the hunting around here?" I asked.

"If you want to shoot some of those Bugs Bunnies, they're all through the almond orchards. You could kill a slew of them in an hour," he said.

"You've done it?" I asked.

"Hell no, I don't shoot guns. I used to know a lady with a house in an orchard."

In a flash, a jackrabbit appeared at the edge of the road and bounded once, clearing the road and disappearing in the darkness.

"The buggars can jump," Camion said.

Jaeckel and his wife Ruth were in the Oaks bar. I had met her at the Democratic Club meeting. She was as petite as Jaeckel was burly, her auburn hair wrapped in a bun at the back of her head, and she had green eyes. Her left hand was slightly deformed, and she wore dresses with pockets, so you seldom saw her left hand. She knew the history of California cold, and she talked slowly with a soft alto voice. John Jaeckel was not as brusque when she was with him.

We sat down and Jaeckel introduced me to Abernard Bannister, a tall, rangy man with black hair who looked like Charles Coburn with glasses. "Call me Ban," he said and sat back down.

"Ban is our Senator Clare Engel's man here in Chico," Jaeckel said.

I was beginning to think that everyone in northern California was involved in politics.

"More important than that," Camion said, grinning, "He's vice-president of the Bank of America."

"*A* vice president," Bannister said, obviously pleased.

I knew of Clare Engel only because he was dying of cancer and it was in the paper, and I wasn't interesting in evaluating Bannister's pleasure. The vice presidencies of banks were created for dull people who approve loans for people they don't admit they know. When that thought occurred to me I realized I needed to get to work on something. Cynicism is the mask of the creative urge. I decided that I'd get out my drawing board when I got home.

I was missing some of the table conversation, wondering if there might be a *San Francisco Chronicle* in the lobby when I left the bar. Maybe it would actually contain something about northern California. I'd been reading Herb Caen's column off and on since I arrived, and didn't understand the fuss over him. Only one out of five Californians had to read his column every day because they all told everyone they met that day what Herb Caen said. I'd also been reading the *Chico Valley Advocate* every day.

I realized that I hadn't been listening. They had been talking about Engel, whose home town was a little further up the valley in Red Bluff. I tried to tune back in to the conversation. Engel's seat was considered a Democratic seat because the other senator from California was William Knowland, a Republican. I could tell from the conversation that Engel was an untouchable for them, and the nomination for his seat was going to be a fight. Party loyalists didn't want a split between the south and the north.

"Alan won't make a move as long as Clare is alive," Ruth said.

"Clare won't resign as long as he's alive," Jaeckel said.

"He will if he thinks it will help the Party," Camion said.

A short man with blond hair and glasses and a pastel green sport shirt was standing next to our table.

"Sit down, Don," Bannister said, reaching over and pulling a chair from the next table.

"Can't," he said, smiling, acknowledging my presence, "got to get back and put her to bed. I just walked over for some air and a Seven Up."

"*Her* is the *Valley Advocate*, not his girlfriend," Jaeckel said to me. "This is Don Way, meet Bill Armature." He said to Way, "You need him. He's a free lance editorial writer, and his political cartoons have been in the *Bee*."

I almost corrected it to *one was*, but said to myself, what the hell.

"Oh oh, competition," Don said, extending his hand to me, laughing. When Don Way laughed, his eyes became merry. He had a good handshake.

"I've been on the verge of coming over and saying hello," I said. "I've also been reading your editorials".

"Jesus, don't judge him by that," Jaeckel said, and everyone laughed.

Don Way knew he was standing in enemy territory, and that the enemy liked him. Jaeckel had told me that he also knew that they hated his boss, Sandhill. Don was a loyal Republican and a good family man, and he made his living working for a conservative son of a bitch. The only people in Chico who didn't like Don personally were some of the college liberals who thought political adversaries were bad people. All the liberals disagreed with what Sandhill told Don to write in his daily editorials, but some of them hated him for it. It was easy for them.

"Come on over, any time," Way said, "Love to talk to you. So long, everybody." He walked through the dark oak archway into the hotel lobby.

"I wonder what it'll be for tomorrow," Ruth said.

"Today's was a beaut," Bannister said. They were talking about Way's editorials.

"No surprises there," Camion said.

Pat and Joan Jay Henry came through the oak archway and walked to our table.

"What are you heathens drinking?" Pat asked. Joan Jay's brown hair was swept up and coiled on top of her head, and she was wearing spiked heels that were loud on the oak floor. With the heels, she was two inches taller than Pat.

"Hello," Joan Jay said, smiling brightly. She talked fast, telling us where they'd been, and her style was to give a lot of details. The more she talked, the faster she talked, and saliva began to form in the corners of her mouth so that she had to slow down to swallow the saliva now accumulating in her mouth. They had been to cocktails at the home of the chairman of the political science department, Wade More, where the young wife of one of the assistant professors had passed out. More's wife had waited so long to put the king crabs on to boil, the martinis she was mass-producing had done their work.

"She was smashed out of her mind," Joan Jay said. "They had to put her on the bed upstairs. The men carried her. Wade shouldn't have fed her those martinis, Pat. He's always doing that. He's not a good chairman."

"You mean *served*, Joan Jay?" Pat winked at me. He had a way of being tolerant of other's opinions, especially Joan Jay's. Part of it was that he didn't take her seriously when she announced conclusions off the top of her head, and part of it was his instinctive enjoyment of controversy. He was a perfect political scientist. He also was fond of Joan Jay, and he admired her personal commitment to her teaching and her grass roots politics. Joan Jay had a big heart and a big mouth, and she had the hutzpah to put her money where her mouth was. She was also tenacious, and she was worried about Pat's other interests.

Everyone at the table was drinking dark draft beer, and Pat ordered "whatever you're all drinking."

Joan Jay said, "I'll have an ice water, I'm just following Pat around." She giggled, and having just finished her sentence, swallowed.

Everyone at the table knew about Pat's affair except Bannister.

"We're talking about Sandhill," Bannister said.

"Teapot stuff," Pat said comfortably.

"Tempest or Dome?" Jaeckel asked, grinning. John liked to show off his versatility whenever college professors were present, especially Pat.

Pat winked again at me, ignoring John, and said it didn't make a hell of a lot of difference what they named the Oroville dam, the subject of today's editorial.

"It means a lot to Pat Brown," Camion said, "It's the biggest landfill dam in the world.

Big anything that's named after a Democrat will stick in Sandhill's craw," Ruth said in her soft alto voice.

"How'd we like it if they called it the Ronald Reagan dam?" Pat said.

"Oh Jesus, that's all I'd need," Joan Jay said, giggling. "I'd move back to Iowa."

"You would?" Pat said.

Joan Jay sipped her ice water. "Not without you, Pat dear." She put the frosted glass on the table, as if to punctuate her resolution. Then she picked up the small napkin from underneath the glass and wiped the tips of her fingers.

"Brown Dam sounds pretty good to me," Camion said.

"Unruh would have to give up too much," Pat said. "He'll spend his chits on himself, not Pat Brown. It'll be Oroville Dam, count on it."

"Sandhill wins again," Bannister said.

"If you want to call it a win," Pat said. "You don't have to wait until it's over to be over. It's already over."

"I really hate that man," Ruth said, so softly that it was hard to believe she meant it, but she meant it all right.

"Gotta go," Jaeckel said. "We working stiffs have to get up in the morning, unlike you college types." And then he added, and you bank executives and inheritance tax appraisers. You look like a working stiff to me, Bill." He was holding out his hand to me. Taking it was like taking a meat cleaver.

"I fit at least half of that expression," I said.

Outside, a little later, Camion walked me to my car.

"How about riding over to Oroville some day and seeing how the dam is going?" he said.

"Sure. By the way, what we talked about at dinner, you think I ought to just wait for the college to get in touch with me, or should I go to see Willard somebody who runs the college?"

"No, for Christ's sake don't do anything with Mooney." Camion's first sentences always jumped out as if he were angry, but it was only pent up feelings about the other things on his mind that he didn't talk about. I never got the sense that he was angry with me. After he blurted out his first sentence, he leveled off. "That property transfer will show up if it hasn't already, and the money boys who work for the college contractors will have it on the Trustees' agenda for the next meeting, count on it. Let me see what I can find out. If you're smart, you'll play hard to get, and I know you're smart. I'll call you before the next Club meeting."

I wouldn't hear from him for three weeks. I was doing other things.

An hour later, sitting on my patio, I was watching an extra inning Giants game on TV, turned down low, and I heard the phone ring inside the house. It was the phone call I wasn't sure I was ready for and the one I was waiting for. I had gotten to like Chico and was on the verge of doing some work for a living, ready also to extend my lease. I liked the relaxed in-between atmosphere of my marriage, and I was calming down from the things I had left behind in the east. The phone conversation lasted an hour.

Back on the patio, *The Jack Paar Show* was on. Jonathan Winters and Buddy Hackett were on together. I stared straight ahead watching them, and nothing struck me funny. Ceil had put Puss and Boots on the phone even though it was late back there. Ceil said Puss couldn't sleep and asked Ceil to call. Ceil said they wanted to come to California.

Chapter Nine

THE HOOKER OAK SCHOOL was located four streets from the near corner of Violet Way and Fourth Avenue. The school was surrounded on three sides by giant Walnut trees and the fourth looked out on wide playing fields and beyond to dried yellow lowlands of grass and weeds and then the western foothills of the Sierra Nevada mountains four miles away.

School had been in session three weeks when I took Puss and Boots by the hand and walked her over early one morning, early for me, and she was nervous.

"What if they won't take me, daddy?" she asked.

"They'll take you, why wouldn't they take you? They'll be lucky as hell to get you, Puss."

"Are you going to tell them my name?"

"I have to tell them your name, oh all A's one, how else can I prove you were born?"

"They can see me, can't they? Why do we have to prove something that's obvious? You're always telling me to be sensible. That's not very sensible."

"That's true but we have to do it."

"Just tell them my name is Boots Armature and you're my father and we can produce my mother if they want to see her." Puss then kicked a walnut and got it so squarely it lifted six inches off the ground and bounced off the tire of a parked car.

"That's not too hot for the toe of your shoe," I said.

"Do you think they'll have soccer? I left my gym shoes in my bedroom."

In the school principal's office, we found out that she should bring her gym shoes the next day.

After leaving Puss in her fourth grade room with Mrs. Pigeon, I walked up Lantana to the flood control ditch and studied it for a while. The rain would come in January, they said. I walked a couple more blocks and turned left on Sinclair Boulevard. There was a billboard that showed a Volkswagen Bug and a lady with a shopping bag. The billboard featured the words, "Mother's Little Helper." Camion had told me about it but I hadn't seen it. He said Kennedy saw one of the billboards when he was in Whiskeytown and told Larry O'Brien to hire that advertising agency for the upcoming Goldwater campaign. It was a pretty good ad. It struck me that the agency would never come up with anything as good as that. Kennedy would do better to hire Oscar Levant.

I followed Sinclair Boulevard for two blocks and turned back down Lantana. Ceil would think the school wouldn't admit Puss and that I was behaving badly. Ceil's word for it was "unpleasant," which she used whenever I objected to what I considered to be unjust or stupid, the anti-Bill Armature behavior of the world. I had at times been plenty unpleasant, I knew that. I had also been plenty justified, I was arguing in my mind again. I was starting the fight with Ceil again.

I walked by a ranch house under construction. A tall athletic looking guy in a business suit was holding a squirting hose, splashing the new concrete sides of the frame. Redwood planks stained with cement lay piled on the ground in a heap.

He saw me watching him and smiled as if to say, yeah I know, I look like a nut in my business suit watering a house. He said, "Morning."

"Hi," I said. "Pretty good job for a hot California day."

"Sure is, especially if your workers come to work when they're supposed to." He turned the nozzle to increase the pressure of the water and had to back up not to get splashed. I watched, remembering my best days with a hose, standing still, watching the spray for hours. It got me a room in the president's residence at Boston University when I was a graduate student. The house was an old Gothic building called The Castle. I was working one summer for Building and Grounds and was sent over to the president's house by Mike Halfpenny, the crew foreman. He said he had twenty complaints from the president about his lawn and flower beds needing more water and he didn't care if I drowned every plant in the yard.

"Jesus, do a good job, will ya? I send Russ and Alky over there and they come back in an hour telling me it's all done. Those two drunks could get more water on the president's lawn if they just pissed out the beer they drank the night before. So water the goddam place, will ya? I don't care if you don't come back till four o'clock this afternoon. Take your lunch. Just don't lie down around the corner of the house. The president comes out at nine fifteen every morning to walk to his office. The thing that makes or breaks his day is if there's any mud around the roses, so make it muddy, pal, Billy boy, king hose-holder for the day. OK?"

One morning the president came out when I was watering the roses. I had been on the job for three or four days. He wanted to know if I was the one watering the last few days. I said I was. He said I was the only one who had done the job well. I said "Thank you" and he crossed Bay State Road and headed for his office. I kept watering. In late morning, a black butler came out the front door to check the mailbox. Earlier I had seen a Chinese student going in and later another student coming out the side door of the medieval house. The butler watched me and said, "Soak it good, the old man is a nut on watering."

"Do students live in this house?" I asked.

"Two grad students live here. One's in med school and the other plays the piano."

"How do you get to live here?" I asked.

"You don't," he said pleasantly. "Remember, soak it, man."

"I'll soak it," I said.

A week later, I was standing and watering in the same place a little after nine in the morning when the president came out on his way to work. He was wearing a light tan suit and he looked like he hadn't slept, big puffy bulges under his eyes. He came over to me. I was spraying water around the base of a giant orange-red rose bush, and he took off his horn-rimmed glasses while looking at the dark muddy base of the other roses. "Morning," he said.

"Morning, sir," I said.

"Ollie tells me that you might be interested in living in the house."

"That'd be great, sir. Yes, I sure would."

That's how it was, no frills. Two weeks later I moved out of the graduate dormitory where I had a summer room, and into the basement of The Castle, a small alcove off the kitchen.

Remembering that incident ten years before took only a few seconds, but I must have seemed to be staring because the tall man watering the house in his suit said, "You wouldn't be interested in a job, would you?"

"I'm sorry, I was thinking about something. I didn't mean to stare."

"Hey, I'm serious," he said, smiling.

He turned off the hose and dropped it, walked over to me shaking the water off his hand, trying not to get any water on his suit, and said, "I'm Larry Bourke. I build these things."

He had a Boston accent. He offered his hand. "It's a little wet, but the water's clean."

I shook his hand and almost regretted it. His grip was iron. I told him I lived down the street.

"Yeah, I saw that someone had moved in down there. That's a nice house. The people who lived there before did a nice job. Good for the buyer, not so good for the seller. California doesn't count shrubbery when you're selling, so I have to spend a lot of money putting them in but they don't count in the estimate. I hope you got a good deal."

"I'm happy. I'm from Boston too."

"It shows, does it? I been out here just a year. I got a card here somewhere. He fished through his pockets and found a card in the inside breast pocket of his jacket, and handed it to me.

"I have to wash this bugger down before it gets hot so it won't crack. My guy took the forms off yesterday afternoon and then headed south. I think he's on a toot. He disappears for a couple days every other week. I got to get back to the office."

He got in his truck and I headed down the sidewalk. I had gone about twenty yards when he pulled up beside me. "You like fishing?"

"Sure do, anytime," I said.

"I'll be down." He drove off.

At home I went directly into the back yard by the walkway on the side of the house. I passed under the grape arbor, opened the redwood gate to the patio, spent some time looking at the bamboo on the back side of the fireplace, walked over and felt the firmness of a grapefruit, wandered over to the scrawny olive tree by the fence between my house and the Garrisons and found three small olives. I went to the rice paper trees and reached behind the large spreading leaves to pick out the dry withered ones covered with white silvery slime, then walked to the screen door to open it and go in the house to see Ceil. She was standing on the other side of the screen door watching me.

"Oh hi," I said.

"You want to know something, Bill?" she said, "not at rare moments, but most of the time, you totally puzzle me."

Chapter Ten

I MET CEIL AT a poetry reading one spring at a university in western Massachusetts. She was wearing a white t-shirt with a William Carlos Williams poem on it, something about blue plums and a refrigerator, and dungaree shorts with torn edges, and she was with someone else. I was standing in the back of the crowded, wood-paneled Memorial Hall, and she came in late with the poet and several people who smiled their way through the standees, squeezed past the legs of those sitting in the wall sofas to the front row where they all sat in saved seats. During the reading I could see only the back of her head, but I had seen her come in. Her hair was swept up in the back, and from where I was standing, I could see her neck. During the reading, I concentrated on the wispy ringlets at the base of her neck.

Poetry readings are next in line to funerals for me, but at least funerals begin on time. I had picked my spot near the door so I could leave early, and a half hour after the thing was supposed to start, I was regretting my agreement with the editor of the student newspaper to do a caricature of the poet for next week's art section, and just then the poet walked in with his merry band, the anointed few who had been culled from the masses for dinner and drinks. Ceil was with a tall guy who I thought for a few minutes was the poet because his head was shaved. I didn't like him. Then I saw the poet with his own shaved head, and it occurred to me to wonder who she would end up with later. The poet also had a patch over one eye. I couldn't wait for the poems. I was enjoying my mood. My editor had made me promise that I'd draw something "sensitive," as he called it, not my "usual." He went on to point out the obvious about my views on life.

After the first three or four poems I stopped wondering how I could do a drawing of a bald headed poet with a patch over one eye without being cynical. I'd have to see what came out and just try to fix it. I was thinking of Ceil's flashing eyes when she came in, and how the flashing stopped when she saw me staring at her. The audience was snickering and smiling and laughing at the fun parts in the poems and I was missing it all. The audience was right with him and they were all having a fine time.

Later, in one of our fights, Ceil raised the point about my references to the fun parts of poetry readings. "You always have to get snide," she said, "you can't see the good in things. If you can't share yourself, why can't you at least lend out some of that ego-cherished space you covet, just for once, and try to appreciate other persons' interpretations? You might for once let other people co-exist in your vicinity, Bill." She came down hard on *Bill*.

We were talking about a lawyer we knew, who also had a crush on her, but somehow it always came down to my attitude about poetry and poets she knew.

"If people are delighted at comparisons and witty connections," she continued, "why do you have to put them down? You call them 'fun parts' because you don't want anything to do with aesthetic experience."

Often, Ceil went a little too far, even when I was trying to lend myself to her chastisements, and I would zero in on her exaggerations, ignoring the truth of the point she was making. I was good at making things worse.

"What's aesthetic about three word monotone lines in the weak passive?" I asked.

"He was making fun of the way people are and the way they talk, all at the same time. He's writing in a new way."

"That's why I call them the fun parts."

When we started shouting, we got back to the lawyer subject, and we hammered each other, Ceil cursing my tone of voice, and I pressing my proprietary claims. Over a period of time, the more I pressed, the more defined my tone became. I perfected the hit and run technique in a domestic quarrel, and it was helping me become a fairly good political cartoonist. I always knew where the weak spot was. It wasn't helping the marriage, which was being held together by the thread of a growing girl child we both adored. I finally cornered Ceil into a state of mind where the poetasters and the bald headed aesthetes and the artsy lawyers, all of whom I considered to make up the clown population of the world, offered her more solace than I did, and she had a brief affair. She did me a favor though, she didn't pick a sensitive type.

Somewhere along the way I drew a cartoon of two brawny dissolutes sitting on a curbstone, one was bald with a few chin hairs, holding a sign that read, "Penny Poems for Sale," the other a crew-cut type with bulging biceps, holding a balloon with the words "A.C.L.U. for the Rights of Prostitutes." The first is saying to the other, "Sometimes I think I'm sensitive." *The New Yorker* bought the cartoon but Ceil didn't think it was funny. She didn't even ask me how much they paid me. They paid me five hundred bucks.

The guy she picked wasn't someone she felt sorry for, or wanted to make a point about me with, or was even attracted to. She just wanted to be distracted for a while. What I've just said didn't occur to me at the time, and it wasn't until my late night solitary patio culinary experiments in Chico that it all occurred to me. I started thinking of her distraction as her dry powder rebellion.

Nonetheless, my at the time response to her rebellion wasn't dry powder at all, and I put the object of her affections into the intensive care unit of the Detroit General Hospital. The emergency room doctor, a young woman intern from Australia who didn't believe that I had driven myself to the hospital, kept telling me that I had been knocked about a bit and should have called a lorry earlier. She insisted on arranging a bed for me, but when she stepped out of the room where I was lying on a thin table with a thin hard pillow, it occurred to me that my sparring partner might be dead, and I left in my stockinged feet. I woke up at five o'clock in the morning behind the wheel of my car in the emergency parking lot. I drove home.

Ceil had taken Puss and Boots somewhere, so I drove to a motel on the edge of the city, and checked in, wondering whether I would be booked for assault or murder.

It was my first real brawl since elementary school. I remembered that as I kept getting off his apartment floor and tackling him chest high in order to try and get him out of his Jim Jeffries boxing stance, thinking *if thine eye offend thee, pluck it out, and if it doesn't offend thee you prick of misery it offends me.* I was feeling very mean, and wanted his eyes. I was not proud of it later.

He had a great jab and he was a southpaw, so I couldn't get my right into his face or the steel apron where his belly was supposed to be. Meanwhile, he was destroying me with his jab, his fake right cross, and a quick left hook that put me down several times.

Luckily for me he was a baseball player, though no second baseman. The weights he lifted were in the hallway, and they gave him the physical equipment of a Welsh rugby player. The baseball bat in his living room kept his swing grooved.

When I was waiting for the ambulance to pick him up, I saw Ted Williams' book, *The Art of Hitting*, on the coffee table. There were several drops of blood on the dust jacket. I didn't know if it was his blood or mine. His eyes were closed, and there was blood on the corners of his mouth. I thought of getting rid of the bat but I remembered a Dashell Hammett story in which a hockey player killed a guy with a hockey stick, then broke it in two and dropped it down a barred sewer main, but the police found it. *At least I shut his fucking eyes.* I was trembling from the letdown after the mayhem, blowing off inside my own head as if I had been justified in the business at hand. When the ambulance arrived, I admitted the fight and ducked out. The next afternoon I checked out of the motel and headed west.

When Ceil opened the screen door I said, "I puzzle myself. Have you ever heard of the Hooker Oak?"

"Darn it, Bill, is Puss in school? Does it take two hours to enroll a nine and a half year old in primary school?"

"She's fine. She can bring her soccer shoes tomorrow. They have a swell view of the mountains from her gym."

Ceil stood shaking her head at me, deciding whether to be mad at me or charmed by my apparent guilelessness.

"Is her teacher nice?"

"Nice. Very nice teacher. Mrs. Alcove. She's chubby, but she's OK. She'll do."

"Why didn't you come home and tell me? I've been on pins and needles. I'm a little shaky, Bill, and all I need is for you to keep running off on your little jaunts."

"Hey, I'm right here. I met a guy up the street from Boston. He was hosing his house and he wants to take me fishing."

"Up the street is not where the school is, Bill. Do you think I'm an idiot? Do you know what you just said sounds like? Have you been off to some hooker place?"

"No, no no. Wouldn't do that, Ceil, you know that. You might not think so right now, but deep down you know it. The Hooker Oak is the tree that Errol Flynn and Whatshisname jumped out of in *Robin Hood*. I thought we might take a ride over and look at it. Maybe do the sights, a little bit of Chico. Oranges falling around the town square, stuff like that, maybe the college. There's a big park with two different outdoor pools they call One Mile and Five Mile. There's even a town called Paradise near here up in the mountains. Name your fruit, they got orchards of it, and nuts. A prehistoric man even walked out of the mountains a few years ago over in Oroville. Oro for gold, you know, goldville. Even Chinese stonewalls. Do you remember my Aunt Ellie?"

"You're all wound up, Bill. What's going on? I let you go on just to see how much you worked in before you took a breath. You've made some decision and you want me to agree with you. You're so transparent, Armature. You want me to go see a big tree so you can jump out of it and pretend it isn't an ambush. OK, I can wash our kitchen floor later. Does Puss come home for lunch?"

"They feed her. I made out a check."

"For how many days?"

"A couple weeks, I forget."

"Bill?"

"It was a month, I remember now. They only take checks for a month at a time."

Later that morning I told Ceil that I sold the land that aunt Ellie's house was polluting for eighty-six thousand bucks. I asked her if she'd like to live in Chico for the foreseeable future.

"Is that how Californians talk, 'foreseeable future?'"

I said something inane that I don't remember, stalling, and Ceil elbowed me in the ribs, looking straight at me, smiling. I looked at her looking at me.

"Calm down, boy," she said, "I'll stick with you."

We drove to Bidwell Park and walked beneath the Hooker Oak and sat in the small wooden stands behind home plate at the children's baseball diamond. We talked through lunch and into the early afternoon.

When we left to be home when Puss arrived from school, we agreed that it was a very big oak tree.

Chapter Eleven

I SET UP MY drawing board in the back room of the house where I could look out and see the dangling lemons, from chrome yellow to pastel green, and the sun-baked and faded red ocher of the tall redwood fence that blocked off all but the cedar shake roof of my neighbor's house. I had heard from Larry Bourke that my next-door neighbor was the high school football coach. He had five kids. I had stopped complaining about their dog because I bought a pair of earplugs at Ceil's insistence one day when I was on my way over to praise the virtues of dogs that snoozed on rugs all day. Larry told me it was a Brittany spaniel, and that it was a hunting dog.

With the ear plugs in, and a special pair of muffs I made by gluing small squares of black silk over two inch blocks of balsa wood on the ends of a thin sheath of strapping metal bent to fit my head, I worked on a cartoon of Goldwater. Ceil liked several versions but said that they weren't finished she didn't think, but what did I think? I also drew a couple of Dean Rusk, and one of Pierre Salinger, but I didn't show them to her because cartoons betrayed my view of humanity that I was trying not to remind her of. Ceil was a Democrat, but I was merely a voter who had an instinctive antipathy towards Richard Nixon. I voted for Jack, as all Massachusetts residents or former residents called him. Before that, I voted for Ike in his second term, having had enough of Stevenson's pomposity. I looked forward to the Kennedy-Goldwater campaign as a means of elevating my income. The cartoons would show Salinger and Barry Goldwater on the scene. Reagan was already stomping California for Goldwater and the upcoming Republican convention in San Francisco.

Ceil made fun of me as I sewed the silk around the balsa wood. "I've got some panty hose with holes in them," she said as I sat in front of my stand-up tilted drawing board.

"Bring 'em in," I said, calling her bluff, but she only shook her head and left me to my sewing as the dog barked next door.

A few days later, Ceil got a morning job in an upholstery store downtown, buying fabric from dealers. Puss made the fourth grade soccer team at school, and Ceil signed up Puss for ballet lessons on Saturdays. When she got home from school every day after soccer, we played Scrabble or Chinese checkers for a half hour. Sometimes I squatted on the back lawn and held out my first baseman's mitt as a target, and Puss practiced her softball pitch. After that I'd jog over and continue jogging around the school's athletic field two or three times before switching to walking-then-jogging, my old boy scout pace. After a week or so, I was alternating between sprinting and jogging. I was getting into shape.

One late afternoon at the field, I met the writer who rode in Camion's car to Whiskeytown when we saw Kennedy. I remembered that his first name was Luke but I'd forgotten his last name as soon as I heard it. He said "Hi Bill," so I said "Hi Luke." He had a football with him, and said he'd seen me in the field a couple times, so we threw the ball around, at first just back and forth, trying to impress each other with our spirals, then hitting each other running at long range. Soon we forgot about competing and took turns centering the ball and running cuts and turnouts and buttonhooks, and finally long bombs.

When we finished, we sat on the dry grass and let the sweat drip off our chins onto our already darkened, soaked t-shirts.

"You played," he said.

"Yeah, you did too," I said.

"Just high school."

"Jesus, I loved practice."

"Except in the spring. Illinois was cold in the spring."

"Same in Massachusetts," I said. "I'd look at my cold hands and they'd be all orange and purple."

"Do you know Ken Morrow?" he asked. "He's in the art department at the college. He lifts weights, and he can throw a football a mile."

"Ask him. The only people I know are the ones who run the Democratic Party around here and went to Whiskeytown that day. And I know a guy up the street named Bourke who's from Massachusetts," I said.

"I live across the street from Larry," he said.

"I'm going hunting with him when the season starts," I said.

"Larry's a good guy," he said.

"They sure like him at the Exchange Club downtown," I said, "He took me there for lunch last Thursday and they fined him three times during the meal."

"Is that good or bad," he said.

"Good. It's all in fun."

"Met his wife?"

"Never laid eyes on her," I said.

He picked off a piece of yellow grass and chewed it, looking toward the Sierras. Puss and Boots was standing between us. She had approached from our backs.

"Dinner, dad. You said forty-five minutes, remember?"

"This is my alarm clock," I said, "Puss and Boots."

"Hi, Puss and Boots," he said.

"Hello," Puss said.

"Tell me your last name again. This time I'll remember."

"Gardner. Like the guy who weeds the garden.

"Mine's Armature."

"I remember." We shook hands and agreed to meet again at the field two days later, same time.

Chapter Twelve

ON THE THIRD SATURDAY in November, Larry Bourke took me and Boots goose hunting near the Sacramento River, and when we returned later in the day I met Larry's wife Eartha for the first time. Ceil had put up a protest in defense of Puss's ballet lesson but Puss fought hard for the goose hunt and Ceil gave in. She was pleased that I'd take Puss on such an ordinarily exclusivly male mission.

Larry's truck was already parked in front of our house when I shook Puss's foot and wakened her. It was still dark outside and I could see Larry's parking lights through the front window of Puss's bedroom.

Larry was sipping coffee with the motor running when I put my old double barrel shotgun into the back and we squeezed into his wide front seat. He handed us a white paper bag with fresh crullers and a jimmy-sprinkled doughnut. He had a large coffee with a lid on it for me and a cup of cocoa for Puss.

"Good thing Klingman's opens early," he said. "I've been out here for a half hour."

"I saw you," I said. "I thought you said six."

"Do you like jimmies?" he asked Puss.

"Yes I do, and I love cocoa. Thank you very much Mr. Bourke, sir." She turned to me, "Did I say it right, daddy?"

Before I could reply, Larry said, "You sure did, honeybun."

As Larry drove route 99 south, I bent back the sipping seal on the extra coffee in the second white bag and picked out a cruller. "Where's my jimmies?" I said.

"You'll get your jimmies later," he said, laughing.

The sun came up behind us as we headed through the rice fields along Ord Ferry Road, then past a large stand of cottonwoods, and then we were in almond orchard country. The rows between the trees had just been ploughed and the soil was ripply and black.

"There's eighteen feet of rich topsoil in this part of the valley," Larry said. "You'd never get up a skyscraper out here."

"Good," I said.

"Sure is. Only thing wrong with these almond trees are the blossoms. Walnuts too. Blew out all my anti-bodies the first fall bloom last year. I had an allergy so bad it put me on my back for a week," he said. "Hits people from the east real bad."

"I'll look forward to it."

"Take pills, that's all," he said.

"The inheritance tax appraiser who helped me with that old house I inherited told me that the almond orchards are full of jackrabbits."

"Every place else is too."

"Can you eat them?"

"If you don't mind the blisters."

"Say what?"

"Blisters. You find them when you're dressing them out. They give me the willies. I don't eat jackrabbits."

Puss was asleep, her head nuzzled against my side. We were on a dirt road on a low flatland. There were small ponds on both sides of the road, then tules and a bigger pond. Overhead, large flocks of water birds were flying.

"Are those geese?" I asked.

"Sand hill cranes," Larry said.

"They're huge."

"They'll be plenty of geese."

In another minute the road ended and Larry turned left and drove along the edge of a lake, putting up what seemed like a thousand snow geese. "There's your geese," Larry said, stopping and turning off the key and dropping it on the floor.

Puss woke when he turned off the engine. When we got out, another flock lifted out of the water and the sky was filled with swirling honking geese, high-flying, curving down in trailing cones, landing, sometimes almost landing and exploding upward again in a ballooning surge. The sky was black with birds, more flocks passing overhead at different heights.

"Most of the geese fly about seventy yards above the ground, just out of reach. We might reach them with number one buckshot, but it does too much damage. I brought number twos. Plenty of them will come by low enough."

"Look, daddy," Puss said, and a mass of swans were passing overhead so low that we could have hit them with sticks, their long necks reaching in front of their wings like spears. "We're not going to hurt them, are we?"

Larry said, "They're too pretty, and they're also illegal. They're special, aren't they?"

"Those over there look like ducks," I said.

"They are. They'll stay just out of range. Some of the geese will come down lower."

More sand cranes passed overhead.

"We can look all day, but we won't get any goose breasts this way," Larry said, reaching in the back of his truck for the shotguns. He handed me mine, an old Shurtleff twelve gauge my aunt Myrtle gave me when my Uncle Howard died. As Larry changed into high-soled boots and filled his hunting vests with shells, and Puss was staring overhead at the waves of soaring waterfowl, I was mentally lost in my own childhood memories of my father's single-shot .12 gauge Winchester. My father had bought it during the war, just before my cousin Bob left for New Guinea as an aerial gunner on a B-24. He told my father to fire it when he shot down his first Jap Zero. A few months later, we received one of those small V-mail letters that the government photographed and reduced in size, and my cousin said my father could fire the gun twice. My father went upstairs and got the gun from the back of the closet in my bedroom where he kept his hunting clothes and gun cleaning kits. I followed him out to the front lawn and watched him break open the barrel and push in a green twelve-gauge shell. He pointed it above the top leaves of the maple tree beside the hydrant in front of our house, and pulled the trigger. The boom was so loud in our little Cleveland Avenue neighborhood that Mabel Wormstead came out of her front door across the street to see what the noise was.

My father called to her that he was celebrating, and explained.

"God love him," she exclaimed. "That boy's half way around the world savin' us all. Shoot one off for me, Ralph."

My father broke open the barrel and the shell popped out with such force it landed several feet in back of him. He pushed in another shell and handed the gun to me. "You want the second one?" he offered.

"Sure," I said.

He handed me the gun with the barrel facing down toward the ground and told me to always carry it that way unless I was aiming at a target or an animal. "You could kill someone in an instant," he said, "especially another hunter."

I said OK and raised the gun, pointed it at the sky, made sure that the butt was snug against my shoulder, and waited. My father told me to squeeze the trigger slowly and the gun would fire. I squeezed and the gun boomed. The backfire almost knocked me down, and my father laughed at the expression on my face. Mabel Wormstead clapped from her porch across the street and my father took the gun. "That's all until Bob gets another Jap," he said.

Neither of us thought to pop the empty shell from the gun. The next day I took the gun from my closet and was practicing holding it up to my shoulder and sighting down the barrel. I decided to look through the inside of the barrel and pushed the lever in front of the safety and the barrel opened and popped the shell into my eye. I couldn't see for a while out of that eye.

Now Larry was watching me in my revery, and when I smiled at him he handed me several .12 gauge shells. Larry turned his gun away from Puss and me and pushed seven shells into his gun, his barrel pointed at the ground. I pushed the spring lever on my Hastings-Shurtleff double barrel and it clicked open, exposing the two chambers. I inserted two shells, and when I closed the barrel, locking it into place, the gun went off. Both barrels emptied with loud explosions into the ground next to Larry's feet. Puss was standing at my right. I had missed Larry's legs by a foot.

Larry looked at me and smiled, "Practicing?

Puss grabbed my arm with both hands. The noise of both shotgun barrels going off within a few feet of her scared her. She was looking up at me. She didn't say a word.

"Jesus, Larry, I'm sorry," I said. "I don't know why the gun did that."

"Just old, probably," he said. "I brought two guns, if you want to use my .20 gauge."

"Yeah, I better," I said, and Larry took my shotgun and got his other gun from a tightly fitting gun case behind the front seat of his truck.

"I don't have as many shells, but I think there's enough here." He handed me a shell vest with several rows of yellow twenty gauge shells.

"Let's go over the rise by the pond and see if some low strays come over," he said.

We walked to the highest ground we could find and watched the incoming flights raise their flying levels when they spotted us. Some of them came in almost low enough. "We've just got to be patient. There are always dumb birds around."

We shot six geese that day, five whites and one Canada goose. Larry got four, including the Canada goose. Puss knew that Canada geese mate for life, and when the lone mate came back several times and circled, looking for its mate. Puss said, "I know what she's doing, daddy."

"Me too," I said.

"We could fix it if it wasn't flying just out of range," Larry said, watching the goose. He fired twice, but the goose was too high.

For a long time afterward I was troubled by the narrowness of Larry's escape from death that morning. I kept seeing Larry's legs next to the blasted earth and Puss next to me. I don't believe in omens, but it was to become a month of bad things.

Driving home from the river, I remembered the sunrise of the early morning and the innocent looking rice fields and freshly ploughed almond rows and the rainbow jimmies on Puss's doughnut. But the blasted earth from my uncle's defective gun kept eliminating the rainbow. When Larry dropped us off, I met his wife Eartha for the first time. She had walked down the sidewalk with their two kids, a girl Puss's age, and a boy toddler.

She was wearing a red and white cotton jump suit and she had blue eyes with heavy black eyebrows. I noticed the eyebrows. She had walked down to see if we were back yet, and to meet Ceil. She was striking.

Later, Ceil said, "She seemed nice. Certainly your brand of eyebrows." Ceil was in good humor.

"Never noticed," I said. I was remembering Luke Gardner sitting on the field, looking across the late fall yellow grassland of the valley toward the mountains, chewing the stem of devil's grass. He had just asked me if I had met Larry's wife. I wondered what it was all about.

Chapter Thirteen

THE FOLLOWING THURSDAY, KENNEDY was murdered in Dallas. Looking back, I can see now that it was the first of two turning points in my story. The other one comes a long time later. I know that the Dallas shooting figures in some way in the life of every American who was alive that day and knew enough to know or feel that something huge had taken place. That's my theory anyway, and that's what part of this story is about. I've never been to Dallas, and I don't intend to ever go there, but I know what it looks like because I've seen the Zapruder film and the route of the president's open limousine as it moved slowly from the hotel to the wide boulevard near the grassy knoll, and with increased speed to the Dallas Memorial Hospital. That day and the next two I spent in front of my television set, Puss and Boots and Ceil next to me until they couldn't watch, and then they brought food for me and sat down and watched with me some more.

The morning of November 22nd I had been in the humanities building at the college where I had agreed to meet Luke Gardner and talk to his creative writing class about political cartooning. I didn't see how a cartoonist could help a beginning writer but Luke insisted that the creative process is the same for all who "imagine and create," as he put it. He said that the cartoon caption had to be juxtaposed just right to the visual portrayal in the cartoon frame, and that juxtaposition played off the same transitional movement that occurs in fiction and poetry. I didn't understand what he meant, but I was happy to play along. I think he merely wanted a visitor to liven up his class, and that was OK with me.

I was sitting in his office, wondering how I could convey to his students that I didn't reason out anything at all, I merely listened and waited and put down images that occurred to me. The English department secretary had unlocked his office for me because he had earlier called her in case he was a little late. Luke suddenly came through the door, very agitated.

"Kennedy's been shot in Dallas," he said.

"Is he dead?"

"I don't know. There's a TV in the Hotel Oaks."

We ran across Pinecrest to the Oaks parking lot and into the lobby where a small crowd was watching Howard K. Smith on NBC. I edged between two people standing in back of a small child sitting in a large leather-covered stuffed chair. The room was absolutely still and Howard K. Smith was listening to the phone plug in his ear as he talked about the motorcade and the hospital. He seemed to be listening to an interview with a Texas state trooper who was sitting on his motorcycle near the emergency entrance to the hospital. Howard K. Smith was giving details from the interview as he listened.

Then Howard K. Smith put his fingers to the earphone, as if the interview had been interrupted. He listened intently and nodded his head slightly and looked into the TV camera and said, "The President is dead."

I left the hotel and crossed the street to my bicycle in the long rack outside the humanities building. I unlocked the bicycle and pedaled through the streets of Chico, past 5th Street where I could hear the tolling bells of the Episcopal Church. I pedaled for several minutes and I could still hear the bells. All I could think of was getting home. I tried to imagine John Kennedy dead. Who could have killed him? Who killed cock Robin? Who?

I passed Raley's drugstore on the corner of Maple, and pedaled. I wondered if Ceil knew at work, and if they told Puss at school. I passed the courthouse on Broadway and the flag was already at half-mast. I wondered if they let Ceil go home and if she would be driving the car, and if she'd be OK. When she got her job we flipped a coin to see who would drive the car and who would ride a bicycle, and I picked heads. I always picked heads. Ceil took an accelerated driving course from someone who taught driver education at the high school. She wouldn't let me teach her. How could John Kennedy be dead?

I pedaled onto Manzanita and crossed Palm and Juniper. I passed the big walnut tree on our corner. My bike tire spun a walnut off to the right. Our car was in the driveway. I pedaled past the car and let it fall on the grass between two giant staked-up rose trees. I opened the front door and fell into Ceil's arms. "He's dead," I said. Ceil was crying, and the television showed Kennedy making a speech at the hotel before he was shot. Mrs. Garrison, our neighbor, slipped out the front door when she saw me. She had come over to be with Ceil.

Puss was between us, hugging both of us. We sat down on the living room floor in front of the television set.

Four days later I dropped Ceil off at work and drove through several towns in the northern Valley. I drove almost to Paradise where I pulled off the road at a scenic view and could see the northern valley for miles. I could see the Sacramento River and the Coastal Range. I got back in my car and drove through Paradise to Megalia where a sign said "Nov. 15—April 1, *Chains*

Required from This Point." I went on to Stirling City where I got out of the car and walked through a meadow where there were bluebells and white puffs. I could see snow on a further range in the Sierras, glistening in the sun.

Driving back through Paradise, I read Chamber of Commerce signs telling me when the Rotary and Kiwanis Clubs met each week. Other signs told of church services, and a billboard listed the bank branches and the real estate agencies. I parked again at the scenic turnout and looked at the valley spread below me like a pastel puzzle. The water in the rice fields shone in the sun. The almond and walnut orchards, lined squares, were orderly and safe. There was Chico with its church spires and county roads winding around it like baling wires, sprawled in the late fall air, waiting for winter when it would rain. I could see the airport and the dump and the fairgrounds, still and unmoving and self-contained in a bustling commerce invisible from this scenic view. I thought of the thousands of pheasants I couldn't see in the rice checks and corn fields, the thousands of jackrabbits in the orchards and the weeds of the creek beds by day, leaping the county roads by night, and the thousands of small black and white California quail in the heavy cover of the orange orchards and creek ditches. I couldn't see the people making love in their houses, or the clerks at typewriters, or the kids in their classrooms. I couldn't see the black widow spiders under the benches in the town square, I couldn't see the rattlesnakes in the canyons above the foothills. I couldn't even see the canyons. I remembered my Wallace, Idaho friend who told me the story of the black cloud over the valley when the smudge pots were lighted in the winter to protect the almond orchards.

I thought of Puss and Boots in school and the friends she left in Detroit so she could live with me. And I thought of Ceil whom I had betrayed by accusing her of betraying me.

The next day I drove to Oroville to see the migrant worker shacks, and the next day to Red Bluff to see the Chinese coolie stone walls, and the next day to Marysville to walk by the offices of the newspaper whose editor urged the county deputies to shoot the migrant workers who picked from the Feather River the potatoes dumped by the farmers *in The Grapes of Wrath* to keep the prices up, and who still went to the fields there every day.

The following week I went down on Thursday night and joined the Chico Democratic Club.

Orchards *of* Almonds

BOOK TWO

Chapter Fourteen

WINTER IN THE NORTHERN California valley comes slowly. First comes the cool rain, then the heavier rain that brings life to the creek beds, then the long steady rain that raises the levels of the Feather and the Sacramento Rivers. The fishermen stay at the rivers and the salmon keep coming as the waters rise, as dispassionate as computers, passing up through the cold downstreaming waters, and the temperature drops into the low forties, sometimes into the high thirties, and the skies are stucco gray.

Each morning I checked the thermometer before walking Puss and Boots to school. It snowed an inch one day in December and Virginia Garrison came over and told Ceil that it was the first snow they'd had in ten years. It was gone by early afternoon.

The snow in the near mountains became permanent, however, and the more I looked at it each day, the oftener I thought of the Donner Party in those mountains in eighteen feet of snow, eating each other. Some mornings, if it wasn't raining, I'd bike with an umbrella strapped to the frame to the Oaks for coffee. Camion was usually there, sometimes Jaeckel. Occasionally Will Curling showed up. We talked politics and club gossip and if Curling was there, women. One morning after Curling left, Camion said, "Curling thinks fucking was just invented."

One morning Jaeckel took six of us to a marina on the Sacramento River where he knew the owner, to fish for salmon. We got into two boats with the outboard motors running. The river was high and it was moving very fast with branches and limbs of trees flowing past in the current. When our boat moved out into the river the current swept us very quickly downstream until the guide turned the boat back into the current and throttled the motor. Someone joked about falling overboard and the guide said, "Don't. The current will suck you down in a second and you won't come up for a long ways. When you do it won't matter."

We slowly trolled upstream for an hour, then turned and came back down in several minutes. We did this three times. Each time we turned to change direction the guide increased the throttle to counter the current. No one had a strike. Back at the marina we each drank a beer and ate a hamburger.

One morning at the Oaks, we were talking about wives and kids who were political widows and orphans. After a while, Curling said, "I love my daughter but she's not going to interfere with my love life." He looked pasty and eager and hung over when he said it. He was sitting on the inside of our booth against the green wall of the restaurant. Jaeckel asked him if he was feeling OK.

"I'm fine," he said, "why?"

"You don't look like you're getting much sun is all," Jaeckel said.

"Hah!" Camion cackled, stoop-shouldered, sipping his coffee.

Curling turned his head a little sideways, squinting as if to shade the light, and thought about it. He didn't say what he thought.

I asked Jaeckel if the road to Stirling City was passable in winter. He said it was if I put on chains.

We talked about Lyndon Johnson in the White House. Nothing was the same since Lyndon became president. Everything about the Democratic Party felt different. Camion said that Johnson wasn't Kennedy but he *was* a Sam Rayburn Democrat. That was something, at least. Jaeckel said he should quit sending people to Vietnam. Curling said they were only observers. Jaeckel said, "Observers my ass."

Pedaling home, it started to rain and getting my umbrella open I rode no hands. Rounding the curve on lower Manzanita across from the little mall next to Safeway, it started to pour. I crossed the mall and leaned my bike against the plate glass window of a Kodak shop, and went in. Larry's wife was there with their little boy. He was just starting to walk and she held him by the hand. He was looking at a large colored photo of snow in the mountains.

She was wearing white slacks and a peach orange soft woven turtleneck. We talked for a few minutes. She still had a deep tan and she wore silvery orange lipstick that made her lips look wet. She asked how Puss was doing in school. She asked if Ceil liked it in northern California.

That night when I told Ceil that I had seen her, she asked me what I thought about her.

"Everything's just hunky-dory. She uses the word 'great' three times in every breath."

"Virginia Garrison told me she's seeing a psychiatrist in Paradise."

"Larry mentioned that to me. He thinks about her all the time."

"He said that to you?"

"That she's seeing a psychiatrist?"

"No, that he thinks about her all the time."

"No, but I can tell."

"I don't even know her name."

"Eartha."

The following Saturday night, the seven Bourkes and Armatures had a cookout under the grape arbor on our cement patio. That morning it had rained hard and steady while Ceil shopped at Safeway's and then took Puss to her ballet lesson in the old school on the west side of the Esplanade near the big stand of cottonwoods. Ceil told me that if they hadn't had the umbrellas they would have been drowned.

Luke Gardner had picked me up in mid-morning and we drove to Ken Morrow's house to see his paintings and lift weights in Ken's barn studio. Ken had been bitten by a black widow spider two weeks before while moving a pile of boards beside the barn, and he had had no feeling up to his elbow for ten days, but he didn't look like he was impaired. He was pressing two hundred pounds and doing squats with almost twice that much weight. Luke did some bench presses and I did three sets of curls with sixty-five pounds. After a while I pressed a hundred and ten five times, twice.

I had lifted in high school and it interested me. When I was in the seventh grade I saw the Charles Atlas advertisements showing the bully kicking sand all over the skinny guy's girlfriend, and sent away for twenty-five cent booklets telling how to develop a strong grip and big biceps. My friend Ray Maes up the street had weights in his father's barn-garage, and sometimes we lifted together when Ray was recovering from rheumatic fever. I was playing football on the junior varsity team and I could curl sixty-five pounds ten times.

Ken could curl a hundred and fifty pounds with ease. He was a strong guy and he could paint. He painted with white glue that he mixed with colors and he gave us a demonstration. Later, he gave Ceil and me one of the paintings, on the back of which he wrote in red ink, "An armored man from a man with no armor." His paintings were in a lot of California museums.

Before the dump north of Chico closed at four, Puss and I drove to it with the trash. As we took turns throwing paper bags of trash on the pile for the bulldozer, the rain became a light mist.

"It's going to stop, daddy, I know it's going to stop for the cookout," Puss said.

"Got my fingers crossed, Vanilla Ice Cream," I said.

When Eartha and Larry and the kids arrived at five-thirty, the gray sky had become blue with low dark clouds moving fast, and Ceil had all the stuff that people eat at cookouts piled on a table in the TV room that opened on the patio. Eartha had brought sweaters for her kids, and Puss and Semantha led the cheers for moving it all outside.

They went out and wiped off the redwood table and piled food on it. Larry and I fooled around with some damp wood for awhile and then I broke up some long thin molding that was in the garage, and we got a fire going in the outside grill. The air was nice and the sun was alternating in and out among the moving clouds. We opened one of the four bottles of Napa cabernet that Ceil told me to get on my way home from the dump. I also brought out an unopened bottle of DeWars and a half-bottle of Jim Beam. When Eartha saw the DeWars, I saw her face, and I asked her pleasure, wine or whiskey.

"I'd *love* a Scotch on the rocks," she said, with smiling, neighborly Saturday night intimacy, and I took three cubes from a bowl of ice that Ceil had gone after when she saw me come out with the whiskey, dropped them in a whiskey tumbler, and poured Eartha a good one. I saw Larry looking at the size of the drink that I poured for Eartha. She took a polite sip and said, "Great," avoiding Larry's eye and pretending to watch the kids who were in their bare feet playing tag on the brown and yellow grass that would turn green in the spring.

Larry and Ceil were drinking the cabernet and I poured myself an inch of Jim Beam. The two girls were guiding young Jamey and poking around under the grapefruit tree. Puss called over to me and asked if they could pick some for bowling balls and I yelled back, "Two."

Ceil had bought two huge chuck steaks and we listened to them sizzling and spitting on the grill. I switched to wine and we went through two bottles in the next hour, talking and eating and supervising the kids who were eating and playing at the same time. Eartha was lowering the Dewars in the bottle. I told her to help herself, but she never did. Each time I offered her another, she said, "I'll have a little one."

It got colder and we went inside. Ceil suggested we christen our fireplace in the living room, so I used some pieces of molding to start the fire, adding dried bamboo that I had cut up after thinning the patch between the far side of the fireplace and the redwood fence. More bamboo shoots were needling up through the grass, and Larry warned me that if I didn't get rid of the bamboo I would have a losing battle on my hands.

The fire was going good and the four of us sat around on the floor. The girls were playing Battleship across the room. Jamey got fussy and Eartha picked him up. She was holding him in one arm and her Dewars in her other hand, jouncing him to quiet him when something in the fireplace blew up. The explosion was loud enough so that we all ducked our heads. It sounded like a shotgun going off, and pieces of burning wood shot against the back and the sides of the fireplace and up the flue, and some of them out into the room. Larry got hit on the shoulder. The little boy screamed and we were all on our feet, unnerved and wondering what had happened, when Larry, who had picked up the glowing piece of wood and tossed it back into the fire, said, "It's the bamboo. The air pockets between the sections contracted and exploded. We need a fireplace screen. Another one may go off any second."

I went to the garage and got the old screen that came with the house. We were standing around talking about it when another piece exploded, but not as loud.

Eartha's two-year old stopped screaming but was whimpering and wanted to have some of the drink in Eartha's hand. Eartha held the drink toward Jamey as if to ask him if he really wanted to taste the Scotch, and when he nodded she put the glass to his lips and raised it. Jamey took a swallow. Within three or four seconds he retched and vomited it onto her white angora sweater. Larry, who was heading for Eartha as soon as he saw her offer Jamey the Scotch, took the boy and walked him around the room.

"I guess that was a mistake," Eartha said.

When they had gone, I read Puss the next to the last chapter of her *Prince Valiant* book, and called Ceil and she came in and kissed Puss goodnight. Puss asked us what happened that made Larry want to go home, and Ceil told her that Jamey had gotten sick.

Chapter Fifteen

JAECKEL TOLD ME OVER coffee one morning at the Oaks that he got a buck that morning, and I was so removed from the real world that I thought he was talking about money. I told Ceil about it and she wondered what it would be like for Puss this winter without snow.

That afternoon I bought chains for the car. On Saturday we drove to Stirling City in the mountains beyond Paradise where an old man operated a small ski lift. Driving back down into the valley that afternoon I felt as if we were re-entering another version of Paradise, one in which we had found a way to live together without testing each other's breaking points and in which Puss could live something like what the world calls a normal life. Ceil was being promoted to a full time assistant managership at the fabric store, and I had begun to go to Exchange Club with Larry and a lot of Chico's middle managers and young business entrepreneurs. In one way or another they were all on the make, and since they assumed that I was too, we got along. They even started to levy dollar lunch fines at me. At night I read to Puss from *Wind in the Willows*.

Larry talked a lot about Eartha. They had come from the South Shore in Massachusetts a couple years before we arrived, with a seven-year old girl and a baby on the way. Eartha was homesick from the first day. After two or three months Larry was taking her to a family counselor in Oroville on Wednesday evenings, but she never told Larry what they talked about and she never seemed to be any happier. People they spent time with never knew that Eartha was homesick. Larry said that he didn't know homesickness could last two years. I said I didn't either. He started coming to Chico Democratic Club meetings with me once a month after Kennedy died, and soon was talking about going with Camion and a small group of us to the California Democratic Council convention in Long Beach in the spring.

The winter rains stopped at the end of February and some of the March days were bright and warm. Ceil and I planned a trip to San Francisco, and when Puss lobbied to stay with Semantha, I fixed it with Larry. When I told Ceil it was OK with Eartha, I tried to make it seem as if we were doing them a big favor by letting Puss stay with them. Eartha had some nice qualities, and one of them was that she was good with kids. We hadn't seen much of them since the bamboo exploded in the fireplace. Larry's seeming interest in politics was all Camion needed to open what he called the "grass roots doors of our great party," and when I asked Camion where the hell he got that metaphor he accused me of being an English teacher in disguise. He had asked me to be Butte County chairman of Cranston's '64 campaign in the California primary for the Senate, but I wasn't ready. I was moved to do good for the Democratic Party, but I didn't know anything about running a political campaign. I suggested Luke Gardner. Camion ejaculated "Hah!" and I thought that was that until I saw him at the Club meeting a couple of days before Ceil and I were leaving for San Francisco. He asked me to sit in his car with him for a while when the meeting ended. I said I came with Larry and he said bring him, he wanted to talk to both of us.

"I talked to Alan about this fellow Gardner. Do you think he'd do it?"

"Ask him," I said, "he comes to all the meetings."

"Alan was an English major at Stanford," Camion said, "He's an all around guy."

Then Larry said, "If he won't do it, I will." Larry looked at me. "We'll do it together."

Camion said, "Done, let's go to the Onager for a drink."

"Wait," I said, "wait a fucking minute. We're a couple of innocents from the east. Sandhill will eat us for breakfast in the paper."

"Don Way will tone it down. I'll talk to him. He likes you."

Larry said, "Maybe it would be bad publicity for my business. I just thought of it on the spot. It could be a bad idea."

"Bullshit," Camion said. "It would be good for business. Good publicity.

All the lawyers and half the businessmen in town are in politics because it's good business."

"I don't know," I said, "I don't have a business, I just don't want to make a fool of myself. Everyone will think I want something."

"You do. You want to do something for your country and this is just the place to do it. Californians are partisan in their politics and open-minded about their money and their friends. Lawyers in the same law firm work against each other in political campaigns just to show the world how open-minded they are. It's all bullshit."

"I don't know," I said. "I have to think about it."

"Look at Bannister," Camion said. "Everybody in northern California knows he's Clare Engels' man in Chico. Art Mallory is Bannister's brother-in-law and he's Bill Knowland's man."

"They're both incumbents," I said.

"So's Alan. So what if he's running for U.S. Senator. Everybody still thinks the inheritance tax business is a Republican office. It'll be great for business." He was looking at Larry. "Let's get that drink."

We parked in the light rain down the street from the Brazen Onager. Larry and I jogged while Camion walked stoop-shouldered next to the sidewalk buildings. We waited for him and went in together. The place was almost full of college kids. We took a table near the far side and Larry and I ordered dark beers. Camion had a bourbon with soda.

Larry looked at me and said he'd do it if I would. I said I'd help him if Camion would tell us what needed doing and how to go about doing it. Camion said Cranston's office in Sacramento would get out an announcement next week and we'd all go down to the paper and tell Don Way it was coming. Don would like that.

As we were leaving, I saw the redhead who gave me directions that first day in Chico, sitting with the chippy bartender with the blonde hair. I thought about going over and saying hello to her to devil him, but I let it go.

Chapter Sixteen

THE VALLEY WAS TURNING green, and Ceil and I drove route 99 south, past Durham toward Yuba City and Marysville.

"I feel as if we just drove out of a strange dream," she said, "Chico is like living in a foreign country."

"Is that bad or good?" I said.

"I don't know, I don't think it's either. It's just Chico."

I felt very good, and she looked very good. Maybe, I thought, we're holding this thing together. I knew I didn't talk to her enough, and she had to guess at my feelings, but I didn't trust myself or her or the world. Maybe this was just an excuse to cover up not knowing what I felt. I should have at least told her that I was on the edge of something, that I had crazy dreams of flying at supersonic speeds between buildings I had never seen, with Puss in my arms, passing over factories and martial fields in the countryside, so fast that everything we left behind fell together in a narrow cone. But I didn't tell her.

"Puss is happy to be staying with Semantha," I said.

"Eartha seemed happy to have her."

"Eartha's happy about everything except everything."

"Larry calls her 'Thee' once in a while. It's a funny nickname. I wonder where it comes from," Ceil said. We were south of the Marysville Buttes, passing between peach orchards with red buds. It was fun to talk about nothing together.

"It's probably short for Earthy," I said.

Ceil socked me on the shoulder. "That's pretty. You can be clever sometimes, Army old boy. I might just think about falling in love with you again."

"San Francisco here we come," I said. I was thinking about Larry and me running a political campaign.

"Let's stay at the Mark, Bill," Ceil said, "I've always heard about the Top of the Mark."

"The Fairmont's a beautiful hotel," I said, "everyone says so. The elevator rises on the outside. You can see the Golden Gate and everything."

"You choose, oh great listener to others, just bunk me in the same room."

"I already have a reservation at the Mark. I was just kidding. Herb Caen had something about the Crown Room in his column last week."

"Let's go there too, Bill, let's do everything."

That night we ate at the Top of the Mark and the city spread before us like a pastel tablecloth. We pointed out Telegraph Hill. The last rays of the sun were soft layerings in the clouds. We ate slowly and very well, and were glad to be married. For dessert we ordered sliced navel oranges and chunks of fresh coconut in glass goblets so large we couldn't finish.

From our room on the sixteenth floor we could see the lights of the Golden Gate Bridge and the darkness of the peninsula beyond, except where street lamps traced roads winding into the hills. We undressed slowly and lay down on the bed with the bathroom light on so we could see each other.

I knew what Ceil liked and tasted her for a long time. She was very good to me and we were alone in a hundred rooms at once and everything was easy and kind and we loved each other very much. Neither of us knew when the other fell asleep.

On Saturday morning we walked along Union Street. West of Van Ness the houses were tar stained and old and very bright in the early air, made of Maine lumber, black as live lobsters. Azaleas burned spring red in gardens. We walked past little galleries and shops and pointed out quaint doorways. The air was ocean air and we were back in our lost childhoods in New England.

"Let's move to San Francisco, Bill." We were sitting in the back courtyard of a small gallery where they served gourmet coffee and home made breakfast cakes. Our table was round and iron, painted glossy white, and we drank cappucino from little china cups. At the center of the table was a silver bowl with Perugina chocolates.

"Let's buy an airplane and fly down every weekend."

"Whichever. You choose. I'm easy."

"You were last night."

"Oh ho," she laughed, "You want to talk rough."

"Just appreciating the terrain," I said, unwrapping a Perugina chocolate. I offered it to her, but she held up one she chose, so I ate it in one bite.

In the afternoon we rode up the outside elevator of the Fairmont and sipped whiskey sours in the Crown Room. The chairs were Victorian velvet, the drinks were orange and yellow and red, and the sky was very blue with very white clouds. "I can see where they filmed *Vertigo*," Ceil said.

"There's Alcatraz," I said.

"Let's ride the cable cars and then take a cruise in the Bay."

"Let's go to Chinatown for lunch and then the zoo."

"Oh Bill, it's all treasure."

"Look at the clouds," I said. They were big and white and baggy, like white magic genies with hidden heads.

"Why isn't everybody happy?"

"They haven't paid the price," I said, but I was wondering as I said it if I had paid enough myself. Things were going very well.

Chapter Seventeen

IN APRIL, PUSS GOT pneumonia, and two weeks later, Ceil came down with it. I cooked for them and read to them and while they slept I worked on an article for Don Way on the upcoming vote in Sacramento on re-districting northern California on the basis of population. I also drew several political cartoons that I didn't like when they were finished, and threw them away. Sitting in Puss's room, reading to her, I could hear the bubbling in her chest when she breathed. Outside, a few oranges and lemons still hung in the green leaves from last year, orange balls and giant yellow drip pearls. It was warm and sunny and the skies were blue. Gardenias and camellias bloomed in the bushes along the front of the house. Virginia Garrison brought over casserole dishes, more than we could ever eat, and told me that there was wetness in the air from the flooded rice fields south of town, and that many people from the east had died in their first two years in California. She said that Puss and Ceil would recover because they had gone right to bed and they were being taken care of.

I had given up going to Long Beach for the convention, but one day I couldn't hear the bubbling in Puss's chest as she breathed, and within a few days Ceil wanted to get up from bed. Their appetites came back. Ceil said I should go to Long Beach to keep Camion company. He was gracious and gentlemanly with Ceil whenever he saw her, always calling her Mrs. Armature, and she liked him. She said he was an old fashioned gentleman. "You're his political pal," she said, "he depends on you. Besides, Larry would never go if you didn't."

Two weeks later, I was in the front seat with Camion, Larry in back with Will Curling, driving through the wine country east of San Francisco, then the hot Central Valley and Bakersfield, the Pasadena foothills, San Diego, the oil wells of Long Beach. It took us almost eleven hours because Camion made us stop in Pasadena for Mexican food. Larry and I called home to tell Ceil and Eartha that we were OK and almost there. Ceil said she was showing the girls how to make tapioca pudding, and after dinner she was going to take them to a Walt Disney movie. Larry left a message with Terry Garrison who was babysitting Jamey and the girls.

When we drove into the parking lot of the Hotel Imperiale, the Jimmy Roosevelt signs were hanging from some of the windows.

"He'll give Alan a tough fight," Camion said, "but he can't win." Camion told us to support either Roosevelt or Cranston as long as we also supported the winner. We could have gotten a suite for the three of us but Camion wanted his own room. Larry and I shared a double.

When we were checking in, Joan Jay rushed over and asked me, giggling nervously and swallowing to keep the saliva from collecting in the corners of her mouth, if I had seen Pat, and before I could say no, if he was with Dottie Bentley. That was when I found out who Pat's friend was. I told her I hadn't seen him.

"He came down yesterday," Joan Jay said, "I should have come with him, but I had to teach." She was both gay and disconcerted.

We put our bags in our room and found Jaeckel and Pat in the happy hour lounge. They had joined Luke Gardner and Jake Toothacher from Chico State's political science department, and a short, stout political scientist from the University of California at Davis.

"We ran into Joan Jay at the registration desk a half hour ago," I said. Pat and I had become friends. He knew I knew as much about him as everyone else, and we never went into detail. I joked with him in a way that avoided direct references to his affair with Dottie.

Pat smiled his open, bespectacled smile and said, "We've met somewhere." Then he looked at Jaeckel: "Did she ask you if Dottie came down yesterday?"

"Of course," Jaeckel said, sipping his beer, looking at Pat, his eyes twinkling through almost closed lids.

Camion came in and sat down, blowing air from between almost closed lips. "Everybody's here that signed up."

"Where's Ruth, John?"

"She's with Jake and Dottie, working the delegations for Cranston. You won't see them for the next two days, until we vote."

The short stout professor was holding court about issues. Larry said privately to me, "I thought Bannister was coming. He signed the list at the last meeting."

I said, "Hey Bob, where's Bannister, he signed the list?"

"Not coming," Camion said, tightening his jaw, shaking his head once, almost imperceptibly. He looked at his bourbon, picked it up and sipped it, and set it down, not looking at anybody. No one seemed to care whether Bannister was there or not, and I looked at Jaeckel who I knew would not miss the opportunity to make a comment about Bannister, and at that moment I realized that the others, except the short stout professor, all knew something Larry and I didn't know. Jaeckel was looking at his drink. I then also realized that I didn't know whether Larry knew something about Bannister he wasn't telling me.

I thought about Bannister and the small jokes I had heard about him being a lover boy, but they seemed inconsequential, just political gossip in a community addicted to salacious talk about one of their own. But it occurred to me now that there was also a hard edge to some of it. Once I heard Don Frontbridge say, "Did you ever watch him eat?" But I had never seen Bannister eat and I forgot it until now. Bannister laced his black wavy hair with an oily hair tonic, and he wore thick eyeglasses and spoke with an air of pretended intimacy and indulgent officiousness. He owned several almond orchards south of Chico and he turned in his Cadillac Grand Prix every fall for a new one. During election seasons he hosted county Democratic gatherings at his ranch home off the highway to Paradise. One fourth of his spacious ranch was a screened-in sitting porch with white leather sofas and glass cocktail tables, and the room was equipped with a sophisticated telephone speaker system. Senator Engel always called from Washington during these gatherings, and Bannister's guests listened over the amplified speaker system. Bannister would talk softly and suavely to his friend "Clare" with engaging tones of insider loyalty and respectful middleman professionalism. Bannister would carefully articulate the names of all those present in order that the Senator's staff could write down the names for personal letters of thanks, letters that were already in the mail, the carefully screened guest list having been sent to Washington by Bannister weeks earlier.

Clare Engel's Democratic voice in the U.S. Senate had been a strong asset to the party for years, and a crucial offset to his powerful almost-friend, Bill Knowland's Republican leadership on the other side of the aisle. As a banker and an almond magnate and politician, Bannister as Engel's northern valley man was a powerful moneyman with many interests. Some of these interests were beautiful women. Many people in Chico already knew that the current woman in Bannister's extra-marital life was Eartha Bourke.

Chapter Eighteen

LARRY AND I WORKED for Jimmy Roosevelt at the convention in Long Beach and didn't see much of Camion during the next two days. Camion was smart. Larry and I were amateurs. Camion knew that if we got hooked on this political game out of conviction, we'd work for the Party, and if Jimmy Roosevelt provided the bait, fine.

The Cranston people were insiders, committed personally to Alan, some out of conviction, some because they owed him, some because they were party loyalists who knew that an incumbent office holder was a safer bet than an outsider. Jimmy Roosevelt, however, almost fooled them. He held no political office but he was the son of Franklin Delano Roosevelt, and he had his father's silver tongue. Jimmy worked the delegations. Both Cranston and Roosevelt pledged to withdraw from the race and support the other in the general election if he lost here at the CDC convention. It was all or nothing, the grass roots way.

By the eve of the vote, the uncommitted were leaning toward Jimmy, and some of the uncommitted were Cranston's own people, not the hard core inheritance tax appraiser base, but the local CDC Club members around the state who had caucused in their cities and towns before coming to Long Beach, and who had never seen or heard Jimmy Roosevelt in action. They were listening to Jimmy talk specifics, and the more they heard the more they drooled.

Around 2:00 a.m. on the early morning of the day of the vote, Jimmy's staff called a general meeting in the lobby of the Imperiale, and the room was jammed. There was a tremendous excitement in the room because the crowd felt that a huge upset was churning. Jimmy started to talk, first in sweeping terms about America and democracy and the historic presence of the Democratic Party in California. He never referred to his father, or the White House, or his intimacy with the American presidency. He didn't have to. He looked a little like his father, and he sounded a little like his father, and he told funny and engaging and moving family stories about his mother without mentioning her name. Everyone in the standing-room-only crowd knew the names. If the vote had been taken when the meeting broke up at 3:00 a.m., Jimmy Roosevelt would have won the endorsement of the California Democratic Council for the general election in the fall.

The vote of the delegates was scheduled for 9:00 a.m. the following morning. As soon as the 3:00 a.m. meeting was over, the Cranston people went to work again, counting committed votes and lobbying the uncommitted. Whatever they had to do to retrieve the soft vote, they did, and sometime between 4:00 a.m. and 9:00 a.m., Jimmy Roosevelt lost the edge he had gained a few hours earlier.

Larry and I went to bed after Jimmy's speech with all of the applause and excitement of the early morning crowd still in our ears. Over breakfast, we believed we had participated in a momentous upset that would send a Roosevelt to the United State Senate. Maybe Jimmy would run for president. And we were here at the beginning.

Camion joined us as we ate our blueberry muffins and drank our second coffee. I had seen him at Jimmy's final speech, standing against a pillar in the ballroom, watching. After he ordered coffee and toast, I said, "What do you think, Bob?"

"Close."

"How close?"

"Alan's got a fight on his hands."

Lobbying was still going on in the delegates' rooms. I expected right up to 9:00 a.m. to be pressured, but I found out a year later that Camion put out to the word to Cranston's organizers not to put the hard sell on Larry and me. I never found out how Pat voted, he always smiled when I asked him. Ruth Jaeckel and Dottie Bentley voted for Cranston, and Joan Jay and Jaeckel voted for Roosevelt.

When the delegations were polled in the main ballroom, Cranston won by fifty votes. Jimmy Roosevelt made a gracious concession speech, and he kept his word and withdrew from the race. The next day's paper carried Pierre Salinger's announcement of his candidacy for the California senate seat.

After we returned from Long Beach, my political interests burgeoned. Puss and Ceil recovered completely. I forgot the lethal mists of the Golden State and waded into the wet political grasslands of northern California politics. Larry was my sidekick and Camion was close by. I was eagerly seduced into believing Jack Kennedy's comment that politics was a noble undertaking, and I even believed that running for office at least once was the duty of every citizen. Though I was only peeking with blurry eyes above the wet grasslands of mundane local politics, I nonetheless joined the long citizen journey of the sixties into troubled waters.

Larry and I were named Butte County co-chairmen of the Cranston for Senate campaign. No one remembered or knew about or cared that we voted for Jimmy Roosevelt at Long Beach, and we thought that Pierre's candidacy was a joke. We talked with Don Way in his office at the paper, even told him of our renegade status in Long Beach, which amused him, and he took our picture and printed it in the paper. Camion rented a storefront walk-in on the lower Esplanade and we decorated it with balloons, and Cranston sent his sister and her husband to Chico for a grand opening. Don Way sent over a photographer and printed a photograph on the front page the next day of Larry and me holding two ends of a string of crepe paper in the walkway of the front door under a sign that read "Cranston Headquarters," with Cranston's sister and husband cutting the crepe with an oversized pair of scissors. Larry and I were razzed at the Exchange Club meeting, and Larry's business picked up. Everything was going fine. Politics was easy.

When Puss got out of school in late spring, we took her to Lake Tahoe for a week and swam, and sat on the beach, and then drove to Reno where Puss had to stay behind the sidewalk lines at the casino entrances, so we didn't go inside. We crossed the mountains through Donner Pass where I told Puss about the Donners and the Reeds and how the mountains defeated them.

"Why didn't they start earlier?" Puss asked.

I told her that they started as soon as they could, all the way back in St. Louis in the spring.

"But why did they cross the big salt desert?"

I told her that somebody fooled them.

"Why didn't they look at the map?"

I told her that there weren't any maps then.

"Why did they leave home anyway?"

She was at the bright age when all the answers ended up as questions and all the questions ended up as answers.

"It beats me," I said.

After a long silence she said, "You really don't know?"

"Nope."

Another silence, then "Why did you come to California, daddy?"

Ceil elbowed me.

I thought about it. "You know that big old house I took you to see over by the college, the one I told you I sold?"

"Uh huh."

"I needed to sell it. Remember I told you?"

"If you kept it, we could have fixed it up and lived in it."

"Did you forget I told you about that?"

"No, I remember."

Long silence.

"Are we going to live in California for all time?"

"All time is a long time."

"I know. Are we?"

"Would you like to?"

"I think so. If Semantha does."

"Don't you think Semantha will?"

"She doesn't know. Her parents are talking funny about it."

Chapter Nineteen

THAT SUMMER, I WENT fishing with Larry twice, both times in the mountains, but he never mentioned Eartha. Pierre Salinger barnstormed southern California where the big vote was, and Cranston never had a chance in the September primary. On the eve of the election, Channel 6 in Chico ran an hour film of Pierre's life, showing stills of Pierre with his dog in the backyard when he was a kid, and wearing a sailor hat on a submarine in World War

II. The Chico paper ran a photo of Larry and me on election day in polling booths on either side of Trudy Solstice, a blonde looker who was Pierre's chairman. The photo was a side shot with our faces turned over the shoulder to the camera as we were marking our ballots and saying "cheese." Trudy was a dead ringer for Debbie Reynolds. Salinger beat Cranston hands down in the primary.

The day after the election, Larry told me that he was relieved, that he needed to spend all his time on his business. He said it in such a way that I knew both that his mind was made up and he didn't want to talk about it. It was obvious that Larry's and Eartha's troubles were escalating, and I let Larry go without a protest. I began to bask in the limelight of California politics.

Democrats were hooting about the Republican nominee, George Murphy the Hollywood actor, gloating over Pierre's candidacy, especially after Clare Engel died and Pat Brown appointed Pierre to be U.S. Senator. Big billboards appeared around the Golden State with the words, SENATOR SALINGER. It didn't go down with the voters. Too much Pat Brown.

In September, Camion and I drove to Sacramento to see Don Blair, the Party's political director, and Camion made a case for me as Lyndon Johnson's Butte County campaign manager. Camion told Blair that I was also interested in running against Howard Handle, the local state senator. It was the first time I had heard about it. Camion was shrewd. He knew that if he said it here he wouldn't have to talk about it with me until the idea had some sun on it and I might be softened.

Blair was ice cold. He said that there wasn't much rural political capital in easterners, but he'd think about it. We didn't know that Orrin Oliver, a prominent Chico lawyer who had been Kennedy's campaign manager in 1960, had made phone calls to Blair complaining about my political ambitions. Blair also knew that Oliver hadn't lifted a finger in the Kennedy campaign and that no one in the county even knew that he had been Kennedy's campaign manager. Oliver had never talked to Don Way. Camion in the meantime had gone to Pat Henry to find out why Blair was holding back on appointing me, and Pat told him. As a newcomer and an easterner, I was poison. Camion suggested to Blair that they name Oliver honorary chairman and me chairman. Blair waited another two weeks and made the appointment. I was the last county chairman for Johnson to be named in California. Don Way ran the photo, Oliver on one side of a large picture of Lyndon, and me on the other. We were smiling our best smiles.

About a month later, well into the campaign, I called Oliver on the phone to invite him to introduce a former state Democratic chairman at a campaign luncheon we were planning. As soon as I identified myself, he told me I was the most ambitious man he ever met. It dawned on me too slowly that he had had a few drinks. I raised my voice when he told me that he had been Kennedy's campaign chairman and how the hell did I get off lobbying for the Johnson chairmanship. I was about to tell him to go fuck himself when Ceil lifted her hands at me, and I hung up. She said it wasn't such a hot idea to talk to old time local political brethren I didn't know well during the cocktail hour.

After dinner, Terry Garrison came over to baby sit and Ceil and I drove to Democratic Headquarters on California Street. The day after Blair announced my appointment as Johnson's county chairman, Camion rented the large vacant storefront that became Johnson Headquarters. We went to the five and dime and bought crepe paper and streamers and blew up balloons and swept out the place and put up a big red, white and blue Johnson sign. We put the balloons in the windows and hung Johnson's picture all over the place and a large hand-printed notice about Thursday dance night fund-raisers for Lyndon. Camion bought another coffee urn and several packages of paper cups and five pounds of sugar. I called Larry at his office to come on down and drink some coffee with us.

"Don't tempt me," he said, and hung up.

Camion asked me to keep house and got in his car and drove one block to the Episcopal Church where he hit up the rector for the loan of some chairs. An hour later a pickup truck pulled up in front with thirty folding chairs from the church basement. The following Thursday night we put on the first Dance for Lyndon, an informal headquarters open house with no admission charge to dance to phonograph records. Drinks were a dollar. Ruth and John Jaeckel brought the phonograph and a stack of Glenn Miller and Tommy Dorsey and Al Hirt records.

An hour after we opened on the first Thursday night, Larry and Eartha showed up. When I caught Larry's eye, he looked at me as if to tell me something, but when I asked him in the men's room what was up, he said, "Nothing, forget it."

"Are you pissed off at me?"

"No, I'm not pissed off at you. What do you think I am, a jerk?"

Larry wasn't dancing, so I got him to alternate with me as bartender. When I was pouring, Ceil danced with Pat and Jaeckel and Luke Gardner, and even Bannister. Joan Jay wasn't there, and when I asked about her, Pat said she didn't dance but that she'd be over later after she corrected a civics test on state primaries. He implied that she'd be over to check on whether Dottie Bentley was there. Pat was having a good time. Joan Jay actually stuck her head in the door at 9:30, looked around and disappeared until almost 11:00 p.m. Dottie never showed up. The only time I ever saw her was at Club meetings and conventions.

During the evening, Camion played the role of sergeant-at-arms. He stood stoop-shouldered near the improvised bar sipping his drink, watching the dancing, nodding and listening without changing his expression when someone came over to talk to him. He also bought a lot of drinks for others.

"Have a drink on the Democratic Party," he'd say, "to celebrate the coming defeat of that local Arizona policeman." He would peel off the dollar from a wad he kept in his shirt pocket. Occasionally I'd hear him blurt out "Hah!" and I'd look over and see his eyes twinkling, not looking at the person he was talking to. Camion never seemed affected by how much he drank. He was single-minded at a party or on the road, his eyes straight ahead, his shoulders bent forward with both hands on the wheel, driving fast and straight.

Luke Gardner came in with Roxanne about 9:30 and Eartha stopped dancing with Larry to greet Roxanne, who was overweight and pretty. I could hear Eartha's "Proxy!" half way across the room. Roxanne took Eartha's hand, laughing, guiding her to the bar and holding up an open palm to Eartha to ask her pleasure. Eartha ordered a Dewars.

Roxanne said, "Make it a double, on me, and I'll have your best rye and ginger. Make it a double also, I'm behind all you handsome politicos, and we have to help the party. Hi Bill. It's Bill isn't it?"

"It's Bill, at your service," I said, and poured their drinks.

Camion raised his glass an inch to recognize Roxanne and Luke's arrival. If he were wearing a hat he would have tipped it. Luke went over to talk to him, and Camion steered him back to the bar and peeled off a dollar and handed it to me. I took the cap off a Hamm's beer for Luke. A little while later I saw Eartha dancing with Bannister again, long-into-the-party cheek to cheek stuff. Larry was tending bar for me and I was dancing with Joan Jay who had poked her head in the door and was withdrawing it again, saying "Back later," when I called to her for just one dance, and she tilted her head sideways and looked at me and came back in.

"Just one," she said. "I'm a lousy dancer, I'll ruin your shoes."

"I'll get another shine," I said. "Trust me."

"All men say that," she laughed.

Two hours later, driving home, Ceil said, "It's Bannister isn't it."

"Looks like it."

"I don't like him."

"They say that other women do."

"Isn't he married?"

"Pat says that she's a nice woman."

"Kids?"

"Two, around eleven or twelve."

"Jake Toothacher told me tonight that the divorce rate in the California Democratic clubs is higher than it is in the English department at the college."

"That's a beaut of a statistic. He's in the wrong profession. He ought to be a divorce lawyer instead of a political scientist."

"I hope you know what you're getting into."

"Trust me," I said, "I just want to see where my civic duty takes me."

Chapter Twenty

I WAS SOON PRESSING Larry to get back into the Johnson campaign and help me, but he wanted nothing to do with it, he had too many things on his mind. The President's Ball in Paradise raised $700.00. Every couple in Butte county with a tuxedo and an evening dress danced away an evening. I was getting ideas about a life of politics.

Ceil was puzzled at first, and dealt with it by kidding about my wanting to sleep in Lincoln's bedroom in the White House. But she made friends with Ruth Jaeckel and Joan Jay. She also began to spend more time with Eartha. Ceil told Eartha that the only other person she knew of who was named Eartha was Eartha Kitt. Eartha said that for the first six months she lived in Chico she couldn't cash a check because everyone thought she was a Mexican. Ceil repeated Eartha's saying, "I had my hair in a pigtail and I had a terrific tan from two weeks at Hyannis at the Cape before we moved here."

I asked her if Eartha told her why she plucked her eyebrows.

"Why would I ask her that?"

"Because women talk about those things. Don't they?"

"For crying out loud, Bill."

"Don't they?"

"That's very personal. No, women don't talk about why they pluck their own eyebrows, they talk about other women who pluck their eyebrows. They don't mention the plucking. Besides, Larry obviously isn't turned on by eyebrows like you are."

"Don't be so sure," I said.

Chapter Twenty-One

THE POLLS SHOWED THAT Johnson's lead was big in California, except in
Orange County. In 1960, Kennedy carried Butte County with no campaign
at all, and I was determined to carry the county bigger for Lyndon than for
Jack, for my own purposes.

I organized a yard-sign party behind the Chico art gallery, tapping
teenage kids to help make the signs and pound them in offered front lawns.
Pat and Camion stood around watching Luke Gardner and me and John's
kids, Pat's kids, and Ken Morrow's kids, all stapling Lyndon's picture to box-
sides and nailing them to sharpened lathe stakes. Camion got the posters
from Sacramento and was enjoying himself at the center of a "real goddam
political grass roots campaign." Pearl Kenneally and Ruth Jaeckel were on the
phones all morning and got forty-five party loyalists to accept more yard signs.
Within two weeks, we had a hundred-and-fifty yard signs scattered around
Chico. Everyone who took a yard sign took at least one bumper sticker. We
had the same kids in the streets of downtown Chico on Saturday mornings
handing out bumper stickers. We also distributed them at Party headquarters,
and volunteer hawkers from the Club passed them out on Broadway and the
Esplanade during the week.

Camion was in a state of ecstasy. He said we ought to go after some real
money. I said, "Let's go, where do we get it?"

The Broadpenny and Heatherton Construction Company was an
upcoming firm in California's contracts for public works. They had done two
freeways in the San Diego area and they had been awarded the contract for
the construction of the Oroville dam. Camion called for an appointment and
we drove over the following Wednesday mid-morning.

We sat in a small compartment just inside the door of a temporary office
trailer about a quarter mile from the site of the dam. The trailer was one of
those portable house sections that wide-load trucks pull slowly along highways.
Enlarged black and white photographs of gravel trucks with oversize tires and
full loads in various stages of hauling and dumping at the dam decorated the
walls, the snake-curling causeway to the dumping platform teeming with
trucks, the landfill site rising load by load to one day becoming the largest
landfill dam in the world.

We were waiting for Gordon Breakwell, head construction engineer for
Broadpenny and Heatherton, to acknowledge and invite us into his office. An
auburn-haired secretary with thick glasses sitting at her plywood desk said he
was on the phone and would be with us in a few minutes. I was nervous. I had

never tried to extort money before, and didn't know how it worked. Camion said not to worry, it was only a political contribution.

"If it wasn't for the Democratic Party," he said, "there wouldn't be any dam. It's another great project of our great Party."

A constant stream of Broadpenny and Heatherton trucks gear-shifted past our window view.

"They own a lot of trucks," I said.

"This is the biggest contract in California right now," Camion said. "It's a bread and butter contract. They've got the trucks because they have to deliver the goods. They've also got to do plenty of public service stuff."

"Like what?"

"Viewing platforms, facilities for school bus trips, documentary films, guides, all tax write-offs."

"Donations to political parties?"

"This Breakwell fellow knows the score."

"You think he's a Democrat?"

"Dunno. Won't matter. He'll just be the middle man if the upstairs boys say yes."

"Won't he worry about tracing the money?"

"If they give us anything it'll be cash in an envelope."

The door opened and Breakwell was holding it half-open, motioning for us to come in.

"Gentlemen," he said, "sorry to keep you waiting."

He walked around a large old mahogany desk with scratches on the legs and sat down beneath more construction photos of the dam. Several engraved safety awards hung beneath a long rectangular engineer's drawing of the Aswan Dam, with the pyramids in the background.

"What can I do for you gentlemen?" he said, lighting a cigarette and tossing his pack on the table and pointing to it, gesturing to us to help ourselves.

Camion said, "Mr. Breakwell, I've brought over a young man to meet you. This is Bill Armature, and he's working hard to make sure that our great President gets re-elected in November."

Breakwell looked at me and nodded.

Silence. Camion and I hadn't talked about silences.

"Mr. Breakwell," I began, having no idea what I would say next.

Breakwell was studying me, waiting.

"I'm the Butte County chairman of the Johnson for President campaign, and we were hoping that your company might make a contribution to our campaign."

"Who's we?" he said, inhaling and exhaling cigarette smoke. He said it flatly, almost smiling.

"Mr. Camion and myself," wondering where that would lead us. I was in no man's land, and wished that Camion would break in and help pull the cannon. He didn't. Camion was watching Breakwell.

"Mr. Camion," I said, intending to bestow on Camion the official title of finance chairman of the campaign, but Breakwell cut me off.

"I understand that Mr. Camion is one of Alan Cranston's inheritance tax appraisers," he said. "I'm curious whether all of Mr. Cranston's tax people are soliciting funds for the Democrat Party. Can you help me with that?"

Camion, without moving anything but his head, turned it slightly, keeping his eyes directly on Breakwell, and coughed. "In my capacity as a private citizen, and as a member of both the Paradise and the Chico Democratic clubs, I'm helping young Mr. Armature in our Butte County effort to help our great President. All the money we raise stays in Butte County."

"I see," Breakwell said. He was enjoying giving the impression that he was educating himself in the political arena, a place that was quite foreign to him, a civil engineer merely fulfilling a contract with the state of California, one, to be sure, that had been awarded only by an accident of history, by a Democratic administration. He edged forward in his soft-edged but poignant manner, apparently hoping that we would make the connection for him between the Brown administration and the Broadpenny and Heatherton contract. "And so you're hitting up all the businessmen in Butte County whose state contracts were awarded by the Democrat administration?"

"We're not hitting you up, Mr. Breakwell, we're asking for legitimate contributions from anyone who might help us." My vision of a few thousand dollars contribution was evaporating. I felt awkward and naive. Breakwell wasn't a Republican, he was a John Bircher. His second use of the word 'Democrat' in 'Democrat Administration' in 1964 was the key. There wasn't any use talking further to this guy.

"We understand your reluctance," I said, "and we won't take any more of your time. The other part of our trip was to see the progress of the dam, so we'll be taking one of your guided trips. No hard feelings about the contribution. Some people give and some don't. We wish you all the best with this project."

"Exactly how much money were you thinking about," Breakwell said.

"We didn't have a dollar figure in mind," I said.

"I'm sure you'd agree that whatever we did for one side, we'd have to do for the other side also. Our company has no political preferences."

"Of course," I said.

"I'll tell you what gentlemen, let me have a few minutes to check the protocol in these matters with some of our people, and see what they say. Maybe our public service monies fit this sort of thing."

Camion and I stepped into the front cubicle with the thick-glassed secretary and sat down. Her buzzer rang and she excused herself and stepped into Breakwall's office, closing the door.

"The John Birch son of a bitch," Camion said softly.

Trucks outside were grinding into lower and higher gears, going and coming to the dam site. I got up and looked out the window. "It's a massive project," I said.

"Goddam right it is."

The secretary came out of Breakwall's office and left our building.

"Where the hell did she go?" I said.

"To the safe."

"What do you think he'll give us?"

"Twenties."

"I mean, how much."

"Are you holding your breath?"

The secretary came back in ten minutes with a briefcase and disappeared into Breakwell's office. She came out and sat down behind her desk. She offered us coffee, apologizing for not having real cream. We shook our heads, thanking her.

Breakwell opened the door and invited us back into his office. He closed the door and handed me a blank white envelope.

"I hope this helps," he said. We thanked him, shook hands, and left.

Inside the car, I started to open the envelope.

"Wait," Camion said, "The son of a bitch is probably watching out the window." He started the car and we headed up the curving dirt road toward the dam site.

I opened the envelope and there were twelve twenties and a ten. "Do you think he'd have gone higher?"

"He might have. It wouldn't have been worth it. Better to grab the chicken feed and run than try and round up the whole flock and feel the buckshot in our ass."

"Who do you think he called?"

"His boss in L.A., and his boss called their lawyers."

"Why two hundred and fifty?"

"Because it's chicken feed, that's why. They give, don't worry, but they give at the office, and the office is in L.A."

"So we don't mention this to anyone?"

"Not a goddam soul. If Blair found out we just hit up Johnson and

Heatherton he'd be pissed off at us for trying to cut ourselves in on the Central Committee's statewide money. Butte County's a hick place to them.

At the dam, fifty trucks were moving up and down the dumping sites. We parked in the visitor lot and sat in one of the tour buses that went to the viewing platforms. They left every fifteen minutes. We stopped at three different spots and watched the dump trucks back up to the men with red flags, crack in the middle to raise their bins and ease out their loads. They dumped at intervals as precise as incoming flights landing at the San Francisco airport. The Feather River gorge was growing a mountain.

"They ought to name it Brown Dam, god damn it," Camion said.

Chapter Twenty-Two

A MONTH BEFORE, AT the Democratic National Convention in St. Louis, Bobby Kennedy and Carol Channing had dramatized the raw and the cooked in the Democratic Party that would, four years and three months later, help elect Richard Milhous Nixon President of the United States. The convention had bristled with delegates as divided in their loyalties as public officials in Washington and Richmond during the Civil War. Bobby, forlorn and frail, spoke to the convention from a box distant from party dignitaries, with Jackie sitting at his side, and remembered his brother Jack. The country wept again.

Carol, velvety and grainy, belted out Broadway for Lyndon, the perfect Dolly, oh so glad to be invited back home to the White House. Democrats, half-embarrassed, almost chipper, cheered themselves by poking fun at Goldwater. It was barely tolerable for most Democrats outside Texas to see Johnson's people poised to move back into the West Wing. But it was also unthinkable to imagine Goldwater people there.

Two weeks later, while the rest of the country watched the Republican convention on television, several of us drove to San Francisco to see for ourselves. Joan Jay had gotten a dozen first day gallery tickets for her civics class, and six of us became her students for the trip. Years later, in a quieter and less zealous time of my life, I came to see both Johnson and Goldwater in different lights, and regretted my dismissive scorn of Goldwater the man, but it remains also a part of history, however, that in July 1964, the Republican Party was in the hands of the John Birchers with their cadres of well-dressed beady-eyed young men, zealous to get some order and discipline back into patriotism in America.

Meanwhile, I was willingly being tempted by all the ego goodies that political cheerleading sucks into one's path. I was ripe for the political picking.

Those of us who drove down for the opening sessions of that convention did so with all the confidence that Lyndon would swamp Barry in November, and we were cocky and carefree. Pat and I and Luke Gardner and Jaeckel squeezed into a 1959 sedan owned by a Chico Republican who taught history at the college, Old Hutch, an old time Republican who supported Nelson Rockefeller, and Larry, who, when he found out that I was going, asked if he could come along. I didn't know what that meant, because he wasn't showing any signs of getting back into the campaign with me, but everyone was glad to have him. Old Hutch's real name was W.W. Hutchinson and he had written a two-volume study of the California career of Thomas Robert Bard, *Oil, Land and Politics*.

"Why is Larry going?" Ceil asked me, the night before we left.

"Search me," I said, imitating my mother's expression when she was truly puzzled.

"Doesn't he know he's playing into Bannister's hands?"

"He probably doesn't think of it in such literal terms."

"He ought to."

"Should I tell him he's a dope to leave Eartha alone up here?"

"Of course not. Who the hell knows?"

Joan Jay got two extra tickets at the last minute and squeezed seven students into a Dodge station wagon loaned by a Chico businessman, a middle-aged old-fashioned Oklahoman from Oroville, a car dealer who owned the Motor Raceway. His family rattled across route 66 in the thirties and worked their way to the northern peach orchards with the Joads of Steinbeck's *Grapes of Wrath*. His name was Lemuel Loter and he ran twice against Rufe Granger for senator from Butte County. Loter lost by big margins both times and was bitter that Iowa Democrats in Butte County rejected an Okie working stiff in favor of a black-haired smooth talking Republican whose father made his money from cotton picked by his Oklahoma relatives. Loter liked kids and liked Joan Jay because she was for the kids and got her name in the paper all the time for taking kids to political conventions. Loter always had loaners for Joan Jay and her field trips.

Chapter Twenty-Four

LARRY AND I HAD heard that Goldwater's suite in the Mark Hopkins was on the 22nd floor, and on the afternoon we arrived, we decided to walk over and see if we could get up to the 22nd floor in hopes of seeing Barry. When we got there, a crowd had gathered in front of the hotel, and we pushed through far enough to get a glimpse of him walking from a black limo with a cordon of bodyguards and police escorts into the lobby of the hotel. We were close enough to see that he was deeply tanned, and in his dark blue suit, and with his silver wavy gray hair, wearing his horn-rimmed glasses, he was impressive. We watched him disappear into the hotel. His personal guards were very serious, focussed, ready for trouble. Young men in the crowd were yelling "Barry, Barry" as I had yelled to Kennedy when I saw him four years before in Boston on the eve of the election. I almost knew how they felt.

Larry and I worked our way into the hotel. We were drawn in by the old fascinations with power, and history in the making, and possible intrigue, and to give ourselves the illusion of participating in the lives of the famous. All unfulfilled yearning comes down to that enigmatic book title of the fifties, "*The Meaning of Meaning*." I doubt now that Paul Tillich would have seen any meaning at all in our curiosity about Barry Goldwater.

Standing near the elevators inside the Mark Hopkins, I noticed a group of men, five or six of them, who seemed to be guarding one of the four elevators. People using that particular elevator were being carefully screened, and only specified Goldwater insiders were being allowed to proceed upstairs, presumably to the 22nd floor.

All of a sudden, two men tried to get through the cordon of security guards and actually got into the elevator, but the scuffle that followed was quick and effective, and the men were strong-armed from the elevator. Larry said, "That's a Goldwater elevator and this is sure as hell a Goldwater hotel. Look around. Do you see any Rockefeller buttons?"

"Not one.

"Let's get out of here. The place gives me the creeps. These aren't happy people here."

"You ever been to Sausalito?"

"Nope. I ain't been anywhere except Eureka. I took Eartha over there to cheer her up last year, but it didn't."

"There's a ferry from the waterfront. Let's take it. You're right about this place."

We took a cab to Fisherman's Wharf. When he saw DiMaggio's, Larry asked the driver to stop.

"Let's go in," Larry said. "I heard about this place. Joe's father used to own it."

We went in and sat at the bar. Single customers sat alone at random tables.

"They have a big kind of a scallop out here," Larry said. "The name sounds something like baloney, did you ever eat it?"

The bartender overheard him and said, "Abalone. We got the best. I can serve you here." He was tall and bald and wore a black silk half-unbuttoned shirt with the sleeves rolled up. A gold medallion on a thick gold chain glistened in his chest hair. "You want?" he said neutrally, wiping the bar in front of us. He was a good-looking kid. He had shaved his head.

I nodded at Larry and he nodded back. "For two," I said.

When he brought the abalone, he explained that it was lightly fried in very hot olive oil. "Just a few seconds, both sides," he said.

We ate it all and had a couple beers. The abalone was better than good. Larry asked him if business was slow.

"This is so-so time, early. Goes good at six, six-thirty, then late. The necktie freaks with Deutsch haircuts are in town. Last night not good, tonight will be better. Next two nights wall to wall midnight crowd."

I asked him where to get the ferry to Sausalito.

"Two wharfs over."

A looker came in and sat at the other end of the bar and he lost interest in us.

On the ferry, Larry said, "He thought we were queer."

The boat passed within two hundred yards of Alcatraz. The prison buildings looked as if they sprouted from the island rock, tuberous and yellow and pocked.

We looked at the buildings. Smoke curled from a small roof pipe in one of them.

"I thought the place was abandoned," I said.

"Two weeks ago," Larry said, not hearing what I had said, "Bill Richards called me and asked me if I knew people were talking about Eartha and Bannister. He said he heard two women in the store talking, and thought I should know. I told him I didn't think there was anything there."

I nodded, and Larry held up his hand as I started to reply.

In Sausalito, we went in a bar, looking for a pay phone. Four motorcycles were parked outside. Larry had called Eartha from the Mark Hopkins, but the line was busy.

The one pool table in the bar was empty and I set my bottle of Coors on the edge and picked a cue stick and tapped the cue ball a couple of times, bouncing it off the bank. My stick was slightly crooked but it didn't bother me. Larry left the wall phone and came over, picking a cue stick from the rack. He rolled it on the table and picked another one.

"Did you get her?" I asked.

"Terry was there baby sitting." he said.

Larry hit the cue ball solidly, testing the banks, and it ricocheted around the table. The motorcycles were watching. One of them said, "It's an eastern game, fellas, bouncey the ball." He had recognized Larry's Boston accent. I knew Larry heard him but he didn't take his eyes off the cue ball. His jaw tightened and he pursed his lips without opening his mouth as he struck the cue ball with his stick again, hard, and it traveled the length of the table and cut the seven ball at an almost impossible angle into the corner pocket.

Larry had everyone's attention. Three of the four bikers were standing at our end of the bar, and the one who had spoken was half-sitting, half-standing at the closest bar stool. They were all drinking Budweisers from bottles. I knew Larry wanted the fight, so we had the advantage even though we were outnumbered. It was now a question of luck.

"Couple you fellas want a friendly game of pool?" Larry asked as he bent over the table, lining up to shoot the yellow one-ball that he had "spotted," not looking at them. No one replied.

Larry drilled the red three-ball into the corner pocket. He hit it so hard that the cue ball streaked off six banks before it rolled to a stop. Still no reply.

"Too bad," Larry said, almost to himself.

He walked over to me. "One game?" he said quietly, "just to make a point, then we'll go. OK?"

I nodded and picked the triangular ball rack from under my end of the table.

The four bikers mumbled something between themselves.

Larry took the rack from me and rounded up the balls with the corner of the rack and enclosed them, picking up several and plopping them inside so that the odd and even balls were distributed. He pressed the back row with his two thumbs so that all the balls were tight together.

"Break?" he asked me.

"You go ahead."

Larry drilled the cue ball and four balls dropped on the break. It was the best break I'd ever seen. More than two thirds of the balls were at the other half of the table.

"Nice break, Lar," I said.

"Piece of cake," he said, expressionless.

I never got the chance to shoot. Larry racked the table except for the eight and now had the cue ball positioned behind it, six inches directly in front of the side pocket nearest the four motorcycle boys. One of them said something I couldn't hear and they all laughed as Larry chalked his cue and lined up to shoot the black eight.

The shot Larry had left was the easiest pool shot in the game. The cue ball was at half table, two feet from the eight in a perfect line to the side pocket.

When they laughed, Larry looked up from the shot, directly at them behind the side pocket. All he needed to do was strike the cue ball softly, just below the mid-point of the ball, to sink the eight. If he struck the cue ball higher than its mid point it would follow the eight into the pocket for a scratch, and the eight would have to come out and be spotted for my chance to win the game. He also had to be careful not to strike the cue ball too hard or it might cause the eight to hit the leather backside of the pocket and jump the table. Side pockets do not hold the balls on hard shots as well as the end pockets do. Larry looked up at their laughing, and bent over the table.

"You sure you jokers don't want a game?"

The biker with the mouth said, "Maybe we don't play games." He was tall and angular, and he wore square-toed alligator boots. He was smoking a cigarette and when he lifted his right hand to inhale, the silver bracelet cuff on his wrist flashed in the dim light of the bar. The other three bikers were smiling at Larry.

Larry shifted his body slightly and drilled the cue ball into the eight so that the cue ball stopped dead where it made contact. The eight ball ricocheted off the back of the side pocket and headed straight for the head of the tall, ropey talker. If he hadn't ducked, it would have hit him in the face. The ball crashed off an antelope head hanging on the wall, then slambanged off a wooden table and rolled across the wooden floor.

Several things happened at once. The bartender yelled "Hey!" and the tall angular biker headed for Larry with the other three behind him, but they had to go around the table to get at us, their leather boots slipping on the waxed floor. The closest one coming around my end slipped one knee to the floor and grabbed the table to right himself. The other three were in a line heading for Larry.

Larry swung his cue stick like a baseball bat and caught the lead rusher on the side of the temple, just above the ear, and he went down like a potted plant. He was short and burly and out cold on the floor, bleeding.

I hit my man, who was off balance from circling and slipping, a straight jab to the nose, breaking it. I felt it go soft against my fist.

When Larry's second rusher stumbled over the cripple on the floor, Larry brought up his right knee into the rusher's face, and he went down.

Larry and I were standing side to side now. There was a clicking noise, and the fourth biker, a short burly fellow with beady eyes was holding an open switchblade, gently tossing it back and forth to each hand, the ends of his fingers moving slightly. Larry was still holding the small thin end of his broken cue stick. The jukebox music stopped. The bartender said, "Put away the blade, Haskell, or I'll call the cops."

I felt Larry groping behind him for my cue stick and I picked it up from the floor and handed it to him.

The biker ignored the bartender.

"You might as well come on, if you're coming," Larry said, now holding the good cue stick with both hands, as if he'd just stepped into the batter's box.

"I got the phone in my hands, Haskell," the bartender said. Neither Larry nor the biker looked at the bartender, but I did. He was holding the telephone up with his left hand, his right forefinger poised over the rotary dial.

The biker said, looking at Larry but talking to the bartender, "We go first, and we'll go."

The second and third to go down had cautiously gotten to their feet and were watching Larry, who nodded agreement, stepping back to keep swinging distance as they dragged the first to the door. He was conscious, but he was not in good shape. The knife backed away. Once they were all outside, I heard the click of the telephone being replaced in its holder. Larry leaned the cue stick against the table. One by one the motorcycles were starting outside. We counted three engines. After several more seconds the fourth coughed and started. Another twenty seconds and they roared off.

"Twenty bucks for the cue stick, and you guys can head out too, if you don't mind a hell of a lot," the bartender said. "The Coors and the pool game are on me."

Outside, Larry asked me if I had any more tourist spots we could hit, "Maybe something quieter, but it doesn't make a hell of a lot of difference."

I said I knew a place, but we'd have to rent a car. Down the street, we found an outside pay phone and called a car rental company. In another hour we were driving toward Muir Woods. It wasn't far away, but it was a long way from the Republican convention in San Francisco.

Chapter Twenty-Five

WE DROVE OUT OF Sausalito, up onto the main highway leading off the Golden Gate Bridge, and rounded the long slow curves through the eucalyptus forest that took us immediately into Marin County. The trees were dark and green and cool, and we paid at the entrance to Muir Woods and drove to the second parking lot.

"Are there bears in here?" Larry asked.

"You mean in addition to you?"

"They were assholes."

"They took to you right away," I said. "You owe me a knuckle."

"You break it?"

"Maybe," I said, "It's swelling."

"We'll tell Camion we took on some of Goldwater's elevator watchdogs."

We stepped along a forest trail and were immediately in dark woods. The redwoods were massive, and the woods were dark. Occasionally the late sun found its way in narrow slanting shafts, and we entered a small clearing where sunlight brightened the bases of several giant trees. The cool forest smelled clean.

"This is nice," Larry said.

"They say these are giant ferns, not trees," I said.

"It doesn't matter much to me, it beats Chico all to hell," Larry said.

We sat in the silence of the woods. The damp earthy smell brought me back to a Saturday morning and a crevice between two huge outcrops of rock above a valley in eastern Massachusetts when I was a boy scout. Two friends and I had cut white-pine branches and spread them over the top of the rock opening and we snuggled together in the cave we had made. I remember the feeling of lying there on my back, hidden from everything. Then I remembered my clarinet lesson and I half-ran, half-walked home."

"California's different from the east," I said.

"New York got screwed when the Giants came to San Francisco."

"Brooklyn got screwed worse when the Dodgers went to Los Angeles".

"Boston got screwed when the Braves went to Milwaukee."

"I had forgotten that. Then they went to Atlanta."

"Imagine playing baseball in Atlanta?"

"Old Peachtree Street. You ever see it?"

"No

"It's wide, just like in *Gone with the Wind.*"

"Good old Gable. He didn't give a damn," Larry said.

"I lit a match during that movie."

"You lit a match in the movie?"

"It was in the Paramount theatre in Lynn. I was with my older sister. I had some wooden matches in my coat pocket and I took one out and scratched it on the leather seat beside me. It flared and a lot of people around me made noises. I blew it out but it scared me."

"We were all kids once."

"My sister took the matches away from me. It was right after the Coconut Grove fire in Boston and nobody could smoke in theaters."

We didn't talk for a while.

"Do you remember the little girl's name?"

"What little girl?"

"In *Gone with the Wind.*"

"No. Wait a minute. It was Connie or something."

"Bonnie. Gable couldn't see anything but that kid."

"I remember the other guy, the guy that got wounded on the way home from the Klu Klux Klan meeting. Ashley."

"There wasn't any Klan meeting in that movie."

"Yeah there was. It was changed from the book. They had gone to a Klan meeting, and it was broken up by Union troops and Ashley got wounded. They made believe he was drunk. He was a fucking wimp, though."

"Melanie was worse," I said. "I didn't know you were an expert on *Gone with the Wind,*" I said.

"I'm not. I saw all of Gable's movies about ten times. *It Happened One Night* was the best."

"They say that he was screwing Marilyn when they made *The Misfits.*"

"What else is new?" Larry got quiet again.

"Do you think that the Giants can win it with just Marichal and Mays?" I said.

"They've got McCovey once in a while."

We were quiet again.

"They want to make me president of the Exchange Club," Larry said.

"Do it. It'll be good for business," I said.

"Everything's good for business."

"No it's not."

"Maybe not."

"It's like church in here," Larry said.

"It *is* church."

"Yeah, it is. Do you guys go?"

"We started to, back east, for Puss and Boots, but we haven't out here yet."

"Earth's Catholic, and I grew up nothing, so we compromise and go to the Episcopal Church. Right now Darrell's too young to go, so we take turns staying home with him every other week."

"We should probably go once in a while."

"I'd rather come here."

"Bidwell Park's OK," I said.

"It's still Chico," Larry said.

"You think this isn't still Chico?"

"I've been thinking about going back east, but my business is going good."

"One of the first things you ever told me was that Eartha is homesick. She'd probably want to go back."

"Women are fucking nutty," Larry said, tossing a stick against the deeply grooved trunk of a redwood."

"What else is new?" I said.

"I shouldn't have come to San Francisco."

"You said she told you to come," I said.

"Yeah, she did."

Silence.

"We can go back if you want, right now, all the way to Chico. We can drop the car off there, or Oroville, or anywhere."

"Shit." He pronounced it with two syllables.

We drove the winding road down to the Golden Gate Bridge. San Francisco spread before us on the other side. On our left across the bay we could see the lights from one end of the Bay Bridge, and Berkeley up in the hills behind it.

"Let's find that Irish Coffee place near Fisherman's Wharf that Pat told us about," Larry said, "and get drunk and ride the fucking cable cars till we get hungry and then eat some more of that west coast baloney."

We put the car in a parking garage and found the Irish coffee place. We had three and an hour later got a cab to Barnaby Conrad's restaurant called Matador. Larry wanted to eat bull steak but they didn't serve it. We ordered two Maker's Mark bourbons. Barnaby came over and we got talking about bull steak and he pointed out Herb Caen. I had read *Matador*, Barnaby's novel, but I could see that Larry didn't want to talk about bullfighting. We ate abalone sitting at the bar. It was better than at DiMaggio's.

The next day Larry and I drove down to Palo Alto and walked around the Stanford campus. Larry asked me if we were supposed to envy college students because he didn't. I didn't envy them either so I didn't say anything. That night we sat in the highest gallery of the Cow Palace and listened to Rockefeller. We heard from others in the Chico group that someone had spiked the punch with LSD at the Rockefeller party that afternoon. When he was introduced by Senator Ed Brooke from Massachusetts, there was mild applause from the floor. Several times during his speech, boos sounded from the crowd, and we saw people in the gallery holding their thumbs down.

"We're in the Roman goddam Forum," Pat said.

"They're having their day all right," Old Hutch said.

When Rockefeller's speech was over, Larry and I left the Cow Palace and drove all the way to Chico, skipping the rest of the Convention.

It was almost one o'clock in the morning when Larry dropped me off at my house, and as soon as he pulled away I remembered that I had put my toilet articles on the floor in front of the back seat. I called him on the phone, but no one answered. Then I saw through my front window the lights of his truck next door. I saw Terry Garrison get out of his truck and then Larry was walking her to her front door. Obviously, Eartha wasn't home yet.

Chapter Twenty-Six

AS FALL ARRIVED, CEIL lived the downtown life of business Chico during the day, and I became a stringer for the *Sacramento Bee*, getting off a couple articles a week on northern valley political affairs. To keep us in touch with our real feelings about each other, Ceil and I took occasional weekend trips to the Trinity Wilderness or Mendocino on the Coast, and once we drove to Reno.

I bought a second hand Nash station wagon from Lem Loter at the raceway, and drove alone a couple times a week as far as Redding and Oroville, and sometimes Marysville, thinking up political cartoons and political articles about northern California. Mostly, I just looked at the scenery. Once I drove to Walnut Creek.

Luke Gardner was teaching three days a week and spending his weekends in the Sierras above Sacramento tramping around the woods where the Donner Party got stopped in eighteen feet of snow in the winter of 1846, and Ken Morrow was spending his afternoons teaching painting and sculpture labs at the college. I went over to see Ken once when I heard that he had been bitten again by a black widow spider while cleaning out another pile of lumber in his back yard, but he was laughing it off when I showed up, more interested in showing me the carmine red hourglass on the dead spider's underbelly. He said the paralysis had reached only to his elbow and had lasted merely twelve hours. He was mostly annoyed that he couldn't lift weights until the poison got diluted in his system. He also told me that if I wanted to see some live black widow spiders, all I had to do was to go down to the main square in town and look under the park benches. I don't know how he knew they were there, but it fitted perfectly into my theory about lethal things lurking around every corner in the northern valley. I had no interest in looking for black widow spiders under park benches on my knees in downtown Chico.

I was learning about precinct politics from Camion, who also began at this time to show up at party gatherings with a girlfriend. Camion told me he was living at the Hotel Oaks and went home occasionally, but he was having trouble with his wife, a teacher in the Chico school system. His girlfriend was a Linda somebody in her late thirties, but I never found out where she lived or what she did for a living.

Larry and I hit the Feather River a couple times in the early evening for steelhead, and once we drove into the Sierras to a lake where we fished for trout. When the pheasant season opened we hunted in the rice fields. We also shot black and white California quail in the dry creek beds that ran alongside the almond orchards on Ord Ferry Road. We talked about a double family trip to Mendocino on the coast after the election was over. Pat told us about a place where a friend had cabins at the mouth of the Russian River, and we could dive offshore for abalone. Larry and I never talked about our wives, but Larry often mentioned his kids, and when he did, he got quiet and changed the subject.

We talked a lot about the campaign, which always interested Larry, and I got the feeling that he wished he was in it. He still came to club meetings and seemed interested in politics, but he was never curious about political power the way I was. I was developing intimations of some kind of personal destiny. I didn't talk about these feelings with anyone, not even Camion or Ceil, but they were in my head. The thought even streaked across my mind a couple times that the California legislature might be a stepping-stone to a run for Bizz Johnson's 2nd Congressional seat when he retired, if he ever did. Actually it was all a pipe dream concocted in the grief forest of post-Kennedy doldrums, merely another form of the childhood fantasy about heroes. The golden coin I was flipping in my mind had a copper underside with all the tail-ends of the political life, but it kept coming up heads when I contemplated the California legislature and the U.S. House of Representatives in Washington. I bided my time, met my deadlines at the *Bee*, dropped rainbow birds out of the sky standing next to Larry in the rice fields and the dry creeks, and made an effort to be a good husband and father.

One Saturday morning in the fall, I brought Puss and Boots with Larry and me when we hunted for pheasants in a rice field belonging to one of Bannister's friends, south of Chico. Bannister's obsession with Eartha was now obvious to many of Larry's friends, and Bannister became a special object of study for me. He was almost charming in the way a clumsy tall man can be when well dressed and focussed on something he wants. If you liked Bannister you would tend to say he was smooth and politic; if you didn't like him he came off as unctuous and overly solicitous. If you liked him he came off as tall and dark and well groomed; if you didn't he was flashy in a southern-

European way, his pants were always a little too long, breaking heavily over his shoes. If you liked him, he dressed well and carried himself with the slow movements of the powerful; if you didn't he was overly meticulous in his chocolate brown, double-breasted suits, and too loud in his ties with hand-painted scenes imitated from Renaissence museums. Most of the Democratic Club members kept friendly distance, and his reputation with women trailed him. Those who held Bannister in scorn made fun of how he ate, slothfully and loud. That was somewhat of an exaggeration, but there was something disproportionate about him.

Once, Jaeckel confided to me the backroom assertions about a certain Bannister anatomical measurement, one that Jaeckel had double-checked with more than one of Bannister's ex-girlfriends. The measurement Jaeckel quoted was astounding. Being unaware of his sexual virtues I had my own prejudices about his fake gentility, his ostentatious use of money, and his blubbery lips. His thick eyeglasses added to his seeming scrutiny of things too carefully. He wasn't obsequious, but he was on the edge of oily, the too smooth attribute of an experienced politician frequently admired by women with special needs.

Bannister went out of his way to offer Larry his well-groomed almond orchards, two of which bordered rice fields that he managed for an investment group in Sacramento.

"Say, Larry," he said at one of the Thursday Democratic Club meetings in the fall, "I hear you hunt pheasants." He rarely attended meetings where Larry was likely to be present and Eartha absent.

"I'm managing a couple rice checks out on the Dayton Road that could do with a little well-aimed pheasant weeding," he said.

Larry was watching his lips move.

"If that interests you, please enjoy yourself down there. Just let my secretary at the bank know, and she'll make sure that no one in the banking business in Sacramento or San Francisco will be down there when you are."

"Sure, thanks a lot," Larry said as Bannister turned to talk to someone else.

Larry turned to me. "What do you say?"

My impulse was to tell him that he was a goddam fool, but I said, "Sure, OK. Maybe I'll bring Puss."

Chapter Twenty-Seven

ON SATURDAY, PUSS AND BOOTS watched me break open the new box of locust green Winchester #6 shotgun shells and grab a handful from the top row. She insisted on carrying some herself, so I gave her two to keep in her pocket. Then she saw my khaki jacket with the rows of little pockets for the shells and she wanted to wear it. She filled the pockets until the jacket was as heavy as a bulletproof vest. The oversized cloth bulked around her thin shoulders and she trooped behind me as I walked along the sides of long ditches where the cover was thicker than the cut fields. Larry had loaned me his pump .12 gauge Remington.

We had a dog for the day. Skip Garrison loaned us his chunky and enthusiastic Brittany spaniel that exulted in the exercise. The dog's name was Brit and he was both eccentric and innocent of field training. When Puss opened the car door where we parked, the dog leaped out and galloped across the first field, following the squared edge, nose to the ground, flushing two pheasants and a rabbit that led him out of sight for another ten minutes. When he returned, panting and drooling, Larry and I looked at each other.

"Let's try another field," I said.

When the dog saw us heading into a new field, he raced ahead, leaping and bounding, and put up a cock pheasant about eighty yards away. Puss put her fingers in her ears when she saw the bird rise and stream away but it was too far for a shot and I explained in range and out of range to her.

"I liked to see it fly away into the sky, daddy, but I hope we catch one to bring home to mom."

Brit tired and stayed closer, and we walked the cover at the field's edge. The newly cut stubble glistened in the early morning sun. The birds were nervous because of Brit, and we saw a couple running ahead of him, not wanting to fly, and by the time they did go up, he was a hundred yards ahead of us again. He pranced back, happy that he had done a great thing.

"We should have brought a leash," Larry said.

"Did you ever try to hold a dog on a leash if he smelled a bird?"

Just then a huge pheasant flushed almost under Larry's feet and veered off to the left. The bird had let Brit run by it on its last run, but when Brit returned and the bird found himself between us and Brit, it flushed. Larry sighted the rising pheasant along the bead at the end of his barrel and dropped it like a basket of flowers. Puss ran to the clump of feathers and stood over it.

"Can I touch it, daddy?"

"You can pick it up if you want to," Larry said.

"Is this a keeper?" she asked.

"It's not like fishing," I said, "we only shoot the ones we can keep."

"It's way big," Puss said, petting it on its wing.

"It's a Mongolian pheasant," Larry said, "He's bigger than an ordinary Chinese ringneck. I've seen only one other like it. You can tell them by the burgundy color on the upper breast feathers."

"Puss lifted the pheasant with both hands and Larry offered to put it in the back of his light brown hunting jacket, but Puss wanted to carry it.

"Let me tag it, sweetheart," he said, and tore off one of the pheasant tags from his folded hunting license inside the plastic cover on his hat, then attached it to the bird's ankle bone. Puss carried the big bird upside down by the leg, one wing half spread, the green head dragging across the yellow stubble-cut fields for the next two hours.

Brit put up eight more birds that morning, and we got shots at three of them. I shot too quickly at the first two and missed both, but Larry's long shot with his full choke Stevens shotgun brought down one of them. On my third chance, I waited, beaded the rising bird, then led him by a foot and dropped him.

This time Puss let Larry put the bird in the loose back pouch of his jacket. She wouldn't give up her Mongolian pheasant, switching from carrying it by one leg to tucking it under her arm like a loaf of Wonder Bread, its green head dangling shiny in the sun.

On the way back to the car we cut across three large rice checks. Twice Brit took off after rabbits loping along the distant edges, and came back with hot saliva dripping from his mouth, again elated that he had driven the enemy from the field.

At home, Larry gave Puss the Mongolian bird and he kept the other two. When I plucked it in the sink for supper, Puss watched and made a collection of colored feathers. She was disappointed that the scarlet red circles around the eyes were not made of feathers. When I opened the body cavity, I told her she didn't have to watch, but she didn't budge from my side.

"It'll be just like the inside of a fish, won't it?" she asked.

"Only it will smell as sweet as herbs."

"I want to smell it, daddy. If it's beautiful on the outside, it has to be beautiful on the inside."

"We'll see."

I showed her the heart and the sponge-like lungs, the liver, and the gizzard, watching her to see how far I ought to go with the anatomy lesson.

She wanted to touch the lungs.

"Are my lungs like this?" she asked. She was pushing the pheasant lungs with her finger.

"A lot bigger."

"I thought lungs were hollow and full of air, and that's where the water was when I had pneumonia."

"The water was there, hon, and your lungs are like sponges which fill up with air each time you breathe."

"I'm going to be a doctor when I grow up, daddy, I already know that sometimes the blood isn't important when you're fixing somebody."

"It's important for you to know that, even if you're not going to be a doctor."

"I am, though."

I had slit open the gizzard and turned it inside out, dropping the mush of sweet berries and leaves and rice into my hand.

"You can smell this if you want to, Puss, this is what the pheasant has been eating. The gizzard mushes it all up before it goes down into his stomach."

She dipped her head and smelled.

"It's sweet, like chicory a little bit," she said. "It *is* nice on the inside."

That night Ceil cooked the sweet chicory pheasant from Abernard Bannister's managed rice fields in a large pot, with a thick consomme of herbs, olive oil, and orange slices, until the pink flesh peeled from the bone at the touch of a fork. I wondered as I ate if Larry and Eartha and their kids would savor the treasures of the day's kill as much as Puss and Ceil and I did.

Chapter Twenty-Eight

IN LATE OCTOBER, THE Secretary of the Interior of the United States came to Chico for the Johnson campaign. Everyone knew that Stuart Udall had been one of Kennedy's first cabinet appointments, and he was perfect for a campaign with plenty of Johnson head, but whose heart was still with Jack.

Camion had suggested it to me early in September. I wrote the letter and fussed with it for a day or two and sent it off registered mail. Camion had gotten some official Democratic club stationery printed with my name on it and a couple weeks after we mailed it, Udall's office called me from Washington and said he'd come. Camion had some fancy embossed invitations printed with raised blue lettering, and the union bug in the lower left corner underneath the words "Donation $25." We sold about forty and gave away sixty. On the night of the event, which was televised on local Channel 6, we admitted everyone who showed up.

I should have anticipated Bannister's move, but I had other things on my mind, and Larry got outfoxed again. At the club meeting the week before Udall arrived, Bannister stood up and offered his Cadillac Grand Prix, with himself as chauffeur to pick up Udall at the Chico airport and squire him to the Oaks and on to the Valley Lodge for the dinner across from Bidwell Park. The club president, Farley Fanning, a Chico orchard owner who taught in the social science department at the college, accepted Bannister's offer immediately. Later, Larry told me that Bannister asked him to ride with him in the car as a successful local businessman and Democratic loyalist, and Larry fell for it. Bannister hadn't mentioned Eartha, and Larry thought that Pat or Camion or Jaeckel would also be in the car, but two days before Udall arrived, Bannister's secretary called Larry's office and left the message that Bannister would pick up Larry and Eartha an hour before Udall's plane arrived at the Chico airport.

Larry told me later that Bannister was chatty and suave as he drove the car, calling Udall Mr. Secretary.

"Eartha's favorite car is a Cadillac Grand Prix. Bannister would be surprised if he knew that," Larry said.

The hell he would, I thought.

The Valley Lodge was a wooden structure built in the twenties, with dark shellacked walls and simulated gas jet lighting and a high open-timbered ceiling. The room seated 150, and we filled it with party regulars from Democratic Clubs from as far away as Redding, Oroville, and Red Bluff, and Chico Channel 6 TV was there with their main newscaster, Paul Breckenridge. Because of certain events that transpired later that evening, Breckenridge was no longer working for Channel 6 by the following noon. It turned out to be one of those political evenings that began with festive anticipation heightened by a kind of gay curiosity, rolled along with help from the cash bar into celebrative hoopla, and fragmented later into various personal and private indulgences and endings. The personal party ending that didn't remain private got Paul Breckenridge fired.

Earlier, Udall made a speech about Jack Kennedy's unfinished agenda, with some praise for Lyndon thrown in at the end, and Channel 6 made the most of it and televised it all. Channels 3 and 5 from Sacramento, San Francisco, and Los Angeles all showed spots picked up from channel 6, on the eleven o'clock news. After Udall had been delivered safely to the Oaks, including an on the way stop at Bannister's home for a special tequila cocktail which Udall left untouched, he was in his room watching himself on television.

By this time, the party at the Lodge was in full force for the leftover dancers who alternated between the cash bar and the dance floor and the fresh outside air. Some wandered into the shadows of the nearby park before rejoining groups leaning against parked cars with drinks in their hands and joviality in the air. The women of the Chico Democratic Club cleaned up the kitchen and folded the spaghetti-stained tablecloths into small bundles to take home for their washing machines. Even Ceil joined the cleanup effort and told me that she overheard some private kitchen gossip when Eartha arrived with Larry in Bannister's Cadillac. No names were mentioned but Ceil knew that "he" was Bannister and "she" was Eartha, and "they" were Eartha and Bannister. Eartha had volunteered to work with the other women in the kitchen, cooking and serving, until Bannister confirmed airport pickup-time and made it clear to Larry that protocol required his wife to join the head table with the husbands and wives of the officers of the visiting valley Democratic clubs. Bannister managed to sit between his own wife and Eartha at the dinner.

When Udall left the Lodge with Bannister and his Cadillac party, I hung around the kitchen waiting for Ceil and got drafted for table-dismantling detail, including packing the wooden tops and horses into one of Jaeckel's pickup trucks for transport back to the Episcopal Church. The party revelers were in the carefree stage. Luke Gardner had returned from the Sierras for the occasion and was dancing with Ken Morrow's wife. Ken was dancing with Roxanne Gardner, and the Channel 6 newsman, Paul Breckenridge, was dancing with Rona Mackenzie, a newcomer to the Democratic Club whose husband Clete was helping us with the Episcopal tables. John and Ruth Jaeckel danced with each other between John's trips in the pickup with the collapsed tables to the church. I didn't recognize any of the other guests except the president of the Redding club and her husband. Will Curling had left his wife at home and was wandering in and out of the lodge with a beauty queen from Paradise who had just gotten a divorce from her real estate husband. The beauty queen came with a friend who was jitterbugging with a tall thin man with a goatee. Someone said he was from Oroville.

On one of my trips carrying table tops outside to the pickup I saw Curling trying to smooth his dry gray hair as he led his beauty queen out of the shadows next to the parking lot and into the glare of headlights of leaving cars.

A pair of blonde twins from Paradise, in their late twenties, wearing white shorts and ice-blue v-necked cotton blouses tight over sixties bounce bras, their blonde hair in upswirls, jitterbugged together under a buttonball tree. Curling had that pleased, glazed look, blinking back into the parking lot where couples leaned against cars, drinking highballs or beers, laughing and joking loudly. Someone called to Curling's friend and asked her how she felt. She called back, gaily, throwing her head back, "I feel like I'm going to live forever." It was that kind of crowd, and that kind of night.

Ceil finished in the kitchen, retrieved our washed blue enamel spaghetti pot and glass pie plate. We drove to Larry and Eartha's house and picked up Puss. Ceil said, after we tucked Puss into her bed, "That was fun. I guess politics isn't so bad."

The next morning I called Larry early and we went for coffee at the Oaks in his truck. Bannister had planned to pick up Udall at eight, and our small crowd of Democratic loyalists sat in a booth and talked. Camion said we made over $300. at the cash bar. Everyone was in a good mood. I asked where Pat was because he said he'd meet us. Nobody knew. That wasn't like Pat.

We all crowded into Bannister's Cadillac and went to the airport with Udall, making small talk, except Jaeckel, who waited for an opening to ask Udall what he thought Johnson's plan was in Vietnam. Udall said something carefully praiseworthy about Johnson and Jaeckel said something carefully critical of McNamara. Bannister said something oily about the national interest, and Larry and I said nothing. Camion was in his stone-silent mood. Jaeckel kept pushing Udall on Vietnam, but he didn't take the bait. We stood at the edge of the tarmac and waved to Udall's departing plane.

Back at the Oaks, I decided to go over to Pat's house. I had a deadline for a *Bee* article about Udall's visit, and I wanted Pat's input. He was an old fashioned cynic who liked the game of politics as much as he cared about outcomes. I trusted Pat's cynicism. He always gave me something I could use.

Clete Mackenzie was in Pat's kitchen when I got there. Pat lived two streets in back of the west side of the campus in an old three story wooden house built in the late nineteenth century. His kitchen was half porch, a large rectangular room with a soapstone sink and a large old box refrigerator, and wall-to-wall dish closets. It adjoined a smaller, narrow room with three different kinds of stoves. Pat saw me coming up the sidewalk and when I got to the door, said, "Come on in, it's unlocked."

As I came through the door, Clete and Pat said some things I couldn't hear, and Clete stayed just long enough to try to make me feel that I hadn't driven him away. He said, "I got to go, Pat, I'll check in later."

Pat told him to stay loose and Clete walked down the steps to his car and drove off. Pat watched him go and then looked at me and shook his head. "Have you heard yet?"

"Udall's plane crashed into the Marysville Buttes," I said.

"Worse," Pat said, "Clete caught Paul Breckenridge fucking Rona in the Channel 6 TV truck at 1:30 this morning."

"People know about it?"

"Breckenridge was fired at 7:00 this morning."

"How did Channel 6 find out?"

"Clete called them. He couldn't find Rona at some point in the party and drove around town checking the late bars. Apparently Breckenridge and Rona left the lodge and drove off in his truck. Someone who saw the truck leave told Clete as he was looking for Rona outside. Clete spotted the truck in the second parking lot behind the engineering building."

"That's a mile from the lodge."

"Clete drove around for an hour before he saw the truck. When he opened the back door they were on the floor."

"Jesus. It's a wonder Clete didn't kill him."

"Clete said, 'Hey, that's my wife you're fucking,' and Breckenridge jumped up and went out the front door and kept going. Rona was drunk and didn't know where she was. When Clete got her home he called Channel Six and told them where their truck was and how it got there."

"Is she OK?"

"This morning when Clete told her what happened she went in the bathroom and locked the door and swallowed a bottle of aspirin. When she didn't come out, Clete knocked down the door."

"He left her to come over here?"

"She's at Enloe Hospital, pumped out and sedated. Clete almost broke his shoulder breaking down the bathroom door. He can't raise his left arm."

"How is he?"

"How would you be?"

That afternoon, Don Way ran several photos in *The Valley Advocate* of the dinner the night before. One closeup of Udall showed him speaking, with Bannister just off to the right sitting between his wife and Eartha. It was a good picture of Udall, alert and vibrant in his crew cut.

A week later Breckenridge got a job as a roving reporter for Channel 12 in Marysville. His rovings never brought him back to Chico.

Rona and Clete stopped coming to Democratic Club meetings and I didn't see Rona again for over a year. When Ceil and I met them together at a Ricky Nelson concert at Chico State, Rona still looked sad. She wasn't wearing makeup and she looked tired. Her wavy shoulder length hair had been cut short. Clete was embarrassed and very kind to her. We exchanged hellos and talked about the concert, but Rona's eyes never brightened.

Chapter Twenty-Nine

THE FOLLOWING WEEK, THE Republicans trumped the Udall visit with Ronald Reagan's appearance in the town park, stumping for Goldwater. Reagan had been all over California making his standard speech, and it was a good one. If you heard it in person, it seemed brand new. You had to give it to Reagan, he put on a classy performance. Even Jaeckel admitted it, and Pat said he had more fun listening to Reagan than the Republicans did, though Pat was always skeptical of Republicans enjoying themselves. Camion watched Reagan in silence, chewing gum, once in a while shaking his head. Later he said to me, "He's running for governor. Nothing can save Barry in November, but next year Pat Brown is in trouble."

Reagan spoke from a small temporary grandstand erected between the elms in the town square across from city hall. The street gutters beneath the trees surrounding the square had been shoveled clean of fallen oranges, and the red, white, and blue bunting draped around the park by the Butte County Republicans would be enough to drape most of Candlestick Park if the Giants won the pennant.

Reagan was late arriving and the square was impressively jammed with Republicans and Democrats alike. Democratic club members spread themselves in various small groups to avoid looking conspiratorial, and I stood with the Jaeckels and their two young boys. Pat and Joan Jay, whose coven of high school students seemed to surround us, stood with Camion. Ceil walked over from the fabric store and found me.

"I've been looking for you for twenty minutes. What a jam of people," she said.

The temperature was in the seventies and it was sunny, a typical northern California fall afternoon with a wispy smell of yellowing trees in the air. The electricity in the crowd was real, a kind of stirring, an anticipation that something monumental was about to happen, part self-generated illusion, part yearning, part anxiety fired by impatient boredom.

I had my own reasons for being curious about Reagan. I was becoming a student of charismatic politicians. Years ago, in the early fifties, I had driven from Worcester to talk to Kennedy when he was a young congressman visiting the University of Massachusetts in Amherst. A young, overweight, political science major, Dave Sokol, chairman of the young democrat's club, had brought Kennedy to campus to speak in the top floor lecture hall of the old chapel. Kennedy's charm was natural and infectious. He had just returned from India, and he talked about the hazards of diplomatic travel, where as Nehru's guest at a state dinner he had been served the eye of a lamb, while everyone else was eating roast leg. He spun out the story, beginning with his hunger and his delight upon discovering that lamb would be the evening meal, and his shock at seeing the plate he was given with the eye staring at him. To the applause of the students he described how he got it down, pretending that it was just the thing to satisfy a hungry American's appetite.

I talked to Kennedy afterwards, on the front steps of the chapel, and asked him if he would be president someday. He smiled and said that as a member of a certain religious faith, the odds of his being elected president were a bit thin. He said it with a relaxed, easy-going and ironic elan that caused me to instantly believe that not even his being a Catholic would prevent him from becoming president. When I saw him again on election eve as he rode the open convertible along Tremont Street bordering Boston Common, I remembered his pleasant ironic smile that afternoon on the steps of the chapel.

In the Chico park that day, Reagan got out of a big black car that appeared along Camelia from the parallel streets that had been blocked off on the east side of the park, and then along Broadway, and stopped just at the back of the platform stairs. He waved and looked out at the crowd, tilting his head and smiling, and Nancy, carrying a bouquet of red roses, looked out over everyone's heads and at the people in the front row, and waved happily. The mayor of Chico, Stan Fennerman, introduced him in three sentences, having been told that he could make the introduction but that its merits would be evaluated on its brevity.

Reagan talked about America and about Goldwater and it lasted forty-five minutes. No one stirred a muscle, and no one heckled. It was a fine afternoon to be an American in Northern California in the fall of 1964.

Ruth Jaeckel looked over at me and Ceil twice during the speech, and then looked back at Reagan. At the end, if it had been a song, the crowd would have demanded an encore, but he had said it all, and turned and walked down the steps of the platform onto the park grass, where he turned and held Nancy's hand as she descended the final two steps, and they disappeared into the big black limousine.

Our little group stayed and watched the crowd and talked. Ruth Jaeckel said, "He's too good. I'm scared." Camion shook his head and chewed his gum.

I said, "He's no bad actor."

"He wasn't acting," Ruth said.

"I'll be out of a job and I'll have to become an actor if I don't get back to work," Ceil said. She walked back across the Esplanade toward the fabric store. Pat and Joan Jay had gone off with Joan Jay's students.

Jaeckel suggested we go to the Brazen Onager for a drink.

"Come on, Mr. Camion," Ruth said, "Join us, he's not governor yet."

At the bar we found Ken Morrow and Pearl Kenneally and her husband at one table and Curling and three other men I didn't know at another table. When Curling saw Camion he left the other men and joined us. We ordered two pitchers of dark beer and began the post mortem.

"God damn it," Camion exploded, "We're a week from re-electing our president and you're all acting like we just lost the next governor's election. It's a hell of a damn thing."

Pat and Joan Jay had come in just in time to hear Camion, and Pat, who was always happier when there was a controversy, but who was also fond of Camion, said, "Give 'em hell Bob. We need a Harry Truman talking to."

Joan Jay was smiling and giggling nervously and swallowing, exclaiming over Reagan's presence. "My god, he was impressive," she said, and added, "Really impressive."

"For Christ's sake, Joan Jay, you talk like we just had a visit from Zorro. Take off that dark brown suit and ruffle his hair and he's just another undressed Republican mannikin." Pat winked at Jaeckel. Joan Jay believed with all her heart that a vote for the Republican Party was a vote for the Nazi Party in Hitler's Germany.

My favorite blonde bartender brought the two pitchers of beer, recognizing me. We exchanged looks.

"Thanks," I said, as he started back to the bar.

He stopped and looked at me.

"For the beer," I said.

"No problem," he said, and turned and started again for the bar.

"And for an inspiring afternoon," I said.

Larry had come through the door with Luke and Roxanne Gardner, and heard the blonde bartender say, "I hope you Democrat Party people heard real good today, because you heard a prophet talking." He turned and this time he made it back to the bar.

"What was that all about?" Larry said, pulling out the last chair at the table for Roxanne while Luke was dragging over two more. "How's about we buy into some of that dark brew?"

"Finish it and I'll get two more pitchers," Jaeckel said and got up.

"Don't you devil that boy, John," Ruth said.

John smiled. "He's cretinville," John said.

"Just the same John, you're itching to get it on, just mind what I say." John snickered and walked toward the bar.

"I wish I could control Pat like that," Joan Jay said, giggling.

"Your every wish, Joan Jay, is my-you-know-what," Pat said, bowing his head to her.

"I know," Joan Jay said, bravely and almost cheerfully, "everything but my command."

"Where'd everyone go?" Larry said, after downing half his beer in one tip of his glass. "Man, I thought he'd never stop talking. We looked around, then we went to the Oaks. Then we figured you'd be here."

Everyone talked like that for another hour, and went home to their real lives.

Chapter Thirty

A WEEK BEFORE THE election, nothing was happening in Butte County for Pierre. I don't know who was unraveling more, Larry with his Eartha problems or me with the campaign. I saw him every five or six days and we managed to skirt both the Johnson campaign and his wife. Pierre's county campaign manager, Trudy Solstice, was seemingly sitting out the election. Not a single campaign event for Pierre in Chico or the northern valley. I pleaded with Camion to call the big boys in Sacramento and squirt a needle in our direction. Camion said, "Get that damn campaign movie on Pierre and run it up here."

A week later the movie arrived and we got Sacramento to pay for a showing on Channel 6. Then we heard that Pierre was coming to Chico. I kept waiting for Trudy to call and tell me to mind my own campaign, but she never did. Then we heard that Pierre was bringing a bunch of movie stars. Camion and I went to see Don Way at the paper.

Pierre landed at the Chico airport on Monday, October 26 with his wife and the actors Dan Blocker and Barry Sullivan. Blocker was then playing Hoss Cartwright on the TV program "Bonanza." Everyone recognized Barry Sullivan from Hollywood. There was a good crowd, and Pierre's speech was all restrained tough guy.

Don Way ran three photos on the front page of *The Valley Advocate*, one of the crowd of 2500 people, one of Camion and me and Hoss and Barry Sullivan, and one of Pierre looking sideways at the crowd. When the plane took off, I saw Pierre and his wife saying goodbye. He'd see her sometime later in Sacramento. She didn't strike me as a happy campaigner, and as they kissed perfunctorily, Pierre was all business. They later divorced.

On the night of the election, the Democrats had a victory party at the downtown Chico headquarters, but it wasn't much of a party. Johnson's landslide was secure by the time the six o'clock news went on in the East.

Chico's Goldwater headquarters was closed up and abandoned by late afternoon. Both CBS and NBC gave California to Johnson before the polls closed. All the pre-election talk about winning the election for Jack Kennedy turned out to be, when the results were in, merely a victory for Lyndon Johnson.

The results of the Salinger/Murphy Senate race were still indefinite, and it wouldn't be until the following day that Salinger would concede defeat. Camion was the only deep-down happy person in the place, and he bought everyone a drink. While everyone was standing around with drinks and speculating on the Butte County final tallies, Camion and I went to see Don Way at the paper, then to the Channel Six television station where I made a victory statement, and we went back to party headquarters. Jaeckel was putting dance platters on the record player, pretending that happy days were here again. He danced with Ceil and I danced with Ruth and Larry danced with Eartha. Pat and Camion talked. We couldn't get Jaeckel to stop playing Glenn Miller, and John was smiling and dipping Ceil with all the grace of a fat person dancing delicately. Ceil said to me later, "John is certainly light on his feet for a big man."

Bannister came in around nine o'clock as we were winding it down. Pat had invited us all over to his house, and said something softly to Camion who blurted, "Hah!" Joan Jay had calls in to San Francisco and Los Angeles about the state returns, and for Pat it would be the most interesting part of the day. When he saw Bannister and said something to Camion, he shot me a look. Camion tried to buy Bannister a drink, but Bannister insisted on buying a round for everyone.

John opened some beers, a ginger ale for Ruth, and Eartha had a Dewars on the rocks. Then Bannister was dancing with Eartha, and people pretended not to notice him whispering in her ear. Eartha listened to what he said without changing her expression.

When the dance was over, Jaeckel turned off the machine and said that the bar was closed due to a local ordinance that prohibited public celebrations after nine o'clock in outlying election headquarters if the Democrats won. No one told Bannister we would reconvene at Pat's and Joan Jay's and he went off by himself. We all thought that Larry and Eartha were going to meet us there but they never showed up. When Larry told me the whole story a year later, this turned out to be the night when Bannister asked Eartha to run off with him to Mexico. On their way over to Pat's, Eartha told Larry that Bannister was in love with her. Larry turned the car around and drove home and they sat in the car for a long time and talked. Larry told her she'd be giving up everything she cared about if she left him. He talked softly and calmly to her and she listened. Eartha was a good listener. Larry thought at the time that

Bannister was only infatuated with Eartha, but Larry didn't know that the affair had been going on for months. He thought that if Eartha ever slept with Bannister she would be repulsed. He was confident of that. It was the thing that kept him from suspecting that they were going to bed as often as they could manage it.

At Pat's we walked into another family crisis, although it was not a crisis for Pat himself, who was more amused than upset. Their boys had gotten into some beer and were silly drunk when Joan Jay surprised them in their room. Nobody could get hysterical like Joan Jay. She developed an immediate fit-like nervous laugh, shrieking and giggling at the same time, blaming Pat for lacking personal discipline and sneaking off with that snipey Dottie Bentley behind her back. Pat, caught in the public embarrassment of Joan Jay's hysteria, stayed steady and reasonable about the boys' foray into the beer, and tried to calm Joan Jay as he soothed the embarrassment of the rest of us. Camion slipped out immediately and went back to the Oaks to watch the late California returns.

Jaeckel watched the television through Joan Jay's tirade, amused by the comedy of it, and Ruth left the room with Joan Jay after she finally broke down and cried. Ruth knew that Joan Jay was more upset about Pat and Dottie, and that the beer and the boys only set it off.

Ceil asked me if we shouldn't leave, and I said we would, but Pat persuaded us to stay, and we stayed an hour and watched the returns that were suggesting the Democrats had lost Clare Engel's senate seat to the tap dancer, George Murphy.

Joan Jay returned, calmed, and asked for everyone's forgiveness for saying stupid things. Before we left, she checked the boys upstairs three times to see if they vomited, but they didn't. "I know they're going to throw up," she said, "they're only babies." Apparently, they weren't, much to Pat's relief.

Chapter Thirty-One

A WEEK BEFORE CHRISTMAS, something happened that I wasn't sure I ought to mention to anyone, but I changed my mind when I saw Jaeckel. He knew more gossip than anyone, and he was the most close-mouthed.

For Christmas itself, the Jaeckels sent us a gallon tin of garlic almonds, and we made the drive out to Ord Ferry Road and visited them on the afternoon of Christmas day. Ruth served Ceil and Puss and Boots fresh persimmons, along with four different varieties of salted almonds, and John and I took a walk through his orchard. He showed me where he shot the buck on the first day of deer season, and we put up several coveys of California quail. I liked being in the orchard and I told him I had once seen the freshly ploughed black furrows between the trees, but the next time I saw an orchard the between-rows were lettuce green. I wondered why they ploughed the orchards. He explained the almond cycle of ploughing and harvesting, how they spread the tarpaulins to gather the nuts when the knockers dislodged the fruit from the branches, and he told me to bring Puss over in harvest season and watch the operation.

"I'm not sure we're going to plough next year," he said. "There's a theory around that the roots of the trees turn up to get the irrigation water and it sounds right to me."

Then John made what I at first thought was a joke about Camion going to Washington for the Inauguration, but then I realized that Camion was really going.

"He's actually going?" I asked.

"So I hear. Pat saw the list. Cranston got invitations for all the inheritance tax appraisers. Bizz Johnson gave out a few. Larry got one for being county chairman for awhile."

I got one for being Johnson chairman, but that came from Sacramento.

"Larry's came from Washington."

"That bastard Bannister," I said. "You think he's fucking Eartha regularly?"

"That's what my sources tell me. You know Ray McIntire the attorney?"

"Not to talk to about fucking."

"He's got a client with a lien on some property Bannister owns in Walnut Creek, and they've had a tail on Bannister for four months. It'll cost Larry some money, but if he ever wants the facts, they're there in Ray's office."

"He's still tailing him?"

"Every day."

"Why every day?"

"Bannister goes to the house."

"The neighbors must know."

"Everyone in town knows."

"Ceil heard gossip at the store, but I thought it was gossip."

"It wasn't."

"All Larry said to me when I told him I had an invitation that I'd put in a scrapbook, was that it would be fun to go but that his business was backing up and he had to hunker down for awhile. I don't know how much he knows. He's spending a lot of time with his kids, but he doesn't talk about Eartha. Who's Camion going with?"

"Probably that June something broad he shows up with every now and again."

"I'm worried about Camion."

"You thinking maybe he's nuts?"

"Something happened last week that makes me wonder. He called me and asked me to come to his room at the Oaks. I didn't even know he was living at the Oaks. He never got up from the bed when I knocked. He looked terrible. I asked him if he was sick and he said, 'Sick at heart, Bill, sick at heart.' He reached for a plastic prescription bottle on his bedside stand and handed it to me. It was half full of capsules and pills, some of them broken and half disintegrated. I handed it back to him and said 'what is it?'"

"I got this letter yesterday, with these pills, delivered to the Oaks desk, downstairs."

He held up a letter, typewritten on old folded paper, and he said, 'The bitch, the dirty goddamned bitch, read it Bill, read it. I'm in trouble and I don't know what to do.'"

I took the letter and read it. It was the goddamnedest thing I ever read. I can't remember all of it, but it was supposedly from his wife, signed. The gist of it was that he was a louse and she had taken a lover and they took dope together. She sent the pills to prove it. The last line said that she was going to deliver the letter and then meet her lover and practice dirty sex with him.

"That's a new wrinkle," Jaeckel said.

"Not a chance it's real?"

"Not a chance. His wife's a damn fine woman who teaches in Chico Junior High School."

"You know her?"

"Sure I know her. Camion's in one of his screwy periods. He must have flipped out. He'll flip back in. Curling has probably been telling him stories. Camion gets stuck with him on inheritance tax stuff a lot. Maybe seeing Lyndon dancing with Lady Bird will shock him back into the real world."

When we got back to the house, they were all on the porch eating pomegranates from a tree close enough to the porch railing so they could reach out and pick them. Ruth had let Puss take two big ones, and Puss had red pomegranate juice all over her mouth, even though Ruth sliced them in half and they ate the blood red seeds with spoons.

The Jaeckel orchard was only three miles from the Sacramento River and after a while we took a ride and looked at the River. Jaeckel said, "If it floods this month, we'll be four feet under water back at the house." A week after the Inauguration in Washington, the rains came and the river flooded.

Chapter Thirty-Two

LUKE GARDNER ORGANIZED A film festival at the college, and it provided the first of several events that changed our lives. The club meetings continued and the CDC Convention in Long Beach was again on the agenda for the spring, but the drama of Kennedy's death plus the urgency of Johnson's exploitation of the nation's stunned grief and guilt had left everyone but the zealots in need of a breather from politics.

Larry was anything but zealous, however, and Eartha's affair kept him in a kind of no man's land of hunting and fishing and worrying, and the longer he postponed doing something about it, the more desperate became his grasp of politically meaningless straws. He suddenly got it in his head to run against the northern valley representative in the California Assembly, Jake Toothacher.

Camion, back from Washington, never followed up with me on his bedside conversation about his wife and dirty sex, and became again his usually stoney self. He drove Larry, however, to club meetings in Redding, Red Bluff, Oroville, and Marysville, and Toothacher's staff was angry and worried. Ceil and I worried about Larry, but decided that I could be more help to him if I just left him to himself and Camion.

While I had my own illusions about an increasingly undefined political future, I was also having faint intimations that the truly political life consisted of more than election night fanfare. Ceil and I were closer than we'd been since the first year of the marriage, and I was becoming a ballet and soccer father.

Gardner got us invitations to an etching and woodcut show at a Professor Dandridge's home on Woodlawn Avenue across from Bidwell Park, and we bought a colored etching of a Dublin street scene by an Irish artist from western Massachusetts. We also bought a woodcut of two woodcocks, one in the moment of hovering after his whistling rise from a thicket, and the other falling in mid-flight from a hunter's shot. Dandridge's living room was spacious, with a high-domed ceiling and a long end-wall covered with framed modern prints. He explained to Ceil and me that a professor's salary prohibited the purchase of original oils or watercolors, but it couldn't squelch the enthusiasm of a simpatico collector of fine but comparatively inexpensive etchings and intaglios.

Jaeckel was there because he was known in Chico as a collector of western prints, including one each of Remington and Charles Russell. He also wrote short stories of his own which he showed only to me and Gardner. His stories didn't seem to be publishable but I liked them, probably because I liked John. They were raw and pure John, who was always needling Gardner about the provincial nature of the English department. He didn't buy anything that night, but he looked at everything that the agent had spread on tables and two couches in the living room. The agent represented a gallery in Baltimore.

Bannister was there because he had money and because he pretended an interest in art. He walked around with a drink in his hand, talking with the lawyers and bankers who were there, keeping his eyes peeled on the front door. Once, he came over to me and asked if I'd seen Larry lately. I told him I hadn't, though I'd been to the Exchange luncheon with him the day before. I knew he wanted to know if Eartha was coming to the print show, and I refrained from telling him that Larry wasn't interested in prints at the moment. Halfway through the evening, Bannister left.

The next time I saw both Jaeckel and Bannister was at the film festival showing of Rashomon, a Japanese film that portrayed three versions of the same violent event. On the way out, when I asked Jaeckel as a pleasantry which version of the story he thought was true, he said "All three of them. History is fiction."

At that moment, Mrs. Camion was on one side of me, having introduced herself and probably wanting to talk about Bob, but Bannister was so pushy that she drifted off when we got outside.

Bannister had heard John's comment and took the bait. "You mean what happens isn't real, John?"

Jaeckel sort of snorted and said, "It's real all right, but the evidence is only an interpretation. What do you think I am, Bannister, an English teacher?"

Bannister had waited for Mrs. Camion to walk ahead, then offered to buy Jaeckel and Ceil and me a drink. John said he had to see an orchard about some almonds, and Ceil and I said we had to get the sitter home.

Bannister said, "These movies are quite good. I thought *The Well Digger's Daughter* was quite charming. I see that *Birth of a Nation* is coming up next week. That's W.D Griffiths' famous movie, isn't it?"

"Griffiths is his name, I think," I said.

In the car, Ceil said, "Gardner should rent *La Dolce Vita* just for that Bannister creep."

Another flood occurred the following week and the whole valley was glistening. By mid afternoon, there were three inches of water on Violet Avenue, and it was seeping up our driveway and into the garage where the washing machine and dryer were plugged into low wall sockets. I unplugged both and moved all our boxes of storage stuff up off the floor. Ceil called from the store to tell me that the water in the city square was rising and wondered if she should drive home. I told her to leave immediately and drive slow. Then I walked over to the Hooker Oak School to meet Puss, but school had already been dismissed before I got there and she met me halfway. That afternoon, there were a lot of kids in Chico stomping through the waters of the Sacramento River.

Birth of a Nation was scheduled to be shown at the film festival several nights later, and as I watched the water slowly covering my lawn in the front yard, I got a call from Gardner.

"I just came out of a meeting," he said, "There's a hell of a row going on about the movie." He wanted to know if I'd come down and support him. I told him I didn't think a townie should get involved in college business.

"It's the townies that are raising hell," he said. "Abe Goodnow and his vegetarians walked in on Willard Mooney this morning and said the film was racist. Mooney agreed to a public meeting tonight. All the Chico San people will be there." The Chico San people were a group of vegetarians who had moved to Chico three years before and ran a vegetarian store on Hollow Hill Road on the north side of town.

When I met Gardner outside the conference room of the administration building, he told me that Mooney's assistant, Joe Bugwell, was inside with the college attorney, and nothing was on the record yet. Don Way wanted a statement from Mooney because the Chico San people had showed up in his office asking the paper to support them. They were just trying to embarrass the paper, Don said, because they knew Sandhill would never support the Chico Sans in anything. All they wanted was to make the paper look racist.

"I talked to Andy Flood this morning," Gardner said, "and he's all riled up."

Flood was a black trumpet player in the Chico San group who taught part time in the college music department. I knew Andy and his wife from the Democratic Club.

"Has he seen the movie?" I asked Gardner.

"No one has seen the movie except me. It came yesterday and I stayed up until three this morning looking at it after Abe called me last night."

"Is it racist?"

"Maybe. Probably. I don't know. What's racist? It was made a thousand years ago when the country was racist. There's a scene with a white mob and a lot of scared black people running around. It's half documentary, half stage play, yet it's also half colossal, half gimmick. It's supposed to be the first important movie ever made. I'm running a film festival, not a fucking political action group."

"Who are these Chico San people?"

"They're pacifist vegetarians, diet people. They came from New York about eighteen months ago. They're all professionally *nice*, they make a point of doing the *right* thing all the time. They despise the *Valley Advocate* because it's pro-business and criticizes the Sierra Club."

"Looks like they've staked it out pretty well."

"At this point I just want to show the goddam film and get it out of town. The talky-talk is a pain in the ass."

"Sounds like the talky-talk is the terrain. You don't need me in there with your college attorney. There isn't any legal issue, he's wasting everyone's time. I'll come to the meeting tonight, though. It sounds like not so friendly cartoon stuff."

I called Larry and Pat and Jaeckel and we all showed up that evening in the humanities lecture hall. Don Way came and took notes. Mooney sent Bugwell who read a statement about the college's support of public forums on issues of contemporary significance. Abe Goodnow stood up and said he believed that a public institution of higher learning ought not to be in the business of dramatizing aspects of American life that degraded the black community. Some people clapped and he sat down.

Jaeckel asked how many people in the audience had seen the movie. Goodnow and Don Way and two people I didn't know raised their hands. There were fifty or so people in the room.

Gardner whispered to me that one of the hand-raisers was a journalist from Oroville. Jaeckel got up and said, "How about showing the film right now, and we'll all know what we're talking about?"

For the next half-hour, people were for and against that idea. Andy Flood got emotional and said it wasn't right to show a movie that degraded black people. Gardner got emotional and said the issue was about freedom of assembly and discussion, not about degradation, that the protesters had already shifted attention from the movie as an art object to a movie as political propaganda. Before he could finish what he wanted to say, Goodnow was on his feet.

"Any movie or anything else that shows the terrorizing of black people is incitation to riot, and ought to be suppressed." He sat down and a few people clapped.

Jaeckel got up and said, "Anyone stupid enough to get sucked into a riot by a movie showing racial injustice ought to have his head examined."

Goodnow said, from his seat, that he resented what Jaeckel said, and Jaeckel said from his seat that he resented anyone trying to choose what movies he could see.

Goodnow got up again. "The question has to do with human sensitivity, not freedom of speech." The same people who clapped before clapped again. Goodnow sat down.

Jaeckel stayed seated, and shot back that if you want to talk about human sensitivity you ought to try to sensitize people to human injustice. "I know morons who know that it's better to be kind than to be nasty to people."

Goodnow again resented Jaeckel's metaphor and the way he tried to simplify the issue of human sensitivity.

Jaeckel said that he resented Goodnow's complicating a simple constitutional question with sentimentality, and the maligning of people already more sensitive to the mistreatment of black people in American history than the do-gooders who sucked up to special interest groups whose major interest was in self-perpetuation.

Goodnow was on his feet shouting and pointing his finger at Jaeckel. Bugwell was on his feet trying to keep the peace, and others shouted at Goodnow and Jaeckel. John was red-faced in his chair, his jaw set, his beady eyes blazing. Don Way took notes furiously, head down. I looked at Pat whose brow was furroughed, but he was amused, studying Jaeckel. He caught my eye and pointed to Don Way, still writing, bent over in his chair against the wall.

The next day, Don Way's description of the event appeared in his editorial, and I thought he got it straight. He didn't gloss the issues and he kept it straightforward. Goodnow and Jaeckel had made it easy for him.

On the following night, the movie was shown as scheduled. The auditorium was filled, half of the crowd there out of curiosity.

Gardner talked Bugwell into conducting a discussion after the film ended, but only a handful of people showed up. The Chico San people had boycotted the showing, and no one else wanted to discuss anything. Ceil and I thought the movie was dull.

Early the next morning, Gardner mailed the film back to the distributing company in San Francisco.

As cleanly as the water had appeared and disappeared in the streets of Chico, the civil discourse of America in the mid-sixties, with its accompanying enmity and abrasive tones, had visited and departed Chico. Three months later, the first anti-Vietnam War Teach-In in the United States was held on the campus of Chico State College.

Chapter Thirty-Three

I WAS WALKING ACROSS the college campus in mid-April when I heard a loudspeaker blaring from the quadrangle on the west side of the administration building, halfway between the tennis courts and the physical education building.

Spring was a nice season in Chico. All the hills were deep green from the rains, and the fields were full of daisies. The inevitable heat wave was two months away. The dichondra grass that had been brown all winter had lost its yellow-green March hue, and had become the deep conifer green of well-watered golf courses. When I heard the loudspeaker, I was comparing the college grass with my own backyard. Then I heard cheering, and headed for the loudspeaker.

Joe Bugwell, whom I got to know during the *Birth of a Nation* squabble, had called me a month into second semester and offered me a temporary job teaching in the journalism department. Kent Sprawling, a retired ex-editor of the *Fresno Bee,* and the chair of the three-man Journalism Department, had dropped dead the day before, and Bugwell offered me $10,000 if I'd teach Sprawlings' four courses for the rest of the semester. I politely turned him down flat for what occurred to me at the time to be good reasons. I had no intention of trying to teach anything to anybody. The next day, Bugwell called me again and said the college was in a jam. They had called around and couldn't find a qualified person, and President Mooney would regard it as a personal favor if I'd teach two courses, both of which met only twice a week, at half of Bugwell's own salary, $7500. I liked Bugwell and said I'd talk to Ceil.

Bugwell was humorless and sincere, and he had the efficient certainty of academic administrative assistants whose success depended on personalizing functionary duties in a way that transformed them from administrative tasks into personal favors to his boss, the president. I'd met Willard Mooney himself once, at Dandridge's print party, and I thought him to be smooth and perfunctory, but Bugwell bridged the impersonal gap with his flattering urgency, and when I told Ceil about the offer, she started calling me "Professor."

Puss heard us talking that evening and asked me what a "perfessa" was. I told her that it was someone who professed to be something he wasn't. Ceil thought it was just the thing for me. I didn't know what that meant and didn't want to know so I didn't ask her. We joked about it and I took the job.

Walking toward the loudspeakers and the cheering, I was an innocent part-time college lecturer, teaching a class of twenty-five students in a course called, "Introduction to Journalism," and a class of eight students called "The Mysteries of Copy-editing Revealed." When I saw the crowd of college kids I figured it would be grist for my own students' intellectual journalistic mills, and if anyone had told me then that I was witnessing the opening salvo of a new kind of war that would topple an American president, I would have doubted it very much. Standing there at the edge of the small crowd of students, I got my first glimpse of former U.S. Marine Sergeant Edward DiTullio.

DiTullio had been wounded and decorated for bravery in Korea, and he taught history at the college. He was articulate and dramatically straightforward in his opposition to Lyndon Johnson's war in Vietnam, and he said he was enlarging his classroom in order to say so. His voice boomed over the loudspeaker that the war was both morally wrong and strategically stupid. The United States had no business in Asia and ought to get the hell out of Vietnam.

At this time, I was neutral on the war, mostly because I hadn't thought about it much other than to evade the issue while trying to get Lyndon a big Butte County margin in the election so that the Democratic Party people in Sacramento would notice me.

Ed DiTullio was passionate, and the fervor of the crowd carried a spontaneous urgency. It was academic, but it was interesting. Ed's straight talk was compelling; he argued persuasively. He had verve, and he spoke with an easy focussed manner that was attractive.

In retrospect, later, I remember thinking that even at this first public meeting, it was clear that Ed was not a rabble-rouser, and he was not up to "liberal" mischief. He was to be branded, however, by both Democratic Party loyalists and conservatives alike, for exactly those two offenses. As the weeks passed, and Ed kept up the pressure in his public meetings, I held out hope for some kind of military solution that would save Johnson's face, but I still admired DiTullio for his bravery and for his refusal to quit his cause when the heat got turned up against him.

I stayed that first day and listened long enough to both hear that a public anti-Vietnam War teach-in was planned for the Chico Town common on the coming Saturday, and to witness a personal beef between a couple of students. Several feet away from DiTullio, in a small crowd of partisan supporters, a young man and a co-ed were obviously upset with each other.

The co-ed had auburn red hair, and I recognized her as my earliest Chico acquaintance, the young woman who urged me to the Brazen Onager after my visit to the real estate office. The young man was the surly blonde bartender at the Brazen Onager. From a distance of fifteen yards, I could see that they were in serious disagreement about DiTullio's speech. The blonde bartender walked away clearly unhappy, and my admiration for the redhead skyrocketed.

Chapter Thirty-Four

THE FOLLOWING SATURDAY, SHE was in the small group standing behind DiTullio at noon in the town park. A couple hundred students were milling around when Larry and I got there. I spotted Jaeckel standing with Pat and Pearl Kenneally and we went over. Pat said he'd seen DiTullio earlier at the college and he'd been to the city hall and had the town permit. Police cars lined the square on the Esplanade and Broadway and South Montana Drive.

"Have a few police cars," I said.

Pat said that he smelled something.

The town fathers were old California and conservative, touchy about controversial events that dramatized the new views of college kids.

By 12:30 there were several hundred college-kids and a few townies. DiTullio blew into the loudspeaker system to see if it worked and the crowd moved nearer to him. He said that he taught history at the college and that he had fought in Korea as a Marine. The Vietnam War was illegal and immoral and the American people ought to tell the government to get out of Vietnam.

People walking on the sidewalks of the Esplanade and Broadway stopped and crossed over to the park. Four county sheriff cars pulled alongside the local police cars and double-parked. Deputies in two-tone brown uniforms stepped out and stood by the cars.

Jaeckel asked us where the sheriff cars were when Reagan talked. "In the motorcade," Pat said.

A small group of students in the front row began heckling DiTullio. They wore football practice t-shirts that were cut at the shoulders. One of them was the blond bartender from the Brazen Onager.

Don Way had come up to us and stood with a note pad in his hand, but when the heckling began he said that he was going to move closer. I went with him. We got to within twenty-five feet of DiTullio and could see that a close band of DiTullio supporters standing several feet from the hecklers were giving signals to each other and nodding. I could see my favorite redhead. She was staring at the blond bartender, her seeming ex-boyfriend. The loyalists were not responding to the hecklers who were calling DiTullio a pacifist wimp. DiTullio was giving a history lesson on Southeast Asia, French Indo-China, Dien Ben Fu.

Blonde Crew Cut yelled, "Why don't you join the French Foreign Legion?"

DiTullio looked at him, stopped his speech, and said he preferred the U.S. Marines where he already served.

Someone yelled "Traitor!"

DiTullio said he wasn't a traitor, he had served his country in a patriotic war and he was still serving his country by speaking his mind. It was a citizen's duty to criticize the government if he disagreed with it.

Townspeople were urging the hecklers to let up and they quieted. DiTullio said that the Vietnamese people had a long cultural history and that the United States was behaving like a bully. He had been speaking about fifteen minutes when he gave the sheriff's department what they wanted.

"American prejudice against Asians is behind the war," he said. "We even call the Viet Cong, 'gooks.'"

One of the hecklers yelled, "They *are* gooks."

DiTullio pointed to the heckler and kept talking. He said that during the Pacific war with the Japanese, Admiral Halsey had urged the Americans to "kill the yellow bastards."

Eight brown uniformed deputies from the Butte County's sheriff's office moved on DiTullio, took his microphone and led DiTullio to one of their cars with its big blue star on the front doors. As the deputies had been moving toward him through the crowd, DiTullio saw them coming and urged the crowd to remember exactly what they saw today. The deputy who had taken the microphone had said that the meeting was over and everyone should go about their business.

Jaeckel called out in a booming voice, "This is our business. What do you think you're doing? Did you ever hear of free speech?"

The deputy, who knew John from the Farmer's Grange, said, "Come on John, we can't be allowing swearing in a public talk now, just settle down and we'll get it all straightened out."

"You ought to be ashamed of yourself, Chick, John said, "You want your own boy to be blown away in a Vietnam rice field?"

"Come on John, you know I don't. We're just doing our job now, don't make it harder for us."

By now, DiTullio was inside one of the sheriff's cars, heading away from the park.

Don Way was talking with the small group of students who were DiTullio's friends, and Larry and I walked over to listen. Pat had headed for his office at the college to make some phone calls. Jaeckel was on his way to find the town counsel.

Don Way was asking the students what DiTullio hoped to accomplish by teaching his history class in public.

The redhead said quietly between her teeth, "He wants to stop this fucking war."

Don looked at her and said, "Tell me more, I want to get it straight."

"Johnson is McNamara's stooge," she said grimly, opening her teeth slightly, "and nobody seems to care. The whole country needs a history lesson."

Don wrote on his note pad, flipped a page and wrote some more.

I went over to the redhead. "Remember me?" I said.

"No," she said.

"About a year ago you gave me directions to the Brazen Onager."

"You were looking for a real estate office."

"Right. I also found the Brazen Onager."

"I don't go there any more."

"It's a nice place, except for some of the help."

"What's going to happen to Ed DiTullio?"

"Looks like he's heading for the county lockup. Depends on how fast a lawyer springs him."

"Who's going to do that for him?"

"All he has to do is make a phone call."

"Obviously you trust the system."

"The college attorney ought to be right on it. It's none of my business, but I teach part time and I can call Joe Bugwell and see what's up."

"When?"

"Anytime. Now, if you want."

"Promise?"

"Scout's honor."

"Right now, OK?"

"OK."

"I've got to go."

"Bye."

Larry was standing close by, waiting. He came over.

"What do you think?" I said.

"DiTullio's a fortunate fellow."

"I told her I'd call Bugwell."

"I heard."

We crossed the Esplanade and walked down Fifth to The Green Walnut Leaf, a new restaurant that specialized in Caesar salads and home made soups.

I called Bugwell from their pay phone inside the front door. The line was busy for five minutes. I called Pat twice but his line was busy too.

Larry said he promised to take his kids to the One Mile swimming pool in Bidwell Park.

"In April?"

"Sure. We might even take the inner tubes to Five Mile and float down the creek. Get Ceil and Puss and we'll do it together.

"I can't. Gardner and Rozanne are coming over for a cookout and Ceil's waiting for me to go shopping for it. We promised to buy Puss a plastic pool for the yard and I have to go get it."

I drove to Safeway to buy the cookout stuff but I could see the long lines at the registers and went home to try to reach Bugwell. No one picked up in the President's Office. I called him at home but the line was busy. I called Pat and he answered and said that a general faculty meeting had been called for Monday afternoon. I asked Pat how that happened. He said, "Search me." Pat was secretary of the Faculty Assembly, and he'd been busy, obviously. I asked him what was going on with DiTullio. He said he was in stir in the Oroville jail.

"Why doesn't Mooney get the college attorney to spring him?"

"He says he will, on Monday morning."

"Why not now?"

"You tell me."

That afternoon Ceil and I bought a plastic swimming pool for Puss and Boots at Johnson's Garden Emporium, and went back to Safeway for the cookout stuff. I filled the pool on our green dichondra grass. The sun was very warm and I put on my bathing suit and let Puss squirt me with the garden hose, sitting in her plastic pool. I wondered what the inside of the Oroville county jail was like on a Saturday afternoon in northern California in April.

Chapter Thirty-Five

ON MONDAY AFTERNOON I entered what I expected to be the friendly fray of collegial discourse and made a brief speech to the general faculty of the college at the special meeting called to discuss the situation generated by DiTullio's Saturday morning teach-in and weekend in the Oroville jail. DiTullio was being detained on an 1880 county statute that forbade the uttering of obscenities in public. That he was quoting Admiral Halsey didn't

matter to the county sheriff, Fred Cliffset, and when DiTullio made his one
phone call from the administrative office of the Oroville jail, no one answered
at the other end. The only further communication Ed was allowed was with
deputies who brought him his meals. Pat made several unsuccessful calls and
then organized an informal meeting of the faculty assembly rules committee
who called the emergency meeting of the general faculty. My speech was
short, but not sweet.

My first draft was mostly a reaction to Pat's outrage at President Mooney's
weekend snub of DiTullio's imprisonment, but as I wrote out some ideas it
began to be fueled by my own instinct for drama at a time when I thought I
had nothing to lose.

"What are you going to say?" Ceil asked me when I hung up the phone
on Sunday afternoon.

"Call for the public hanging of the sheriff, and putting all the deputies
in stocks and pillory."

"You better know what you're doing, Billy Boy," she said, "it'll be in the
paper."

"It's a closed meeting of the faculty. Don Way can't get in."

"You think he won't know word for word what you say?"

Out in the yard I thought about what Ceil said. I let Puss spray me with
the hose and then we tossed a grapefruit back and forth, Puss pretending it
was a softball.

"What's One Mile?" she asked.

"It's the swimming pool in Bidwell Park."

"All the kids at school talk about One Mile and Five Mile."

"Five Mile's the other swimming place, further up in the park."

"Why don't we ever go there? Larry takes Semanth and little Larry
there."

"He must be a really good dad."

"He is."

"You want to go there?"

"When?"

"Now."

"You know I want to."

"Go ask your mother."

She did, and the three of us stopped by Larry's house to borrow their big
black inner tubes. The Bourkes were gone but Larry's garage was unlocked
and the tubes were stacked in a corner. We piled three into the back seat with
Puss.

Within a half-hour we were drifting down Chico Creek through the
scenes of Errol Flynn's *Robin Hood*. We passed the spot where Little John and

Friar Tuck battled with long staves on the little bridge, now long gone. The Creek moved us along at a good pace, and we sometimes separated and then came together and joined hands. Drifting in the tube, I remembered Eric Partridge's *Dictionary of American Bawdy*.

On Sunday night I called Dottie Bentley. When I started to tell her what Pat had told me on the phone about Ed DiTullio still being locked up in the Oroville jail, she said she already knew and how could she help. I told her what I intended to do, and that I needed a copy of Partridge's *Dictionary*.

I met Dottie at the Reserve Librarian's desk in the library on Monday morning, and she laughed when she saw me. "I guess I can still recognize a faculty emergency when I see one," she said.

The copy of the book under my arm that afternoon when I entered the campus auditorium was a reserve desk copy from the library, one illegal for removal.

I listened as my well-behaved colleagues rose to discourse on the current campus crisis. The repartee, except for Pat's was uninspired. I was reconsidering my intentions to discuss DiTullio's obscenities with my fellow academics when a full professor from the engineering department rose to attack Ed DiTullio as a threat to both the security and dignity of the campus. As he elaborated, my pique began to mushroom into a larger irritation, and when he was followed by a tall angular squinter from the sociology department who said that a cooling off period in a quiet place might be the best thing for someone advocating turning the academic profession into a public circus, I again became eager to lay my body across the barbed wire of academic no-man's land.

A few minutes later I was holding up my library reserve copy of Eric Partridge's *Dictionary of American Bawdy* and announcing that I, a newcomer to the sacred halls of academe, felt obligated as a teacher of journalism to remind everyone present of the virtues and versatility of the American language, codified in our dictionaries, the usage of which was protected by the First Amendment to the ("dare I use the over-used phrase") Constitution of the United States. I knew that I had everyone's attention, though I later remembered feeling pompous and over-extended.

As I read out "bastard" and defined it, I could hear Ceil's cautionary words the night before, telling me to go slow lest I blow my chances of reappointment. Her voice, however, faded in my inner ears as I heard in my outer ears my own voice calling out and defining other words that Admiral Halsey and Ed DiTullio might have privately used to describe the Butte County Sheriff in his inappropriate, misguided, and unlawful arrest of Ed DiTullio, to say nothing of those powers that be in the college administration who allowed our colleague to sit for almost two days in the county jail when the college attorney could have procured his release in a matter of minutes. I had over-cooked my goose.

I stepped away from the podium to a thunderous silence, albeit also to several grinning faces in the audience, and bumped into Bugwell as I moved to sit down in my vacated seat in the front row. He was standing with members of the faculty rules committee, and he acknowledged me with a serious look and dip of his forehead. We were eyeball to eyeball and I said softly, "I guess I got carried away."

"You're upset," he said in a tone that suggested that my remarks were, if not wholly appropriate, not wholly inappropriate. I liked Bugwell very much at that moment, though I found out later that Willard Mooney's own assessment of his newly acquired lecturer in journalism was not as generous as Bugwell's.

I had expected some sort of tangible result from the meeting, such as a statement from the faculty vindicating DiTullio, or one chastising the college president for failing to defend his faculty member in a crisis, but none was generated, and the meeting adjourned. At the Oaks bar, Pat explained to me over a drink that college faculties do not take votes on issues that have not been filtered through the committee process, and he added, "Resolutions that threaten the status quo do not survive the filtering." He said that his view was somewhat cynical, but I ought to take some comfort from a process that revealed so nakedly the courage of some and the cowardice of others.

"Academic politics make the public boys look like kids on the playground," he said, "It resembles the operation of the Council of Ministers in a monarchy during the feudal age."

"Mooney could have sprung DiTullio?"

"In one second. He didn't want to buck the two Republican County Commissioners, Hagwell and Burnett. Our own guy, Harley Davis, worked it as hard as he could, but he couldn't get one of the others, and he needed a majority. Sandhill was in it too. He's always in it, but you never see his name. Don Way's editorial tomorrow will spell it out."

The next day's afternoon edition carried full coverage of Saturday's events on the front page, with photographs of the crowd, and Ed speaking, but no photo of Ed being led away with the deputies. The article said that a few partisan college students and a history professor were opposed to the Vietnam War, and that student opinion was divided, as evidenced by the dialogue in the audience during the professor's remarks. It noted that DiTullio was a veteran of the Korean War but did not mention his decoration for bravery or his wounding. It concluded that the demonstration was suspended by sheriff's deputies when the professor's language became obscene.

At the bottom of the editorial column on the left side of the next to last page of the paper, in a column devoted to flood control in the northern valley, Don Way's secondary editorial said that the symbiotic relationship between the college and the town could best be preserved and furthered in a time of national debate by preserving tradition, insofar as conventional wisdom argues effectively that college classrooms remain within college buildings.

Chapter Thirty-Six

IN THE WEEKS THAT followed the DiTullio event, campus unrest deepened and both the town and the college began to slowly divide on the question of the growing war in Asia. I was surprised when Luke Gardner asked me if I noticed any difference in my classes, which I hadn't, and he told me that some of his creative writing kids were smoking marijuana and a few were experimenting with heroin. I was ignorant of their weekend parties but he apparently was not, so I taught my classes and was oblivious to the social changes in student life. I didn't know any students very well and underestimated the energy that was generating on the campus about the war.

When Luke invited me to go with him to a Friday night gathering of some of his student writers, I didn't feel strongly one way or the other and said that if he really wanted me to, I would. Ceil was surprised that I was going to a student beer party but was a good sport about it and only kidded me a little bit about co-eds on the hunt for young faculty members. I had told her about DiTullio's redhead.

The party was held in a seven room wooden house on the north edge of town. Most of the college upper classmen lived off campus in old houses such as this one that were built in the twenties and sold to real estate companies when the new residential communities on the east side of town were built in the early fifties.

The real estate companies rented the old houses by the room to college kids for prices competitive with student housing, and made only modest annual repairs. By the time Ceil and I were living on Violet Lane in the early sixties, the second-hand furniture market in Chico was almost non-existent because old furniture that surfaced in tag sales was immediately snapped up by real estate people for these houses. Ceil asked me if she should wait up for me and I felt flattered and said "Sure." It would give me a good excuse to leave early.

Luke picked me up at 8:30 and we had a dark beer at the Onager where I asked him why he invited me. The question came out more abruptly than I intended and as soon as I asked it I realized that I was really questioning my own decision to go with him. He said it was either of two reasons and I could choose which I preferred. He wanted to show me weekend extracurricular life and had himself been putting off student invitations for weeks, and now that he had accepted he didn't want to go alone.

"It's not too late to back out," he laughed.

"I feel uncomfortable being watched by students when I'm drinking beer, that's all," I said.

"The good part is that it's not mutual. They really don't care what anyone sees at their parties as long as the anyone is invited."

"Sounds salacious."

"It probably won't be, not if we leave early. If we stay out the party, anything could happen."

"Anything?"

"Anything."

"Drugs?"

"You won't see them, but they'll be there."

We arrived at 9:30 and the porch light was on and the front door open. The music was loud. We walked into a dark living room with fifteen or so students sitting in sofas and on the floor or on the stairway leading upstairs, rattling gourds, clacking sticks, slapping the backs of pans with their palms, all to the beat of the loud, slow fifties jazz that was booming from a record player somewhere in one of the corners of the room. When the first student recognized Luke, he got up and welcomed us. Several students heard the welcome and came over and Luke introduced me as the faculty member who read from the dictionary at the faculty meeting a couple months ago. They exclaimed "all right" and "way to go, man," and a co-ed named Betsy handed me a pan and a wooden spoon. I sat down on the floor with it and accepted a can of Coors from a young man named Hugo, who had a goatee. Not being much of a pot banger, after a few minutes I put it down and Betsy back in her seat on the staircase didn't seem to notice. The party seemed more like group meditation with no director, and I tried to look interested and with it.

As I sat there on the floor, I realized that Luke had disappeared, so I entertained myself by remembering back to the beer parties at Lambda Chi during my own undergraduate days, where the drinkers and songsters stayed close to the beer keg in the downstairs dining room. Close-locked dancers moved in the darkened first floor living room where the furniture had been pushed to the walls and the rug rolled and stored behind the couches in the library, and the make-outs were quiet on the second floor study room couches or in the third floor sleeping dorm.

Both Betsy and Hugo had called me "Bill" after Luke introduced me, and

Betsy had whispered that I should just do whatever I felt like doing, the main thing was to be myself. I didn't know what that meant, so I was trying as I sat there on the floor, remembering my undergraduate past, to look inconspicuous doing nothing and being myself. I saw Luke leave the room and realized that he hadn't disappeared at all but had been sitting in the far dark corner near the record player. I figured that he went to the bathroom and forgot about him. I was thinking of the Sadie Hawkins dance at Lambda Chi in the spring of 1952 when I saw Louise Walden and Fonky Ford go out the back door of the songsters' room during the singing of "That Son of a Bitch Palombo," not to return for about an hour. I said to Louella, my date, "There go Fonky and Louise," and she said, "Let them go," touching me on the lips. Behind the fraternity there was a field that sloped down to a brook, and a line of trees, on the other side of which was the practice football field. I was remembering how Louella had fixed up Louise, her roommate, with Fonky, and the next-day details which Louella related to me, when all of a sudden I smelled marijuana and was immediately back in Chico. I had finished my beer but hadn't put the can down lest Betsy or someone would hand me another one. I was sure that they could all see me in the dark and were watching me.

Luke was no longer in the corner and the pan and gourd knockers were still meditating when I got up to go to the bathroom. As soon as I tried to untangle my legs and push myself to my feet without appearing to be as out of squat-sitting shape as I was, Betsy was beside me asking if she could do anything for me, and I said I was OK for the moment. "The bathroom's next to the kitchen," she said softly, "You'll see the kitchen light if you go through there." She pointed to an opening in back of the stairs.

"Thanks," I said, feeling the pins and needles in my left leg, and thought of DiMaggio stepping out of the cab, not realizing his foot was asleep and tearing his tendon. I concentrated on the pins and needles, trying not to put too much weight on my leg but also trying not to limp. I felt old, in the wrong place. The life of co-eds chasing college professors wasn't very romantic at the moment. I waited at the bathroom door, and took my turn.

"How're you doing?" Luke said when I found him in the kitchen, leaning against an old Brigham stove.

"Just being myself," I said.

He introduced me to Lee Green, Slim Row, and a small dark man called Karo, editors of the English department magazine, *The Tasty Tidbit*. Lee was smoking a joint and held it out for me to take a drag. I shook my head and tried to look like I was being myself, and he withdrew the offer and took a drag himself. "Slim's the editor, he puts everyone he publishes on the masthead of the next issue. He's also the tidbit."

I looked at Slim and tried not to smile too intimately.

"How about drawing a cartoon of yourself reading from Partridge's dictionary to the faculty, and we'll publish it anonymously?" Slim had wavy blond hair, neatly trimmed, with long blond sideburns and a blond outcrop of hair between his lower lip and his chin. He also had a blue and orange bracelet tattooed on his wrist.

I looked at Luke. "You didn't warn me you had told them my life story," I said.

He borrowed Lee's joint for a drag. "Ask them if I told them anything," he said.

I looked at Slim Row. He said, "When you took over Greenclough's classes and they ran that story on you in the campus *Gazette*, the cartoonist thing caught my eye. I went to the library and Mrs. Bentley showed me the two cartoons in the *Bee* and one in the *Chronicle*.

"I'm flattered," I said, feeling like a part time jerk instructor who takes compliments from aesthetes.

"How about doing one for us? We'll call it 'New Lecturer Lectures Faculty,' and we'll post-date it."

"Let me think about it. I called a lot of attention to myself with that, I don't know if I want a re-run."

"It's Andrea's idea," Luke said. "She'll be over later to make the case."

I looked at Luke.

"Andrea Jelleneau, Ed DiTullio's girlfriend," he said.

"The redhead?"

"Don't call her 'red,'" Lee said, "she doesn't take to it."

"How much later?"

"Depends on Ed," Slim said, "He'll probably skip the poetry reading."

I looked at Luke.

"There's always a poetry reading. Limit three to a customer, none longer than a page," he said.

Karo slipped out the back door.

"If Ed shows for the reading, he'll read a Dylan song. He teaches Dylan in his history classes." Lee rolled another joint and we all watched. He was good at it. He lit it, inhaled and exhaled slowly, and offered it around.

Luke said,"Just one hit," took it and inhaled and passed it back.

A brunette in navy blue shorts and a Chico State t-shirt appeared in the kitchen. It was clear she wasn't wearing a bra.

"God," she said, brushing several strands of hair away from her face, "Don't take a nap after drinking red wine, I almost fell down the stairs."

"Ash," Slim said, "This is Bill Armature, he teaches journalism. He's the one…"

I cut him off. "He's the one is good enough." I was half-laughing and I put out my hand. "I'm a friend of Luke's. How are you?"

"Groggy," she said. "I live here, and I half-slept through my own party." She hadn't looked at Luke yet.

He said, "Hello Ashley," and she looked at him and raised one eyebrow.

"Professor Gardner. I know you from somewhere. You were in the Donner Party, weren't you?"

"I walked through eighteen feet of snow and brought relief, but they had to amputate."

"Serves you right for getting cold feet," she said.

Karo slipped back into the kitchen through the back door and when he saw us looking at him said, "Great moon." In that half moment I caught the glance between Ashley and Luke, and she raised the eyebrow again in a question. He barely shook his head and looked away. I decided it was a good reason for me to leave early, but we had come in his car. I wondered when Andrea Jelleneau would arrive.

For the poetry reading in the living room they set up a box crate with two lighted candles and turned the music off. Karo sat behind the box crate and started to read. He had an attractive unkempt look, needing a shave, but he had that suave look popular with Italian male models a generation later. As he read, he unconsciously kept pushing up the sleeves of his silk shirt as they flopped back down again. I saw the marks on his forearm. It was the only animated part of him as he read quietly and lovingly three poems about amanita mushrooms. When I asked Luke later, "What's with the amanita mushrooms?" he told me that amanitas are beautiful but could be deadly.

When Karo finished reading, he sat as still as a statue, with his head bowed. Then a girl in a dark purple leotard read two poems about a field changing color during the seasons, during which Karo left for fifteen minutes and returned. He had a quart bottle of mineral water with him. A gallon jug of Gallo burgandy kept making the rounds, and everyone drank from paper cups. Another girl read a story about a man killing a dog on a rainy day. She was gangly and intense, and leaned to one side when she read. At one point her hair brushed the candle flame and almost caught on fire. The smell of her singed hair permeated the room. I heard someone say "shit to hell," and looked over to see napkins being passed to a girl soaking up a cup of spilled wine on her skirt and the floor. The girl with the singed hair kept reading.

During the next forty-five minutes, Slim, Lee Green and two gangly co-eds wearing black lipstick read their poems. When it was over, the last reader, Slim, blew out the candles and the music was on again, first the Tijuana Brass, then Roger Miller, then Dylan. I went to the bathroom.

Betsy met me as I was coming out and asked me if I needed anything. I said I was holding together OK, and she said, "Let me know, the colder the snow," and began whistling to herself as she lightly touched me on her way into the bathroom.

People were moving up and down the stairs and I could hear music coming from upstairs rooms. Part of the party had moved outside, both in front and back. I looked in the kitchen for Luke. Slim said he hadn't seen him since the reading started.

"You already know Andrea," he added. I turned around.

"Hello," she said.

"Hello."

"You don't have much pull with lawyers."

"Unfortunately not. Am I forgiven?"

"You were great at the faculty meeting."

"You were there?"

"Spies."

Her hair was cut and shaped so that it fell straight down, covering her ears and intensifying her high cheekbones and light blue eyes. Her red eyebrows were dark, almost brown. She was standing close enough so that I looked for the lines of an eyebrow pencil but there were none. She was the best looking redhead I'd ever seen.

"When I heard the Dylan records I wondered if you two were here," I said.

"He's out back. The records are Ed's substitute for a poem. He says he feels inferior around creative writers."

Slim was talking to Lee and I told him to find me out back if he saw Luke. Andrea and I went out into the back yard. It was a warm spring night and the moon hadn't risen and the yard was dark. I thought of Karo and the moon marks on his arm. Ed DiTullio was standing in a small group beside another small group sitting on the grass, drinking wine. Dylan's monotone voice came clearly through the open living room windows. I thought it was too early for mosquitoes, but I heard the students sitting on the grass slapping flesh.

For a while I made small talk and then brought up the cartoon.

"About that cartoon, Andrea…"

She cut me off.

"Don't make any promises, cap, Andrea's first rule is do it or don't do it, but don't promise anything. It was just an idea."

Luke appeared from nowhere. "Everybody being themselves?"

He drove me home and I told him Karo was in trouble.

"Ah, Karo. Karo's in deeper than trouble."

"He seems like a nice kid."

"Who isn't a nice kid?"

When I got out of the car I had the feeling he was not going straight home.

Ceil was watching a re-run of a Perry Mason show as she was making a skirt out of taffeta for Puss and Boots's ballet class.

"How was the party?"

"They read poems about poison mushrooms to the smell of burning hair."

"You're kidding."

I told her everything except about Ashley and Luke, and we both ate a bowl of cornflakes. When the Perry Mason show was over we went to bed. Karo's story made her a little sad, but the story of Betsy the whistler made her laugh.

Chapter Thirty-Seven

THE NAVARRO RIVER ENTERS the Pacific after cutting a swath through the west slope of the California Range and sweeping through the grooved alluvial plain that contains the raging river in flood stage during the rainy season. When the rains are heavy and the snow melts in the mountains, the Mendocino riverside cottages near the outlet are abandoned. Ten years before, they were swept away, then rebuilt. Ceil and I planned a long weekend with the Bourkes in June and drove from Chico down and across the valley, then through the mountain pass west of Yuba City and Williams, past Clear Lake to Ukiah, and then route 128 northwest to where the Navarro River enters the Pacific just south of Albion. From the coastal ridge we could look down on the sandy plain below, cut by the light blue river with its brush-strewn banks pocked with half-covered logs as thin as pencils. The surf was white-lipped and undramatic, and the Pacific was deep blue. Larry pulled over and parked on the ocean side and I pulled up behind him. We all got out and looked.

"We're here," he said. "The cottages are tucked back against the underside of this hill, beneath us."

"Let's go," Ceil said, and we descended to the first side road along the edge of the brush-littered plain. After a couple hundred yards, four white wooden cottages came in view. Larry drove past them to the restaurant and parked, and he and I went in and got the keys. It was mid-afternoon and overcast, and I told Ceil I hoped the cottage had a wood stove.

"That would be special," she said.

Larry and Eartha tried their key and it worked. We all agreed to meet at the restaurant for a drink after we got settled, and Ceil and I went next door and mounted the unpainted steps of our small wooden porch, and our key worked also.

Puss asked if she and Semantha could go swimming and we both jumped at her at the same time—"Not on your life," then we both laughed. I told her I'd take her wading after we unpacked. She asked if she could see if Semantha could go too, and disappeared toward Larry's car.

We could see across the silvery stream flowing through the wide, sandy riverbed, the coastal highway disappearing above the crest of the cliff. The river looked wadeable where it leveled to a silent dribble into the surf. The air was wet and cool and I could see the fog hanging offshore.

Inside the cabin, Ceil said, "It's nice, Bill. And you got your wish. There's even a woodbox with actual driftwood. Somebody was nice to us." She held up a piece of a tangled tree limb, whitened and dry.

I was testing the double bed. "Let's move the cot into the kitchen," I said. Ceil pursed her lips and looked at the ceiling and laughed.

The bedroom walls were whitewashed and the cabin smelled clean and damp and oceany. As I was pulling the cot through the doorway, Ceil called, "The refrigerator is cold and the gas stove works!"

Puss came through the door with Semantha and asked if they could start on their walk if they didn't go above their knees, and I could catch up.

"Not above your ankles," I said, and they disappeared. I went to the door window and watched them running across the sandy plain toward the frothy edge of the grayblue water. People further down the beach merged into the jagged boulders and outcroppings of granite that stood starkly against the base of the northern coastal cliffs.

"It's a big ocean," Ceil said, watching beside me.

We put on sweatshirts, and walking along the sand could see the girls playing along the edge of the beach, barely into the water. As we neared the restaurant we could hear the jukebox, Roger Miller singing "King of the Road." Ceil said she was glad we brought our soft wool turtlenecks for later. "I hope we're fogged-in the whole three days," she said.

"It's sitting right offshore," I said. "It'll come in in a couple hours."

"Do you think they'll join us?"

"Sure they will. Larry's had it up to his eyeballs with her in Chico. He's counting on this trip."

"He's talked to you?"

"Not a word. Maybe a little bit around the edges. Something good has to happen."

"Like what."

"A miracle."

Inside the restaurant, Larry and Eartha were dancing, and Larry was being fancy, dipping and doing slow swirls with Eartha. She was smiling and they were whispering together.

Ceil and I sat at the bar and Ceil asked the bartender if he could make a lime velvet.

"Sure," he said and smiled at me. "Yours?"

"I'm a bourbon man," I said, "but the fog is calling 'Brandy Alexander,' across the water.

"What the hell is a lime velvet?" I asked Ceil.

"I don't know," she said, "I saw a picture of one in *The New Yorker* about ten years ago, and I've been waiting for the right place and the right time.

We turned and watched the dancers and clapped when Larry smoothly dipped Eartha backwards.

"I wonder what they're saying to each other," Ceil said.

"I don't," I said, and turned to watch the bartender who was returning with our drinks.

"I like Eartha," Ceil said.

"Everybody likes Eartha," I said, "except Bannister's wife."

"I wish we could help."

"We can. We are. We're here."

"I guess so."

"I know so."

"Here's mud in your eye."

"Here's to you, kid."

"Oh, it's quite good."

"Mine too. Reminds me of my first mother-in-law, it was her favorite drink."

"Your *what* mother-in-law?"

"Remind me to tell you sometime about my first marriage. My mother-in-law was a pip, and I was a yearling. In one evening I had my first raw oyster, my first cigar, and my first brandy Alexander. I've been a drunk ever since."

"You're crazy Armature, but you're loveable crazy. Where has this place been all our lives? You're actually having a good time and we just got here."

"It's the gospel truth, but that's another story."

"Another mother-in-law?"

"My second or third, I've forgotten. It was on the Isle of Skye, we had just taken the ferry that morning from the Kyle of Lakalsch. We were in a driving rainstorm…"

Larry and Eartha took seats beside us where they had left their scotches.

"Thank god you've come back," Ceil said. Bill has lost his mind. He's enjoying himself."

"Sounds good to me," Larry said, raising his scotch.

"Here's to Bill and a good time," Eartha said, raising her scotch.

We clinked glasses all around.

"The abalone pickers are coming in the morning," Larry said. "Jake said if we wanted to go with them, we could ask. All they can do is turn us down."

"Go *where?*" Ceil asked.

"Abalone picking," Larry said. "Jake says they're right out there in twelve feet of water." He pointed to the ocean.

We had another round of drinks and walked back to their cabin. It was misting already and I looked to make sure the girls were still in sight. They were in approximately the same spot, heads down, dancing slowly in the shallow water. Eartha had said as we left the bar, "I hosey getting dinner tonight for all of us," and I was relieved when Ceil said immediately, "Wonderful." I was tired of the "Oh let me do that" game, and we all needed to be kind to one another and see where it took us.

Larry got his little boy and we left Eartha and Ceil cutting up potatoes and sipping scotch, to join Puss and Semantha on the beach. Larry lifted young Nicholas from his shoulders and he ran ahead of us across the moist sand toward the beach fifty yards away. We neared Puss and Boots and Semantha trying to scale round rocks across the water, but each one plopped and sank where it landed.

"They have to be flat, sweetheart," I called.

"If you catch it just right, sometimes it jumps," Semantha explained as we joined them.

Together we searched for flat rocks to scale across the water, and soon all of us except Nicholas were making little splashes in the Pacific Ocean. Nicholas bent over to pick up a rock, and when he got it, he fell back and sat in the wet sand. Larry showed him how much fun it was to dig sand with his fingers, and by the time we started back, Nicholas was drenched on his backside, covered with sand, and Larry got sand down his own neck as he took great strides with Nicholas on his shoulder, pretending he was Gulliver heading for Lilliput.

Larry and I had a friendly competition over how to build a fire in a wood stove, and Larry won, and after a while we had to open the front door and the windows to let in some cool ocean air as the salmon sizzled in the big iron spider that Eartha brought from Chico. Ceil coaxed me to go with her to the restaurant bar for another lime velvet, but I demurred long enough that she had to settle for a Jack Daniels with milk. It was a new drink for all of us, and by the time we sat down to eat we were booing and hissing at each other's suggestions for invented drinks exotica. Larry's final proposal was campari and chocolate walnut ice dream, and mine was dry vermouth and bananas blended with orange juice. Ceil was fixated on what the bartender put in the lime velvet, so we agreed to find out later, by god. Eartha proposed a double Dewars on a Johnny Walker Black Label on the rocks.

Nicholas was asleep by nine and Larry and I were doing the dishes when Ceil and Eartha stepped out on the porch for Eartha to smoke a cigarette. In a few minutes they came back in to report a campfire on the near banks of the stream, a little way up from the quiet surf. They said that our cove was fogged in. The girls pleaded not to have to babysit, and the group decision went for Nicholas being safe, with periodic checks, and we trudged across the sand to the fire.

The abalone pickers had arrived early and the five of them sat around their small bonfire. When we approached, they asked us to sit and have a drink or a beer, pointing to three stacked cases of Hamms and one of them holding up a bottle of Union Jack. An opened stack of paper cups in a cellophane wrap leaned upright against a log rolled close to the fire.

We sat on two other driftwood logs around the fire, and the leader, Jamison Tandy, urged the girls to throw pieces of the piled driftwood on the flames when they had a mind to. The girls took turns and giggled when they didn't toss the piece of wood close enough and Jamison had to lean in close to the heat and retrieve it for a second try. Sometimes the new wood on the fire crackled with sparks and sputtered and sizzled for several seconds with different colored flames.

Jamison said to call him "Tan," and made a joke about us not really wanting to watch him put on his wet suit and see his chalk white skin. He introduced Burly, Kenny, Skid, and Beans. He said this was their annual abalone hunt, and before we had a chance to ask, invited Larry and me to join them at 5:30 the following morning.

"We got two extra wet suits, but without the helmets," he said.

Larry looked at me and I looked at Larry, and we grinned the grins of neophytes.

"We'll be here *I* guess," Larry said, emphasizing the "I," shaking his head in pleasure.

"I guess too," I added, and a half-hour later the four of us left the fivesome drinking by the fire, and walked back to our cottages and our alarm clocks.

Chapter Thirty-Eight

IT WAS STILL DARK at 5:15 when my alarm clock began its series of short beeps. I felt for it, found the notch to shut it off and rolled out of bed. Ceil said, "Don't get wet," and I put my tongue on her neck and kissed her ear lobe and she shivered and said, "Thanks a lot, pal."

The idea of a beer crossed my mind but I prayed instead for the divers to have a pot of coffee at their fire. I slipped on a pair of shorts and my pants, then into my sandals and a sweatshirt. When I stepped outside, Larry was standing on his porch drinking a beer. The fog covered the cove but it was lifting and I could see the fire and the divers.

"You're probably smarter than I am, I'm praying for coffee at the fire."

"I'm dumber than you are, you mean," Larry said.

We walked across the sand and gravel bed of the delta.

"We're nuts, you know that, don't you?" Larry said. "You know how cold the ocean is? I won't know a fucking abalone if it bites me."

"Tan said they have wet suits for us."

"Not for our heads and feet they don't. If my brains freeze I'll drown."

At the fire, Tan said, "Right on time." He got up and got the wet suits and flippers from two cardboard boxes. "We each bring two wetsuits just in case."

"In case of sharks?" Larry said, joking.

Tan and Beans laughed. Skid said "Sea lions," and tipped a rum bottle to his lips.

"You guys sleep OK?" I asked.

"Not so's you'd notice it," Tan said, putting on his wet suit. A large pile of empty beer cans glistened near the fire, some crinkled and mashed, some whole. The divers were putting on their wet suits. "We come over here to have some fun. The abalones are just frosting. First night's always an all-nighter."

I pulled on the wet suit and watched the others pulling on their rubber helmets. Tan said, "Once your head is under water you'll forget about it."

"I'm so dumb about this, I don't know what I should know," Larry said.

"Just do what we do," Burly said. "We'll stay together."

Tan gave Larry and me inflated inner tubes with burlap bags tied inside, and tire irons. We walked to the water's edge and up the beach another fifty yards and put on our flippers. Before I got mine on, Burly and Beans were swimming, pushing their inner tubes before them. I should have drunk the beer, I thought. My other self said, you should have stayed in bed with Ceil.

I breast-stroked after the divers, Larry behind me, for about seventy-five yards, rising and lowering with the swells. My hands and my head were cold at first and then I forgot about it.

Then I couldn't see Tan. His tube was ten yards in front of me but he was nowhere in sight. "Where's Tan?" I called out. Kenny was the nearest to me, and he said, "He dove to see if we're deep enough."

He was gone for what seemed like a long time, then surfaced next to his inner tube and dropped an abalone into the burlap bag hanging down from the middle of the tube. "It's only ten or twelve feet but it's OK. They're there, you just have to look around."

"If you get another one of those, let me see it, will you?" Larry called, paddling toward us.

"Sure," Tan said. "They look like round rocks six or seven inches across. You can see 'em easy, it's nice and quiet down there, all purple and pink. Take a couple practice dives and make sure you look coming back up. You don't want to get tangled in the kelp."

"What kelp?" Larry said, treading water beside his tube.

Kenny and Skid had dived, and their tubes were floating several yards from us.

"If you do get caught, pull the release on your weight belt and it'll drop," Tan said.

Burly was holding the side of his inner tube and vomiting.

"Seasick already?" Tan called.

Burly shook his head and vomited again. "Fucking seawater and rum don't mix," he said. "I got a mouthful coming out."

I saw Kenny drop an abalone into his burlap bag, then disappear.

"I better do this if I'm going to do it," Larry said, and I watched him gulp air and go down.

I was getting up my nerve, treading water, hanging on to my inner tube, worried that it would drift away if I dove. But the other tubes seemed to stay in place. Tan surfaced and held out an abalone for me to see.

"They're attached to rocks and you have to pry them off with the iron. We can't legally take more than five apiece."

"I guess I'm not worried about being illegal," I said.

"You'll do OK," he said.

I took a deep breath and headed down to the floor of the Pacific Ocean, thinking dramatically and with an overblown sense of my personal worth, that this was as good a way to go as any. I could see well through the goggles, having obeyed to the dotted i Tan's instructions to spit into them before going down. I was astonished at the lavender kingdom I had entered. As soon as I made it to the bottom, I was out of breath, and surfaced for air. I started up, remembering to look overhead for the light, and came up next to my tube.

Larry was close by, holding on to his tube and slowly treading water. I hadn't been down thirty seconds.

"Where the hell is the abalone?" he called. "You were down there five minutes."

"Christ, I haven't even seen one yet, and these guys have probably got their limits. I got all out of breath getting down there. Have you?"

"What do they look like?" Larry said, laughing.

Ten minutes later, both Larry and I had abalones in our bags. I felt very professional. Tan had four, and Kenny had already swum ashore with his five.

"How do they know how many we take?" I asked Tan before descending again.

"Maybe they're not watching, but they might be. They stay up on the highway with glasses. Don't think they can't count."

I went down again and spotted the biggest one I had seen so far. I tried to work the tip of the tire iron under the edge of the abalone shell that looked like a rock except that it was almost perfectly round, like a large turtle shell seen from the top. I tried twice but couldn't spuck it from the rock where it had clamped itself. I felt out of breath but I didn't want to leave the abalone. I had taken such a big gulp of air I had to fight to stay at the bottom in the right position to get leverage with my arm. This time I felt the pressure at the edge of the tire iron and pushed hard and the abalone flipped over and lay on the bottom. I kicked hard with my flippers and got down to pick the abalone off the bottom and started up, wanting air badly.

Air was the only thing on my mind. I had the tire iron in one hand and the big abalone in the other. I kicked my flippers to increase my speed to the surface of the water.

At first it didn't occur to me that I was caught in the kelp, and when I realized it, I had forgotten that the kelp moved back and forth many yards at a time, like great long strands of ocean hair flowing in and out with the swells of the waves, and I panicked. I was sure I was going to drown. I was out of air and puzzled and annoyed that someone wasn't coming down to find me. They must know that I'm missing, I thought. I had been gone from the surface a long time, way too long. I threw the abalone and the tire iron and grabbed for my leaded waist belt, but I couldn't find the release. It had moved from my left side several inches further as I thrashed around, but I couldn't locate it with my left hand. All of a sudden I felt it with my right hand and it dropped off. I knew I was going to drown right there beneath Larry and Tan and Beans. This is it, I thought.

Then I was on the surface breathing air. I grappled for my tube, and it was right next to me.

127

"Where's the abalone?" Tan asked.

"I got caught," I said, trying to sound casual. "I thought I was a goner. I threw the abalone and the tire iron, even the belt. I didn't look up. You were right."

"You will next time. I got my five. You want me to stay here awhile, and you can get one more?"

"Let me see if I can find the one I tossed away, and my iron and belt. I won't hold you up."

"I'm OK here. I aint been swallering any water like Burly."

"Where's Larry?" I called.

"Right here," he called back. "The fuckers are hard to locate. I want one more. Are you going in?"

When we emptied our burlaps near the fire and lined the abalones on an old door that Beans pulled out of the sand, we had twenty-eight. The divers each got their five, Larry got two, and I got just the single. I never found the one I tossed though it was lying on the bottom upside down somewhere right beneath me. I dove three times for it, found my tire iron and my weight belt on the first try. Later, reasoning out my kelp entanglement, I figured out that I was sprung free when the tidal flow reversed and the outgoing water swept the long kelp arms back over my head. I felt very inconsequential.

Larry and I pulled off our wet suits and Tan told us to come back in the afternoon and they'd show us how to clean the abalone. He said they were lock-tight rigid now from the handling, as if rigor mortis had set in, and they needed several hours to relax. We said we'd be back, and headed across the sand to the restaurant for coffee.

Sitting at the bar, we drank coffee and Larry put a quarter in the jukebox and played "King of the Road."

"That was fun," he said. "Fucking abalone-picking in Mendocino County."

"You guys never knew I was caught in the kelp, did you?" I asked.

"Whyn't you give a holler?" Larry said, grinning at me.

"Right."

"Now I want to eat some of it," he said. "Another coffee?"

"Why not."

"You got any doughnuts, Jake?"

"Delivered an hour ago. Lady makes 'em up the road. How many?"

"Three," Larry said, "and one for my friend. He's celebrating being alive after the great kelp escape."

"You get caught in the kelp?"

"For about twenty seconds. It felt like five minutes."

"Man, I wouldn't go down there for nuthin. You gotta have to like that sort of thing. Those guys out there with Jamison, they got the bug. They come every year and drink like hell and stay up all night and don't bother anyone. They're good guys, but they're a little crazy and they don't give a damn. Really good guys. I knew they'd take you along. I don't charge 'em anythin. They'll be over here later this afternoon and they'll eat like hell before going home tomorrow. They're good guys."

Chapter Thirty-Nine

PUSS AND SEMANTHA WERE making morning sand castles and fortresses on the beach when we left the restaurant with large coffees for Ceil and Eartha, and I started over to see if they had eaten any breakfast. Before I got there Puss saw me coming and stood up and called "Rice Krispies" and made a round motion with her hand on her stomach, then pointed to Semantha who was digging and piling sand. Larry was up in front of me, waiting, and I told him they had eaten. He nodded and went into his cottage.

Ceil pretended not to hear me when I came in but I knew she was awake because she woke up if a moth fluttered against the window screen in summer.

I stood in the bedroom doorway taking the coffee out of the white paper bag, and then to devil her sipped the coffee. Ceil said, "That's mine you beach bum." I handed her the coffee and she took it and sat up and sipped. I kissed her and she said, "You taste like an anchovy."

"I have explored the Great Salt Lake."

"Was it nice."

"It's very pink and purply and quiet at the bottom."

"No mermaids?"

"Two, but there was something fishy about them."

"How did you find out?"

"Secrets of the deep."

"The coffee's divine. Remind me not to drink any more of Eartha's scotch. I can hardly see you."

"I'm going to shower. Don't go away."

Later, we spent the morning walking the beach and looking for driftwood and shells. Larry was with Nicholas at the water's edge. I showed Ceil and the girls the abalones piled on the flotsam door. All the divers were snoring in sleeping bags except Burly who sat drinking a beer and occasionally throwing a piece of driftwood on the fire.

"They're calming down," he said when he saw us. "We'll sneak up on them in a couple hours."

We walked north on the beach and rounded a bend where the water's edge got rocky and the cliff steep. Puss asked why the man at the fire was going to sneak up on his friends.

"He meant the abalone."

"How can a anabaloney calm down?" Semantha asked.

'Search me," I said.

"Did you catch any of them?" Puss asked.

"One."

"That's not many," Puss said.

"I'm not very good at it."

"How many did my dad catch?" Semantha asked.

"He got two. We need practice."

"Never say die, daddy," Puss said.

"Never say it," I agreed, remembering the kelp, trying to free the release on my lead belt, then throwing the abalone. Tan had described the kelp flowing in and out like hair, thousands of strips twenty feet long.

"Tell them about the mermaid, old salt," Ceil said.

"You saw mermaids?" Semantha asked.

"Daddy, there's no such thing, you know it. Semanth, don't believe him, he's making it up."

"Don't be so sure," Ceil said.

"Don't encourage him, mommy, you said so yourself."

"Hey, I didn't say there were mermaids did I?"

"You did this morning, big boy," Ceil said.

"That was different," I said.

We found a path leading up the side of the cliff.

"That was before breakfast and I had just emerged from the deep. Then I remembered it was all a dream."

"You always say that daddy, it was all a dream."

"Can we go anabaloneying?" Semantha asked.

"Someday you might, sweetheart, but you have to be bigger, so you can wear a heavy belt and sink to the bottom." I could see her thinking about what I said, but she didn't ask further.

We climbed up the path until it began to be steep and we stopped and looked down. We had rounded a bend on the beach and couldn't see back to the river or the fire or even our cottages, just the fog over the water and the small waves frothing as they broke on the narrow rock beach below. There were bushes and clumps of grass growing all around us, and up the coast we could see where the highway curved around the top of the cliff and occasional cars were moving along the rim. The cliffs were several hundred feet high and the coast highway went along the top ridge.

Early that afternoon we ate BLTs at the restaurant and then walked over to the driftwood fire. The divers were forking sardines out of cans and making sandwiches, folding the sardines inside single pieces of bread and dipping the bread in the oil. There were several empty cans in a pile by the log where they were sitting. They offered us beer.

"When are you going to sneak up on them?" Puss asked Tan.

"This is as good a time as any," he said.

We went over to the old door with the abalones and Skid sharpened a knife with a curved blade on a small honing stone that he spit on and worked carefully against the surface of the knife. When he finished he slipped the stone into a leather pouch and put it in his pocket.

"Once you pick them up, they tighten, so you have to work fast," he said. "If you cut the main muscle when it's tight, you have to pound hell out of it, but if you wait until they're relaxed and cut the muscle quick before it contracts, you can slice it and fry it and cut it with a fork."

He did the first one so fast I didn't see what happened. If he hadn't explained what he had just done, I would have missed the next one. He set the first abalone shell on a driftwood log with the muscle lying next to the viscera and then reached to pick up the second one. I moved to get a front view. He held the knife in his right hand several inches from his left, poised over the shell. Then he picked up the abalone, palming it in his left hand as if he was picking up a cantaloupe, turned it over, inserted the knife in a scooping motion and severed the main scallop from the shell in less than two seconds. Once his left palm touched the shell, the whole operation was over in a flash. He was careful not to set the cut abalone back on the door and alert the others, and placed it on the log next to the first one. Skid even talked in a whisper. "They're finicky creatures," he said.

He did five more and offered them to us for dinner. "We got plenty here," he said, and we'll get a pile more tomorra mornin. You kids can throw the guts to the seagulls. No need for you to watch the rest of this less you want to."

We thanked them all and Nicholas and Semantha and Puss each carried an abalone, muscles and viscera together in the shells, back to the cottages, as if they were carrying a king's crown on a velvet pillow, Nicholas chanting, "Throw the guts, throw the guts." Later, the gut-throwing ceremony was not as popular with Ceil and Eartha, who begged off. Ceil took a walk back up the stream-bed, and Eartha took the car and drove somewhere to buy some Parliament cigarettes. She said the restaurant didn't have kingsize filters. Ceil told me later, after her walk, that she went back to the restaurant for a coke, and out of curiosity looked at the cigarette machine, and the kingsize filtered Parliaments were there.

Later, we piled the visceras in two shells and walked down to the beach. An overhead gull spotted the intestines in the shells and began screeching and circling, and soon there were a dozen, all making a racket.

It was Nicholas's high moment of the trip. At the water's edge, Larry gave him the go- ahead, and he reached into one of the shells and grabbed a handful, then shouted, "Throwing the guts!" and heaved it into the water. Several gulls dropped in a flash of wings and spray onto the intestines and darted and picked with their open beaks at the colored mass. The first one to get a beakful tried to ascend with the whole mass trailing out of its beak and it became a gull circus as two other gulls got dangling ends in their beaks and the whole mass dropped again. This time a great gray gull got it and with most of it in its mouth rose and floated away. Several gulls bobbed on the water at the scene of the crime, beady-eyed and alert, as if not sure what had happened, hoping it might happen again.

Nicholas made sure that it did, repeating his battle cry each time, until the shells were empty. We washed them in the water and continued down the beach, Nicholas on Larry's shoulders and the girls running ahead, trailing driftwood branches in the sand, pretending to leave a trail for the rescue of shipwrecked immigrants.

We left for home the following noon. The fog cleared during the night, and heavy dark clouds swept in off the water and it got warm and humid, unseasonably, Jake said, and it began to rain. It rained harder as we said goodbye to Jake and crossed through the Coastal Range, and then the sun of the Northern Valley shone down on us as we drove into Wilbur Springs on the way to Williams. There were blue skies all the way into Chico. That night Eartha told Larry that she wanted a trial separation.

Chapter Forty

IT OCCURRED TO ME later why Larry called Pat instead of me, but at the time I was sore about it, actually more worried about Larry than sore. He needed Pat's light-hearted and philosophic cynicism more than he needed my own defensive mood. And Pat had a room in the cellar of his rambling old house.

Larry didn't tell me about it for three days, and then all he said on the phone was that he had moved in with Pat and Joan Jay and did I and Puss want to go fishing with him and Semantha for a couple days in the Sierras. Dottie Bentley and her husband had a cabin on the Feather River and offered it to him any time he wanted it.

"For Christ's sake, Larry," I said.

"It's pretty short notice, I know," he said.

"For Christ's sake, Larry," I said, "What the hell."

"You don't want to go?"

"Sure I want to go, what the hell's going on? You're *living* with Pat and Joan Jay? For Christ's sake, Larry, do you need anything?"

We talked longer but it was mostly me sputtering. It was clear, as usual, that Larry was not going to say anything else. In the meantime, I ran into Pat on the campus after I cleaned out my office for the summer, and then stopped in to see Bugwell about teaching again in the fall. I liked the teaching and the money.

Bugwell was sympathetic and told me he thought it would be good for the college, but why didn't he hold off going to Mooney for a while and see how things played out in the department during the summer. He was really telling me that Mooney was still burned over my yellow bastards speech and he, Bugwell, would talk to the other journalism guys and see if he could get them to ask Mooney for me rather than go outside and hire someone else. I asked him if I should talk to Joe Fennel and Nat Burger, the other two journalism professors.

"Why don't you let me do it, it might be cleaner that way," Bugwell said.

I met Pat on the walkway leading down from the administration building. He said he just saw those two pirates, Camion and Jaeckel, at the Oaks.

"How's Camion?"

"Close-lipped, hunched over, and humorless."

"Par."

"He's getting restless with Lyndon and McNamara."

"What's with Larry, Pat?"

"Good question. He's sleeping in my cellar with no windows. Says he doesn't mind. When he showed up the other night he had one suitcase and all his guns."

"What the hell."

"How well do you know him?"

"I don't know, pretty well I think, we're friends."

"What's with the guns? Joan Jay's spooked about the guns. She told me last night that Larry might be a secret gun nut, and that Eartha's probably afraid of him."

"That's a crock," I said.

"Joan Jay's daily contribution. I don't care how long Larry sleeps in that cave, he's got his own entrance through the bulkhead, but if Joan Jay gets him in her sights she can make it hard for him."

"How come you attract all the cuckolded guys in town, Pat?" I was grinning at him.

"Joan Jay says I'm the Mother Hubbard of the Chico Democratic Club."

"I'm going with Larry to Dottie's cabin over the weekend. We're going to take the girls."

"She told me. It's hell and gone in the middle of nowhere," Pat said, "I was there once but I'm no fisherman. You guys might like it."

"Thanks Pat, for helping Larry out."

"I don't know how long it will last. Let me know how you like the cabin."

When Ceil and I talked that night she asked me if I thought she ought to do anything about Eartha.

"What do you have in mind?"

"Nothing. I don't know. Should I avoid her, call her, or what?"

"Make an appointment at Enloe Hospital for her for a couple zaps of shock treatment."

"Good, Bill. And for me too?"

"Hell, you got me, you don't need shock therapy."

"I saw Eartha downtown with Luke's wife last week. They were in the store for about five minutes and left. Bill saw them and called them the drinking duo. What did he mean by that?"

"That we live in a nice town with people who never gossip and who always give each other the benefit of the doubt."

"I know. Bill's the darndest gossip. It's what he does all day."

That weekend, Larry and I and the girls drove into the Sierras on highway 43, and headed for the town of Holdenville. We asked directions and followed a dirt road to a fork, turned left on another dirt road in a thick tamarack forest, took a left when the road split in a V, and turned at the second power pole onto a pine needle path just wide enough for Larry's truck to pass. We came to a large log cabin with a screened-in porch that overlooked a brook.

"Jesus, that's not the Feather River, is it?" I said.

"River's down through the trees," Larry said. "Pat told me to walk seventy-five yards straight down the incline from the wood pile."

"Mind if I take a quick look?" I asked.

"Go ahead. I'll unpack the stuff and see about the beds. Pat said there's a room with bunks, and I'll get the girls squared away. I hope the refrigerator works. I brought a bunch of food."

I walked down the incline through the trees, and after fifty yards or so heard the water. The trees were tall and further apart, and the ground was soggy in places. I stepped past two or three holes between tree roots and realized that I was in a semi-swamp. When I came to the river, I was at the edge of a meadow looking across moving water to tall green grass and scattered dead trees, and beyond the trees a rising hill with a patch of alders, and beyond that another higher hill covered with dark conifer trees. The river was thirty yards across, swiftly moving and clear. I could see the boulders on the bottom beneath the moving swirls, and there were dark places underneath the bank where I was standing. Downstream, the river narrowed and the banks were solid, the river deeper, and further down there were deep holes on the far side where the water seemed not to be moving and I could walk along the bank at the water's edge.

On the way back to the cabin I wasn't watching where I was stepping and almost fell into a hole a foot wide through which I could see water. The whole banking stretched back twenty-five yards from the stream, a roots and grass covering over the east side of the river that had obviously flooded the lowland earlier in the spring during the snow melt. Now the water moved slowly in the crevices and small caverns underneath the roots. The girls would have to be careful. I decided to bring them down and show them the terrain.

They were playing jackstones on the floor of the porch when I got back at the cabin and Larry was trying to get the refrigerator to work.

"Pat told me this thing is temperamental," he said. "I better go back into Holdenville and call the gas company."

I asked the girls if they wanted to see the river, and Larry left in the truck. We walked down through the trees.

When the girls heard the river they wanted to go faster, and I pointed out the meadow grooves and bog holes and they acted very sober and grown up, and together looked for more dangerous places. As we reached the bank, four ducks came flying upstream over the middle of the river. I sighted the lead duck with my eye and shot the first two with one shot, swung my imaginary gun on the third as he passed, led him and dropped him, and bagged the fourth as he kept a middle course upstream where the banks narrowed and the dark trees closed on either side of deep water.

"Are there big trouts in here?" Semantha asked.

"Trout, Samanth," Puss said. "It's for one or a bunch."

"Are there big trout Mr. Armature?"

"I sure hope so," I said.

"Me too," Semantha said. "My dad catches steelheads and we eat them."

"Steelhead, Semanth," Puss said.

"Steelhead, I mean," Semantha said.

""Mr. Henry says there are rainbows and browns in here," I said.

"Daddy!" Puss said. "Rainbow and brown. You told me and now you don't do it, and I've been correcting Semanth. I feel silly."

"No, you're right. Rainbows would mean there's a lot of rainbows in here, the colored ones when the sun comes out after the rain."

"I bet when the water's just right you could see that kind too," Semantha said.

"I'll bet so," I said. "Let's go downstream a ways and I'll show you the deep pools in the river where there might be some rainbow."

"Very *good*, dad," Puss said.

We walked downstream about fifty yards and I showed them the pools. While we were there, a swirl occurred on the surface of the biggest pool, sending ripples.

"Look, they're feeding," I said. "There's been a hatch of white moths, and they're taking them."

There was another swirl in the middle of the dark pool.

"Boy, they like the white moths," Puss said. "Is it good now for fishing?"

"Really good, if we had a fly rod and some good flies. You have to find exactly the right fly to fool the fish into thinking the fly is a live moth."

"That's why you have so many flies in your fishing box, right daddy?" Puss said, showing off.

"My dad's got zillions of flies. He makes them all the time," Semantha said.

We watched for several minutes the trout feeding on the new hatch, then we carefully walked over the soggy, dangerous bank and into the darkness of the trees, up the hill to the cabin.

Larry drove his truck into the small clearing a half-hour later. The girls and I were playing Crazy Eights on the porch.

"I made the call," he said. "Somebody'll be out this evening if we're lucky. If not, tomorrow mid-morning. I got some Off for the mosquitoes."

"Dad, we saw a moth hatch and the big trouts jumped for them," Semantha said.

"Trout," Puss said quietly.

"You made your point, Puss, that's enough," I said.

"I know," Semantha said, "*trout, trout, trout.*"

"Three of them?" Larry said, smiling.

"More than three," Semantha said, "They were jumping all over the place."

"Sounds good to me," Larry said.

Larry fixed hot dogs and Boston Baked Beans for supper and we had yellow pudding and Virginia Dare cupcakes for dessert. Then we all played Monopoly, lying around the board on the living room floor.

After we tucked in the girls for the night, Larry and I sat in the living room and talked about nothing for an hour, going through a six-pack. Larry sat back in his pine rocking chair and popped the cap on another beer and looked at me. "I can't talk about it, Bill," he said. "If I do I might break."

"Talk about what?"

He nodded and we made a plan for the morning before the gas people arrived.

Chapter Forty-One

WE CROSSED THE BOGGY meadow at 6:15 the following morning and the air was clear and smelling of larch even though we had left the forest behind us at the bottom of the path down through the high trees. The morning was filled with the sounds of the moving river, and as we stood on the bank, the river was bright and quicksilvery in the shallow places where the water furled and eddied without rapids because the mid-stream rocks were small. Downstream, the pools were dark and the girls were giddy with the idea of catching rainbows. We had agreed that nouns describing trout could end with or without the s, and that we would not correct each other while fishing, but could discuss it later. The sun would not clear the crest of the mountains for two more hours, and the river landscape was bright and cool without direct sunlight as we walked downstream along the east bank. Larry decided to fish upstream and said he would return to the cabin by nine to meet the refrigerator people.

I said to the girls, "I want to take one cast across this open water before we leave it," cocking my spinning rod overhead and slinging the miniature daredevil spoon almost to the other bank where it dropped into the moving water without disturbing the rippling surface. As it hit the water I was already retrieving it, jerking the tip of the rod slightly as I reeled. I didn't see the trout hit, but I felt the weight as he hooked himself and raced sideways into the upstream current toward the center of the river.

As the trout made his first run in a wide arc across the middle of the river toward the east bank above me, I gained several feet of line, then thought I lost him as I tried to turn her from the dark underbank, extending my rod out over the water. He fought all the way in, but he came steadily and I asked Puss to unhook the hand-net from my belt.

"Lower the net into the water," I said, "and push it right at him when he's almost to it," and he did, and the foot-long brown trout was inside the net. One barb was implanted so securely that I had to turn it with my small fishing pliers to extract it.

"Just like the dentist," Semantha giggled.

"How about if I toss out the spoon a couple more times and you two fishermen take turns reeling it in?"

"Then we'll know, won't we, if this one is a fluke. That's the word, isn't it daddy?

"That's the word, honeybunch."

"You go first, Pussy," Semantha said. "I don't know if I can do it."

"I'll go first but you *can* do it," Puss said.

"We better hook them first," I said, and lofted the little red and white spoon almost across the river. I gave Puss the rod and told her to reel quickly so the daredevil wouldn't snag on the bottom. The exchange went nicely and Puss reeled steadily with her left hand.

When the trout struck, it almost ripped the rod out of Puss's hands. "Reel it if you can, babe, and try to make her fight the tip."

"What does the tip mean, daddy? I'm only ten." She started to cry.

The rod was bent and nodding deeply as the trout fought.

"Semantha said, "You can do it, Pussy."

"Fighting the tip just means hold the rod up toward the sky," I said.

When the line was parallel with our upstream bank the pole stopped nodding and Puss couldn't reel. The trout was under the bank and the line was tangled.

"Did I lose her, daddy?"

"No, you didn't lose her but she's pretty smart and she's tangled the line in something. We might get lucky."

At the spot where the trout went under the bank I knelt down and leaned over the water, holding the line in my hand and trying to see the tangle. The bottom was pebbly and clear and I could see the trout hovering above a little sandy rise. The small red and white daredevil dangled from the corner of her jaw. She was at least fifteen inches long, a beautiful fish. The line was curled around a half-torn root beneath me, and then tangled around another root two feet in front of the trout. As long as I did nothing, the trout was secure. If she felt pressure on the line, she'd probably explode away from me and break it.

"Don't fall into the water, daddy, it's only an old fish," Puss said.

"A pretty nice one though," I said, "I can see her."

"Is she big?" Semantha asked.

"She's big," I said.

"A whopper?" she asked.

""A semi-whopper," I said.

"Maybe this is the time for clear thinking," Puss said. "You always tell me when it's decision time it's clear thinking time."

"OK gang," I said, "I'll tell you what we'll do. You're right. It's decision time. I'll hang over the water and you guys sit on my ankles to weight me down, and I'll try to reach in and unwrap the first tangle. If I get that one, there's only one more. But I'll talk to you and explain the problem."

The girls were staring at me. If I said "Boo," they would have fallen into the water. I was enjoying myself again. Ceil would be proud of me. Hell, I was proud of me.

My plan almost worked. I lay down and the girls sat on my ankles. I grasped the spinning rod above the reel and reached it toward the tangle around the other root. I could see the trout barely swaying sideways in the current, and then everything was white water and swirls and I felt the line still tight against the finger stump and then it was loose. I swung the pole free and the trout was gone.

"Darn, darn, darn," Puss said.

"Double double darn," Semantha said.

"Well, we gave it the old college try," I said.

"What'll happen to the red and white thing?" Semantha asked.

"It'll take a long time, but the hook will rust and fall out of the trout's mouth."

"She'll have to go to the trout dentist," Puss said.

"That she will," I said.

"Well, there's always a rainbow," Puss said.

"Remind me to always take you fishing with me to cheer me up," I said, and I took her hand and shook it.

I led the way downstream to the deep pools, and we fished with flies and worms with the two poles Jerry and I brought for the girls, for a longer time than we needed to discover that whatever was rising late yesterday afternoon was showing no interest today.

"I should have eaten the banana from breakfast, daddy, I can feel what you call 'the old pangs,'" Puss said.

"How about you, Semantha, do you feel the old pangs?"

"I'm a little hungry."

I produced three Milky Ways from my fishing jacket pocket and we sat by the river and chewed and listened to the grasshoppers coming awake as the sun dried the grass on the other side of the river beyond the pools.

On the way back to the cabin, we crossed the bog upstream and the sun was hot in the open terrain. We pointed out the bog holes to one another as we saw them. Then the air filled with dots and we were walking through a red cloud.

"They're ladybugs, daddy," Puss cried, "zillions of them."

The ladybugs were landing on our arms and our clothes.

"Don't squish them," Puss cried, "It's bad luck."

"They're pretty all right, but they're everywhere," I said, watching them land on my arms.

"Hold out your hands," Semantha said, "They land right on them."

"I squished one," she said. "I didn't mean it. It was between my fingers. My hand stinks."

We reached the further side of the bog and got through the hatch, now stepping on round brown conifer cones and needles of the larch trees, then tromping up the forest path in a single line.

"This is Billy Hawk Feather," Larry said as we approached the cabin. He and two men were standing by the gas company truck. They were looking at the trout hanging from my waist, tied to my belt through its gills. Billy said, "This is my dad. He's caught a few of those, but that's a real good brown."

"Hello," his dad said, "Call me Sam. It's always a privilege to land a good fish in a good place."

The girls scampered onto the porch and disappeared.

"The refrigerator's percolating," Larry said. "I'm trying to entice Billy and Sam to come back and try the river after Billy gets off work."

"Sure and hell do," I said. "I'll show you some stepping holes to avoid and the river's all yours."

"It sure is a pretty place," Sam said.

"He means he'd like to test the waters," Billy Hawk Feather said. "We'll drive out after supper if it's OK."

They drove off and Larry looked at me and then at the trout.

"There must be more where that came from," he said.

Chapter Forty-Two

BILLY HAWK FEATHER AND Sam Beaver and Bird Wing, Billy's wife, came back in Billy's pickup truck as we were finishing our fried chicken thighs and spaghetti, and Larry and I walked the men down to the water. Billy carried a

Wilson flyrod case, but Sam wanted only to look at the river. Bird Wing stayed with the girls, who told me later that they walked up the little brook and found water cress, then picked the mountain bluebells and Indian paintbrush that we later found in the water glass on the table when we returned from the river at dusk.

Billy and Sam wanted to walk upstream, and where the trees grew almost to the deepwater bank Billy unpacked his fly rod from his carrying case and dangled a green and white fly over a dark eddy. When the fly touched the water, the surface exploded and Billy's fly rod bent in half for two seconds and then straightened as the rod dangled a broken leader over the water. Billy looked at Sam and an understanding passed between them as Sam nodded. Billy smiled at Larry and me and shook his head.

"Can't catch 'em all," Larry said.

"It was my fault," Billy said, "I wasn't ready." He separated his fly rod into lengths and returned the sections to his case.

We walked upstream through the dark trees and entered a grass meadow with a small stand of aspen on the other side. Following the east bank, we came to a lowland area where the main channel flowed through a burned-over swath with new alders rising, and the water moved darkly and quietly.

"I've never seen this section of the river before," Sam said. "One could spend some good hours in here."

"We're only going to be here tomorrow," Larry said, but you're sure welcome to come back as far as we're concerned."

"You have a nice access, that's for sure," Sam said. "Maybe we'll find a time some day."

"My father's very sensitive about other people's property," Billy said.

When we arrived back at the cabin, Bird Wing and the girls were playing jackstones on the porch. When the Indians left, Larry and I played Parcheesi with the girls, and then Larry and I popped open a couple cans of Hamms' beer.

"What do you know about Klamath Indians?" Larry asked.

"Not a damn thing. Oregon is all I know. I think they're an Oregon tribe."

"Nice people."

"Did you see the old man's hands?"

"No."

"Huge wide fingers."

"I'll bet he was a strong guy."

"I'll bet he still is. I wonder why he didn't bring a fishing pole."

"He's in no hurry, that's why. Pleasure and hurry don't mix for him. He goes easy but he's not slow. He takes his time and he's got that quiet dignity that old Indians have."

"Thanks for taking Semantha, Bill. She told me about the grasshopper and the ladybug hatch."

"Christ, it was sprinkling ladybugs. I had to spit one out of my mouth. I spit six times so I wouldn't taste it."

"At least you could spit it out."

There was a silence.

I got up and went to the refrigerator and got another Hamms. "You too?"

"Yeah."

I popped mine and Larry drained his first and popped a new one.

"I'm thinking of going back east," Larry said.

"Alone?"

"Maybe. I don't know. I talked to Old Hutch the other day. I've got to get Eartha and the kids out of Chico. I shouldn't have gotten involved in politics."

"Maybe," I said.

"What the hell's the point?"

"That's the eloquent way to say it, I guess."

Larry almost smiled. "Yeah, that's me. Anyway, I told Camion."

"What's back east?"

"New England. Eartha grew up there. She's been homesick since we got here."

"So she'll go with you?"

"She says she can't. Maybe she'll change her mind."

I sipped my beer.

Larry said, "You're happy with California, I take it?"

"What's 'happy'? We're here. We get along. Something might come of it. I'm waiting for the big surprise. I can wait here as well as anywhere."

"You think some big thing will happen?"

"I don't know what I think. Ever since I was a kid, I thought I was different. Everyone probably feels that way. It's just a feeling, like some day I'll have the power. I don't even know what I mean, but it's like when I'm flying in a dream. I have this power in my chest and I hold out my arms and take off. I even go into outer space. Christ, I've dropped down through long shafts and come out into another world millions of years ago and I fly over these old civilizations"

"I don't even dream."

"Then I wake up, and I'm lying next to Ceil, and Puss is in the other room, and outside the screens there's no sound but the snails are all the time climbing in the rice paper trees, sucking the juice out of the leaves where you can't see them. In the morning the phlegm-trails gleam on the grass, and if you pull back the inner folds of the big leaves, they're hiding in the rotten folds."

"It's the trail to the governor's office."

"Sometimes when I'm flying, Puss is in my arms and we're going at a supersonic speed past great buildings, curving over the world. Sometimes I'm in the cramped nose of a jetliner taking off between tall narrow buildings, afraid of crashing any minute. Then I wake up and it's like slipping into a giant cartoon that I'm drawing myself. I look up at the square corners and they get bigger. I push against the side and it moves. Then there's all this space and I walk into fields of gladiolus as far as I can see. Then I wake up again and there's another woman in bed with me, and I wake her and she's old, and I can't move in the bed, and someone's coming through the door, and I'm frozen. I can't move my arms and it's coming. When I wake up I'm really awake, and I can hear a dog barking somewhere, and I'm far away in California, and it's dark in the bedroom and dark outside."

"Your night life is a hell of a lot more interesting than my day life."

"Mine too. That's why it's nice to know the fish are there in the river and when I catch them they're still real fish."

"I guess so."

There was a long silence.

Larry said, "I don't know why I like to fish and hunt. I just like it. It ought to work so you can do everything, but it gets all fucked up."

The next day, Sam and Billy and Bird Wing came back in the late afternoon. Sam went with Billy who caught a two pound rainbow upstream across from the stand of aspens. Bird Wing brought a leather Indian dress decorated with beads and shells to show the girls. They went on a wildflower walk and Bird Wing told them about the daughter she lost in a river in Oregon a long time ago.

Chapter Forty-Three

CEIL AND PUSS FLEW back East for a month in mid-summer to visit her mother and an aunt who was dying of lung cancer, and I played doubles tennis with Dwane Ranke, Pat's colleague in the political science department, Phil Boggs from the journalism department, and Roxanne, Luke Gardner's wife. She had a good left-handed serve, but I felt more relaxed throwing the football around and chasing fungos with Luke and Ken Morrow in the Hooker Oak School playground. The heat was killing, but the boredom was worse. I drove once to Sacramento to have lunch with Jack Reed from the *Bee*, and once to San Francisco to see a Giants-Dodgers game with Slim Row the student magazine editor. Slim told me that Karo over-dosed but was getting better, though he didn't say what getting better meant. We drove down and back the same day because Slim's wife didn't come home the night before. I didn't want to know why and he didn't tell me. In the game, McCovey hit a home run with one on in the last of the 8th and the Giants won 2-1. The park was full and it took me two hours to get out of the parking lot. I bragged too much about Fenway Park in Boston and the '46 Red Sox while we sat and waited for the parking lot to clear.

Two days later Camion took me to dinner. He insisted on driving all the way to Walnut Creek to a restaurant he knew there. On the way he said I ought to declare against Rufe Granger for the Butte County senate seat. There would be a state re-districting convention in Sacramento in September and Camion said I could show myself around and maybe make a speech on the floor and get myself in a position to run. If they redistricted by population instead of geography, I didn't have a prayer against incumbent democrats from Lassen and Trinity counties, but then I could always run against Assemblyman Jake Toothacher. The Assembly would stay the same because the Democrats were in power and they already had the seat. Toothacher was a dimwit and even his staff knew it, and the party power boys would get over their problems with me as soon as I beat him in a primary. Camion made it sound easy and I was naive enough to almost believe him.

Larry and I went up in the mountains twice and caught golden trout at 8000 feet. Larry had moved into a little house a hundred yards off a narrow road that ran along the outside of Bidwell Park. Joan Jay had told Pat that she heard a woman's voice in the cellar and she would feel better if Larry found another place. Pat told me he scoffed but lost the fight and had to tell Larry to look around for another place. It was the only time I saw Pat all summer. He told me I could ride with him to the re-districting convention in September, but I had already promised Camion.

When Ceil and Puss came home, they were tanned and happy and I forgot politics for a while. Joe Bugwell had called two days before Ceil and Puss flew into the Chico airport and Bugwell told me that Willard Mooney authorized a one semester visiting appointment for the fall. I told him I'd take it, but the money wasn't much considering I had done the college a big favor the previous semester.

"I'm well aware of that," Bugwell said. "I did the best I could. You have to be aware that Willard thinks he's being a hell of a fella just re-appointing you after your speech."

"Tell him thanks a lot."

"I'll make a point not to tell him," Bugwell said, and added that I should give it a little more time. "When he gets to know you better, it'll be a lot easier. I leaned on your student evaluations, which were pretty high-powered by the way, and that helped."

For Labor Day weekend, Ceil and Puss and I flew to San Diego to show Puss the zoo, and we swung back into the life of Chico by attending two Friday night high school football games between Chico and Oroville and then Red Bluff. We got to sit on the fifty-yard line because Skip Garrison, our next-door neighbor, was the head coach.

In the middle of the Red Bluff game, I asked Ceil what she would think if I ran for state senator or assemblyman. She asked me if it might change our lives much. I said I didn't know, but didn't see why it should. I said I was only considering it. She made a joke about being a political widow.

"Just as long as you don't become a black widow," I said.

"How about a merry widow?"

"I thought you already were."

She said one on the street was enough and we left it at that.

When I saw Pat I asked him how strong the democratic senators from Lassen and Trinity counties were. "Too strong," he said. "If Camion told you that, he's right. The trouble is, they're going to eat each other up. Neither one will back down, but Lassen's got more voters and Gerry Lakewell will win it. They're both good guys."

Chapter Forty-Four

THE PROBLEM WITH RUNNING for political office was that I didn't know what I wanted out of it. Butte County was too conservative even for me, a Yankee outsider. Down deep, I knew I was bored and merely wanted something to show for my days, but I didn't want to rock Puss's boat.

Late summer was the hardest. Chico was a furnace, and while Ceil and Puss went to One Mile in the park, I drove out to the river and fished, knowing the salmon runs wouldn't start until the fall. I got bored with fishing and took to walking the dry bed of Chico Creek ten minutes from the house. It cut across Manzanita after a twenty-minute walk, and I imagined the black and white California quail with the little black crests jaunting up from their foreheads, bursting from the dried vines draped at the turns in the creek.

None of it helped. I was looking to be distracted, and I had no agenda. I thought about black and white birds falling from the sky, pheasants dropping in clumps in rice fields, deer with blazing eyes in the V sights of my father's .32 Special carbine, even of the redhead giving me directions to the real estate office, her brown freckles and white shorts, that first drive into Chico, beginning something unknown. I thought about dying, being nothing forever. I forced myself to think about Ceil and Puss at the park, lying on towels on the ground next to the swimming pool across from the swings where I pushed Puss the first week they were in town, when I was afraid to be alone with Ceil. The swings were on the edge of the thick park woods where the vines hung down from the oak trees and the summer air was dry, and the black widow spiders never moved until the sun went down.

Ceil was trying very hard in the marriage. We were like kids together. Every day at five-thirty in the afternoon she would send me over to Klingman's on Manzanita to get a half bottle of red wine for dinner. "For eighteen cents, how can we miss out?" she said. We talked a lot about our first year of marriage. It was like playing word games with close friends on swimming parties, treading water.

My mind kept going back to the creek beds, weeds burgeoning between the bedrock, drying in the semi-tropical heat, the parched boulders hot enough to fry eggs, the crevices filling with dust and blown soil and the mud from last year's floods caked as hard as rock. Northern California was seductive and dangerous—its semi-tropical poisons, its easy life of plenty—summer wildflowers, yellow and prickly, the agents of a force so indomitable and natural and insensate that discussions of their beauty became models of triviality and sentimentality.

I did my morning pushups, skimmed the *Chronicle* except for Herb Caen who treated the city as a neighborhood, with his conversational self-applause disguised as public chatter. He began every column as if he were on the telephone, flushing all birds with the same song. Then I walked the creek bed for an hour. I did this until the end of the summer.

Ceil was very beautiful that summer. She had let her hair grow and it was now shoulder length, the short neck curls of fuzz growing into waves of coal black sheen. When she wound the black strands into pigtails she looked like a Sioux Indian. Puss begged to imitate her and began to look like her adolescent twin. When I nuzzled Puss's hair at bedtime and whispered "Princess Valiant," she protested, "Prince, daddy, prince."

Later that night I nuzzled Ceil's shoulder tresses, seeing the quarter moon outside the bedroom window, and asked if she could imagine being dead.

"Oh Bill," she said, "you're a crazy guy. I can't imagine anything about things that don't have to do with us. Death is only an idea, it isn't real. Besides, I expect to die first and that's how I want it. If you died I wouldn't know what to do."

Chapter Forty-Five

THE NEXT DAY CEIL was doing the dishes, and the windows were open. I could hear Puss's leather shoes shuffling and tapping on the cement patio under the trellis of grapevines. Light blue grapes hung down in clumps. Puss was showing Semantha how to do a soft shoe routine she had watched on TV, Brando and Sinatra in *Guys and Dolls*.

I thought, it's not an idea when you're dead, but I didn't say it. Ceil's cotton jumpsuit was unbuttoned in the back and she had wound her hair into a single black pigtail that made the open V of her back seem browner than ever. Little flecks of perspiration glistened on her back.

"How come you expect to die first?" I said.

Ceil quietly rested her hands in the dishwater, not answering me, looking straight out the window at the yellow rose tree with the giant blooms, then half-turned and flecked soapy water at me.

"Because I don't do pushups, big boy," she said.

I moved her pigtail aside and kissed her neck. She shivered and raised her butt into me.

"You planning on getting a quick babysitter?" she said.

The screen door slammed.

"Semanth says I should change my name to Pyrocantha, mama, so's we can be name twins. Am I interrupting?"

Semantha stood behind Puss in the doorway to the kitchen with her hand over her mouth, giggling.

I backed away from Ceil and raised my arms in a machine gunner's stance.

"Rat a tat tat!" I said. "Hell no, Valiant One with squire. We're just having a water fight. What could you be interrupting?"

Ceil flicked more soapy water at me to prove my point, and the water stung my eyes.

"See?" I said. "You've made me cry."

"You're faking daddy," Puss said. "What's pyrocantha? I don't want a name that means something bad."

"What do you mean 'faking'? Am I a fake, your true-blue father? That is legitimate dirty soapy water and these are legitimate tears. And as for you, young neighbor fair, it's 'Oh oh' time. I'm just going to have to bring this up with your father."

"Yes, you're a fake," Ceil said, scooping a handful of dishwater at me. "Don't mind him, Semantha, he's full of beans. Pyrocantha is a lovely red berry and it's a perfectly nice word."

Semantha was still giggling with her hand over her mouth as Puss led her out to the patio, letting the screen door slam behind them.

"How about taking your hands out of that water so I can defend myself?" I said.

"You mean so I can't defend myself," Ceil said.

"Yeah, that's sort of what I mean," I said, holding Ceil by the elbows, yanking her pigtail gently between my teeth.

Ceil bent her head back, nuzzling my cheek, as Puss called from the patio, "Semanth and I are going to her house, is that OK mama?"

"If it's OK with Semantha's mom," Ceil called, and I followed Ceil into the bedroom. She was wiping her hands on a dishtowel that she brought with her.

Later I lay dozing and heard Ceil pronouncing the names of towns south of Chico: Gridley, Biggs, Glenn, Live Oak, small towns to pass through on 99 going to San Francisco or Sacramento or coming home.

"All nowheresvilles," I said, looking at the late summer sky through the spaces formed by the rice paper leaves brushing the half-turned open windows.

"People live and die in those towns," Ceil said. She was looking at the ceiling.

"They're Oakie towns," I said, "the growing fields of northern California. The topsoil is eighteen feet deep. Livingsvilles and Dyingsvilles, all the same."

"When we were driving home from San Francisco last week, I felt so alone going through those towns, slowing down and speeding up again, the blown-out tires on the sides of the roads, the butternut squash fields half-picked, the rice storage bins in Dingville. How can that be a real place?"

"Ah, but it is."

"Oh Bill, I thought where would I be if you and Puss weren't here in Chico? All of a sudden I got scared. It was all so beautiful and lonely. Not because of the flattened rabbits on the highway lined with yellow sycamores, or the tractor dust blowing over the tilled fields, but something I can't explain. We're in such a new place out here, not for the people who have always lived here, but for newcomers, and Puss doesn't know anything about it, and I don't know anything about it, but I want to hold on to it for as long as I can. Do we have to let go of it someday, Bill?"

"Hey, come on Ceil." I was wide awake. "Was I that lousy?"

"You were lovely, Bill. It's something else. I don't know what it is. But as we were driving home last week, I didn't know where we were driving to. It was like my dream where I know where my destination is but I can never get there because it's always different. Every time I come home to Chico, I know where it is on the map, and I've memorized the way, but the shadows are all hid in the daylight—all those marvelous rows of poplars and palm trees and orchards of kiwis and avocados and oranges and then those ugly Sutter Buttes. I don't know what I mean."

"They look like bombed pyramids, and they remind you that you're entering a strange country."

"They really do. Then those lava outcrops around Yuba City, and just south of Chico all that black lava in the soft hills, and the brown stonewalls with no trees at all. And all of a sudden I was driving too fast because we're all here and we have this home with giant roses and bamboo and a gardenia bush and a scrawny olive tree and mistletoe dangling from our own ash tree in the summertime. I don't know. I should be ecstatically happy."

"You're not?"

"I'm content, Bill, I really am, but deep down inside I'm waiting to get the bad news. I don't mean about you or from you, just something that's coming that will change everything. I want Puss to be safe, but there are always the spidery live oaks in the foothills surrounding us, and I don't know what's come over me. I'm sorry to spoil our time together, you were so nice today. I'm so sorry."

"It's OK. Ceil. I'll try to do better. I should spend more time with you."

"You don't have to. It's not your fault. It's not you, Bill. It's not even Chico. I don't know what it is.

We dressed and walked up the sidewalk to Eartha's house. The girls were alone in the kitchen, making cookies. Eartha had left a note for Semantha saying that she had gone for a walk and her brother was with Terry Garrison and that she would be home later. We told Puss to come home as soon as Eartha returned, and we walked up Sunset to Damon Road until it crossed Iris where there are three weeping willow trees and a long field, and we looked across to the foothills of the Sierras. Then we walked home.

Chapter Forty-Six

THAT EVENING WE DROVE out the Ord Ferry Road to the Dayton Four Corners for fried oysters at "Mother's."

Puss hadn't come home by 5:30 so Ceil called Eartha to check on the girls. Eartha wasn't home yet so Ceil told Puss to bring Semantha home, but be sure to leave a note for Eartha telling her that we were taking Semantha with us.

"I hope you didn't eat all those cookies," Ceil said, when the girls arrived.

"Well, we ate some," Puss said, "and then we talked about it."

"You discussed the quality before you ventured further?" I asked.

"No, Mr. Bill," Semantha said, "Pyrocanth thought we should save the rest for my mother."

"I see," I said.

"But we burned a couple," Puss said.

"Yes, we burned four quite seriously," Semantha said.

"And?" I said.

"Well," Puss said, "we had eaten six," and we only had six left."

"So you couldn't decide whether to eat the good ones and leave the burned ones for Mrs. Bourke, is that it?"

"No, Mr. Bill, you see, the burned ones were causing a problem. If we ate two of the burned ones, half of the leftover ones would still be burned and it would look like we couldn't make cookies without burning half of them, because it wouldn't be reasonable for us to cook a dozen cookies and only burn two of them. Besides, we weren't very hungry."

I looked at Ceil, who was laughing.

"Mama," Puss said, "Don't make fun of Semanth, it's perfectly reasonable. Isn't it, daddy?"

"Sure," I said. "Why eat two burned cookies if you're not hungry. I can see that."

"No daddy," Puss said, "it was four burned ones. We didn't want to eat four but you shouldn't throw food away, don't you see?"

"Well, all I know is, you did the right thing, finally, I'm sure of it." I said.

"We crumpled them up, Mr. Bill, and dropped them over the fence for Mrs. Grotkill's dog," Semantha said. He doesn't get to come outside much, only in the morning for a little while, and sometimes in the afternoon."

"I'm sure he loved them," Ceil said.

"Dogs usually love burned cookies better than unburned ones," I said.

"Yes," Puss said, "and the food wasn't wasted and we were too full to eat the two good ones so Mrs. Bourke won't think we're lousy cookie cooks."

"OK, well that's that for the burned cookie saga," I said.

"Let's just hope they don't burn the fried oysters at Mother's tonight."

"What's 'saga?' Mr. Bill."

"Story," Puss said, "he uses words like that all the time."

"My father uses words I don't understand sometimes," Semantha said. "What's a 'grost creepo' Mr. Bill?"

"I'm solid on 'creepo,' but wavery on 'grost,'" I said.

Ceil looked at me and said "gross."

"Oh yeah, 'gross,'" I said, "Well I guess that means someone who exaggerates things that should be subtle and who slurps his soup when he eats."

"What's 'subtle?'" Semantha said.

Ceil was staring at me. She said, "'subtle' means hinting rather than making a big deal about something, but we don't know anyone like that, thank goodness, and I'm hungry so let's all get in the car and drive off into the cool summer countryside for a wonderful meal. I'm going to be the first one in the car." Ceil went out the door.

"Why did she say 'cool' when it's hot as blazes outside," Semantha asked Puss as they filed in front of me and followed Ceil into the driveway and the car.

"She was making fun. She meant it's hot as hell," Puss said.

I tapped her on the shoulder and gave her my do-you-want-me-to-get-in-trouble-because-of-your-language look. Puss elbowed Semantha and they giggled in the car as we drove down Violet Lane.

I picked up 5th Street on the Esplanade across from the town park, and followed it to Ord Ferry Road, passing several almond orchards with magpies in their branches. The white painted lower trunks of a young orchard resembled old army puttees and shin wrappings.

We came to yellow rice fields with low circling hawks, and then flatlands as far as we could see. The road was straight into the distance and telephone poles went by one after another. Cornflowers were dots of blue on the sides of the road, and there were orange-yellow clumps of California poppies.

At the Dayton Four Corners, cars were parked all over the open lot next to the restaurant, and oleander grew as high as the windows.

"Why do they call it 'Mother's'?" Puss and Boots asked.

"It was either that or 'Father's,'" I said, "and the old man was probably a lousy cook."

"Where do they catch the oysters?" Semantha asked.

"Did you see those little canals along the edge of the rice fields?" I said.

"Semantha honey, don't mind him," Ceil said, "Something got him going and he's just going to talk through his hat all evening if we let him. Let's pretend we don't know him. The oysters come from somewhere in the ocean, but I don't know where."

"It was the burnt cookies," I said, "I was just thinking of Mrs Grotkill's lucky dog."

"You're the lucky dog, lover boy," Ceil said. "You don't need any more oysters. Why don't you try the sweetbreads?"

Halfway through dinner I said to Ceil, "Camion wants me to go to the reapportionment convention in September and declare my candidacy."

Ceil looked at me for a long time, and then nodded her head.

"Do you think I shouldn't?" I said.

After a while Ceil said, "No, I don't think you shouldn't. I think you should do whatever comes up next. If that's what's coming up, check out your colors and paint it."

"What's a 'candidacy?'" Puss asked.

"I didn't think you were listening," I said.

"I didn't mean to," Puss said, "You don't have to tell me, daddy."

Ceil was looking at me, waiting for me to speak.

"'Candidacy' is like when you're skiing well on the easy slopes and having a nice afternoon, and you get in the line for the steepest mountain."

Chapter Forty-Seven

THE SEMESTER STARTED AND I met my first class and fall was underway. I was liking this time in my life. I liked thinking of running for political office some time in the future. I liked Puss's soccer games on Saturday morning and watching Ceil run up and down the sidelines cheering when Puss had the ball. I liked the times with Larry at the river in the evening even though Larry was going through the motions. I liked riding my bike through the early morning streets of Chico, stopping off at the Oaks for coffee with Camion or Jaeckel or both, racking my bike in back of the Humanities building, and walking across campus to the journalism building or the library.

One morning in the library I got in a discussion with Dottie Bentley's colleague in the research room. I was looking up something about the Civil War battle of Drewry's Bluff in Virginia where a couple of my ancestors from Maine had been killed, for an assignment I had given my advanced journalism class. I wanted them to compare the newspaper accounts of the battle with current newspaper coverage of the Vietnam War. Jackie Blanchette was the other research librarian and she had been divorced the year before and several times had hinted that she wanted to tell me how much fun she was having as a liberated woman. She was not unattractive and had a pleasant glint in her eye, and was always offering me Certs, so often that when I went home later I would ask Ceil if my breath smelled.

On this particular day I lingered longer than usual on my way to the stacks because we got talking about the nice rides one could take above the foothills in the mountains just north of Chico on route 32 above Richardson Springs. I told her about the ladybug hatch at the river and how sensuous it was with millions of red dots all over your body, and she must have thought I meant sensual because within a few more sentences she was telling me how great it was to make love on a pine needle forest, high enough in the mountains that there were no mosquitoes. I didn't know what to say about the image that came to my mind, and as I hesitated to reply I could see her chewing what remained of her current Certs as she peeled back the sides of her green cylindrical package and picked out another one to pop in her mouth. It was all quite academic and I thought of something to say that seemed appropriately sympathetic and brotherly, and slid between the stacks.

As I switched the stack lights on and off, looking for the right call numbers, I felt distantly removed from both wars that I was asking my class to write about. I knew I was postponing even thinking about my still vague plans to enter politics. Changes were in the air, an air soon to become filled with the songs of sad folk singers and airwaves electric with numbers about sorties and tonnage and body counts. I was still disinterested about the war. I wanted to close my eyes when Lyndon flashed the vertical incision-scar of Vietnam on his belly, and I drew and discarded another cartoon, this one of smiling Lyndon astride the globe in cowboy boots, one arm extended over Asia, dripping from his fingers a million combat paratroopers, the other hand behind his back turning on a television set showing a little girl in a field of daisies with an atomic bomb mushroom cloud rising behind her.

Rhetoric against the war was increasing. At the CDC Convention in Sacramento, the delegates voted to petition the president to stop the air raids on North Vietnam and sue for peace. Don Way wrote in the *Valley Advocate* that the grassroots CDC was "as representative of grassroots thinking as the House of Lords." His full page editorial the day after the convention called Willie Brown and John Burton "left wing misfits," and delegates from the real grassroots of California were "out-talked, out-weighed, and out-voted by the noise beatnik faction of the party's ultra-liberal left wing."

Way devoted over half of his column, however, to the reapportionment issue, and I was shocked to see that it featured me. Five consecutive paragraphs began with "Armature... ," and Ceil said "My Lord, Bill" twice as she read it, me standing behind her, reading it for the umpteenth time, as my mother used to say, over her shoulder. Way wrote that I led a gallant floor fight against the big city liberals, and that I had joined forces with state senators Ron Galloway of Los Angeles and Trent Lunardi of Roseville. I was linked with Pat Brown in arguing for a constitutional amendment to reapportion the two houses of the bicameral legislature in a way that protected individual rights and rural areas. I well remembered making the two speeches on the floor, and I knew I asked for it by talking to Don Way in his office when I came back from Sacramento, but I was truly shocked by the feature-quality of such local coverage. It didn't matter that the paper was conservative because liberals and moderates and conservatives in northern California were all against state reapportionment. The big issue was going to be water rights, and how southern California would get water from the north in the years to come.

But the issues didn't matter to Ceil. She thought she saw in the editorial the handwriting of the future of our lives, handwriting with a lot of question marks in it.

"Wow," she said, as she picked up the paper after supper and read the editorial again. "That's all I can say, Bill. Wow. It looks like, reading this, that it was all you and Pat Brown and all those senators like Ron Galloway, with a little bit of Willie Brown and John Burton thrown in."

"People talked for two days. I made two speeches. If I run for anything I ought to get Don Way to be my campaign manager. The whole thing is very mysterious."

"What does your friend Camion think, and Pat and John?"

"I can't wait to find out. I haven't seen them. I got the paper and came home."

All three called that evening. Camion began, "Say, can we meet... ?" Pat began, "How does 'Senator Armature' sound?" Jaeckel began, "Did y'see the paper today?"

Camion was dead serious, Pat was amused, and Jaeckel was curious. The big three wanted me to meet them that evening at the Oaks to bat it around, but I had promised Ceil we'd drive up to Richardson Springs with Puss and Semantha, and stop somewhere for ice cream. There was also a new ice cream store in a dairy market out near the raceway, and it had bubble gum ice cream, Puss said, so we went there instead. Ceil ordered pistachio, and when the young man put the scoop on a sugar cone, she handed it to me, smiling, and asked the young man to put hers on a paper cone. I had planned to order maple walnut, but I settled for pistachio. Ceil was enjoying my good humor these days.

The next day I rode my bike downtown and parked it in the rack outside

Raley's drug store. Inside I ran into Trudy Solstice who was looking at women's shampoo as I was looking at Gillette razors. I had gone in with the intent of definitely buying a ten pack but as I stood there wondering if I should grow a beard, she spoke to me. I had felt since I was a kid that something was not quite right about my face and was trying to imagine myself with a beard.

"Mr. Popularity," she said, smiling her serpentine early morning political smile.

"I read it," I said, "we missed you at the convention."

"You don't need me if you've got Don Way," she said. "Who's you're campaign manager?"

"Actually, I'm a little off guard, this morning. How do you think I'd look in a beard?"

"It'd be a great disguise except that every graduate student in California is growing one."

"A disguise is just what I'm thinking about."

"I'll be reading the papers to keep up to date, see you sometime," she said, holding a pink plastic cylinder of shampoo as she turned to walk down the aisle to the front counter.

"We could meet every once in a while here and I could brief you," I said to devil her.

"Uh huh, that would be interesting," she said, turning back without stopping, then disappeared around the end of the aisle.

I bought the razor cartridges and bicycled to the Esplanade and stopped in front of a new sports equipment store on the corner of 3rd Avenue. I looked at the muscle-building weights in the front window. The circular metal plates were covered with red plastic. I imagined myself curling and pressing and doing squats on my patio every morning. Then I bicycled to the Hotel Oaks where Camion was sitting in one of the side booths of the coffee shop. The waitress hadn't taken his empty breakfast plate that he had pushed aside, and he was drinking coffee.

"Hi Bob."

"That was some article by Don Way, mister."

"Yeah, if I've got those kinds of friends and all that," I said.

"Your lovely wife must be damn proud of you."

"She doesn't know what to make of it. I think she's scared I'm going to ride off into the sunset trying to be John Wayne or Ronald Reagan."

We talked like that for another half-hour. I kept waiting for Camion to announce his master plan, but he never mentioned another word about me running for office. He treated the whole thing like it was just one more piece of political lumber that had been dropped into the right slot in the side of the house we were supposedly building. When he asked me to meet him, he just wanted to celebrate a little. His urgencies to meet me came from loneliness and friendship and comradeship. We were on some kind of an undefined journey, and the idea was to make it intriguing.

I wasn't sure that I was having fun, however, even though I admitted to myself that I enjoyed the five paragraphs in Don Way's editorial that began with "Armature." I had a cup of coffee with Camion and left him sitting in the booth next to the green wall in the Oaks coffee shop.

On my way to leave a note for Larry, who had moved into the little cottage without a phone next to the park, I bicycled down Woodlawn past the stucco mansions with the baked clay Spanish roofs. The vine-wrapped oak trees in the park were deep green and inviting, and I was thinking about Larry and Eartha as I passed Linden and Sycamore. I turned into Park Drive South and the park was brown and green and I passed under route 99 North. Occasionally I got glimpses of Big Chico Creek and I passed a middle-aged woman bicycling with a German police dog running beside her on a leash. I recognized her from the Democratic Club, Dorothy Hatcher, a leather-skinned liberal from New Jersey who had come to town several years ago. Her brown pigtails normally hung half way down her waist, but now bent forward over her pumping knees, they trailed out from her dark blue kerchief and dangled almost to her pedaling feet. I called "Hi Dorothy," and she quickly lifted one hand from her handlebars and waved and grasped the handlebar again. She looked straight ahead. She didn't recognize me. So much for the infamy of the *Valley Advocate*, I thought.

I exited the park and followed Centennial to Manzanita, turned left on Vallombrosa bordering the park, and Larry's little house was on Vallombrosa Lane, about two miles down.

His truck was parked next to a pile of unpainted green shutters. The fallen limbs from two sycamore trees, one across the street and one in his yard, seemed huge in comparison to his dwarf house. Unraked sycamore leaves covered the overgrown lawn. When Larry opened the door in his bare feet and wearing a robe, he said, "Fancy seeing you here."

I kidded him about the easy life, sleeping until noon.

"Don't I wish it," he said, pointing to a chair in the kitchen. I looked around expecting to see dishes everywhere but the place was immaculate.

"What's up?" I asked.

"Good question," he said, "not much, I guess."

I waited. He looked at me and shook his head.

"I have to take these god damn sitz baths. All goddamn day long. My fucking truck is out there in the yard, just sitting there. *It* needs a god dam sitz bath. I've got fourteen fucking contracts and three guys running around falling all over themselves and I'm living in this little pee hole and the fuck with it."

"I'm glad I asked. Obviously you've been to the doctor."

You're god damn right I've been to the doctor. Fred Kazen stuck his middle finger half way up my gooch and I've got a prostrate problem."

"Prostate."

"Yeah, that's what he said, but it ought to be 'prostrate.'"

"Baths do the trick, huh?"

"Yeah, warm water. Old Fred, he's a good guy. He wanted to tell me to get a girlfriend, but he told me the dangers of the clap instead. He said there's an epidemic of gonorrhea around here. Did you know that?"

"There is around every college campus in America."

"Yeah, well, clap or no clap, it'll teach me not to live the celibate life."

"I thought you had a girlfriend. Joan Jay told Pat you were importing women into her house."

"Jesus Christ, Joan Jay with the geiger-counter ears. Pat was great. I never slept in a cellar without windows before. I never slept in a *cellar* before. I'd wake up in the dark and it would feel like the whole house was pressing down on me. Then I'd start thinking about my kids. I listened to a lot of all night talk shows on the radio."

"Looks like you're a lovely housekeeper."

"Yeah, lovely. What else is there to do after I read about my famous acquaintances in the paper at night? I should have encouraged that chick from one of your college dean's offices. If she came over here I wouldn't have a boggy prostrate."

"You read it, then."

"Didn't everybody? Everyone at the Exchange Club wants to know where you're keeping yourself, besides Sacramento and Don Way's office?"

"How the hell did they know I was in Don Way's office?"

"How many people do you think work in that paper who you walk by on the way to Don's cubicle?"

"I guess so."

"So you're going to run for governor?"

"They say the salmon are starting up the river, big ones."

"You name it."

"Tomorrow afternoon. I get out of class at three."

I bicycled to the library and picked up a book I had called Dottie Bentley about, and walked through the rose garden to my office to meet a student. On the way back I sat on one of the benches in the rose garden. The blossoms were deeper in the fall. If I squinted and looked directly into the garden, I couldn't see the dead blossoms.

Chapter Forty-Eight

LARRY CAUGHT A THIRTY-POUND salmon and I hooked two and missed them both. Back at his house, he flopped it in the sink and washed it, put it on a bread board and broke the bone with a meat cleaver. He sliced a two-inch steak for himself from the middle and gave me both halves.

"What about Eartha and your kids?"

"Oh yeah, I better take one of those halves and drop it off. Sorry, I should have thought of it."

"How's it going?"

"Oh, I don't know, shitty. I tuck the kids in every night and then come over here and lie awake. I've got to get them out of town. I've sent some letters back east, but who the hell wants to work for someone else."

Larry told me a year later that when he was living in the little house and visiting the kids at Eartha's during the evening, the phone would often ring shortly before he left for the night. When he answered the phone, no one would be on the line. Actually, it was Bannister calling to see if Larry had gone, so he could come over and stay the night. The neighbors saw his car parked in the driveway and they talked among themselves.

During this time, Eartha got anonymous phone calls during the day that scared her but she told no one. Ceil and I heard about Bannister's car being there all night, but only Larry knew about the nine o'clock calls to the house, and he thought they were mistakes. Larry still couldn't accept the fact that Eartha was sleeping with Bannister.

That afternoon, I drove home with the salmon and put it in the freezer in the garage and set up my drawing board on the patio. It was late afternoon on a Friday. Ceil and I had been to an art show at the downtown Chico gallery the weekend before and I saw a painting I liked, a watercolor of black sagebrush, yellow clouds, and two antelope faces up close that seemed to be looking right through me.

All week I thought about the painting and stopped in the art gallery and bought a set of watercolors and two good sable brushes and a book of watercolor paper. When Puss came home from school I was painting one of the Japanese rice paper trees.

She pulled up a chair beside me and asked me why I was painting the "rotten" leaves. I told her I'd tell her when it was finished. Then she asked me what the black circles were and I realized that she didn't recognize perfectly drawn snails. I told her to go and visit with Semantha. When Ceil came home she didn't comment on my watercolor adventure and merely asked me to go for a walk with her before supper.

"Sure, what's up?"

"Oh, not much. I'll tell you."

We walked down Violet Way, crossing 1st Avenue to Palmetto, and when we passed Ken Morrow's house, I pointed out the woodpile where Ken had been bitten by the black widow spiders. Ceil said that we ought to go for more walks together. She had put her arm through mine, and I wondered what I might have done to upset her, but I couldn't think of anything to feel guilty about. I told her about Larry's prostate problem. She said she knew that a prostate had something to do with sex but she didn't know what. I said that it was a gland that surrounded the urinary tract and that it was the reason old men had to change their underpants every day.

"That absolutely clears everything up for me."

"That's the shortcut explanation. I can give you the psychological or the strictly physiological stuff if you want."

"That's OK, Doctor Armature, we can refer to it in the future as the sex and stinky underpants gland."

"Larry's been living the celibate life since he moved out. Without sex, the prostate gets swollen and boggy because it fills up with sperm, and Larry's hurting now because of too much sperm."

"I want to hear the old psychiatrists's view."

"Larry's punishing himself because Eartha's having an affair. He's denying himself sex, even with himself."

"He ought to get a girlfriend. Maybe then Eartha would see things differently."

We had reached Sheridan and were walking back. The foothills of the Sierras were rounded and yellow against the snow-pink outlines of the distant mountains. Ceil stopped to examine a clump of California poppies growing at the side of the road.

"I would love to take some home, but they'd probably die anyway. I know it's illegal."

She twisted and snapped off some blue chicory.

"I thought you wanted to talk about something," I said.

"Oh, it's nothing, Bill. I had an appointment with Dr. Grogan this afternoon, and he said that my pap smear was positive, that's all. He said it happens all the time, and all it means is that they'll do another test. Ninety-nine per cent of the time, the second test is negative. It's nothing, really. I just wanted an excuse to go for a walk. The prostate lecture was a windfall."

We held hands as we walked back to 5th Avenue and up to Eartha's house where we retrieved Puss and Boots for supper. While Ceil was cooking pasta with fresh basil, she asked me why Larry didn't give us any of that big salmon he caught.

"He did, a whole half," I said.

"Where is it and why didn't you tell me?" she asked.

"It's in the freezer, I forgot about it. We can eat it any time. I'll take it out and thaw it tomorrow if you want me to."

"If we don't, it may stay there forever," Ceil said.

"OK," I said. "I'll take it out tomorrow."

I forgot to, however, and it was there a long time.

Chapter Forty-Nine

FALL CAME AND THE trees turned yellow along the Esplanade. The almond and walnut orchards were lined with tarpaulins, and mechanical knockers rocked their way back and forth between the rows. The salmon runs enlivened the Sacramento and Feather Rivers. High school football games on Friday nights rocked the Chico stadium. Larry and I drove into the Sierras for three days and I shot my first elk. Every night on CBS, Walter Cronkite gave the body count of the daily dead in Vietnam. The Cincinnati Symphony orchestra played Dvorzak's New World symphony at the college. I got elected to the Butte County Democratic Central Committee and was chosen secretary. Larry and I hunted at the Parrot Ranch in Dayton and the skies were filled with thousands of sand hill cranes. The poet Robert Lowell read his poems at the college and then went back to Bellevue sanitarium in New York.

Chapter Fifty

IN DECEMBER WE AWOKE one Saturday morning to a half inch of snow in the yard and Puss stomped around in it and made snowballs and threw them at me, but by noon the snow was gone. Ceil and I went for our walk down Violet Lane toward the park, and swung around and walked back on Sheridan. At the spot where Ceil had picked the blue chicory I remembered the pap smear I had forgotten.

"Whatever happened about those pap smear tests?" I asked her.

"This is where the poppies were that day, isn't it? I picked the chicory instead. You're getting old, Billy boy, but you still have your memory."

"Pap smear," I said.

"I know," she said. "Dr. Grogan says a lot of the time they're not reliable."

"Is that it? They're not reliable?"

"No, I'm having more tests. There's no point in two of us thinking about it when there's nothing to worry about. I feel fine. I never felt better, actually. I'm OK Bill, truly."

"When are they going to do these new tests?"

"Oh, I don't know, sometime next week. It's on the calendar. I may have to stay overnight. Come on, let's not let it screw up today, OK?"

We walked, and Ceil took my arm again with both of hers. "I wish the poppies and the chicory bloomed year round," she said.

We could see the sun-whitened Sierras from in back of the Hooker Oak School, and Ceil said we ought to take Puss and Boots to Stirling City so she could play in the snow. When we got home I drove to Western Auto and bought a set of chains for the car and a round red snow dish. Puss wanted skis so I went back with her and we bought a small pair of skis and ski poles. She wanted clamps and ski boots but I told her that when I was a kid I used stretched strips of an old inner tube to hold the skis on my feet. Puss said, "Daddy, not the good old days again. Besides, where am I going to get an old inner tube to cut up?" Even though I knew I was being a tightwad, I suggested she borrow Semantha's boots this time, and we'd see how she liked it. Maybe next time, I'd get her the clamps and her own boots.

"Semanth and Jamey have gone with their dad. It's Saturday, remember, daddy?"

"We can borrow them from Semantha's mother," I said.

"She's never home," Puss said. "She won't be there. You wait and see."

When we got home, Puss called Eartha, but no one answered, so we found Semantha's boots and borrowed them from Larry's garage.

Ceil packed a lunch and we brought our up to now unused winter jackets and mittens and overshoes and headed for Paradise. After a couple of miles on the Skyway, we began to see patches of white, and up along the ridge, there were several inches of snow. We pulled off at the scenic point and looked back into the valley where Chico was spread before us like a miniature town with invisible dolls making smoke that rose from chimneys, and patterns of orchards someone had lined with rulers. We drove into Paradise where the pine branches were white and the streets were slushy with tire tracks and unploughed snow. Beyond Paradise we came to the sign that said we couldn't proceed further without chains, so I pulled over.

Puss helped me spread the chains on the top of the packed snow behind the rear wheels, and she directed me as I backed onto them. We lifted the ends together up over the tires and fastened the clamps. I kicked against the tires and the chains seemed firm.

"That's the aye," she said, imitating me.

"That's the aye all right," I said, and we drove along ploughed roads for several miles through Megalia where it was snowing lightly, and ten miles further into Stirling City, following a sign that said "Children's Ski Lift."

Ceil and I watched Puss ski the children's hill, sometimes falling and losing her skis, sometimes making it to the bottom, balancing as if she were a full glass of water trying to keep from spilling. Ceil kept telling her to bend her knees, and Puss, going down the hill standing straight up, called back, "I am." The small rope pull, powered by several generators hooked together, could pull a dozen or so children at the same time, and was a great incentive to Puss as she ran after a runaway ski and gathered both skis together in her arms and got in line again. We asked her if she wanted to go with us to an area for sleds and dishes but she didn't want to leave the rope pull.

Ceil and I followed a trampled path across a small field and through a forest of larch trees to an opening where we could see across the Sierra Nevada Mountains.

"Oh Bill, it's gorgeous," Ceil said, taking one of my arms in both of hers. "This is so much fun."

We stood on the edge of a further field that sloped directly down the backside of a mountain a couple hundred yards before the thick woods closed it off. The snow was too deep for sleds but there were two young children sitting on a red snow dish and a man ready to release them down the slope. They were to our right about fifty yards across the top of the field. "There they go," Ceil said, "Let's watch."

"They'll never reach the bottom," I said. "This hill is too steep."

We could see the two riders squatting V-legged against each other in the dish, each holding one of the side straps with one hand. Their red dish was bright against the glare of the snow from the afternoon sun.

They pushed off, and as they passed the imaginary line across from where we stood, they were hurtling too fast, the dish bouncing down over the uneven side of the hill.

The man who had been standing where they started immediately began running after them, waving his arms. He was wearing a blue scarf and it flopped behind his neck as each plunge of his legs broke the top crust of the snow and he sank up to his knees.

"If they reach the bottom, they'll hit a tree and god help them," I said.

We couldn't see them for a few seconds as the long hill dipped, and they were out of sight; then we saw the red dish flying in the air and for a split second, one of the riders. The man kept plunging toward a spot we couldn't see. There was no sound from the woods or the long sloping field of deep snow.

"We should help," Ceil said. We headed down the hill. Ceil could walk two or three steps before breaking through the crust, but I broke through at every step. Ceil got there first and was hidden from my view. I was sweating and grabbed off my knitted wool hat as I clumped through the deep snow.

When I got to the rise where everyone disappeared, I saw the two children sitting up in the snow, fifteen feet apart. The man with the blue scarf was standing beside one of them, and Ceil was standing beside the other. They were about five and eight years old. The girl had tumbled off the dish as it left the ground and was unhurt, and the boy had been thrown free but landed on the back of his neck and was in shock. The dish had continued down the mountain and was somewhere in the trees below.

Ceil talked with the father while I clumped into the woods where it was colder in the shade and I could walk on top of the snow. I found the dish beside a larch tree and carried it back up the mountain. The four of them were climbing the hill slowly because of the disoriented boy, and the father was apologetic. Ceil was quiet, and spoke to the little boy kindly.

Driving home, Puss asked me to stop at the vista again, and we looked out across Chico and the valley. It was as quiet as a dark oil painting.

"When we get home," Puss said, "I will imagine myself up here looking down on me and not knowing what I'm doing down here. My life will be a secret to everyone looking down."

Coming down the Skyway, we saw the first patches of dry ground and Ceil said, "I can't get over how fast they went by us. We could see such a long way and it was so beautiful and calm. Do you think that boy will be all right?"

"I hope so. It was a dumb thing to do."

"But it didn't seem so. It was just sliding down a hill. We never even got a chance to do it."

When we pulled into the driveway, Semantha was coming down the sidewalk to play with Puss.

Chapter Fifty-one

IN EARLY FEBRUARY IT rained in Chico for ten days. In the northern counties of Del Norte, Siskiyou, Shasta, and Humboldt, it also rained hard for a week and the rivers rose, then for three days it deluged, and the Klamath, Salmon, and the Redwood Rivers rose over their banks, rumbling toward the Pacific as the forks of the Cottonwood poured into the Sacramento. Three more days of slow and steady rain in the north and the valley rivers were up to their brims and snarly. During this time, the snow-water from the Sierras swirled into the Sacramento in the Cow, Battle, Deer, and Rock rivers. By the end of the second week, the Sacramento River was spreading over Hamilton City and Nord and Ordbend. Jaeckel called and said that he was six inches under water and it was rising an inch every ten minutes. The water should be in Chico within an hour. I asked him if it was serious and he laughed and said, "Hell no, it's not serious, it's northern valley play time. Put on your rubber boots. We'll all be walking in the Great Central Valley Lake again for a couple days. You'll see your patio and your front yard through a glass lightly."

I almost made a joke about his biblical allusions, but said, "I thought when you called you would say 'It's serious this time.'"

"What's serious? It's just water. It goes away. Row row row your boat and all that. Gently down the stream. Don't you have any rubber boots or did I ask you that? Put on your rubber boots. What you need is a geology lesson. Do you know what a physiographic subdivision is? I'll tell you. Have you got a minute? Put on your rubber boots and I'll tell you. It's pretty heady stuff for a cartoon-drawing-journalist-easterner-maybe-politician, but I'll tell you something about alluvial fans and terraces and flood basins. Hold on a second. Have you got a minute? Hold on a second, I have to get something, I just have to reach over here, I can't, hold on, don't go away."

I waited while John filled whatever he was drinking.

"Are you still there? Did I tell you to put on your rubber boots? Never mind, what would an easterner do with rubber boots? Rubbers yes but not rubber boots. Listen, Billy Army, did anyone ever call you 'Army' before? I'm going to copyright that. I'll be your campaign manager and we'll run you as 'Army Mature,' what do you say? I don't know about this easterner stuff. I like you, you're a goddam good guy, but you have to be an Oakie to run for office in California, that or your name has to be Sutter or Bidwell or Glenn. Do you think a name like Jaeckel could get elected? Ha! I sound like Camion, don't I? Did you read Steinbeck's *East of Eden*? He got it right. Remember that German family in Salinas in World War I? You think it was different in World War II? I'm taking too much of your time. I should hang up. Do you want me to hang up? I better hang up, I just wanted you to know the water is here, and it's coming to Chico, and I'm going to have to wade around in it waiting for it to go away. It's better than the fucking fog, but that's coming too. So I thought you'd want to know. So I called you. I never called you 'Army' before. It's bettern 'Navy,' right? You think I don't remember calling you 'Army?' Listen, Army, we live in a flood plain, the Sacramento Valley flood plain. The Sacramento River goes right down the middle, all the fucking way to the San Joaquin River and the Pacific Ocean. It's great, it's a great river, it's a mile from my orchard. I'm getting irrigated. That's pretty good. I'm getting irrigated all right. You know how wide this flood plain would have to be before we're in trouble? A lot wider. We're thirty fucking miles across, do you know that? Thirty fucking miles, that's a lot of water. You probably know that, you work at that fucking college now. You're an academic, Army, a fucking academic. I'm not an academic myself, nor do I attain to be, he said pontifically, I mean pontifuckily. But you're a good guy. Did I tell you what I called about? I don't remember if I told you. It's about the river in my yard. My orchard is drowning. No it's not, I'm only kidding. I've got my boots on. One thing is sure, I'm not going to die with my boots on. Puss and Boots. You've got a daughter named Puss and Boots. She'll be all right. She'll put on her rubber boots. Tell her I told her to put on her rubber boots. Will you tell her that Uncle John told her? King John. Tell her King John was not a bad man. That's another story. You ought to read more, Army, you don't know these things. Will you tell her?"

"I will," I said.

Jeackel hung up.

It was ten in the morning. Puss was in school and Ceil was at work. I called Ceil and told her to drive home, and as I hung up, Puss came in the front door.

"It's another flood, daddy," she said. "Flood, flood, flood."

"Maybe we ought to build a boat," I said.

"You're not serious, daddy, I know you're not, where would we build it?"

"You're right, I'm not. I guess I can't fool you with Noah's Ark any more."

"That's OK, daddy, I know you're just trying to cheer me up. Can I have Semanth down?"

"Did you talk about it already on the way home?"

"Yup. She said it would probably be OK with her mother."

"OK, call her mother and make sure," I said.

"If she can come, can I go up and get her?"

"You mean you want to walk in the water."

"May I?"

"You have to say please may I, don't you know the rules of Red Light?"

"Please may I?"

"Sure, but you have to put on your overshoes."

"Come on, daddy, the water's really warm. It's no fun in overshoes. That's the whole point?"

"That's the whole point, huh?"

Puss disappeared out the front door in her bare feet and I called Ceil to tell her that Jaeckel said it wasn't going to be really serious, but she had already left. Bill Richards answered the phone and said that there were four inches of water on the Esplanade.

When Ceil arrived, I was looking out the front window, and her car was moving slowly, pushing the water in little wavelets from the tires. She left the car outside the garage and came in the front door holding her shoes in her hand.

"There are cars stalled all over the place," she said.

"Jaeckel called a half hour ago, he was feeling pretty good. He said the water was rising about an inch every ten minutes."

"What was he feeling good about?"

"He'd had a couple drinks, he talked nonstop for fifteen minutes."

"I thought you meant he was feeling good that the river was flooding."

"I think it was the opposite, it was hard to tell. He said an easterner couldn't get elected in California."

"Sounds like a pretty serious conversation to me. You sure he called about the flood?"

Puss and Semantha came through the front door, and Ceil got them towels from the bathroom.

"How deep is the water, you mermaids?"

"Up to here," Semantha pointed above her ankle.

"We want to play in the back yard," Puss said, "It's fun looking at the ground through the water."

The girls disappeared out the back door. Ceil said, "I'm not sure I'm going to have enough towels."

"When I was a kid, I used to love the days in the spring after a hard rain. There was a field behind Wormstead's house across the street, and at the far end toward the trees along the South's dirt driveway, the water got to be almost eighteen inches deep. I loved to walk with my rubber boots on, looking down through the water at the yellow grass on the bottom. My flood pond was different from real ponds because the bottom was firm and grassy, not dark and mucky. I had my father's old rubber boots with the tops cut off, and the water came almost to the top. If I moved in the water too fast, the water would come over the tops and my stockings would get wet. My mother never got mad at me and it was always nice. None of the other kids could come out and play in the water, and I was alone, looking down through the clear water at the yellow grass bottom. I always wished there were fish, but there weren't. The water would disappear in a few days, and the field would be just a field again."

"Build a fire, Bill, and we can sit in front of it and open a bottle of wine," Ceil said, "I know it's still morning but I don't care. We only live once."

I had never seen Ceil drink wine before the evening meal. I went out to the garage and saw the water and realized that I hadn't pulled the plugs on the washer and drier, so I pulled them and put the plug-ends of the cords on top with a brick to hold them from slipping back to the floor, now under two inches of water. I lifted the pile of old newspapers and put them on a wooden box in the corner. Outside the door I took an armfull of thin scrub oak pieces and carried them in and started a fire in the living room.

"No bamboo, I hope," Ceil said.

"Bam-boom," you mean," I said

"When I was a little girl I used to love the rain, especially if there was thunder and lightning. My girl friend Norma was afraid of the thunder, but I loved to sit on the front porch in our green wicker rocking chair, curled up in a blanket and watching the storm. The lightning would flash and streak across the sky and the thunder would crack and sometimes shake the house, and I loved being alone in the rain and the storm. I was warm and I felt like something huge was taking charge. My mother and father used to fight all the time even though each one loved me and I knew it, and in the storms they thought I was courageous to go outside and sit on the porch alone. They helped me put on warm clothes and tucked me in with the blanket, and they would go back inside and sometimes in the storm I could hear them fighting. The rain and the thunder and lightning made me feel safe. Isn't that funny?"

"It isn't funny, but it's a nice story."

I told Ceil about my getting caught out on Great East Lake in a thunder-shower when I was a boy, and rowing back to the camp in the pouring rain because I couldn't get the motor going. Ceil then told me the story of her father's car stalling in an underpass filling up with rain water when they were on the way to her cousin's wedding—her father was driving so fast that the water splashed up inside the engine and the wires got wet. They had to sit there in the car in the middle of the deep water until a truck came and pushed them out, and they were late for the wedding. We thought of other stories and we finished the bottle of wine. Puss and Semantha came in from the back yard and dried off their feet and asked if they could go up to Semantha's house. Ceil made them promise to wipe off again when they got there and to stay out of the water unless they put on overshoes. They agreed and disappeared.

"What do you think, Ceil, that bottle of *Gewurtztraumiener* I've been saving?"

"What did we just drink? It was wonderful."

"A white Bordeaux. The last bottle."

"Bring on the Gewurtz, I'm a little smashed. This is fun."

I opened the wine and put some more scrub oak on the fire, and we lay on the rug and reminisced about the first year we were married, before Puss was born. Outside, the water was rising, and it rose steadily for another several hours before it receded. By the following morning the water would be down to a couple of inches, and by noon the streets would look as if there had been a spring storm, with small debris in the streets. Out on Ord Ferry Road where the Jaeckel's lived, the water covered the orchards for another day. Puss stayed at Eartha's house for supper, and Ceil and I made omelettes together.

On that afternoon in the middle of the flood, we sat by the fire in our house surrounded by water, and we comforted each other in our innocence, for we did not know what we knew later, and the knowing of which could never let us be innocent again. We finished the spicey German white wine and went to bed and loved each other and slept. Later, I measured the water in the front yard at ten inches. Puss stayed overnight at Eartha's, and when I called Jaeckel to find out how much water they had, Ruth told me that he was sleeping.

"Too much celebrating," she said.

"I guess the flood is always a burden for some people, but we just sat in front of the fire and drank some wine," I said.

"Floods make an awful mess," Ruth said, "but what can you do? If it's not one thing, it's another. If you don't go in a flood, you'll go in a drought, but we'll all go, we can bet on that."

Chapter Fifty-Two

When Dr. Grogan's secretary called in late February to make the appointment, she said, "Mrs. Armature, Dr. Grogan thinks that it would be a good idea if your husband came with you."

"Nothing like the good old fashioned direct technique," I said when she told me.

"I guess so," Ceil said, "but it's better than leaving you out. It stinks either way. I think they call it facing the music."

Three days later, on a bright sunny day, with the wind blowing gently from the west, and the snow gleaming brightly across the valley from the tips of the Sierras, we sat in Dr. Grogan's office on Viburnum Street as he told us that Ceil had cervical cancer. Ceil and I looked at each other and then back at Dr. Grogan. He said that early detection was crucial, and that since we found out early, the chances were excellent that Ceil would not only respond positively to the radiation treatments, but that she would resume a completely normal life after the treatment period was over. I asked him what he meant by that and he said that Ceil would have to slow down for the next several months during treatment, and that she would have to take a leave from her job.

"How soon do I have to stop working?" she asked.

"Well, pretty soon, as soon as you can wrap things up for a leave," he said. "The sooner we begin treatments the better. We've got you scheduled for early next week."

That night we decided at first not to tell Puss, then decided to tell her. "I can't lie to her about it," Ceil said. "What would be the point anyway? If they fix me, we win, and if they don't we did the right thing by not springing it on her."

I agreed with everything Ceil wanted to do. What the hell would be the point if I didn't, and I didn't, but what did it matter? What did anything matter? It matters, you jerk, I thought, but I was too angry to argue with myself, and I went to my easel and started a watercolor of antelopes, but not like the one I had wanted to buy at the gallery that day. I remembered seeing antelopes in Wyoming before I turned north to Idaho. They were looking at me with their brown eyes, ready to bolt. It would not become a good watercolor because I didn't know what I was doing, but I did it anyway. As I was mixing the light brown with a dab of purple to make black, I was thinking of the way color merged into the paper to make something different. All I had to do was add more water, and the trace would almost disappear. I was staring into antelope eyes and they kept changing and disappearing as I dabbed the brush full of water. Then the faces disappeared. It was quite an artistic evening.

A week later, Ceil entered Enloe Hospital for her first radiation treatment, and stayed two days. The day she came home, the sun shone late in the afternoon, the first time in weeks. In the morning there had been a dark heavy cloud cover. By noon it had become lighter in color, a cesium bluish gray, with light beginning to show underneath in the north, as if someone had lifted off a blue amanita mushroom cap. By five o'clock Ceil was asleep in our bedroom with an open book on her lap and the sun coming through the window, warming her face. Before she fell asleep, Puss showed her the drawings she had made in school and the notice for a field trip that would take the class to the cattle auction in Durham on a Friday afternoon in early April. When Ceil closed her eyes, Puss came out into the kitchen where I was looking out the window over the sink at the new leaves beginning to show on the rose tree.

"Is mommy going to die?" she asked.

"No," I said. "She's not going to die." I bent down and hugged her. "She's going to get well. She's tired from the medicine they gave her at the hospital, and she's going to sleep a lot, and that will make her better."

"What kind of medicine?" she asked.

"The kind when they take a picture of your chest. X-rays. The doctors point them at the place where the problem is and they kill the stuff that will make mommy sicker if the doctors don't bring her to the hospital every once in a while to do it. It's what made mommy tired today, and we'll have to do it again every couple weeks until the bad stuff is gone."

"Can I go up to Semanth's?"

"*May* you, you mean?"

"May I, please?"

"Sure. Just come back as soon as Semantha's mother starts to get supper ready. I'm going fix something special for us to eat tonight?"

"What?"

"It's a surprise."

"Oyster stew, I bet."

"Oh, you're so smart, aren't you?"

"It is, isn't it? I hope so, I hope you bought a lot of oysters this time so there's more than two or three floating in my bowl."

"Well, we'll see what we can do."

I checked to see if Ceil was still asleep and she was and I lay down quietly on the bed beside her and felt the sun on my face and tried not to think, and after a few minutes fell asleep too. I woke up about twenty minutes later and Ceil was reading John P. Marquand's *Wickford Point.* "How do you like it?" I said.

"How long have you been awake?"

"I haven't been asleep, I was just resting my eyes. How's the book?"

"Since when did you snore when you're awake? I like Bella. I just finished reading about when they went woodcock hunting. My father used to call it 'gunnin' too. I'll bet she gets him in the end."

"I haven't read it but I have something special for supper."

"Oh good. I'm dying for oyster stew, just don't boil the milk."

"Not you too. I can't surprise anyone around here. Maybe I'll go get a pizza instead."

"I take it back. Boil the milk. You may even burn the oysters. You're a darling."

I winked at her and turned to go into the kitchen. "Bill?" she said.

I turned back and cocked my head to one side and smiled, waiting for her to speak.

"Oh Bill, I'm exhausted."

"You should be, you've been drilled with cell-killing x-rays."

"Do you think they can get it?"

"Sure they'll get it. They found it right away."

"It's been three months since the first positive pap smear."

"They'll get it Ceil, they'll get it, I guarantee it."

I turned and went into the kitchen and opened the quart container with the fresh oysters from Safeway's. The oysters oozed together when I tipped the white paper quart container and I remembered shopping with my mother in J.B. Blood's Market on Commercial Street in Lynn, Massachusetts on Friday afternoons where occasionally she would buy a pint of oysters for a stew. I liked the smell of the sawdust on the floor and the fresh vegetables. Sometimes she would buy liver, and sometimes fresh mackerel. The men behind the counter wore white coats and they placed everything in scales in front of them that hung over the counters with chipped ice in trays, and they had hair on their arms and were strong looking and efficient and pleasant. Once I was watching the tentacles of the black lobsters on the chipped ice, and my mother moved away for a moment and I couldn't find her. I was so scared that I lost my breath. I started to cry and a lady took my hand and then my mother was standing there, laughing and hugging me.

I poured a quart of milk into a large saucepan with the oysters and put it on to heat over a low flame. I knew that the milk would burn on the bottom of the pan if the gas wasn't turned down low. My mother always put a slice of butter into the milk when it got hot and turned off the gas before it boiled. The butter would melt and spread. Then she would shake in pepper and it would spread. Just like cancer, I thought, and walked out on the patio and sat down and waited for Puss to come home.

The following morning I left Ceil reading in bed and went to the office for my ten o'clock office hour. I was waiting for the third student when the phone rang. A fellow with a gravelly voice on the other end identified himself as Bill Weeks and said that I had been recommended to him by someone in the Salinger campaign who told him I brought Pierre into Chico and organized a "great" airport rally. I knew what was coming and I didn't want any part of it but I was flattered and listened. He was helping a friend who was running for lieutenant governor. He wondered if I might give him a few tips about Chico because this friend had eight kids and was planning a bus tour of the state with all eight kids and he hoped to come to Chico. I immediately liked this guy on the other end of the phone and made one of those instantaneous decisions that change the next ten years of your life, or maybe your whole life. Maybe it was his gravelly voice. I said, "You want me to help you bring a

bus load of kids whose father is running for lieutenant governor into Chico."
I said it as a statement not a question.

"I guess that's about it," he said.

"And you're not going to try to convince me that this guy will make a
great lieutenant governor." I said it as a statement, not as a question.

"Well, he probably would make a good lieutenant governor, but what I'm
concerned about is this bus and Chico, and these kids. I don't even know if
they have a television station in Chico."

"Yeah, we've got a television station, Channel Six, it covers the whole
Northern Valley, all the way from Sacramento to the Oregon mountains above
Redding. You want television coverage to boot." I said it as a statement, not
a question.

Bill Weeks said, "What do you think?"

"When are you coming?" I asked. One part of me was saying hang up,
forget this guy, you don't need this, you don't want this. The other part was
saying, this guy is interesting. Bring the bus here, get this father of eight kids
some TV time, then it's over. Do it.

Bill Weeks said, "The end of April, the 27th or the 28th or around
there."

I was looking at the calendar in front of me on the wall.

"When, exactly?"

"The 27th, it's a Thursday. We'll arrive at 2:00 o'clock in the afternoon.
We've got a luncheon thing in Marysville at noon and we'll leave at one and
get into Chico at 2:00. Whatever you can arrange for the evening will be a
hell of a lot more than we have now."

"First of all, you won't get here at 2:00, you'll get here around 3:30, maybe
four or five o'clock."

"I guess I can talk to you," gravelly voice said. "Whatever you can do
would be better than great."

I told him I'd get his friend a TV spot and an interview with the editor
of the Chico paper. I didn't know about the evening, I'd have to see. "By the
way," I said, "what's this guy's name."

"Braden," the gravelly voice said, "Tom Braden."

In the next few months I found out that my new friend Bill Weeks had
been the head of a CIA group in East Germany for ten years, until the STASI
got him on the waterfront one night with two-by-fours. He had the scars on
his face to prove it. He was also a black belt karate expert and flew his own
airplane and drank champagne splits. He'd written a spy novel published by
Houghton and Miflin called *Knock and Wait Awhile*, and he turned out to be
the best man I ever knew.

Chapter Fifty-Three

ARTISTS HAVE COMPARED THE light in the north Central Valley in spring to the light in Provence. Bonnard, of all the Impressionists, would have gotten it best, because he understood pink in landscapes. I made this connection many years later when I was living in another valley in the east, but during the time of Ceil's sickness, I was thinking only about Ceil. The long walks we took in the almond orchards surrounding Chico became part of a consciousness that only later I identified with light and color and the eternal nature of landscape. The almond orchards in the spring were magical, and they were all slightly different. Ceil felt the color and the light very deeply, and I became her companion and her student as she pointed out the subtleties and the color variations as the new green grass grew between the rows of bristly, iron-bark trees. I thought the orchards all looked the same, especially as we walked between the long rows sprouting the first colorations of blossoms, but she always saw something different and new and miraculous. I think, looking back, that the miracle was always in the growth itself, and we saw it as we had never seen it before. It was what we had, this new growth. We never spoke of the growth inside Ceil that was trying to destroy her, the mindless cells also trying to stay alive in a way that Ceil and I had no awareness of.

We walked during the mornings of early March and April, whenever we could find the time between my work at the college and her recovery from the radiation treatments. We walked, and Ceil pointed and showed me the changes. We were not aware that the real changes were the ones going on inside her, and we didn't know that while the radiation treatments were killing the cancer cells of the cervix, they weren't touching the ovarian cysts that no one knew about, and whose cells were rapidly multiplying. In the meantime, we dallied hand in hand between the lines of gnarly trees, walking through the soft lime-green fauna that created impressionist paintings of every row. Inside the row, we couldn't see the pink color, but as we turned at the tule ditches at each end and saw the long row again in front of us, the faint glow of pink emanated from the first sunrise of almond blossoms. Then the milk-white orchards blazed in the spring sun and the bees were everywhere.

On a sunny Saturday morning in early April, Larry and I and Ken Morrow went trout fishing in the Sierras. Ceil stayed in bed to rest from her final radiation treatment, and Eartha took the girls to their ballet class. We drove in Ken's open jeep for two and a half hours, and when we got to the stream I was so stuffed up from the almond pollen that I could barely breathe. Following the stream into the mountain terrain, we walked and climbed for another half-hour.

"Don't put your hands anywhere you can't see," Larry said. "The rattlers are spring-blind and they'll strike at anything they feel is close."

He didn't have to tell me to keep my watery eyes and ears open. I imagined a waiting rattlesnake around every bend and over every ledge, and we dropped down into a small canyon to fish. There were deep holes in the river and Larry hooked two big trout but lost them both. I caught a small one and threw it back. Ken was fishing upstream. Larry hooked another and it broke his line.

"I stink as a fisherman," he yelled when he looked over at me sitting on a ledge with my head against a slanted boulder, sick from the pollen, thinking of the long ride home, and held his fly rod to show his dangling broken line. He tied on another leader and changed his fly two or three times and caught a fifteen-inch rainbow. He ate his lunch while I dozed.

"You all done fishing?" he called after disappearing downstream for an hour.

"I'm done all right," I said.

"We'll work upstream and find Ken and head out," he said. "You got it bad."

Driving back to Chico, it was worse, and Ken said I had pollen poisoning. Larry tried to make me feel better by kidding me. I felt as if I had been hit by a truck.

"You easterners are sissies," he said. "Don't you know you're supposed to have fun on a fishing trip?"

"No one told me that," I said.

When they dropped me off, I could barely stand up, and I crawled in beside Ceil in bed as soon as I got in the house.

"*We're* a pair," she said, feeling my forehead and getting up. "I better fix you something to eat."

Ceil told me the next day that she went to Safeway's and bought two New York sirloin steaks and then baked two big potatoes, and fixed fresh tomato slices with a basil dressing, but couldn't wake me up. The steaks and the potatoes were still in the refrigerator the next day because she wasn't hungry either. She ate some of the tomato salad. I stayed in bed all day and ate some pea soup later. She offered to make me oyster stew, but I could see that she didn't feel like going out, so I told her I couldn't eat it.

On Monday she drove me to Dr. Grogan's office and he gave me a shot of something. He also said that Ceil ought to be feeling a lot better within a couple weeks.

I was sick another three days, but I met my classes. We tried to live a normal life. I knew she didn't want to talk about it, but I kept asking her how she felt. One day she said, "I wish I knew."

"I should quit asking," I said.

"No, you shouldn't, you should ask. I think I feel a little stronger," she said," but I've got this tree frog in my ear that swallowed a nail."

We resumed our morning walks in the almond orchards. We had visited eleven orchards, some several times. When the blossoms fell, they floated onto the lime-green grass between the black trees, and we walked through the rows, trying not to count the days until she was supposed to feel better.

On April 12, Thomas Braden came to Chico with his wife Joan and eight kids on a bus. Braden was kicking off his campaign for lieutenant governor. Weeks called me from the Oaks at almost four and I walked over from my campus office. Camion was sitting in the bar and I sent off the bus with the kids and their young British nanny to see where Errol Flynn jumped out of the Hooker Oak in Sherwood Forest, then took Braden and Camion to *The Valley Advocate* to talk to Don Way, then to Channel Six where Braden did an interview to be broadcast on the six o'clock news. Bill Weeks and Joan Braden and Bob Kaiser, Braden's press secretary, signed into their rooms at the Oaks.

For dinner that night I had organized in an upstairs room at the Oaks a buffet spread for about twenty-five prominent Democrats in the Northern Valley, and everyone was happy. Camion told me who to invite and they all came, even though it was Pat Brown and Glenn Anderson territory. Grass roots Democrats in California were very loyal to their incumbents, but were also polite to living and breathing challengers. Braden made his case, not strong enough to sway the loyalists, but Braden himself was impressive. He knew he needed the vote of every malcontent Democrat in California to dent Anderson's popularity. What he didn't reckon on was Lyndon Johnson sending his chief of protocol, Lloyd Hand, to California to split the vote and ease in Anderson. This all came later, and at the time, I couldn't care less for Tom Braden or Glenn Anderson, or Lyndon Johnson. After the buffet, I hung around the Oaks with the Bradens and Bill Weeks and Kaiser, and was home by 9:30 to spend the rest of the evening with Ceil. She said Braden was impressive on the evening news.

The next morning, I joined them for breakfast at the Oaks and saw the bus off for Redding at 9:00 a.m. I had done my job and I felt good about it and I never expected to see any of them again.

Chapter Fifty-Four

NEAR THE END OF April, the first magnolia blossoms on the campus appeared over Larson Creek, showcasing the oldest and biggest magnolia in town. I passed under its branches on the days I went to my office, and sometimes stopped for a few minutes on the little bridge to watch the water from the Sierra Nevadas course beneath me on its way to the Sacramento River. After two weeks, the pinkish white petals began to drop into the creek, floating downstream until they snagged in waterlogged branches or disappeared around the bend at the science building. The petals that snagged in the branches gradually sank, dotting the creek bottom until they disintegrated and the pieces were swept downstream.

When the first blooms appeared, I described them to Ceil, and she wanted to see them, and that afternoon we stood on the little bridge over Larson Creek and looked up into the pink and white blossoms. The sun deepened the pink weight of the overarching limbs.

"I think I'm strong enough to go back to work now, Bill," she said.

"We better check with Grogan," I said.

Two days later, Dr. Grogan told her to wait another two weeks to be safe, so we went on long rides together on the days I didn't have to go to the college. We packed lunches and headed out as soon as Puss trudged off to school in the morning. Ceil wanted me to surprise her, so I pulled out the map each morning and made arbitrary decisions. Our only rule was to be home by the time Puss got out of school.

In the next two weeks we made day trips to Grass Valley, Clear Lake, Chester and Lake Almador, and a little town named Wildwood near Dubakella Mountain in the Coastal Range. We rode with all the windows down and Ceil put her head back and looked out the window for long periods of time. She would pick out the spots where she wanted to stop and eat, and she chose small lakes and scenic overlooks and groves of cottonwoods. Once we drove through a stand of eucalyptus trees and parked by the side of the road and walked behind them to a small meadow and spread our blanket by a little brook.

On the way home that day she studied the map and announced that she would like us to take Puss to the coast for a few days. She wanted to see the Pacific again. "Arcata, Bill," she said. "I want to drive through the Trinity Wilderness to Arcata."

We left on a Friday afternoon as soon as Puss got home from school and we stayed that night in a log motel in a little town called Buckeye, north of Redding on route 299. There was a field behind it and a little man-made lake with alder trees and birches, and we walked after supper. Puss said that she wished we had brought Semantha. "I am going to miss my ballet lesson tomorrow, but I don't mind," she said.

"We have to miss important things sometimes," Ceil said. "Look, it's still light and the moon is up." We looked and saw the moon above the trees. "It's almost full, but I can't tell if it's new gibbous or old gibbous."

"Who's he?" Puss asked.

"It means the moon is one day before full or one day after full," Ceil said.

"Why do they call it that?" Puss asked.

"I don't know. Do you know, Bill?"

"Gibbous means bulgy or humpbacked. I guess that's why," I said.

"How did you know that?" Ceil said. "You know the darndest things sometimes."

"It was a question in a seventh grade geography bee. I missed the question. I remember my teacher's name was Miss Taylor and she was very crabby. Patricia Rockhill answered the question. She was the smartest one in the class. She was my girlfriend in the eighth grade for a while."

"What's a jog gravy bee?" Puss asked.

"You started this, you tell her," Ceil laughed.

"You started it, you said gibbous, not me."

"Yes, but you said humpbacked, remember?"

"OK Puss, geography is what the world looks like, different mountains and oceans and things like that. Bee as in spelling bee, you know, when you have to spell the word right or you don't get any more tries."

"Yup, we had one last year. I know what that is."

The next day we followed 299 through the Trinity Wilderness, passing through Whiskeytown and Weaverville and Burnt Ranch, all the way to Arcata. On the way, Ceil said that the word sounded like Arcadia, and she imagined big forests and the ocean and the long journey in Longfellow's *Evangeline*. She said she read it in the eighth grade.

"This is the forest primeval, the murmuring pines and the hemlocks," I said. "That's all I know."

"I remember his name was Gabriel," Ceil said. "It was such a sad story. They never found each other."

When we got to Arcata, we drove through Humboldt State College and Ceil said it didn't look like Chico but it was still a college town and she wanted to find another spot for the night. We drove along the water to Bayview and across the bridge to Samoa where we parked and watched the breakers rolling in. We stayed in a motel with glass doors and a balcony that looked out on the ocean, and in the morning we drove by redwood trees that blocked the view from the road where the lumber companies were cutting every day. We had lunch in Blue Lake on 299 and stayed Saturday night in Big Bar in a motel surrounded by larch trees. On Sunday we ate the "Lumberjack's Breakfast," sausages and potatoes and eggs and pancakes, and drove through small towns in the Trinity Wilderness. We stopped at the Whiskeytown Dam and then drove all the way to Chico. Lying in bed that night, Ceil said that she wanted to go to the Donner Pass the following weekend. She wanted to see where they finally had to eat each other to stay alive. I had no idea what was going on in her mind, but I said, "Sure, we'll do it."

That week Ceil returned to work at the fabric store, and the following weekend we drove to Lincoln and Auburn and followed U.S. 80 to Emigrant Gap where we walked around and read about the Donner Party. At a tourist stop, Ceil bought three books about the Donners and the Reeds and read all evening in bed in the motel where we stayed in Baxter. Every once in a while she would make a remark and then she would be absorbed in her reading again.

"Tamsen Donner was an incredible woman," she said. Later, she said, "There was actually a man named 'Wolfinger' who killed children and made a stew with their little bodies. My God!"

The following week I got a phone call at the office from Bob Kaiser, Braden's press secretary. Braden wanted me to join his campaign.

"'Get Armature in this campaign,' that's what Tom said to me on the bus ride back to Oceanside," Kaiser said. "You're only part time at the college, you can get someone to cover your classes. If we win this, Tom can be the next governor of California and you can run the whole education department in Sacramento."

"Yeah, that's great," I said, "That's all I ever wanted to do, run an education department in the worst city to live in the United States except Bakersfield."

"Think about it, Bill, we'll fly you down here, pay all your expenses. Take a little time off from your family, you've got nothing to lose."

"That's what you think. I've got a little girl and a wife who's been sick. What do I know about running a lieutenant governor campaign?"

"You're a natural. No one knows anything about running a political campaign, we just do what has to be done. You think it up as you go along. What do you say? You did a great job in Chico with the bus tour. Tom was really impressed."

"Tell him I'm flattered."

"Can I tell him you're thinking about it?"

"Of course, who wouldn't be thinking about it, but I can't do it. Tell him when he comes to Chico as governor, I'll set it up for him."

"I don't think he'll take no for an answer, Bill."

"Yeah he will, just tell him."

"Will you get mad at me if I call you again next week?"

"Make it a month," I laughed.

Chapter Fifty-Five

I DIDN'T TELL CEIL about Kaiser's phone call for two weeks, until one late evening in the middle of the week. Ceil and I were watching a rerun of *Naked City* and the phone rang. Late evening phone calls always unnerved me, but it was only Bill Weeks, calling from his home in Palo Alto, inviting me to join him and Tom Braden on a plane ride the next afternoon. Tom was going to meet with the Shasta, Trinity, and Lassen County Democratic committees and Bill was going to fly him in his Cessna to Redding. Did I want to go? They'd pick me up and drop me off in Chico late the next night.

"Sure," I said.

"I'm going to pick up Tom in Oceanside tomorrow morning," Bill said, "and we're going to be in Sacramento for lunch. I don't know when we'll leave Sacramento for Chico, but it'll be at least late afternoon and I'll call you just before we take off. How's that?"

The next day I called Ceil at the store after Bill called me, and she came home and picked me up. Driving north on Cohasset, Ceil kidded me about being a sucker for an airplane ride.

"I wouldn't get in one of those planes for love nor money," she said.

"I must be doing it for love," I said.

"For Tom Braden?" she said.

"For me, for adventure, I don't know. I've always wanted to fly in one of those little planes. Once when I was a kid, we took my grandmother to the White Mountains in New Hampshire, and we stayed in two little cabins in a place called Twin Mountain where there was a small biplane and a pilot giving rides for ten dollars. I asked my father two or three times and I think he wanted to let me do it, because he didn't get mad at me. It would have been a lot of money for him then. It was 1940, just before the war. He was making about $6000 a year as the General Foreman of building 63 at the River Works plant of the General Electric in Lynn, the good old G.E. I remember it was a cool summer night and the mountains were clear and the sun was going down, but it was still light. We were served rancid peas in the meal at the motel restaurant that night. When my mother told the waitress, she thanked my mother politely, and everyone laughed about it when the waitress went back to the kitchen.

When Ceil and I arrived at the airport, I turned left on Airpark and pulled in next to the small terminal on Invader Street. We sat in the car and waited and talked. Ceil was curious about Braden and I told her he was the editor of the *Oceanside Blade Tribune* and a friend of Jack and Jackie Kennedy.

"You mean a close friend?"

"I don't know how close. Weeks told me he knew them. That's all I know. He said Tom is running for office because of his friendship with Jack Kennedy."

We didn't see the plane until it taxied to within thirty yards of the terminal, facing us. There was a slight wind from the north and Bill landed straight into it. I kissed Ceil and told her I'd be back late and hustled across the tarmac and stepped through the open door of the plane. When I got inside I asked Bill why he turned off the motor: "I wasn't going to walk into it."

"The main reason being that I didn't know that, and I thought you might want to introduce us to your wife, but since you are keeping her all to yourself, we'll have to postpone that to a later occasion."

Bill taxied out and got up speed heading to the north end of the runway and we were in the air. On the way, Braden wanted to know what I knew about the Democrats in the northern county and I didn't know anything about them. I knew Shirley and Wally Custerfield from Whiskeytown but that's all.

"I know her," Tom said. "She's in Sacramento with Fred Dutton and the boys all the time. She set up this meeting for me, but officially she's for Anderson. She's a close friend of Anderson's wife."

We had to shout to hear each other, so we didn't talk. Bill took us up to 7000 feet and kept it there. Off to the right I could see Clear Lake and the Caribou Peak Wilderness, and up ahead Mount Lassen which still had snow at 10,000 feet.

"There she is," Bill said and pointed.

"Lassen," Braden said.

I nodded to show that I heard.

"She must have been some mountain before she blew one third of her top off," Bill said.

We were in the air forty minutes. We could see Lassen until the last hundred feet of our landing. Bill headed straight in and we touched down and taxied over to two waiting cars.

Bill cut the motor and we got out. Shirley and Wally Custerfield and two other people waited until we walked away from the plane and then walked toward us. Everybody shook hands and made small talk. Braden rode in Shirley and Wally Custerfield's car, and Bill and I went with Trudy Stircum and Hank Buckfield. Trudy drove. She was a small woman probably in her mid forties who spoke slowly and chewed gum without opening her mouth. She wore a light brown roughened leather jacket with a thin braid of strip tassels on the back line of her shoulders. She was the chairman of the Trinity County Democratic Central Committee. She introduced Hank as the treasurer of her committee. She called it "my committee" but she said "my" neutrally. Hank asked us how the flight was. He said he was never in one of them itty-bitty planes.

"How do you get 'em down if that propeller conks out?" he asked, turning around in the front seat and looking back and forth between Bill and me.

"Look for the closest field and glide her down," Bill said.

"You mean air field or any old field?" Hank said, turning back around.

"Airfields are easier on the tires," Bill said, "You got a valid point there."

"I heard once, you're sposed to land an airplane nose into the wind even if it's blowing real bad, is that a fact?" Hank turned back around again and looked at Bill.

"That's a fact," Bill said.

Hank thought about it for awhile. "Probably not too much fun flip flopping around in any wind," he said, not turning around. "I flew to San Diego once in one of them big critturs and it sure was smooth."

"Tell us about Tom Braden," Trudy said. "We've got six or seven minutes before we get to where we're going. I know you're his friends and I don't mean to be poking around personal stuff, but he doesn't sound like a troublemaker to me. So what's Glenn Anderson done to him?"

"That strikes me as the perfect leadoff question for Tom," Bill said. "I'm only his friend and his pilot, so I'm probably not your best source in that department. Tom's got his list, and it doesn't stay in his pocket."

"Well, we've got a few people for him, committee and club people. Most people are committed to Anderson, so we had to pretty much scratch around among the regulars who want to be fair to good Democrats. The trouble here's probably the trouble you run into everywhere, all the whiners and bitchers who are against everything and everybody end up supporting people like Braden who take on incumbents."

"Well, that's the same match that we've been striking around the state," Bill said.

"I hear there are some good people backing him," Trudy said, "You don't get people like Paul Fay and Alan Becker behind you unless you've got something."

"We hear he's got Kirk Douglas and Burt Lancaster padding the kitty," Hank said, turning around.

"Political movie stars are like big guns in a war," Trudy said, turning into a restaurant parking lot, "it's your 105 howitzer against your 88 mm. cannon. People like Fay and Becker are different."

The restaurant, "Rancho Madera," sported a large red, green, and yellow neon sign of a giant saguaro cactus. Yucca in large wooden tubs lined the cement walkway with embedded sandstone and rock crystals. On the way in, Trudy waited for the Custerfields and Tom to join us, and we went in behind Tom. Hank was with Bill and me at the end of the line and he said, "Trudy's father was a brigadier general in World War II in Europe."

Shirley Custerfield led Tom and the group into a spacious back room with about thirty people sitting around a center buffet with untouched mounds of chicken and potato salad, various platters of cold ham and roast beef, and when the waitress saw us enter she signaled to the kitchen and a waiter brought out a steaming leg of lamb. The bar was doing a good show, and Shirley was all business introducing Tom and giving everyone a half-hour to eat and the rest of the evening to ask questions. Tom said he was willing to skip the eating and get to the questions while everyone else ate but that was shouted down. Bill filled a plate for Tom who held it as he followed Shirley. She introduced him to the northern county Democratic leaders.

Later, as Tom answered questions and gave his pitch, he talked straight, and he convinced a lot of people that he would make a good lieutenant governor and a good anything else he could get elected to. If Tom could have talked to everyone in California he could have gotten elected to any office in the state. The problem was that he was talking to thirty people at a time in places like Redding and Chico. No one needed to be told that Braden would make a good U.S. Senator, and no one who ever heard him talk ever mentioned it, except among themselves. He talked straight about big labor and education and extremism and conservation, and he talked about imagination and courage. He said that he repudiated Hugh Burns and the California Senate Un-American Activities committee and their attack on Chancellor Clark Kerr and the University of California, and that when he asked Glenn Anderson to also repudiate Hugh Burns, Anderson's state campaign chairman, Anderson said that Braden was "ungrateful." When it was over, the crowd gave him a standing ovation.

On the way back to the airport, Hank said, "That Braden sure can talk. When he talked about Jack Kennedy, I got chilly all over."

No one said anything. Trudy worked the gum in the back of her jaw, then gave it a rest. After a while she said, "Everyone there will vote for him, and he'll lose all three counties by two to one. I'll take odds." She had no takers.

I called Ceil from a pay phone at the dark airstrip, and we took off in the single engine Cessna, Bill curving us around as we gained altitude, then headed south. Bill again pointed to the snow-topped Lassen in the moonlight, and we nodded. In twenty minutes we passed over the lights of Red Bluff, and fifteen minutes later we saw the lights of Chico. Bill circled and descended for the landing. It was late and the field was dark. Bill touched down smoothly and taxied toward the north side of the dark terminal building and I could see Ceil's car. She flashed her lights twice.

This time, Bill and Tom got out of the plane and came over to meet Ceil. Tom thanked her for borrowing me for the evening, and Bill told her that he understood why I was reluctant to join up with a couple of renegades like him and Tom for a long flight into a wholly unredeemable way of life. Tom thanked me for coming with him and said that he'd be in touch with me. They walked back to the plane and Ceil and I stayed to watch them taxi out into the runway and take off into the dark. Puss was asleep in the back seat, and never woke as we drove home, even when I carried her into the house and tucked her in her bed.

Chapter Fifty-Six

THAT SPRING PUSS SPOTTED the Jolly Green Giant on vegetable can labels in the Safeway food market, and he became for Puss and Boots California's patron saint and benefactor. He was Mr. Macgregor and Peter Rabbit and Mrs. Tiggywinkle all dressed in green, and he mythically strode between valleys and sat on mountain ranges and engendered the growing season with magical hormones and human gestures and friendly animal powers. He put the vitamins in asparagus and green beans and iceberg lettuce, and he healed eastern immigrants of pneumonia; he energized little girl soccer players and ballet dancers, and he colored the foothills of the Sierras green green green. When Puss and I went to the Chico dump on Saturday mornings, she pointed out his handiwork as she looked across and canvassed the fields. She told me that the secret seeds were in the ground, Greenie had been at work in the night. She said that the daisies were coming, that the ice plants of summer were in the planning stage, and that the cottonwoods were conspiring to fill the air with white fluff in the fall. Puss was an authority on the Jolly Green giant.

"You should see if he would consider a run for U.S. Senator," I said.

"Daddy, don't be silly," Puss said, "he doesn't care about frivolous things."

"Frivolous, huh? Where'd you get that word? Never mind, don't answer, I think I know."

Puss looked away, trying not to smile.

"Maybe I ought to tell that to Mr. Braden, my friend who's running for lieutenant governor."

"Why should he run after an old governor, especially a new tenant one?"

"Puss, love, tell me something. Do you know what a tenant is?"

"It's someone who lives in a tent. And a new tenant governor is a governor who lives in a new tent. Am I right?"

"Well, yes and no. In principle, you're dead right. In practice, however, it's slightly different. OK, let me see. Actually, it's not new tenant, it's *lu* tenant, it's spelled l i e u t e n a n t and pronounced *loo tenant*. It means assistant. So a lieutenant governor is an assistant governor."

"What does he assist?"

"He assists the governor."

"You mean like he brings him coffee and bagels?"

"No, the governor's secretaries do that. He assists the governor by presiding in the senate. The senate is the place in Sacramento where the people we elect to do our business, sit. Wait—don't ask me what that means. It's very complicated. It's for big people to think about. When you're eighteen you can vote and by then you'll know."

"I understand, daddy, I'm not supposed to know about these things. Can I ask you one question?"

"*May* you."

"May I ask you one question?"

"Shoot."

"Why do the people we elect go to Sacramento to sit down?"

"Last question, right?"

"OK."

It was our turn to back up to the unloading area. Puss got in the back seat and pushed the trash bags to me as I stood at the open hatchback and tugged at the bags and threw them into the piles of waste. Driving along the exit lane with the windows down, Puss asked me if I liked the smell at the dump.

"I never thought much about it," I said. "It's the way dumps smell."

"It's better than pig manure," Puss said. "Remember that field we had to go by when we went to the dump back east?"

I started to answer when she asked me, "Did you go to the dump with your father when you were little, daddy?"

"That was a long time ago. Let me peer into the mysterious mists of the past and see if I can see our old dump."

"What do you see?"

"Don't distract me, I'm peering."

"Come on, dad. You're teasing."

"You know, Puss, for a second I couldn't remember. We actually didn't have dumps for people to use then, just for big companies and the town trash trucks. The town sent trucks around every week and people would pile stuff in front of their houses. Everyone had metal ash barrels to store the ashes from their burned coal. And the garbage men would come around and pick up people's garbage from closed buckets in back yards. Some people kept their bucket under the ground and if you stepped on the handle the top would lift open. We kept our garbage in a bucket hanging on a board nailed to the end of our garage. If you left the bucket on the ground, dogs would come and knock the bucket over and the garbage would smell-up the place."

"What would the garbage men do with the garbage?"

"They fed it to pigs. We had a piggery near our house and in the summer the smell was bad. Some days we couldn't go out of the house."

"Pigs really stink, don't they daddy?"

We were passing through the long sloping fields on the western outskirts of Chico, and the air was clear and warm with the windows of the car rolled down. Saturday mornings had always been special for me, even as a child. Everything seemed fresh and new, and time seemed to stop. As we passed several live oaks clustered on a small ridge off to our left, I remembered one Saturday morning when my father let me ride in his new wooden trailer that he bought from Tom Baldwin, our next door neighbor, and he drove slowly down Cleveland Avenue with me riding alone in the trailer, holding on to the green wooden side board, and I waved to Kent and Buddy Frederikson in front of Maes's house. I don't remember where we were going, but I was completely happy.

Puss's ballet lesson at 10:45 was an hour away, and I had the urge to drive out by the airport and watch the morning plane come in from Red Bluff, but I kept going toward home. Ceil had said she had a stomachache. It was Eartha's turn to drive the girls to ballet class. Maybe Ceil would feel better and might want to take a walk in the park. That afternoon we would visit the Jaeckels. Tonight would be the first demolition derby of the season at the Silver Dollar Fairgrounds.

"Actually," I said, "pigs don't naturally stink. They're very clean animals."

"How come they stink?"

"Smell, honey, smell. They smell bad only when the farmers don't keep them clean. You'd smell too if you had to wallow around in garbage that was rotting."

"Ugh! What's 'wallow,' daddy?"

"Oh, just walk around in. I knew a friend who had three pigs once."

"I know that story, daddy, the three little pigs. One went to market…"

"No, not that story, these pigs were real pigs. My friend Irving Bergstrom owned them. His father bought them up at a farm in southern Vermont, in a little town called Bellows Falls. They were just little piglets, and Irving's father put up a fence in his yard where they lived next to the woods, and there was a big rock in the middle of the fenced area, and when the pigs grew up they played king of the rock."

"Daddy, that's not a true story."

"Yeah, it really is, that's what I'm telling you. Pigs are very intelligent. I knew another family once, they lived on an island off the down-east coast of Maine, and they had an old pig, and they used to play hide and seek with it. I'm really not kidding. I knew those people. They lived in an old trailer on Swan's Island in Blue Hill Bay, and the father drove the school bus. I really knew them. This pig was a big old pig and they played hide and seek with it. And the pig even played a joke on them once when they were playing. Instead of hiding, the big old pig went in the living room and lay down on the couch."

"I'm going to tell mom that you're telling me stories again if you don't tell me that it's not a story."

"No, I'm telling you, scout's honor, that's a true story. Pigs are clean and they're smart."

We were driving down Cohasset. We passed East Avenue, then Manzanita, and Cohasset became Mangrove. "One more thing," I said. Puss looked at me suspiciously.

"No, this is on the level. I'm just reminding you of the question you asked me when we pulled into the dump. It's not a big deal. I am the world's greatest Saturday morning father and I leave no Saturday morning questions unanswered."

"I don't remember," Puss said, "and even if I did you'd just joke with me, but it's OK, daddy, I won't tell mom. I like going to the dump with you. I'm just glad there isn't any pig manure in Chico."

"You asked me why we elect people to sit in Sacramento."

"I remember now. OK, why?"

We pulled into the driveway of our house and I turned off the ignition. "It's just a figure of speech. It means sitting at a desk and doing the work of the government. If we say 'sit in Washington,' it means sitting in one of the desks in the House of Representatives or the Senate. Same in Sacramento. You understand?"

"It sounds reasonable to me, daddy. But I still don't believe it about the pigs being the cleanest animals and playing king of the rock, and hide and seek. I'm only ten. Will you cross your heart that those stories are true?"

"I will. Cross my heart, they are true, they are true, they are true. Some day I will explain to you about mystery and paradox."

Puss looked at me and waited. "I can't remember all your words, daddy," she said.

"Some day," I said. "Not today. Let's go in and see how your mother is."

"OK," she said, and we got out of the car and entered our Saturday morning home in Chico, California.

Chapter Fifty-Seven

WILSHIRE BOULEVARD STRETCHES ALL the way from Santa Monica Bay to downtown Los Angeles, and Braden Headquarters faced east, half a mile north of Watts, in a low-rise undeveloped business area with no trees and a lot of sun. Arthur Wexler, a tax lawyer in his late twenties, had chosen a small back room with two windows and a desk with two telephones and bare walls from which to direct the Braden campaign. He kept his desk clear except for a stack of lists of names, some of which had check marks beside them with dollar amounts next to the check marks. Arthur wore horn-rimmed glasses, and he had perfected a pleasantly wry manner of speaking which accommodated his cynicism and reinforced his willingness to receive negative news without apparent emotion. Although I could sense that it was all the same to him whether or not I added my scintillating and dynamic presence to the campaign, he was respectful of my arrival and introduced me to the ten or so workers at their desks in the large room with an all-glass front. It looked as if the room formerly contained several new car models at one time, and several large indoor-outdoor mats covered the cement floor. My desk was in the corner, although I probably, according to Wexler, wouldn't be spending much time at a desk in the office. He had an idea for a specific project for me to go to work on, if it suited me, after I got my apartment settled.

"What kind of a title do you want, anyway?" he asked me after he had introduced me to the head secretary seated with her back to the front tinted glass and told me that she used to be engaged to Sandy Koufax.

"Why do I need a title?" I asked as we walked back to his cubicle in the back.

"You don't, I was just curious."

"We can skip the title," I said.

"I called someone I know about an apartment for you while you're in town, two rooms in a condominium type arrangement about a mile from here, not a bad setting, and the place is a two floor job surrounding a swimming pool, and you're on the ground floor. You better go over and take a look at it and I can wrap up the deal and we can talk about what you might get to work on. OK?"

"Wheels?" I had taken a cab from the airport.

"Tom wants you to drive a car that's been sitting in his back yard for a couple years. He says it works OK, or it did the last time he drove it. It's out back. I had a kid drive it up from Oceanside this morning and he said it was C+, whatever that means. It's some kind of a foreign car, British I think. Try it anyway. If it's really bad, we'll rent you something."

I found the apartment after driving around in the vicinity of a street called Cactus Way for about twenty minutes, and the landlord, a middle-age woman who seemed bored with her job, asked me how many sets of keys I wanted. When I said "one" she took a deep breath and looked out across the pool and fished a key out of the pocket in her apron and plopped it in my open palm. "Try it and see if it works," she said, and I did, and it did. She asked me for $78 for the first week and I told her it had already been taken care of and she sighed and looked as if she wished she hadn't given me the key, and said, "I'll check at the office and get back to you."

I can't remember anything about the apartment except that it smelled like Head and Shoulders shampoo and the phone worked. I didn't spend ten nights there during the next two months. It was not a place that I could tuck myself in and fall asleep reading a book. There were several good looking women who spent their days lying on the chaise lounges around the pool, looking bored. I never saw them in the water. I remember that it was always sunny and hot and that no one ever spoke to anyone else, around the pool or in the parking lot. I swam in the pool twice in the next two months and both times felt that I shouldn't be disturbing the placid waters.

Inside, I called Ceil at work and we talked for twenty minutes before she said she had to go. "I don't know why I'm here," I said, I'd rather be in Chico with you."

"Buck up, Bill, you just got there, give it a chance. Guess what Eartha told me yesterday morning? Curling's wife filed for divorce. She said it would be in the paper tonight. I wonder how she found out?"

"Bannister, who else? I was just beginning to miss Chico. Good old Curling. Camion will have something to say, you can bet on it."

"I saw Mr. Camion this morning, Bill, he said to tell you that he has good news and he wanted to know when you're coming home. I told him about your arrangement with the college."

"You're OK?"

"I'm fine. I haven't had any really bad pains since you left. When I saw Dr. Grogan yesterday he said it might be my gall bladder, and he's going to give me some tests. He says that the pain is in that area and he can't think it could be anything else."

Back in Wexler's office, he asked me how the car ran.

"It starts hard but it starts. Seems OK."

Wexler said he wanted me to meet Tom at the plane tonight, and that after dinner with Stewart Alsop at the Beverly Wilshire, Weeks would fly us to Oceanside for two days.

"You're coming?"

"I don't travel with the candidate. One of your jobs in the next month will be to make the candidate happy, spend time with him, meet him at the airport when he comes back from trips. Tom likes you. We're kicking around this idea for a possible fly-tour of the state during the last three days of the campaign, and maybe you're the one to do it. Palmieri thinks so. You made a good impression on him at his house last Sunday. Weeks thinks so too, although he thinks he's still flying planes behind the Iron Curtain, and everything in the air appeals to him."

"Sounds fine to me."

"By the way, we're calling you the State Organizational Director in case you want to put it on your vita. Tom and Joan are coming in on Western at 6:30, terminal C, gate 23.

I met Tom and Joan at gate 23 and we met Weeks at the Beverly Wilshire a half hour before Stewart Alsop. The chef offered a special that evening on a certain kind of small pan-fried fish, and everyone ordered it except me. I ordered the salmon.

Chapter Fifty-Eight

I FLEW BACK TO Chico through Sacramento on Tuesday nights to teach my two Wednesday classes. The only time I spent with Ceil was a couple hours on Tuesday and Wednesday nights. I saw Puss before she went to school on Wednesday and Thursday mornings. I took the nine a.m. flight from Chico to Sacramento on Thursday.

When Ceil met me at the airport my first Tuesday return in late May, the sun was setting and the Coastal Range was clear against the yellow and orange sky. Flying from Sacramento to the northern valley, the plane

189

seemed weightless above the dark green Sutter Buttes and the silver rice fields. Touching down, the sun was disappearing behind the mountains, and when I approached Ceil walking toward me from the car she said that Puss was in bed but could stay awake until I kissed her goodnight, and that Gina Garrison was staying with her until we got home, so we had to hurry.

Driving along Cohasset Road, I told her about meeting Stewart Alsop on my first day in Los Angeles, then the cocktail reception with Braden and Arthur Schlesinger Jr. in the Crystal Room of the Fairmont Hotel in San Francisco, strategy meetings with Braden's staff back in Los Angeles, and my assignment to set up a two day fly tour of five cities with Braden and Robert Vaughn, the TV Man from U.N.C.L.E., a couple days before the June election. Ceil told me that Curling's wife had disappeared with their little girl when he got an injunction to take her on weekends, and that Camion called to tell me that Jake Toothacher was not going to seek re-election next year and the county central committee wanted me to run. Camion wanted to see me. Also, Luke called to tell me that a student named Karo was in the county jail in Oroville on a drug charge, and that Eartha had gone to San Francisco for the weekend to meet her mother again, leaving the children with Terry Garrison. "Who's Lloyd Hand?" she said.

"I heard it when I was in the airport in Sacramento waiting for my connection," I said. "He's Lyndon Johnson's chief of protocol in the White House. Lyndon has sent him out here to split the Braden/Anderson vote."

"Is that bad for Braden?"

"It's over. Braden can't win with a three way split. Tom knew it was coming."

"Will he quit now?"

"It was only an outside chance to beat Anderson anyway. His staff in Los Angeles wants him to run for Senator next year against Tom Kuchel. The hell with all of it for now, I'm home. I don't even know what I'm doing down there. I miss you like hell, Ceil. I wish you could come with me on this thing."

At home, Puss begged me to read one chapter of *Prince Valiant* before she went to sleep. "We finished that book, remember?"

"But it's my favorite, please daddy, please?"

I read a chapter and it was forty-five minutes past her bedtime but she stayed awake until I finished. By the time I kissed her and put out her light, however, she was asleep.

Ceil and I sat out on the patio under the grape arbor until midnight. The new leaves over our head were yellow green, and the brown vines had almost disappeared.

"How are you feeling?" I said.

"Some days I feel terrific," she said, "other days not so hot. I've stayed at work every day, and I only had bad pains once. If it is the gall bladder, Dr. Grogan says he'll take it out when I'm stronger."

"How will he know?"

"The pains, I guess. If they keep up, he'll do an exploratory operation."

"Maybe we should go to San Francisco and see a specialist."

We talked like that for an hour and then we sat quietly for a long time, holding hands across two redwood lounge chairs.

"How about a glass of white wine?" I said.

"You're on," she said. "I put a bottle of Emerald Dry in the fridge."

I uncorked the bottle and poured the wine and we sat quietly.

A little later, Ceil said, "It's nice here Bill, in the yard, in the valley, in the spring, in the night, all the neighbors in bed, Puss in bed, safe, happy. It's nice."

"It is nice. I'm crazy to be running around. I don't know about this running for office stuff. I've been doing a lot of thinking about it. It's not much of a life. All the people in it are looking for something. They all think they'll get what they're looking for if their man wins, but in the meantime they're getting something else. There's a lot of money around, and great food, and available women."

"Should I be worried about the women?"

"No."

"Tell me about it."

"There isn't anything to tell really. There probably isn't any more screwing than there is anywhere else, it just seems like it because everything is so intense and there are so many Los Angeles glamour people around. And with them, the best workers are serious even when they're famous. I met Milton Berle's wife last week, and she's really terrific. Spends all day on the phone in San Francisco. She's really good. I didn't even know she was Berle's wife until I'd spent a whole afternoon and half an evening with her. She's raised a lot of money for Tom. We all went for Irish coffee at a place near the waterfront the other night. People work their heads off all day, late into the evening, then they blow off steam. They have to, everything is so intense. But it's not conducive to family life, I can tell you that."

"I can't believe that Braden has eight kids."

"They've got a nanny for them. It's not ideal."

"Nothing is."

"No, nothing is."

We sat without talking.

"Did you ever wonder what we'll be doing in two years, or five years, or ten years," Ceil said. "Or where we'll be, what Puss will be doing?"

"I probably should, but I can't get past tomorrow's classes, tomorrow's plane ride, tomorrow's fishing trip. I just seem to end up doing what the Jolly Green Giant tells me to."

"How does he tell you?"

"He just winks, and points with his green finger, and I look, and then I'm fishing in the river, and then I'm walking in an almond orchard, and then I'm driving an old British car from Los Angeles to Santa Barbara, and in a few weeks I'm going to be flying around California in a single engine plane with the Man from U.N.C.L.E."

"The Jolly Green Giant, huh?"

"Or Puff the magic dragon, or Jack Kennedy's ghost. Maybe this campaign can help me get something out of my system, Ceil. When it's over, I think I'll stay put, right here in Chico for awhile with you and Puss. Maybe I'm just talking through my hat."

"I don't care where you go, Bill, as long as Puss and I can be with you. I don't mean trailing you around, I mean just so that the three of us are together in the big stuff. I'm content. Even having this cancer has made me content. When these pains go away, I will feel as if I have been cleansed of something big, some big shadow inside me. Something else inside me will grow and replace that shadow. This is all happy talk, Bill, this isn't morbid, we're here together under the stars, and it's warm tonight, and it's spring."

"Pretty soon it will be June, Ceil, and this thing will be over."

"Why do you feel so guilty about it, Bill? Enjoy it. We're not going anywhere, we're going to be right here. One more month. You can be good to yourself for another month, can't you?"

"I'll try," I said.

Chapter Fifty-Nine

AND I DID TRY. The next day I met my classes and held office hours, dropped in on Joe Bugwell just to show my face and let him share vicariously in the hi-jinks of state politics, went to the Exchange Club luncheon with Larry, talked my way into the Oroville jail to visit Karo for twenty minutes, ran into Pat Henry on the campus and chatted and laughed with him for ten minutes about Jake Toothacher's health, took Ceil and Puss to dinner at Dayton Four Corners, called Camion several times unsuccessfully, and sat out on the patio again with Ceil until one o'clock in the morning. I told her that Larry was way down and that he had told me he was planning to go back east and work with his brother, that he'd gotten the idea that the only way he'd get back with Eartha and the kids was to go back where they lived before.

"If she won't live with him here, why would she go back east to live with him," Ceil said.

"Larry still thinks she's only homesick."

"It's a funny way to show it. I should think he'd be so angry at her that he wouldn't want her."

"He wants the kids. I don't think he yet believes that she's screwing Bannister."

"If he doesn't know it, he's the only one in Chico."

"He knows it, he just doesn't believe it."

"They're getting closer to something bad. He better accept it pretty soon or she'll force him to walk in on it, and Larry could hurt somebody. He's just setting himself up. She's spending all Larry's money on baby sitters and he doesn't even know it. If he goes back east he's just playing into her hands. I like Eartha a lot, she's bouncey and fun, and she's generous-hearted, she'd do anything for her kids, but she's heading for a hell of a lot of trouble with that Bannister creep."

"I hate to go in," I said.

"Don't. You can sleep on the plane."

"I accept."

"I've got some French vanilla ice cream in the fridge and we can have some of Jaeckel's almonds on it."

"Do it. When I was a kid we used to say 'This is the nuts' when we really liked something. I don't think kids say that any more."

"When I bring out the almonds you can really say it."

I arrived in Los Angeles at one p.m. the next day on Western Airlines out of Sacramento, and by one-thirty I was driving Tom's yellow car on highway 5 toward 101 and Santa Barbara. After Ventura, I drove along the ocean the rest of the way. I passed the billboard that said *Braden Braden Braden*. Tom's campaign director Vic Palmieri wanted those billboards all over the state, but this was the only one the campaign could afford. The last week of the campaign, he also got up three billboards that said *GUTS!*

I fished my directions from my shirt pocket and made my way to #87 Gaucho Lane and one Helen Wainscot, who had sounded pleasant and enthusiastic on the phone. She would be my first contact in Santa Barbara for the Braden skydiving entourage that would fall from the heavens at the Santa Barbara airport on June 5.

I knocked and she opened, and after the first ten minutes I stopped noticing details, and she turned out to be OK. Her boyfriend was a detail, along with a few dishes in the sink, magazines on the baby's empty high chair, a large philodendron plant hanging in front of the window by the kitchen table.

"You're really going to bring sky divers to our airport," she said, "Wow, all that and Robert Vaughn too."

I explained that Braden had been in the O.S.S. during the Second World War and parachuted behind enemy lines, and we were going to build up the courage and daring image, etc, and try to show how much pizazz it takes to run against an incumbent who's soft on McCarthyism. "Four skydivers will jump with red flares trailing from their feet, and we'll pass out toy parachutes to the kids and Robert Vaughn and Braden will make speeches and we'll be on our way. So we need a flatbed truck with some moveable stairs, and we'll need it set up near a fence to keep the crowd back and the best spot to make the crowd look big on TV."

Helen read my list and we talked about flyers, radio advertising, whatever we could get on the local TV station, and we'd probably have to buy an ad in the local newspaper. I was listing our other landings in Sacramento, Fresno, Bakersfield, and Irvine when the baby woke up in another room and Helen went to get it. In a couple minutes, I was out the door.

On the outskirts of Ventura, I parked and watched the surf for awhile, thinking of Ceil, then drove to Wilshire in south Los Angeles and pulled into a surf and turf restaurant, unconvinced that I was doing the right thing.

The sirloin steak was fair and the lobster tail was tough and I got tired of a cigar. I drove to my apartment by the vacant, lighted swimming pool and showered and went to bed.

Chapter Sixty

BRADEN'S OLD YELLOW BRITISH car broke down twice within the next four days, once in Huntington Beach a mile from the backyard airport there, and once in Altadena where Wexler needed a speaker at a Woman's Tea for Braden. By this time I was calling it "Braden's old yellow…" and everyone in the Los Angeles Headquarters would finish the phrase with "British car," as if they were chanting a song title. Weeks called it "Gatsby's Car," and when someone in the office asked him why, he said "It's yellow, isn't it—and that became the standard explanation for anything that went wrong in the campaign. When the handbills didn't arrive from the printer for a "spontaneous" volleyball game on a Saturday morning at Playa del Ray beach, accusations and blame were cut off with "It's yellow, isn't it?" Later in the campaign, when the motor on Weeks' plane cut out with Braden himself at the controls at 10,000 feet, Weeks replied to a reporter who questioned him in the airport when they landed, "It's yellow, isn't it?" and Kaiser had to explain to the press that it was a campaign joke.

The first time the car died, it needed a new starter and had to be towed, so I called headquarters to locate Weeks but nobody knew where he was, and Tom and Joan were going to a private fund raiser in Westwood Village, which meant Weeks would be somewhere else. I called his wife Sue in Palo Alto and she said he was staying at the Beverly Wilshire Hotel, so I left a message there that I was stranded with no car and needed to be entertained for the night and would call back every half hour. The third time I called there was a message for me to meet him for dinner at Sardi's at seven and he had tickets for the Hollywood Bowl and Robert Goulet.

Later that night, with Weeks and a Braden worker named Georgeanne, we edged down the stairs with the crowd in the Hollywood Bowl after the performance. When three heavy-set, open leather jacket types with wide belts and topaz stones in the buckles and around the rims of their boots, shoved Georgeanne aside, she fell onto an old man sitting in his seat. Bill instantaneously grabbed the pusher by the shoulder and spun him around and said, "Apologize, now!" Georgeanne got up off the old man and made gestures of apology and told Bill she was fine and everything was OK and it was an accident, tugging at Bill's arm to not make an incident, she wasn't hurt. The two other leather jackets had come back up the few steps they had descended, and surrounded Bill, who slowly lifted his hand from the first man's shoulder and extended his finger toward the man's face and said softly, "Now!" as he brought his hand back to his chest in the flat, palm down position, and he took a step back, pushing me aside. All this happened within a couple of seconds. The crowd had spread, sensing something unpleasant about to happen. The pusher looked down at Bill's feet as Bill stepped out of his loafers. Without a word, Bill dipped his forehead an inch and blinked, widening his eyes at the offender as if to emphasize that time was running out. The leather jacket on the left who also saw Bill remove his shoes, elbowed the man in the middle and said to Bill, "He's sorry," and the middleman nodded and they backed away and walked down the steps, not looking back.

The second time the car died, I was within two hundred yards of an elegant home with tropical trees and shrubbery in Altadena. I had been drafted without warning to make a speech. I was due back for a staff meeting with Wexler, and we were going out afterward for Italian food. I had just walked out on post-tea cocktails with a small group of wealthy Braden supporters, and when the car broke down, I had second thoughts about trying to get back quickly to Los Angeles.

I knew that Weeks was flying Braden to Sacramento from the Los Angeles airport around five-thirty and that I had plenty of time. I walked back to the tropical mansion, called a tow truck and told them where the car was and to haul it to Braden Headquarters on Wilshire. I called Weeks' hotel and left a message that I was coming and to save me room on the plane. After several drinks, a young rich couple who lived next door offered to drive me to the airport. The young rich couple had never been interested in politics before, and they were very neat and clean. He looked like someone about to book passage on the Titanic, and she could have doubled as a Breck girl. When they dropped me off, they hoped that we would meet again during the campaign.

"Maybe in the governor's mansion in a couple years," he said. "I know Braden is going to be governor someday."

That night Weeks and I flew over the Donner Pass to Reno. There was moonlight snow beneath us and the night was clear. Then the desert was dark. Braden and Kaiser were hooked into Sacramento for the evening and two breakfast meetings in the morning. Bill and I saw Debbie Reynolds in the late show at the Diamond Lil and then went to Harrah's. It was my first time in Reno and I played blackjack for an hour and lost thirty dollars. Bill won $120 at the roulette wheel. I was enjoying the girls in green who came around with drinks, taking orders on the house. I watched Bill throw the dice and wandered over to the slot machines. I played one machine for twenty minutes and had two small jackpots, but was still losing. Bill came over and said, "Let me show you something."

It was after three a.m. No one else was playing the machines that lined the walls of two rooms. "We better get a couple buckets," he said, and we each cashed a paper twenty for silver dollars. The seventh dollar in the first machine rolled three plums for twelve dollars. Bill moved to the second machine and put in fourteen dollars before it rolled to three clowns for nine. The third machine rolled all cherries on the fourth dollar, for forty-one dollars. One after another, we took turns and played all eighty-five machines, leaving each one with three identical fruit showing. At six-thirty a.m., only the jackpot machines were un-played, and we made only one mistake. I put in only one dollar in the jackpot machine instead of filling all five slots. When the machine hit on the eighteenth silver dollar, it paid only $134. Altogether, we made $486.

Flying back over the Donner Pass the following noontime, Bill asked,

"Guess how much we lost because I wasn't thinking at that jackpot machine last night."

"I don't know, how much?"

"$3800."

"Imagine the first guy in there this morning with all those identical lines of grapes and bananas and oranges?"

At the Sacramento airport, we were a half-hour late to meet Braden and Kaiser, and Braden was grumpy. "I got a long day, Bill. Where'd you guys go, anyhow? I called the Townehill House at midnight to see if you wanted a nightcap, but you hadn't even checked in."

"Shall we tell him?" Weeks asked me.

"No, let's not tell him. He'll never forgive us for losing the money."

"What money?" Braden said.

"You don't want to know, Tom," I said.

"I know I don't want to know but tell me anyway. I'm sick of talking politics. Fuck the lieutenant governorship. Tell me about last night."

"We lost some money at Harrah's."

"Harrah's, for Christ's sake. No wonder I couldn't find you at Townehill House. You bastards. I haven't had any fun for two months and you guys sneak off the first five minutes I'm out of sight. How much did you lose?"

"$3800."

"We don't have that fucking much money left in this campaign. It's a good thing you didn't have the kitty with you. How much did you really lose?"

We strung him along a little while longer and then told him. It cheered him up.

We were cruising about one eighty at seven thousand feet and Braden wanted to fly the plane. We were on the way to Los Angeles for a Braden dinner with contributors in Redondo Beach, then Weeks and I were going back to Oceanside with Tom for an overnight at his house on the beach. Tom took the controls and wanted to take her up higher so Bill told him to do it. At ten thousand feet Tom started down again slowly and the engine stopped. I thought he was fooling around with the ignition but Bill reached down casually and started studying the map. Kaiser said "Cut the shit and start the motor, Tom."

"She glides beautifully, Bill," Tom said. "Have you found a place?"

"We've got at least twenty minutes, maybe longer."

"What do you mean, that's what we've got?" Kaiser said. "Quit fucking around. I'm not used to this stuff. I wasn't in any fucking OSS or CIA. Just get us down."

"Calm down, Kaiser," Tom said. "This thing lands as nicely on a glide as it does on power."

Bill called the inland naval air station in Lemoore in the San Joachin

Valley, they cleared us, and we were on the ground in twenty-five minutes. Kaiser got to the nearest phone and called in to the AP wire services that Tom Braden and his small party narrowly missed death this afternoon when their engine failed at ten thousand feet. I called Ceil at work so she wouldn't hear it first on the evening news. A ground mechanic asked Bill how long since he'd changed the spark plugs and Bill confessed that he hadn't thought about spark plugs lately. The mechanic said he didn't have any new ones but he had six used ones that were better than the ones we had so Bill asked him to put them in. We flew to Los Angeles for a staff meeting, left Kaiser there with Wexler and Vic Palmieri and several others, and flew to Oceanside. Bill landed the plane in the dark on a small airstrip 2000 feet long. I never felt the wheels touch the ground.

"You're getting better, Weeks," Tom said.

The British nanny was waiting in Tom's Chrysler, and within twenty minutes we were swimming in the ocean in front of Tom's house. Tom swam a long way out in the water alone, and then swam back. The water was warm and the low waves shone white in the moonlight.

On the beach level of the house, sliding glass doors opened on a long room with leather furniture and a billiard table, and built into the wall an open liquor cabinet with cut-glass decanters and various shapes of brandy snifters and whiskey glasses. A telephone was fastened to the wall beside a dumb waiter. Tom pressed a button beside the phone and a bell inside the dumb waiter rang. Within a minute, the door of the dumb waiter opened on frosted bottles of British and Canadian ale, and frosted glasses on cork place-squares. Tom sent the dumb waiter back and it came down two minutes later with German potato salad, hot sliced ham with raisins, huge black olives and artichoke hearts, and cold lobster tails and mayonnaise.

"Ask Tandy if she can fit into that dumb waiter," Bill said.

"Go for another swim, Weeks," Braden said. He had a sense of humor about everything except sex.

"Just because you've got eight kids, Braden, doesn't mean the rest of the world has been shut off," Weeks said, grinning. "Don't you have any champagne splits, for Christ's sake? What kind of a place are you running here, anyway?"

Tom was the most unguarded I'd seen him since I met him in Chico when he arrived with the bus full of kids. We talked for a long time that night with the glass doors open on the beach and the sounds of the ocean a few yards away. Tom talked about his friendship with Jack and Jacqueline, and the night he met the plane from Dallas with Jack's body. Jacqueline talked with Tom for eight hours in the White House later that night. He said most of it was personal and he didn't think he'd ever talk about it. But that was a long time ago and Jackie herself is dead now. Maybe Tom has even forgotten much of what she said. One thing though, has stayed with me, and I remember it exactly as he quoted her. She had said that Jack was hit from the front with the first bullet and his head jerked back, then he was hit from the back, and his brains splashed onto her dress, "and he looked at me with that beautiful quizzical look, and died."

Chapter Sixty-One

I CALLED CEIL AND PUSS every other night at dinner-time, from Fresno and Bakersfield and San Francisco, in whatever city I found myself during the next weeks. I missed Puss and Boots' two spring soccer games and her spring ballet recital, and she and I made a deal that I would take her and Semantha to the San Francisco ballet when the campaign was over on June 7. Ceil and I planned a trip to Lake Tahoe if Eartha would take Puss for a few days. I got Camion on the phone once but he sounded distant and seemed to ramble. When I mentioned Toothacher's health, he said that there was nothing wrong with Toothacher that cancer couldn't kill. I called Pat and asked him what was wrong with Camion. He said, "You mean aside from being himself?" Then Pat said he hadn't seen him in Chico for weeks. I called John and he said that Karo was out of jail but that Lee Martin was picked up for possession. John was always good for the college gossip.

That afternoon I went to three novelty shops in Los Angeles before I found the paper parachutes. The owner said he could get me two thousand at twenty-one cents apiece if I put fifty bucks down. I charged it with Alan Becker's voucher for the Braden campaign.

The fly tour was shaping up. Wexler scheduled a private reception with Robert Vaughn for the evening before we took off. I read in the paper that Allen Dulles had left Washington and was in San Francisco for a meeting with the South Korean ambassador, and Weeks disappeared from the campaign for six days. Tom and Joan began flying commercial airliners. Wexler had me meeting their planes and driving them to their room at the Beverly Wilshire. Tom wrote me a letter near the end of May that said, "Of all the people I have known in this thing we're in, the doughtiest and the brightest and the best is you. Thank you for sticking with me. I want you to know that I'll stick with you."

The next week, Wexler asked me to write a draft of a letter to be sent to CDC Democrats, and I took two days off to do it. I sat by the pool at my apartment, in the sun, and wrote for a couple hours. Then I dove in the pool and sat under an orange and green umbrella, perched on the end of a strung-rubber chaise lounge, and wrote for another hour. Then I went inside and took a nap, and when I woke up I felt the sunburn on my back and neck, and stayed inside and wrote for two more hours.

Wexler read it and said that some of it was OK maybe, but it needed work. Two days later I had five paragraphs that ended with Braden being like John Kennedy, and Wexler approved it, but after the mailing I knew it lacked something.

Three days before the fly tour, with everything set and committees in place, airports cleared for crowds, security arranged, Robert Vaughn groomed for takeoff in the single engine plane, Wexler called me into his little back room and said he was calling it off. A new Field poll had just been published that said Tom was running third behind Anderson and Lloyd Hand, Lyndon's stand-in to split the vote. Wexler didn't think we could get enough publicity during the last days of the campaign with the fly tour. I blew up. Arthur listened but was unconvinced. I asked him what the hell else he was going to do with Braden the last two days of the campaign, walk him on the beach, take him to the zoo? Wexler said he wasn't sure, he wasn't making a final decision, he just wanted me to know that he might cancel if something better came up.

When I exploded, Arthur was composed and said that I should be calm, that he would let me know. I told him to do that, and to make it quick because as soon as he canceled, my ass would be on the first plane to Chico. I went back to the big room with my desk and the other workers, and no one looked at me, busy at their own desks. They obviously had overheard my response. When they saw me smiling, however, they all smiled, and we all pretended that nothing had happened. I called Weeks at home in Palo Alto and he hadn't heard anything, but said that if Wexler was folding in the bananas at this late date, he was not only trifling with Bill's own schedule, but it didn't say much for Wexler's attitude toward Mr. Vaughn's schedule.

"Do you feel like calling him?" I asked.

"No, but you can let it be known down there, especially in the little back office, that if Wexler cancels the fly tour at this late date, he'd be advised to negotiate the cancellation through someone other than himself if he wants to avoid some unpleasantness. By the way, you might want to advise the candidate himself of Wexler's late flirtation with insanity."

I left with Tandy a simple message for Braden at Oceanside, that I was awaiting instructions whether to proceed to San Francisco for the pre-tour evening with Robert Vaughn or to proceed to Chico with my best wishes to all for the rest of the campaign.

I took Sue Broccoli, Koufax's ex-girlfriend, or the other way around, to my surf and turf restaurant for lunch. She told me that I yelled a lot but I was a good worker. At first I felt patronized, but I ended up taking it as a compliment. She apparently had been that straightforward with Koufax. When we got back, there was a note on my desk to see Arthur in the back room. I went into his office and stood and looked at him. Arthur was on the phone and he motioned for me to sit down. I did so, and took a deep breath and stared at the lists on his desk. He hung up and smiled at me. I did not smile back.

"OK, we just have to stay calm. Everything's just as planned, nothing's been changed. The fly tour is on. I've got some ideas that might attract more press, but Braden says we can't let down the people involved. So that you know, all that stuff before was part of the process, and there's a lot of give and take in these things. Nothing was ever in real jeopardy. I presume you're going up to San Francisco for tonight."

"Arthur, you're full of shit, but I accept your apology."

That night I met Robert Vaughn in a quiet upstairs front room of a small restaurant with a balcony and lots of large potted plants. He was drinking coffee with Joan Braden among several crowded tables with single-lighted candles, and a violinist and pianist quietly playing "Tea for Two." Vaughn was pleasantly formal and committed to Tom Braden. He said he was doing a doctorate in political science at the University of Southern California. I liked him.

The following day, when Vaughn made his first speech on a flatbed truck parked in a corner of the Sacramento airport, he was intent and respectful of schedule. We had climbed the moveable stairs to the flatbed truck as the crowd was being directed to watch the plane with the skydivers climbing in circles to 20,000 feet. Then three tiny specks appeared, then red smoke trailing from one, yellow smoke from another, until the four parachutes opened and the chutists guided their ballooning silk tents toward the crowd, landing fifteen feet from the restraining fence. Everyone applauded and the skydivers gathered their stuff and waved and tromped toward the parking lot near where their own plane would taxi in.

Volunteers from the Sacramento area worked the crowd with Braden leaflets and toy parachutes for the kids. I introduced Robert Vaughn, who talked for three or four minutes, and he introduced Braden who talked for five minutes. There were five hundred people in the crowd and two TV cameramen. We boarded Weeks' plane and took off for Fresno where we went through the same routine. There were three hundred people in the crowd and one TV cameraman. It was a hot June day and the sun was high.

In the air between Fresno and Bakersfield we talked about the small crowds.

"There were two TV cameramen in Sacramento and one mobile TV truck in Fresno," Joan said. "This is a statewide campaign."

Kaiser said it was enough. Joan Braden was dissatisfied. "They'll show the puny crowds on TV," she said.

"They'll show Tom and Vaughn too," Kaiser protested. "It's the best we can get."

"We need to be where there are more people," Joan said.

"Where the hell would that be?" Tom said.

"Almost anywhere," Joan said under her breath.

Weeks pointed to the ground a mile below. "There's a crowd down there," he said. "It looks like an auto show of some sort."

We all looked out the window of the plane. There were a hundred parked cars at a small airstrip in the middle of nowhere, and a large crowd. "It looks like an antique car show," Kaiser said.

"There's about five thousand people there," Joan said. Why don't we land and Tom can talk to them."

"There's about five hundred people there and we've got people waiting for us in Bakersfield right now," I said.

"What do you think, Weeks?" Tom said. "Could you land there?"

"If you want to land there, Tom, I can land there," Bill said.

"We're running a half hour late for Bakersfield," I said. "Don't even think about it, Bill."

"It's not a half bad idea," Joan said, and sat down in the fifth seat, upset with me.

"It's a crazy idea," I said. "We've got a crowd of people waiting for us in Bakersfield."

It was quiet in the plane until we landed. I had been right but hot-headed, and I knew I was in trouble with Joan Braden. Later that night in the bar of the Ramada Inn at the Bakersfield airport, Weeks said, "Hell, Armature, it could be worse, the spark plugs could have given out again and we would have *had* to stage an impromptu rally at that Republican antique car rally."

"It would have had to be a Republican rally, wouldn't it? Why didn't you say that to Joan?"

"What do you think I am, crazy? You were doing just fine."

"I'm cooked with her."

"Just because she secretly vowed that she'll never have anything to do with you for the rest of her life doesn't mean you're cooked. She might not put out a hit on you, you never know."

"Maybe I can straighten it out with her at the last night party in Oceanside. I'll tell her I over-reacted."

Bill laughed. "You do that," he said, "I know she'll take you back with open arms." He grinned at me and shook his head as if I was finished.

Our last stop was in Santa Barbara the next day and it was set for three o'clock. We left Huntington Beach with plenty of time and arrived early. Helen and her boyfriend had a crowd of two people waiting for us when Bill landed and Tom and Joan and Vaughn went into the small terminal to stay out of the sun until the skydivers began their climb. The field was the smallest field we'd landed on so far, and when we landed we cleared several houses on the north side of the field by thirty feet. Bill said to me, "Come on, I want to watch this. Those guys will never get their plane in here unless they crash-land it."

Fifteen minutes later their plane made a pass over the field without landing, then made another pass without landing and started climbing.

"They're going to jump, so we better get Tom. I don't think they'll bring that plane in here, so we're going to have those four smoke eaters on our hands tonight. I can't fit them in my plane."

When Tom got to the flatbed truck he went up to the fence and greeted the crowd of one hundred and fifty people. One middle-aged man wearing a Dodgers baseball cap asked him where he'd been for the last half-hour. Tom said he had been inside resting, and the man told him he'd given up a whole day to come out here and talk to him and instead of coming out and talking to the people, Braden hid inside for a half hour. Braden told him he hadn't been hiding, he was taking a half hour break in the middle of an exhausting schedule. The fellow said he had some issues he wanted to talk about before he voted for Braden. Braden said he was right here and he could talk.

"There's no time. I came out here for nothing."

Kaiser was standing next to Tom, pointing to the four specks high in the sky. "They're coming down," he said.

"What do you want to talk about?" Braden said to the troubled man. "I'm not hiding and I'm not ducking issues. Let's talk."

"How can I talk when there's sky divers jumping down on top of us? The hell with it, I'll vote for Anderson."

"Thanks a lot," Tom said. "What about Lloyd Hand, why don't you vote for him?"

"Who's he?" the man said.

I urged Tom to get up on the flatbed truck. The divers were coming down around us, the red smoke trailing from the jets on their ankles. A few minutes later while Tom was speaking to the small crowd, Weeks nudged me with his elbow and lifted his head toward the north end of the field. The parachutist's plane was coming in for a landing. Bill was shaking his head. The pilot passed up his first approach and made a wide circle, then came in again on the same approach path. This time as he cleared the last house at the edge of the field he cut his engine and the plane dropped nicely onto the short strip of tarmac and coasted to a stop several feet from the fence at the south end of the field. "He'll never get her up with that crew," Bill said.

When the crowd dispersed, I talked with Helen and her boyfriend while Bill talked with the skydivers' pilot. Tom tried to find the disgruntled issues man but he had disappeared. Vaughn and Joan were inside the terminal, Kaiser was talking to the two mobile TV guys packing up their gear. I paid the skydivers their $2500 fee. Their pilot came over and said the only chance he had to get the plane out was to strip it. The divers said they'd stay with their gear in Santa Barbara for the night, and ship it in the morning with a driver and a van as long as Bill could fly them to Modesto. They wanted to party tonight. Bill said he'd fly his own people to Los Angeles and come back before dark in order to get an early start. He had to bring people from San Francisco for the Oceanside party. The divers stripped everything not bolted down and we watched the empty plane clear the houses at the south end of the field by ten feet.

Chapter Sixty-Two

THAT NIGHT BILL AND I flew back and landed again on the tiny airstrip, and we stayed at the same nearby motel with the skydivers. They offered to buy us dinner, and we had a few drinks together, and they wanted to go in the pool. The restaurant manager said that the pool was closed because there was no lifeguard. The divers insisted and the manager went and got another manager.

"I thought this guy was the manager," the short stocky skydiver called Red said.

"He's the assistant manager," the manager said.

"We want to go swimming," the tall, skinny skydiver called Leon said. "Have you got any more managers back there we can negotiate with?"

"No, there are no more managers. There is only the owner and he is out of town and I am the manager and I speak for him. The house rule is that there is no swimming after six o'clock."

"But we hadn't had our dinner at six o'clock," the skydiver called Rafe said. He was also tall and skinny but he had wide hips and he had red hair and one of his ears was half missing.

The skydivers talked among themselves and sat down and ordered a round of beers. The manager said, "Thank you for your understanding, gentlemen," and disappeared. The skydivers got up and Red said to us, "Don't go away if you want to see some fun." They came back from their room in their bathing suits and jumped in the pool. The managers came out, but by the time they were poolside, the skydivers were leaving the pool. They were more intimidating in their bathing suits than they were in their casual clothes. They all had protruding bellies, but they also showed multiple muscular development and tattoos for emphasis. They convinced the managers that they would settle down, and Bill and I left them to get a cab to go into town. Before doing so, however, Bill led me to the motel front desk and requested a room change. When I asked him why he said, "You'll see later tonight."

We got the cab and asked the driver to take us to the nearest bowlerdrome. I wanted to show Bill how to bowl candlepins, but there were only duck pin lanes. We bowled four strings and walked to a bar with a white cobblestone parking lot and redwood-lined gardens of saguaro cactus plants. When we got back to our motel at eleven thirty, the pool was empty and there wasn't anyone around except the bartender who was reading at one end of the bar and his assistant leaning against the cash register, sipping a drink. Neon lights from the overhead-flashing-oil-rig-in-the-process-of-gushing reflected in the pool. The bartenders said they hadn't seen the skydivers for a couple hours. Bill and I went to bed.

In about twenty minutes, there were whooping noises from the skydivers back in the pool, this time with their clothes on. Bill and I watched from the window of our new room. One of the bartenders picked up a telephone, said something into the receiver and put it down. Within two minutes, the assistant manager was standing poolside, protesting in loud tones. Leon climbed out and pushed the assistant manager into the pool. When he stood up in four feet of water and attempted to climb the metal ladder, Rafe grabbed him back and they played with him like a rag doll for several minutes. He said that he would call the manager and the police.

"You'll WHAT?" Red said, pushing his head under water. When he sputtered to the surface, Red said, "I CAN'T HEAR YOU!" and pushed him under again. When he came up the third time he was crying. "Tell you what," Red said. "We got some partying to do yet, and we don't want any trouble. We got some friends that also might want a swim tonight, so you just hold your water about this swimming business. We been putting out a few dollars at this place, and we aint botherin anyone except maybe you. You notice that them bartenders over there is still dry. RIGHT, BOYS?" One of the bartenders lifted a glass as if to toast the swimmers, and the other swung his bar towel in a circle in the air. "Now you just stop your cryin and settle down, y'hear? Are you listenin?"

The assistant manager wiped his eyes and nose with his sleeve and nodded.

"This here is just a friendly party. You go and get yourself dried off and come on back here like a civilized person and have a drink with us, on us. And as soon as we have a little swim with our new friends in room #26 over there, we'll be right quiet. Y'hear?"

The manager nodded.

"I don't hear nuthin," Red said.

"Yes," the assistant manager cleared his throat and made a real sound.

"OK, now there's only one thing else. If you go back there and call the police, we'll go off quietly to your little Santa Barbara jail, but I'm telling you on my great aunt Delilah's three black Bibles, we'll be back here some night two months or a year from now, and I swear to God we'll drown you. You believe me or you think I'm bluffing?"

The assistant manager looked at Red.

"Which is it?" Red said. "You got about one second left."

"Yes," the assistant manager.

"Yes what, goddam it?"

"Yes I believe you."

"Is it a deal?"

"Yes."

The assistant manager disappeared.

Red and Larry got out of the pool and went to #26, our former room, and knocked on the door.

"Jesus, I hope they didn't rent it," I said.

They knocked and shouted, and finally gave it up, and we could see the assistant manager in a dry set of clothes, sitting at a table with the four skydivers, dripping wet, drinking beers from the bottles. The assistant manager was drinking a tall cocktail of some sort.

The following night, Bill and I were in Oceanside at Tom's house. Tom told Bill that it took him all afternoon to get Joan to relent and let me come to the party. I went to her in the kitchen and told her I was sorry for being abrupt with her in the airplane, and she was almost gracious.

It was a warm June evening and the campaign was over. I called Ceil and Puss and told them I'd be home early afternoon the next day. Paul Fay and Alan Becker and Kaiser and I sat on the beach and talked about the campaign.

We all knew that Tom didn't have a chance but we were glad we had gotten into the campaign and we really believed that it was a beginning for Tom's life in statewide politics. Each of us told stories about things that happened to us, and I mostly listened. They told about friends who betrayed Tom, about contributors who pledged and refused to pay, others who didn't have much money but who gave a thousand dollars.

Finally I told them how I was stranded in Sacramento one Tuesday after the last plane had left for Chico, and hitched a ride with a government plane transporting a prisoner to the state penitentiary in Redding. The prisoner was a sixteen-year old skinny little Mexican boy who had killed somebody. He was handcuffed feet and wrists in the seat behind me, and he trembled during the flight. The pilot was a government agent who had a .45 caliber on his hip and a pump shotgun next to him in the cockpit. It started to rain as we were taking off and soon we were in a lightning storm. Then it hailed, and round pellets of ice banged and popped on the windows. When he dropped me off in Chico, the sun was shining.

We drifted back to the party and I asked Tandy if she would find me a bathing suit. She said, "Sure," and I ate some hors d'oeuvres. A half-hour later, I reminded her about the bathing suit and she smiled and said, "I thought you were kidding." I said no I wanted to go for a swim, and she said could I wait five more minutes and she'd meet me in the children's bedroom at the east end of the house. There was a bathing suit there. I went to the east bedroom and looked out the large window to the sea. It was very calm and I wasn't sure why I was here. I was glad to be going home the day after tomorrow, voting day.

Tandy came in quietly and closed the door behind her and locked it. She went to a long set of drawers built into the wall and opened several and fished various particles of clothing out of each, but no bathing suit. She looked at me quizzically and then opened some more drawers. No bathing suit. Then she smiled and said, "You really want a bathing suit, don't you?"

I nodded, feeling foolish.

"I just remembered, it's in another room," and she unlocked the door and went across the hall and came back with one of Tom's bathing suits.

I swam for twenty minutes, thinking about Tandy grinning at me as she handed me the bathing suit, walked slowly back through the shallow surf, and fell asleep on the beach.

When I awoke, I wondered why I had decided to stay tomorrow for the election. I had voted by absentee ballot.

Chapter Sixty-Three

THE NEXT MORNING I went for a long walk on the beach and was back in sight of the Braden house when I saw one of the Braden kids waving her arms, cross-fashion, and then jogging toward me. I couldn't tell if it was Tom junior, the oldest boy, or Cindy, the oldest girl, they both had shoulder length hair. When she got closer I could see that it was Cindy. She was a runner and was practicing her slow loping stride. I waved to her so she could see that she had my attention, and we advanced toward each other. She ran gangly and easy, as if she were making no imprints in the dry morning sand, but as she approached I could see the light trail of mussed prints from the balls of her small feet, and she was carrying a small white paper bag in her right hand.

"My dad sent me to find you, Mr. Armature, and tell you you have an important phone call from your wife," she said evenly, "and I brought you this Danish. Mr. Becker went out and got about a million of them a little while ago." I took the bag and carried it back to the house, and Cindy continued running down the beach, her long red hair glistening in the California morning sun. I never saw her again, but she became an expert runner, and a few years later when Tom was doing Firing Line in Washington with Pat Buchanan, Cindy was winning school championships in Virginia. I was on my way to the airport in Irvine before she got back to the house.

The phone call had been from Virginia Garrison, our next door neighbor, and when I called the number she had left, the operator at Enloe Hospital answered. I gave my name and she said, "Yes Mr. Armature, your wife was admitted a couple hours ago. Dr. Grogan has left a message here that if you called I should tell you that Mrs. Armature is resting comfortably and he hopes that you can be here with her as soon as possible."

I called information and got the fabric store number on the Esplanade. Bill Richards told me that Ceil collapsed a half hour after she arrived at work this morning.

I called the hospital from San Francisco and again from Sacramento, but they wouldn't let me talk to Ceil, and I left a message at Pat's to find Larry and tell him to meet the 3:30 plane from Sacramento.

Bill had flown me to the Los Angeles airport. Both Bill and the landscape beneath the plane had seemed as inorganic as a colored map that had dropped from a table and lay open on the floor. My swim in the warm ocean last evening, my walk on the beach this morning, the sky divers free-falling for two miles trailing canisters of red and yellow smoke, the motel assistant manager crying in the pool two nights ago, it all happened in another century, another life. I watched the airstrips one after another looming up from below, and felt the restraining brakes on the speed of the planes, and I moved from one plane to another, and then I saw the jagged, unearthly Sutter Buttes, and I was walking across the tarmac toward Larry leaning against the side of his car.

Inside the hospital I found Ceil in a private room, sleeping. The head nurse at the station paged Dr. Grogan through the intercom. I sat next to Ceil's bed and waited. The nurse came in after fifteen minutes and said that he was coming from his office.

Ceil was hooked up to intravenous bottles of clear liquid, one crawling from her arm and one from her nose. I watched occasional bubbles move through the tubes. The television set was on but it was mute. I picked up the clicker on the bedside table and turned it off. I had been sitting on the end of Ceil's bed, and I got up and sat in the easy chair halfway across the room. Through the window I could see high green shrubbery and the corner of the hospital where the left east wing began. I was annoyed that it was taking so long. Several minutes passed. Another nurse came in and said Dr.Grogan would be right along.

"When?" I asked.

"Any minute now."

A nurse's aid came in with a bouquet of cut flowers in a white vase. "Some nice person sent these," she said.

"Is there a card?"

"Right here," she said, pulling it from its triangular plastic holder.

"Open it, please,"

"It says 'Love, Larry.'"

"Thanks." Good old Larry.

Dr. Grogan came in and held out his hand. "I'm glad you're here," he said.

"So am I. What's going on? What happened?"

"Ceil had an abdominal attack while at work and was admitted feeling great duress."

"They said she passed out."

"I believe she was unconscious for a period of time."

"What do you mean 'duress'? You mean she was in a lot of pain?"

"Yes. She's sedated now, and seems to be comfortable."

"What's wrong with her, Dr. Grogan? She's been feeling crappy all spring, ever since the treatments. Is she OK or isn't she? She said you said it might be her gall bladder. How serious is that?"

"It depends on whether it is the gall bladder and how bad it is. I think the time has come for us to go in and find out. I had hoped that we wouldn't have to do an exploratory because it's such an insult to the system and she's been through a stressful time with the radioactivity."

"So you're going to do it?"

"Yes, I've already scheduled it."

"For when?"

"Friday morning at ten."

"Who's going to do it?"

"I am, with Dr. Kazen."

"When will she wake up?"

"In a few hours maybe, I'm not sure. The Demerol didn't give her any relief and I gave her a quarter grain of morphine."

"May I bring our daughter in to see her?"

"Of course."

I drove home and picked up Puss and brought her back to Ceil's hospital room. Virginia Garrison had intercepted Puss as she came in the yard from school and had left me a note. Puss started to cry when she saw the tubes in Ceil's nose, but I told her it was helping and she quieted down. I asked her if she wanted the TV on but she didn't. The nurse's aid came in and saw Puss and asked her if she wanted some strawberry jello, and she looked at me to see if it was OK, and I nodded and she said "Yes please." The aid brought it in a couple minutes and Puss finished it and put the dish and spoon on the bedside stand.

Ceil was still asleep when a nurse brought dinner. I told her to tell Ceil we would be right back if she woke up, and I took Puss to Andy's on the corner of 3rd and Salem for a hamburger and a glass of milk. She asked me if she had to eat the pickle and I shook my head. I didn't eat.

Back in Ceil's hospital room, she was awake and lifted her hand and smiled when we came in. Puss hugged her and tears came into Ceil's eyes. I kissed her despite the tape around her nose and she squeezed my hand.

"Are you in pain?" I asked her.

"I'm on cloud nine," she said, "I feel very wonderful." She said 'very wonderful' slowly.

"You'll become a dope addict," I said.

"I hope so," she said.

Puss looked at me and I said, "We're joking."

"I was in the store this morning and I felt these awful pains and then I was here," she said. "They've gone away."

"Morphine helps," I said.

"Is that what they gave me? It sure is good stuff. Let's buy some and keep it on hand."

"I'll get a pound of it on the way home."

"Did you see Dr. Grogan?"

"He's going to operate Friday morning. He still thinks it's the gall bladder."

"I don't care what it is, I just want them to find it."

"They'll find it mommy, I know they will," Puss said, and Ceil held out her arms to her again and they hugged.

"How did your friend Braden do today? I didn't even get the chance to vote. I was going over to the polls on my lunch break."

"I have no idea. We'll know as soon as the polls close at seven. They brought you dinner, but it must be stone cold. Shall I have them send another?"

"I'd gag if I had to eat. Just stay here with me and if the pains come back I'll have some more morphine and fall asleep. Then you can take Puss home and watch the returns.

And that's how it went. The pains came at eight and Ceil said they were bad and I got the nurse who brought Ceil two tablets of Demerol in a little plastic cup.

"Demerol didn't work this morning, why do you think it will work now?" I said.

"I can't give her anything stronger unless the doctor puts it on the chart," the nurse said.

In a half-hour, the pains were still bad. Ceil bit her lip and held on to the side of the bed when they came in spasms. I told the nurse to call Grogan now or I would. She said she'd call him immediately. In five minutes the head nurse came in and gave Ceil a needle with the morphine. I was holding her hand and she was squeezing so tightly that her fingernails almost pierced my palm. Then she said, "Oh god, it's working," and her hand went limp. Then a few minutes later she closed her eyes and said, "I'm leaving you for awhile," and she was asleep.

I read to Puss the last chapter of *Prince Valiant* for the fifth time and watched the election returns on Channel Six. Braden ran second behind Anderson with 28% of the vote. Lloyd Hand got 20 %. Braden conceded at 11:00 p.m. with Joan beside him at the podium in the Beverly Wilshire Hotel where four hundred Braden supporters cheered. Tom made a good speech. The crowd kept cheering and applauding.

"I want to clap for you," he said. "I don't know of any peacetime test that shows the mettle of men or women as does a political campaign. Your resolution, your courage, your grace have been tested, and all of you passed the test. I am proud of you and grateful."

As he talked, the camera panned the group standing on the platform in a semi-circle around him, and all my friends were there, Wexler, Weeks, Palmieri, Kaiser, and Alan Becker. Robert Vaughn was there next to Kirk

Douglas and Burt Lancaster. At the end, Tom refused to blame the late entry of Lloyd Hand for his defeat. "The steadfastness you have shown," he said, "has given us the energy with which we will light up the California political scene for years to come."

Ronald Reagan won the Republican nomination for governor over Sam Christopher, with 70% of the vote. Pat Brown won the Democratic nomination over Sam Yorty, the mayor of Los Angeles, with 58% of the vote. I called Larry to invite him over for a drink but he didn't answer. I went for a walk, staying close to the house, to the corner and back, for an hour. Inside the house I found a bottle of Gewurztraumiener that Ceil was chilling for us, and took it to the patio. I remember later finding another bottle of wine in the cabinet in the dining room, and opening it. I fell asleep in the living room with the TV on, and got up from the chair at five in the morning and went to bed. The bottle was a Sonoma Valley white burgundy, and I found it in the morning on the floor next to the chair, one third full, uncorked.

After Puss went to school I drove to the Oaks and read the *Chronicle* over coffee. I had hoped to run into Jaeckel or Camion or Pat, but after three cups of coffee, no one I knew had come into the coffee shop. Arthur Hoppe in the *Chronicle* wrote that Braden had done his best in a hopeless cause. He said that on election night when the returns came in, his supporters cried. He said that Braden had campaigned eighteen hours a day, seven days a week, for three months, "as honestly, as energetically as one can in politics." He had talked to Braden last night in Los Angeles when Braden knew it was over. I tore out the article because of one clause—"all in that world within itself." Then I read the ending again: "And as he talked, you suddenly realized how it must have been for him these past months, surrounded day in and out by the cheering crowds, the back slappers, the optimistic managers, the enthusiastic believers—all in that world within itself. And you realized how hard it is to lose, even in a hopeless cause."

Going out the door, I met Bannister coming in.

"Well Bill, I see where your man didn't do so bad," he said.

"No, he didn't do so badly, Ban, he only lost," I said.

"Seemed like a strong candidate. Good campaign to get involved in. As you know, I'm rather on the sidelines these days. I always think it's more interesting if one can play even a small role in an election. Buy you a cup of coffee?"

"Depends on how tough the opposition gets, Ban. Just had three cups, that's down and out for me. Thanks."

It was Wednesday. I had planned to stay in Oceanside and cut my classes. Maybe I would anyway. I drove to Johnson's Florist Shoppe on Memorial Way to buy flowers for Ceil.

Orchards *of* Almonds

Book Three
Western Massachusetts, Early March, 1968

Chapter Sixty-Four

I STRAPPED THE CARDBOARD box of food to the sled with an old belt, handed Puss the two sleeping bags and locked the car. One of the sleeping bags fitted into the open top of the food box and the other fitted in front of it. It had snowed the day before but the runners easily cut through the three inches of untouched snow as Puss tugged the sled behind her. The early afternoon air had the unmistakable smell of more snow, and the sky was overcast. The bottoms of our boots made perfect impressions in the moist snow.

"How far is it daddy?" she asked. "I don't mind, I'm just counting my steps, and maybe I can earn a walking badge for girl scouts."

"About a quarter of a mile, sweetheart. We'll be able to see it off to our left through the trees. How far do you have to go to earn a walking badge?"

"I don't know. Mrs. Pomeroy said we could do it this spring when the weather gets warm. She says we can walk up to the observation tower in Montague. She didn't say how far. I know it's in the book. Do you want to play guessing with me?"

"Sure. What do you want to guess?"

"How many steps till we see the cabin. Then we can tell clues and stuff after."

"You mean like why did we pick a certain number?"

"Uh huh. It has to be an educated guess, not just any old guess."

"Shouldn't we have some kind of a prize to give us an incentive to be educated in our guessing?"

"Yes, that's a good idea. What can be the prize? I've never been to the cabin but you were here last week with Dr. Month, so you suggest a good prize that has to do with the cabin."

"OK, let me think. Since we're going to do maple sugaring, how about if the winner gets to make the first maple snow cone."

"Oh good. That's a good prize, dad. What do you guess? How many steps till we see the cabin?"

"Your steps or my steps?"

"Yes, that's right. I forgot about that. I remembered when I was figuring about the... oh oh, I almost said my clues. You choose, your steps or my steps."

"Are you still counting while we're talking?"

"Yes, I still am. You have to concentrate, dad, make it be my steps, OK? I can do your steps, I have a way to do it, but we'll do my steps to make it easier for you."

"Whoa. OK. I'll start now and just estimate how far we've come and add it on. I say four hundred and fifty steps for you."

"I'll say seven hundred. Closest wins, OK?"

"OK."

The road leveled out and then went up a slight incline, and then went down a steep hill. A couple times Puss had to walk alongside the sled and hold it back. We walked for about fifteen minutes and came to a driveway that curved to the left and stopped. Through the trees about forty yards we could see a log cabin.

"Six hundred and eighty two, right to here," Puss said.

"I'm going to tell Mrs. Pomeroy that you should get a badge for judging, you little squirt, you beat me all hollow. You will get the first maple snow cone, probably around noon tomorrow if we can keep the fire going all night. It's a good thing Dr. Month and I drilled the taps last week. The buckets are probably overflowing. I hope not. It hasn't gone above freezing for the last three days, so maybe not."

"Is it above freezing now?"

It was last night, and it's right around freezing now."

I found the key to the door where Fred Month left it, under the end piece of wood on the right side of the pile. Inside, the cabin was bone-chilling, damp cold, and Puss brought in more heavy chunks as I was starting the stove fire with the kindling in the wood box.

"It's cold in here, dad, I can see my breath." She exhaled and a stream of frozen breath rose in the cold room.

When the inside fire was going good, we went outside and started another fire under the tin sink. I carried several overflowing buckets of maple sap that had been collecting on nearby trees, and the sap hissed as it hit the bottom of the heated tin sink. We collected thirty or more almost full buckets and filled the sink and four ten gallon buckets that we stored in the little hut next to the woodpile. As we were collecting the last of the buckets into the large white plastic containers, it started to snow.

The fire underneath the outside tin sink blazed, and the heat warmed our faces. We took off our gloves, wet and cold from the sap, and placed them on the side of the sink, then warmed our hands, holding them as close as we could get them to the fire without burning our jackets. Puss was perspiring and the hair around her forehead was wet and stringy.

"This is so fun, dad. Can we do this every spring vacation?"

"Sure, as long as Dr. Month lets us use his cabin, but I'm sure he will, that's why we call him Will."

"Come on dad, that's his name. Did you ask him about the pond?"

"That I did. Actually we drilled a bunch of holes last week with his power drill. They're frozen over again, but we can poke through with the crowbar. If we're lucky, we can catch some of his brookies through the ice."

"Can we have pancakes for supper?"

It was late afternoon, and I was hungry too, so I left Puss to mix the batter and showed her how to work the electric stove to heat the black skillet hanging on the wall over the sideboard to the right of the soapstone sink. I took the crowbar, threw some more wood on the outside fire and walked down to the pond. The snow was coming down a little harder. The first flakes had been large and wet, but now they were smaller, almost sleety. When they hit my face, it burned.

On the tiny pond, I took the aluminum shovel that Will Month hung on the side of an ash tree and pushed it back and forth, clearing several square yards, enough that I could see the iced-over holes. Last week Will and I drilled through five inches of ice, but the new ice covering the holes was only an inch and a half thick, and I was able to punch through easily with three or four plunges of the iron crowbar. As I cleared the third hole, Puss appeared with a bamboo basket of ice fishing traps.

"Don't you need these, dad?" she said, holding up the basket as she walked across the ice."

"Sure do babe, nice going. Thanks. But guess what, I forgot something important."

"What?"

"Bait. I was going to buy a couple dozen shiners in Greenfield before I picked you up at school, but it slipped my mind when I left Stop and Shop. We'll have to think fast. What's in our food box that we could use to catch a shivering trout?"

"All I can think of is marshmallows for the Some Mores."

"Hey, terrific. I actually saw a kid catch perch with marshmallows through the ice at Walden Pond in Concord a long time ago, before you were born."

Before the day was over, Puss and I had set three fishing traps with pieces of marshmallow for bait, eaten a supper of pancakes with home made sausages from Pekarski's farm in Deerfield, munched Cortland apples from Clarkdale in Old Deerfield, added split maple and ash logs to the outside fire, then sat down to read by the light of four kerosene lanterns placed together to form a square on the oak table in the large central room of the cabin. Every so often I could hear the sleet whipping against the windows.

"Book report?" I said, looking up from the *Boston Globe* sports page. She held up her thin paperback book so I could see the cover.

"*The Bee Man of Orn*. Mommy gave it to me our first year in California. It's my favorite story. I brought *Heidi* to read for my book report for Miss Puchaski, but I've been thinking of the Bee Man all day, and I always have him with me."

"Your mother read that story to me once a long time ago, did I ever tell you that?"

"Tell me."

"That's all. She brought it on our honeymoon as a gift for me, and on the second or third day she gave it to me, and when I opened it, she read it out loud to me."

"Do you remember it?"

"I remember the old guy had a great jaw in the illustrations, and the Fair Domain character struck me funny."

"Mommy's favorite was the Languid Youth who wanted to get energized."

"There was a Very Imp."

"Yes, and the Lord of the Fair Domain turned out to be a lousy lord."

"Your mother laughed and laughed when she read the part about the Junior Sorcerer doing research."

"I miss her awful bad."

"Me too, skeezix."

"I wish we didn't have to leave her in that cemetery in California. I wish we could have brought her back here with us. I've seen two cemeteries in Deerfield that she would like, I know."

"What we left in the ground in California wasn't your mother, Puss. Whenever we're together she's with us."

"She's the bee lady, daddy."

"That's what she is, Puss."

"Is that why you call me 'honey?'"

"It's what my father called me. I guess everyone's got a little bee man in them. How would you like to read the story to me, and then we bank the fires and blow out the lantern and listen to the storm outside and think of a trout nibbling a piece of marshmallow."

Puss read me the story and we put fresh blocks of wood on the fires and blew out the four lanterns and crawled into our sleeping bags spread on the tops of the bunks. In a few minutes I could hear Puss breathing in a deep sleep. I lay and listened to the wind blowing and I believed that snow was falling and the ice was forming again in the holes in the little pond below the cabin. I got up once in the night and added more wood to the inside fire.

The next morning, it was raining slightly. When I wakened, I could see the drops rolling down the outside of the window next to my bunk. The room was cold and damp, and the top of Puss's empty sleeping bag had been pushed half-open.

I found her outside blowing on the coals under the tin sink. She had placed small slivers of sticks from the bottom of the inside wood box on the burned-down coals from the night before. "That's the way to do it. Good morning, sunshine."

"Morning, daddy, I've almost got this one started. The sap boiled down great."

"I'll get the cabin warm and then we'll fill her up. By tomorrow morning we'll have a couple gallons of syrup."

With both fires going good, and after a breakfast of raisin bran and bananas, we filled two more ten gallon plastic pails from the tree buckets, and walked down to the little pond. Two of our fish traps were sprung but Puss lifted only empty hooks out of the water.

"Let's try sausage this time," I said, and handed Puss an uncooked sausage from my pocket. "Here's a knife, you can cut off a little piece."

"It ought to work, dad, it's got lint from your pocket all over it."

"No comments please, actually the lint is the special added ingredient that produces fish, especially brook trout in a light rain."

The traps set, we walked through the wet snow, following the little brook draining from the pond, to a marshy area with cattails at the edges.

"Look, daddy, there are pussy willows already."

Puss carefully broke off some stems for a bouquet, but as I broke off a couple of the cattails, the molasses-colored heads broke open and yellow wisps floated in the air. I waved my stems at Puss and the air filled with the cat seeds.

"Let's cut some more to go with the pussy willows," Puss said.

"OK, but we have to be careful not to break them."

I cut a cattail and handed it to Puss, who waited until I cut a second one.

"En garde!" she said, smacking the head of my cattail with hers. The brown heads broke into fluff, filling the air with the cottony seeds, sticking to our damp coats and faces as we stood there toe to toe knocking the cattail heads together.

As we walked back to the cabin and the outdoor steaming sink of boiling maple sap, the rain stopped. An hour later the sun came out and Puss went down to check the trout traps. When I went into the cabin to check the fire, it was too warm and I opened several windows. Back outside, I drank a glass of the cold sap from one of the big buckets. I heard Puss calling me and I stepped around the side of the cabin to see her running toward me with two fish dangling from a stick in her hand which was swinging as she ran. "Two," she yelled, "we got two, dad, we need some more sausage!"

She had broken off a thin Y branch from the alder bushes at the edge of the pond and strung the long stem through the trout gills. One was about nine inches long and the other one slightly smaller. "Did I do it right?" she asked.

"You sure did, pal," I said. "You just got us lunch."

We did the dishes together and swept out Will Month's cabin and headed up the hill towards our new home, each carrying a middle-sized container of maple syrup.

Chapter Sixty-Five

MORE THAN A YEAR and a half had passed since Ceil's funeral in early summer. Puss and I had flown from Chico in August and were living in a rented farmhouse on the banks of the Connecticut River in a western Massachusetts valley white-pocked in summer by shade tobacco fields. When the wind blew in the spring the topsoil swirled in brown clouds across the flat open spaces, but by June the farmers had covered the fields with white cloth spread four feet or so above the soil in order to grow the world's best cigar wrappers. By harvest time the tobacco spears punctured the cloth that soon hung in rags on the field poles and the connecting wires.

In the meantime Puss was back in school, being picked up by the long yellow and black bus that stopped each morning and afternoon on the road up the driveway from the side door of the farmhouse, its red STOP sign swinging out automatically from the rear as the bus slowed. She and Semantha exchanged letters often but Puss didn't share with me any news of Chico. I had found a temporary job writing advertising copy for a nearby plastics factory, and had put in my name for a teaching position at a community college nearby that was nestled at the base of a long hill that headed west on the Mohawk Trail out of a neighboring town called Greenfield.

Larry had met us at the plane in Boston when we arrived from San

Francisco. He was living in Brookfield, near Worcester, and supervising a development firm with his brother and brother-in-law, and they had made the contact for me with the plastics factory. From the first moment we both recognized in the other a reluctance approaching refusal to talk about our wives, and it wasn't until later that Larry told me the unfolding story of Eartha's California saga.

In the meantime I was concentrating on Puss's transition east and half-concentrating on my job when I received a call from Tom Braden in California in the middle of Robert Kennedy's run for the presidency. He had called me a week after our new family doctor at the Greenfield clinic, Will Month, had offered us the days in the sugaring season that we spent at his cabin in the woods outside Shelbourne Falls. Tom and John Siegenthaler, Robert Kennedy's administrative assistant in the Justice Department, were running Kennedy's northern California campaign out of the San Francisco headquarters next door to the San Franciscan Hotel. Tom wanted me to come to California and help in the campaign. I could stay at the San Franciscan.

Part of me was immediately wary of returning to California politics with all its memories of campaign hoopla and both private and public losses, all of it overwhelmed by the grief and inaccessible meaning surrounding Ceil's slow death. Tom was persuasive, however, and his own beliefs in another Kennedy presidency argued on behalf of what I had thought were my abandoned political passions. He spelled out the final urgency of the California primary after the Kennedy loss in Oregon, the last chance nature of this huge final campaign, and I could hear again in his voice the Tom Braden of those first campaign speeches he made in Chico and Redding California two years before, and then election night when he lost the lieutenant governorship of California when the first intimations of Ceil's final days were becoming clear.

On the plane out of Hartford on a late Saturday morning, I tried not to think about the past, but being alone again and feeling guilty that I was indulging myself by agreeing to a neighbor family's invitation to let Puss stay with them for the few weeks that I would be gone, my rationalization being merely that Puss was being courageous to roll again with her father's political indulgences, I solicited a drink from the stewardess. After a couple sips of the drink I was back to concentrating on our new neighbor's daughter having befriended Puss in school and convincing her parents to subsequently invite Puss to stay with them in their farmhouse behind the largest sycamore west of the Mississippi. Then memories of the Hooker Oak in Chico replaced my view out the plane window. By the time we leveled off at 35,000 feet, all my thoughts were on Ceil slowly dying while I was flying around in a small airplane over Southern California.

The last thing that Larry had said at the Hartford airport before he left me at the departure gate was that he had something to tell me but that it could wait. I wondered where I'd be right now if Ceil were alive. *Not on this airplane.* Ceil saved me from Chico. I ordered a second drink and began to count: Camion's and Ken and Donna Morrow's funerals (Ken and his wife Donna had been killed in a car crash); Pat's retirement and divorce and move to Sacramento; Luke's divorce; Ruth Jaeckel's funeral and the walk across campus to the Oaks bar and lonesome, angry Jaeckel; the students at Chico State and their new world of drugs; Eartha and Bannister and Larry's kids and their own world. But Ceil couldn't save me from her own funeral. *Do I really want to think about that funeral?*

Ceil's casket was ivory white with maroon gilding and cornflowers and daisies scattered on the top. I wanted the casket open but Puss cried so hard during visiting hours at the funeral home that I told them to close it. The morning of the funeral, I drank half a fifth of Armagnac but it didn't keep me from remembering Eartha's trembling hands. Next to Puss, she took Ceil's death the hardest. Eartha looked very beautiful and haunted, with Semantha sitting between her and Larry, beside Puss and me. Later, I remembered Dr. Grogan standing at the graveside service with tears in his eyes. I wanted to push him into the grave when they lowered the casket.

Chapter Sixty-Six

THREE WEEKS LATER, ON the morning of Robert Kennedy's funeral, I was back in Massachusetts in the little TV room between my bedroom and Puss's bedroom, watching the hearse move through crowd-lined streets. I had come in from my garden to watch the end of many things. The seeds I had planted by the barn during my day and a half furlough from the California campaign to see Puss two weeks earlier had broken ground enough that squirrels had dug into the new sprouts and I was going through the motions of planting again.

On the American Airlines Kennedy campaign plane to Boston with the Los Angeles and San Francisco volunteers, I had sat up front on the left facing Senator Kennedy's still unmade bed, still hoping for good news from the Los Angeles hospital where Kennedy lay unconscious on the morning after the shooting in the kitchen of the Ambassador Hotel.

Jack Galivan, a friend and one of Kennedy's advance men in the San Francisco campaign had called me earlier and invited me to ride on the train from New York to Washington but I thanked him and told him I'd pass. Weeks later, Braden told me on the phone that Sirhan's gun was held directly against Kennedy's head when it fired.

For two days after my return home I had half-restored, half-replanted my garden, and now kept coming back in the house to watch the television coverage of the train. I watched the thousands lined along the tracks, the blacks in Baltimore, silent, motionless, devastated, and I remembered the black Unity League workers a couple weeks before in Richmond, and the overflow crowd at Constitution Hall in San Francisco the night of the shooting, Ted Kennedy singing Irish songs on stage and then John Siegenthaler and I on either arm working him back through the crowd to the cab for the airport where he heard the news that Bobby had been shot, and now the long train was slowly making its way to back to Washington.

I knew that someday I would have to talk to Puss about my three weeks in California with Robert Kennedy. I had called her on the phone every other day, and even returned for a day and a half in the middle of the campaign. When I arrived home as the Senator was lying unconscious in the hospital, I promised her I would someday tell her about my time with him.

It was a good time of the year to live in western Massachusetts again. The first lemon lilies were opening behind Puss's rope swing over the ground grapes, and we counted all the yellow flowering things in the yard, the wild strawberries and the dandelions and the first asparagus shoots. I finished re-planting the garden, and Puss and I hoed it together later when the weeds began to show.

Chapter Sixty-Seven

IN JULY, LARRY AND his girlfriend rented a warm weather house on an island off the downeast coast of Maine and invited Puss and me to visit. During the seven-hour drive from western Massachusetts to the ferry, we switched the radio station back and forth from the Democratic national convention in Chicago where street demonstrations against Humphrey were getting more coverage than the nominations inside the hall, to Puss's tapes of Disney movie soundtracks. After the long stretches of route 2 east, route 495 northeast, and 95 north to the Maine turnpike in Kittery, I gave up the idea of trying to make the last ferry at 5:15 and turned off at Wells to show Puss the old Route 1 north that I knew as a boy.

The names, Old Orchard Beach, Ogunquit, York, were still magic for me and I told Puss stories from summer vacations with my parents in the late thirties and through the war. After each story, she asked me to tell her another, and we turned off the radio and forgot the tapes as we slowly passed through hot summer Maine coastal towns where I took pleasure in the popcorn smells and the look of freezing cold seawater, the memories of summer chocolate-covered ice cream bars, and the seashore movie houses of my childhood. I drove by the Eaton tent-ground at York Beach and remembered my little red folding chair and the Thompson family in the next tent who were fat and jolly and who unnerved my mother with their cases of beer. I showed Puss the movie house at York Beach where I cried so hard during *The Charge of the Light Brigade* that my mother had to take me from the theater.

I drove down the long spit of land to Wells Beach and the low-tide York River where I once dug clams with a much older girl and we walked home barefoot through marshland with half-full clam hods, ogling field spiders and minnows trapped in field tide pools.

We got as far as Wiscasset and found an old-fashioned string of several one-family cabins that had one vacancy, bought two pint boxes of fried clams, French fries and cold slaw from a roadside stand nearby, and ate sitting on the end of the marina with moored sailboats and motor launches as far as we could see. After Puss fell asleep I watched the convention euphoria in Chicago following McCarthy's nomination speech, and do not remember falling asleep myself.

We got an early start and by ten in the morning were driving through Searsport with its white New England mansions and dead elm trees, and the long main street was summer lonely.

"Why did the trees all die, daddy?" Puss asked.

"Somebody brought an insect from Holland that made them sick."

"Did he want to kill the elm trees?"

"No, he just didn't know what he was doing."

"We studied about Holland in school in California. They have lots of tulips with all bright colors. And we read a story about a boy with ice skates."

"Hans Brinker."

"That's him. Did you read it in school too?"

"I did, in the fifth grade."

"I wonder how a little bug could kill all the beautiful trees," Puss said as we left the town. Soon we passed through Bucksport, then Ellsworth where we stopped at the state liquor store and I bought a bottle of port wine and a bottle of Campari. Larry said his girlfriend Sandy drank Campari and soda.

When we approached the causeway at Thompson Island, and all the lobster pounds with steam pouring up from the outside cooking stoves, Puss said she bet the lobsters would taste good, so I pulled in and we ate steamed lobster for lunch. I told her the joke I heard about the Midwest ladies visiting Maine who told the waiter when they ordered their lobsters not to serve any of the "yucky green stuff." Puss was puzzled until our lobsters arrived and I showed her the green paste of the lobster liver. We made the 2:15 ferry with twenty minutes to spare.

The four-mile crossing to Swan's Island took thirty-five minutes. I explained the reason for the red nuns and black cans in the water as we left Bass Harbor, and I pointed out Julia Child's home on Lopus Point. Blue Hill Bay was calm on this summer day, and we could see a long way down the coast. In the distance there were some hills and I went back downstairs to the car on the main deck and got the map.

"They must be the Camden Hills," I said.

"What's that mountain over there, daddy?"

I looked at the map. "Maybe it's Mount Cadillac," I said, "No, it's Blue Hill. It's not a mountain, we can't see the mountains on Mt. Desert Island until we get a little further out in the bay.

"Look daddy, look!" Puss cried, pointing to a school of porpoises fifty yards from the ferry, rolling and diving, black-backed, effortless, miniature backsides of the moon under our summer sun. They stayed with us for several minutes and were gone. The breeze picked up and ruffled our hair, and we could see Mt. Cadillac and Mt. Champlain back on Mt. Desert Island. The ferry swept past occasional lobster pots in the green water.

"Why did mommy die?" Puss asked.

"I don't know, Puss, I don't know. I wish I knew."

"I don't talk about her because I know you miss her and it makes you sad."

"I don't talk about her because I know you miss her and I don't want to make you sad." I said.

"Do good people always die?"

"Eventually, some sooner than others. Your mother misses you, wherever she is, I know that."

"I touched her when she was in the casket at the funeral place."

"I saw you."

"I was going to kiss her, but I got scared."

"I should have talked to you about it."

"Her hand was hard when I touched it."

"I know."

A cormorant flew past the ferry, a foot over the water, and disappeared into the sun.

"Was that a sea duck?" Puss asked.

"Up here they call them 'skags.' They're long-necked sea cousins of the crow, with a hooked beak. They eat fish. The lobstermen think they dive down and eat the lobsters in the traps on the bottom. Some lobstermen shoot them."

Puss thought about that for a while. "We didn't see them in California, did we?"

"No, but they must have been there somewhere. They're as far away as China."

"Do we like them?"

"They're just part of everything else, Puss, and as with all things dark and strange, we live with them."

"But we don't have to like them, do we?"

"We don't have to like anything, but if you see them on a rainy day sitting on a bell buoy or the end of a pier flapping their wings to dry them, you have to wonder whether they're only clowns after all. Stupidity sometimes comes in dark packages, kiddo."

"Stupidity isn't really funny, though, is it?"

"It sure as hell isn't."

We passed a big green bell buoy on the port side and turned into Mackerel Cove, several hundred yards from the ferry landing. As we got closer, we could see a line of cars waiting to board for the return trip, and people standing on the side of the road near a parking lot.

Puss and I went down the stairs and got in our car. Two deck-hands pulled back the chain link fence across the bow, and the barely-moving ferry bumped against the wooden pilings on the starboard side, the pilings creaked, and then the ferry eased against the pilings on the port side, creaking those pilings, then snuggled into place against the narrow wooden mouth of the terminal. A deck hand jumped up on one side of the terminal, holding a heavy hemp rope that he secured around an iron cleat, and the other deck hand reached up and pressed the button that lowered the steel ramp to the bow of the ferry.

We were the fifth car off, and drove along the jetty toward the terminal building, the line of waiting cars, and the few people waiting to greet the arriving cars.

"There's Larry and his friend," I said. "He's the only one not waving."

"What's her name, daddy?"

"Mona."

"Do I have to like her?"

"Nope. But if you try to be nice to her, it would help Larry."

"Can I ask him about Semanth?"

"Sure, he'd probably like that."

I stopped the car beside the two of them long enough to hear Larry say, smiling, "It took you long enough," and then pulled ahead because of the line of cars behind me. I waited on the side of the road as Larry and Mona stepped over the coiled wire fence to the parking lot and got in a car I hadn't seen before. When they passed me, I followed them on a recently tarred road that led around the cove and through a forest of tall and dark spruce trees.

Chapter Sixty-Eight

IF YOU DREW A picture of a robber crab, the top of it tilted sideways to the left, then reduced the right claw to an unformed stump, the result would be a rough nautical sketch of Swans Island. The ferry had docked in Mackerel Cove, a horseshoe-shaped north by northwest body of water formed by the bulky left claw and the right stunted stump. We drove a couple miles down the thorax of the island, turned right and crossed a narrow spit of land along the northern shore of Toothacher Cove, then straight into a private drive which led to a white summer house with a long glassed-in porch on the rim of the southwest claw.

The view across the cove, open to the southwest, of a hundred lobster pots in the afternoon sun, created a scene that would have caught Dufy's eye. One lobster boat was circling selected pots, alternately racing and idling its Chrysler motor, then moving against a background of spruce trees lining the south shore. We pulled off the narrow dirt road, following Larry, and parked behind him on the sloping gravel driveway by the side of the sun porch.

"Hi Puss and Boots," Mona called through the open window before we could get out, "I love your name. I'm Mona. Welcome to Swans Island."

"Hi," Puss said cheerfully, and opened her door. Mona was heading around to her side of the car.

"Well, get the hell out of the car," Larry grinned at me as I nodded my head, smiling at him. "We're paying for this damn place, so we're wasting time. It was low tide an hour ago and the damn clams'll be underwater if we don't get to 'em."

"We came up old Route 1," I said.

"Guess what? This is a dry island. They didn't tell me that when I rented the place."

Mona was telling Puss that she knew where to get sand dollars, and there was a thunder hole on the other side of the island. Mona was a strawberry blonde with freckles and she wore white shorts and a colored t-shirt. She was what we called in high school "a dish." I asked Larry if he was watching the convention.

"What convention? If you turn on the TV set, I'll put sand in your sheets."

"We're going to the beach, daddy, '" Puss said, "It's not even far away."

During the next five days, Mona threw the Frisbee with Puss on Fine Sand Beach, a two mile drive on a bumpy gravel road through the Swans Island wilderness, then a twenty minute walk along a path criss-crossed with exposed tree roots. They also waded hip-deep off Tongue's Beach on the other side of the ferry terminal where they picked up several big sea clams rolling around on the bottom, dug steamer clams in Mackerel Cove and the Minturn flats beyond City Point, and shot hoops at the school playground. Larry and I participated in the first fifteen minutes of each of these adventures, then explored the island and I told him about the California campaign with Kennedy, and one afternoon he told me the Eartha story.

We had brought one of the six-packs that Bonnie the mail carrier brought over on the ferry for a small carrying charge and drove to the lighthouse at the entrance to Burnt Coat Harbor. We lay down on the steep grass slope overlooking the surf breaking on the rocks below, and looked out to Marshall Island and beyond it to Isle of Haut. Occasional lobster boats came in from around the south side of Harbor Island and through the passage into Burnt Cove, and as we talked, we could hear the summer bongings of the mid-channel buoy just inside the entrance. Marshall Island was clearly visible, but a mile offshore a fog bank was hanging, and Larry began his story.

I set it down here because he is my friend, and in a strange way his story became my story, partly because our daughters found themselves within each other at a corner in their lives, then found the corner blurred by all our losses. Also, because young loss foreshadows old loss, and the substitutes we seek to dispel our pain grow into the balm of forgetfulness. All suffering leads us further into the river Lethe, and when we finally pass the mid-point and feel our feet under us again as we go up the other side, we have forgotten our pain, and that is the final reversal of life into death while we still breathe. I am convinced that Eartha's own story leads to the same River, but she would have to tell that story herself.

Chapter Sixty-Nine

LARRY LEFT CHICO EARLY in the summer that Ceil was dying. Eartha acted as if she and Larry were still best friends, and that they would write, and she hoped that he would call. She made him a lunch and turned away as he told Semantha from his truck that he would call her and that he would come and visit her at Christmas time. He got out of his truck and lifted up his son. Larry knew that Semantha and the boy didn't understand why he was going, but he said the words and kissed Semantha again who was holding Eartha's hand and crying. As he drove out of the yard, Eartha ran after his truck and he rolled down his window and she said, "Call me after you get over the mountains. Call me from Reno or someplace before you get too far. Is that OK? Would you mind?"

"Hell no, sure I'll call you," he said, and drove down Violet Way and stopped in front of our house. I had carried Ceil out to the patio on the side of the house where I had put a bed for her to spend the early mornings before the terrific heat, and Larry came out on the patio and said goodbye. Actually, he said "So long," because he knew she was dying. We all knew, even Puss, and we knew it wouldn't be long before the morphine doses became so heavy that she wouldn't have much consciousness during the long days.

"You're a bum to walk out on me, Larry," Ceil said, and she lifted her hand and pointed her finger at him.

"I've always been a bum, I guess," he said, taking her finger and kissing it.

"You're not a bum Larry, you're a good guy. Just don't forget about me going across the desert. I'll be thinking of you and waiting for a call."

"I'll call you as soon as I reach the Massachusetts border."

"That a boy," she said softly. "That's the right border all right."

He put his fist gently against my shoulder and got in his truck and didn't look back: 99 South to Marysville, 65 southeast to U.S. 80 east of Roseville, then through the canyons, Emigrant Gap, and the Donner Pass to Truckee, and down into the desert and Reno where he stopped for gas. It took him five hours to get there. He had eaten his lunch going through the lower canyons on the California side, and entered the gas station, bought some more sandwiches and some cokes, and called Eartha.

"We want to come with you," she said. "Would it be awful for you to drive all the way back and get us?"

Larry had waited so long to hear this, he didn't know how to say yes. "I'd be honored," he said. "I'll be there sometime tonight."

"I'm going to put Semantha on."

"Hello, daddy? Can we live in one of those houses with two floors and stairs?"

"You got it, ladybug, I'm on my way."

He filled his tank with gas and started toward Donner Pass again. He got into Chico at ten-thirty that night, and the children were asleep. Eartha ran out the front door and hugged him before he got halfway across the grass.

"Oh Larry," she said, "I've been so mean to you. You were so good to come back for us."

They slept together that night for the first time in a year, and Eartha said to him in the middle of the night, "It's like learning together all over again, isn't it?"

In the morning, Larry was ready to start out as soon as they loaded the truck with as much as they could take. While he was driving back from Reno, Eartha and Semantha had packed all the suitcases they owned, and Larry wanted to throw them on board and take off. They could call when they reached Massachusetts and hire someone to ship the rest. Eartha, however, said she wanted to just say goodbye to the Catholic priest at St. Margaret's church, and she'd be right back and they could go.

She drove off in the packed truck at 8:45, and Larry did the dishes with Semantha and put them away and had a beer on the patio. When Eartha wasn't back by 11:00, he called the church, but Father Templeton said he hadn't seen Eartha, and when he asked Father Avery, he hadn't either. Larry took Semantha and the little boy for a walk down the street. He made them lunch and took them for another walk. Eartha drove in the yard at 5:30 and told Larry not to get upset but she had to tell him something. They went out on the patio, and she asked him again not to get upset.

"Where the hell have you been all day? I called the church and you didn't go to see any priest. Let's have it. I didn't come back here to play games."

"You're going to get upset, and I don't want that."

"So I'm upset. Are you going to tell me where you've been?"

"Well, I went to Oroville with Art Mallory and got a divorce. It doesn't mean anything, Larry. In California you have to file twice or it isn't final. Art just thought it was a way to protect myself if things don't work out in the East for us."

"You mean Bannister wanted you to get a divorce, that's what you mean. Mallory is his lawyer. You think I'm going to believe that you went to see Mallory all on your ownsies this morning? I called the church. Neither priest had seen you."

"No, I did go to say goodbye to Abernard. It's all right, nothing has changed, Larry, we can still go."

"You want me to go east and we'll be one big happy family now that you've divorced me? Jesus Christ, who do you think I am?"

Larry left the house and walked to the Rio Linto channel, along the dry creek bed, for an hour. He was numb, back in the room in his head where he had been for two years, the little dry room inside his head where the walls were gray skin, and it was dark with empty space outside, and he couldn't reach out and touch his kids because they were floating out of reach. He walked for another hour, but he was walking where he had never walked before because he never felt like this before. He walked back to the house and went in the bedroom and shut the door. He was really going to lose his kids. He kept thinking over and over again, *my little girl, my little boy, they won't even know me after I leave.*

He could see them in the back yard. The boy was naked, riding a little green tank car, pushing it with his feet. Semantha was running on the grass, looking back over her shoulder to see if her ballet cape was flying out straight. Eartha was sitting in a lawn chair with her hands folded on her lap.

Larry left the bedroom and went out the front door, got in his truck and drove across the country in four days. He remembered stopping in a dumpy hotel on the main street of a small Nebraska town one night, sleeping from 2:00 to 7:00 a.m., but he didn't remember the other three nights. He drove to Worcester, Massachusetts and made a pay phone call to his brother who had rented a small house for him on a lake in North Brookfield. He drove to his brother's house and sat in his kitchen and got drunk.

Chapter Seventy

THAT CHRISTMAS, LARRY FLEW back to Chico and stayed a week at the Hotel Oaks, driving over to the house every morning at 9:00 a.m. Eartha was solicitous and seemed glad to see him. She accompanied his outings with the children, and her manner was intimate, except when he attempted to touch her, and she became sad.

"I can't," she said. Once, tears welled up in her eyes.

When the visit was almost over, a heavy fog moved into the northern valley and all flights were grounded. On the morning of his flight, Larry took a bus to Sacramento. When he boarded, Eartha held up the little boy to the window, like an ancient warrior's wife holding up a son to the father on horseback, about to depart for the wars.

In the spring, he went to see a Congregational minister in a neighboring town, and talked about the separation, then broke down. The minister suggested he use his phone to call Eartha, and Larry talked for forty-five minutes. He asked Eartha if they could forget everything that happened and begin over together. Eartha said, "There have been moments when..." and her voice trailed off without finishing the sentence. She thanked him several times and put the children on the phone. She said she was glad he was coming to visit the children in the summer.

In July, two weeks before Larry flew west, he met Mona at a golf driving-range. She was driving balls on the mat next to Larry, using a finely polished wooden three wood, out-driving Larry who was using a two iron. As Larry emptied his wicker bucket of balls, he saw that Mona's bucket was still half-full so he left his iron on the rubber mat to hold his space and bought another full bucket of balls. When Mona finished her bucket, Larry had about a dozen balls left.

"How about hitting most of these?" he said, "I'm finished. You'd be doing me a favor. This is my first time out and I'm getting a blister."

"Sure, I'll hit a couple, for the blister's sake."

And so it went. They became friends.

When Larry said goodbye to her at Logan, Mona told him to do what he had to do.

"I don't know what's going to happen," he said, "I just want my kids back."

"You should," Mona said. "Call me when you get back, or before, whichever."

In California, Eartha and the kids met Larry at the Chico airport. During the drive to town, the little boy said to Larry, "Are you going to shake hands with Ab?" Larry and Eartha both pretended he didn't say it.

At the house, Eartha wanted Larry to stay for dinner. She had made lasagna, a favorite of his, the way she made it with layers of cream cheese and pine nuts. Larry wanted to do the dishes with Semantha but Eartha asked him to sit in the kitchen and talk to her. She saw him look toward the opened pack of Parliament cigarettes on the kitchen table and she said, "I'm cutting down."

Next to the cigarettes was her plastic prescription bottle of birth control pills. There was a silence, and Eartha said, "Dr. Kazen said it would be a good idea to stay on the pills, just to keep everything regular. Later, when Larry asked her whether she would come back with him, she said, "Now's not a good time. We're all used to life out here. We have two guinea pigs and some white mice, and things like that." She became subdued and quiet.

"I'd like to take the kids back with me for the summer," Larry said.

"That would be great, Larry," she said. "They would love that. I'll hold down the fort here for them."

Three days later, Larry called Mona from the San Francisco airport, and she was at Logan when they arrived. Larry's brother had a camp on a lake in southern Maine and Larry and Mona and the kids went there for several days. When they returned to Brookfield, Mona took care of the kids during the day.

A month later, they went to the lake again, and during Nicholas's afternoon nap, Larry took Semantha fishing in a little cove. Larry was showing Semantha how to cast a piece of perch belly and play it across the top of the water so that a pickerel would strike at it. Earlier, at lunch, they were eating spaghetti and Nicholas wound his spaghetti around his fork and said, "This is how Ab eats basgetti."

Larry said to Semantha, "If I'm going to help, Mannie, you have to tell me what's going on in California."

"I can't daddy," she said, "Mummy told me I can't tell." She started to cry.

"It's OK honey, try to tell me. It's nobody's fault. Nobody's going to get mad at you. I need to know, and you can help. You have to tell me."

"Ab lives at our house. When Mummy picks him up at work, he scrunches down in the seat on the ride home."

Back at the lake, Larry whispered to Mona what he found out, and he drove to the general store at Round Pond and called Johnson Appleton, a lawyer Larry knew from the Chico Democratic Club. "It's about time," Appleton said. "Everybody in town has been waiting for you to do something. Do you want me to put a tail on her or don't you want the kids?"

"Do it," Larry said.

He called Eartha and told her that he was keeping the kids in Massachusetts. She became hysterical on the phone. When they returned to North Brookfield, there was a special delivery letter from Eartha demanding that Larry return the children. She said that if Larry wanted her to come back he had to bring the kids back to her. She said that ever since they left, she had been crying. She lay on the floor beneath the air conditioner and just cried for hours. He had to bring the children back.

Larry felt sorry for her. He asked Mona what he should do and she said she didn't know. She asked Larry what he wanted to do and he said he didn't know. In late August Larry flew to California with the children. Eartha hadn't answered the phone when he called and she wasn't home when they arrived. Skip Garrison drove them in from the airport and said he hadn't seen Eartha for a week or ten days. Larry stayed with the children in the house. There was a new mattress on the bed in the master bedroom. The old mattress was leaning against the wall at the end of the bed.

The next day, Eartha showed up. Larry was sitting on the patio in the late afternoon, watching a Giants game on TV and drinking a beer. The children had gone to a movie with Gina Garrison. "Larry!" she said as she came through the open screen door from the house. "I wondered whose car that was. I didn't know you were coming."

"Apparently," Larry said, studying her, not moving from his chair.

"You'll never guess what happened. I've been to Mexico with an old girlfriend. Imagine, me in Mexico, the wonderful Mexican embroidery, the pyramids, Diego Rivera's murals in Mexico City."

"Cut the shit, Eartha."

"I can prove it, you can call Earlene. She's in San Francisco right now."

"Bannister's been gone ever since you've been gone."

"I saw him in San Francisco, it's true. I know you've got a man watching me, Larry Bourke, I'm not stupid, you know. But Earlene and I went to Mexico alone, you can ask her. Call her."

"Yeah you're stupid, Earth, you don't have enough money to get to Oroville by yourself. Quit the game. I want those kids, you either get yourself straight and come back so we can have a family or I'll take them away from you, believe it."

"You'd do that?"

"Yeah, I'm dumb enough to do that. Are you smart enough to do that?"

"I need some time."

"What do you mean, you need some time. You'll do it or you won't do it. What the hell does time have to do with it?"

"Everything. I'm signed up to take two courses in the fall so I can get my certification to teach. I've got a zoo full of animals in the house. I have to go get them right now from next door. Semantha's ballet lessons. Everything."

"You're stalling."

"I'm not stalling. I'm not."

Larry looked at her.

Eartha said, "I know you know about Ab. That happened. I can't do anything about it. I need time to break it off, but I'll do it. Give me until Christmas and we can put Semantha in school in spring term in the east. I'll have my certification."

Larry flew back east. In December, he came back, and Eartha talked him into waiting until late spring. He called every week and talked with Eartha and the children. He bought a round trip ticket on American Airlines and made reservations for a one-way trip for four in late June.

Two days before he was to fly out of Logan for San Francisco, Eartha didn't answer the phone. She didn't answer the phone the next day. He called Johnson Appleton. He didn't know anything. He called Luke and Jaeckel but they hadn't seen Eartha and they didn't know anything. He called Bannister's wife and she didn't want to talk to him. He pleaded with her not to hang up and she listened as he told her the whole story from his point of view. She said that Bannister hadn't been home for three days.

Larry flew to Chico and the house was locked. In the back yard, he pushed aside the leaves of a rice paper tree brushing against a partially open bedroom window and forced it the rest of the way. The clothes drawers and the closets and the refrigerator were empty. The Garrisons down the street knew nothing. He went to the immediate neighbors and the woman across the street saw Bannister's Cadillac in front of the house a week ago.

"You might have saved your family if you didn't run off," she said. "What'd you think would happen, anyway?"

Larry looked at her. "You don't know the half of it, Mrs. Longworth, but thanks for telling me."

She looked at him and shook her head and closed the door.

Larry stayed in the house another day, asking around, but nobody knew anything.

Chapter Seventy-One

LARRY AND I WALKED up the hill from the lighthouse. Blackberry bushes lined the narrow winding road on both sides.

"They'll be ripe at the end of August, looks like," Larry said.

"We won't be here," I said.

"Maybe we should come back."

"For blackberries?"

"For the hell of it," Larry said.

We turned a corner and walked down the hill to where we could see the rest of Burnt Coat Harbor. A boatyard was busy with three hauled lobster boats being made ready for the fall. Men with sanders were working the hull of one, a woman with a hose attached to a bottle was squirting bleach on the hull of another as the old discolored sea grass peeled away and fell to the ground, and a young boy was painting the copper-red hull of another. Across the harbor a schooner had come about and was lowering its dark red sails. Lupin was growing on the side of the hill.

"We better get the girls," Larry said. "Mona deserves a fucking medal."

"You lucked out," I said.

Driving around the harbor to the asphalt playground with the basketball hoop, I asked him if he had heard anything from Eartha.

"No," he said, "but I found out they're in San Francisco. I'm going out in September. It's the earliest I could get a court date. I'm going after the kids."

Mona and Puss and Boots were sitting by the side of the road watching white ducks in a little pond next to the school playground. Each was chewing a piece of yellow grass. They were deep in conversation.

"Hey, you hayseeds," Larry said as we pulled up next to them, "How's everything in the water world?"

"Ducky," Mona said. "We're comparing notes." I say they look like dodgem boats, but Puss says they look like lawn ducks with motors."

"We've got big plans," Larry said.

"You've been hiding the water wings," Mona said.

"Nope," Larry said, "Mussels for dinner. Hop in."

We took a left turn just before the Oddfellows Hall and headed back to the house where we picked up two clam hods and got back in the car and drove towards the dump. About a half a mile up a slow incline, we turned right off the pocked oil and stone road to a smooth dirt road, moist and white with calcium chloride. We passed a large engraved sign telling us that we had just entered Shady Waterside, a private development that bordered the tidal flats on the southwest side of Mackerel Cove. We drove through spruce and birch trees and took a right turn that led down a winding hill to a waterfront recreation building where we parked in the grass. We carried the clam hods and walked out to the orangey flat granite boulders. On the far side, we took off our shoes and socks and carefully negotiated our way to the low water's edge and stepped into submerged places where we could find good footing and reach the clusters of blue mussels on the submerged sides of the lower ledges.

"God, it's like picking jewels," Mona said.

Back at the house we poured them into the sink and left them to fix later for dinner.

Larry and Mona went off in the car to see about a possible trip the next day on a lobster boat, and Puss and I went for a walk around Toothacher Cove.

"It's a funny name, daddy, for a beautiful place," she said. "How do things get their names?"

"You got me, hon. Maybe something happened here once, I don't know. Somebody called it that for a reason a long time ago and it caught on. Maybe some old sailor had a toothache and came ashore. I do know that Indians came through this passage from Mackerel Cove as recently as a hundred years ago, carrying their canoes across the hundred yards of land to the water here."

"Who told you that?"

"I read it in a book about the island. It's dedicated to a man who lives over on the other side of the island, an old captain named Clyde Torrey. Maybe we'll go visit him before we go home."

"Can we come here again next summer?"

"Would you like that, Puss?"

"Maybe someday we could have a boat, daddy, so we can sail on hot summer days. Do you think we could?"

"You want to sail the ocean blue, do you?"

"I do, daddy, I really do."

We had walked halfway around the cove to a little cabin built on the edge of the rocks, about forty feet above the high tide line. An old lady sat on a rocking chair on a small porch that was built out on one end. Puss saw her and waved to her and called "Hi."

"Hi yourself," the old lady called pleasantly.

"Great day," I said as we passed beneath her.

"Gruss Gott," she said, and held up her hand as if to wave.

"What did she say, daddy?"

"She's a very bright old lady," I said. She said something in German. There's an island in Blue Hill Bay we can see from the ferry called Gott's Island. When I said, 'Great day' to her, she answered me with a greeting people say in Bavaria, in Germany, 'Gruss Gott,' which means 'God is great.'"

"You know everything, daddy."

"Oh boy, I wish I knew half of what I want to know. I'd settle for one third."

We came to a place in the rocks where two yellow flowers were growing.

"I don't even know the name of these flowers," I said. "That shows you I don't know everything. I'd like to know how they could grow in the rocks, though. That's quite a trick for a flower to pull off."

"Lots of things are mysteries, aren't they?"

"Almost everything, Puss."

"May I ask you a question, daddy? You don't have to answer it if you don't want to talk about it."

"Sure. What's on your mind on a great day like this?"

"Remember when you went back to California to work for Senator Kennedy and a man shot him and you told me when you came back home that someday you would tell me about it?"

"I remember. I thought then that if I waited, it would be easier on both of us some day, but it still seems like yesterday to me, and maybe it always will. But it's OK for us to talk about it."

"I'm not scared any more at night, daddy. And when I'm with Semantha, California and here seems almost like all one thing again."

"But something is not the same about me, is that it?"

"No, not really, daddy. After we came back here all that way across the country, I knew that mummy somehow would always be with us, and all the things I didn't understand about California seemed OK, but then you were so sad all over again when Senator Kennedy died and I saw you get quiet again, some place inside me got lonesome again and I didn't understand it."

"Everybody has a lonely place inside them, Puss. Even in California, your mother and you and I were filling up lonely places inside each of us, even when we didn't think about it, and now you and I and Semanthe and Larry and Mona are all filling up each other's lonely places as best we can, even when we can't quite fill them all up. I guess that before in California and then when I went back when Senator Kennedy was running for president, I was trying to fill up some of the lonely places inside me just like Senator Kennedy himself and the people I met who were helping him were trying to fill up the lonely places inside themselves.

"Everybody has small lonely places all the time, Puss, but people don't talk about them because they're part of life.

"There are a lot of exciting things when you get to be around a person who runs for president and people's feelings are pretty high all the time, and when something bad happens to the important people involved, there are a lot of hurt feelings. My short time in California was very meaningful to me, especially the time I spent with Senator Kennedy himself on the day before he was shot, and then when it was all over just when Senator Kennedy had won a great victory, it was hard for people to talk about it without feeling sad deep down inside themselves.

"The day before the election, I had been the one who planned the visit of Senator Robert to an airport where thousands of people had gathered to hear him talk near a city called Concord, about twenty miles from San Francisco. As the people waited and cheered, his plane landed and when the runway was not quite long enough, it skidded around in a circle to come to a stop and it was a scary moment because there was a lot of dust churned up from the tires, and then the pilot taxied the plane over close to the crowd. I climbed the steps onto the plane and told the Senator some things about the big crowds that were cheering outside, things like the recent polls in the area and what percentage of people liked Senator Kennedy more than Senator McCarthy who was running against him, and who was going to introduce him. Senator Kennedy asked me if I had any information about how people felt about the debate the night before between him and Senator McCarthy and I told him that many people felt that it was even, and he nodded.

"He had brought with him on the plane some important people like John Glenn who had been the first astronaut to orbit the earth when we were getting ready to send men to the moon, and the great black Olympic athlete Rafer Johnson, and others who were the most important people in the California state government, and his wife Mrs. Kennedy too.

"Outside he walked along the restraining fence and shook hands with the people who were crowded against the fence to touch him and then he jumped up on the big flatbed truck and held a microphone and talked to the big crowd of people and told them why he wanted to be president and made jokes with them and told them that he would come back and talk to them again if he was elected president. Then he climbed up the steps to the door of the plane and turned to wave and smile at the crowd who were still cheering, and he went inside and the plane took off.

"The next day, when people in California voted, I spent most of the day driving from town to town in the places where I was making sure that all the work was being done to help people vote who liked Senator Kennedy. I didn't know that my friend Tom Braden, who I had helped when we still lived in California, had flown to San Francisco to bring me back to Los Angeles to be with him and the Senator that night in Los Angeles, but he couldn't find me and flew back to Los Angeles.

"That evening I was in San Francisco in a building called Constitution Hall where the Senator's younger brother Edward came to speak and together with a Mr. Siegenthaler I helped him walk from his taxi through the big crowd to the stage where he sang a couple of Irish songs and had fun with the crowd. Then I and Mr. Siegenthaler, who had been Senator Kennedy's chief assistant and most important helper when he was Attorney General of the United States and enforced the laws that made all the schools in the southern part of the United States open up for black students for the first time, again helped him walk back through the happy crowd trying to touch him and get into a taxi to go to the airport and fly to Los Angeles to be with his older brother, Senator Robert who by this time knew that he had won the California primary election and was making a victory speech to a big crowd in a Los Angeles hotel.

"On his way to the airport, Senator Ted was still riding in the cab when he heard on the radio that after making his speech his older brother Robert was shot in the kitchen of the hotel.

"I was downstairs in the TV room of Constitution Hall and all of a sudden I saw on TV the pictures showing Senator Robert lying on the floor after being shot. I stayed up all night watching the news and flew home the following morning to Boston where I got a ride home to be with you in Sunderland. Later that day I got a telephone call from a friend in California who told me that Senator Robert had died, and I told you that someday I would tell you about it.

"I know that Senator Robert was trying to fix those things that he thought could be fixed in our country even though if he got them all fixed there would still be a big lonely place inside him because his two older brothers had died, one in the second world war and one when he was president, and even if he had lived and become president himself he would still have his own lonely places that he didn't talk about with anybody, not even with his wife who loved him very much."

"I thought maybe that something else happened in California that hurt you, daddy, not just Senator Kennedy being shot."

"It was mostly, Puss, that when I was back in California I was reminded that many of our friends who lived there when we were in Chico had died in the meantime, and then mummy died, and then Senator Kennedy himself died and all the good feelings that I had about helping him became sad. You were very patient to wait and not ask me about my sadness until now."

"I waited, daddy, because now you're happy again, and you make everything clear to me, and now I won't worry about you any more. We can go back now and fix the mussels for dinner with Larry and Mona. Do you think we'll see the gross God lady again?"

"Let's see if she's still there on her porch."

When we passed below the cabin, she was gone. Back at the house, Mona and Larry were scrubbing the mussels. They had put a large blue agate pan with a little fresh water in it on the stove, and it was steaming. "Peel and quarter that onion, Bill," Larry said, "We're just finished. We'll steam these buggars with the onion and they'll be ready in about five more minutes."

Puss made a salad while we drank gin and tonics on the porch. The sun set behind Irish Point as we dipped the mussels in the mussel water and downed them as if they were the food of gods and goddesses. Puss got the one black pearl in the last mussel in the pot, and said, "I'm the luckiest girl in the world."

Chapter Seventy-Two

THE NEXT MORNING I got up soon after sunrise and found Puss already at the kitchen table, eating cereal. I had a cup of instant coffee and we went for a walk along the beach. It was low tide and we followed the other shore of the cove, passing several areas where clammers the day before had left mounds of sand that had spread during the night tide and left small declivities that would disappear in the next tide.

"Mona's nice, daddy, I wish I could tell Semanth."

"Larry doesn't know exactly where she is, Puss, except they're in San Francisco somewhere. He's going out in September to look for her."

After a while, Puss and Boots said, "Are they with that Bannister man?"

"It looks like it."

"I don't like him."

"It's OK not to like him."

"Do you think Semanth is OK?"

"I'm sure they're all OK. It's very difficult for everybody."

"If Larry finds them, will he bring them back east?"

"He's going to try but nothing has worked so far."

We entered a series of small coves and then rounded a corner and could see further along the shore to Fine Sand Beach.

"How come there are sand dollars over there and none here?" Puss asked.

"I don't know. Maybe the mint's over there."

Puss thought about that as we walked, and then said, "I'm lucky to have you as a dad. I know that."

"I'm lucky to have you as a daughter. I know that too."

"Well, we got that straight, didn't we?" she said, running ahead and jumping to make two solid footprints in the moist sand.

Walking back, she said, "I wish we had our own house on this island. I don't mean not with Larry and Mona, but our very own so that they could visit us. We could have Semanth's mother and Semanth and her little brother."

When we got back to the house, Larry and Mona hadn't surfaced yet, and Puss and I got in the car and drove to the General Store that was supposed to open at eight, but opened ten minutes early. The store occupied the former front room of a house overlooking Burnt Coat Harbor, and was run by a Mr. Sprague, a grandfatherly man who had white hair and smoked a pipe and talked with a lovely Maine accent. He said "Yessir" to all my questions except the one about available property. He didn't know of any. I asked him about Captain Clyde Torrey and he said, "Alive the last I heard."

"Do you think if we drove over to Atlantic he'd be up and about?"

"Since about three hours," he said, and we took the only oil and stone road on the island to Atlantic, six miles away.

The Torrey farm was a ramshackle house blackened by salt weather and roof-pocked with neglect on the road edge of a long cliff meadow of yellow summer grass that dropped off to a rock beach walkable at low tide. To our right, southeast, a forest of spruce; to our left, northeast, a small pond and a gravel road that circled the edge of the cliff to a gravel airfield. From the meadow we could almost make out the individual spruce trees on Placentia and Black Islands across the Bay. The bald granite rounded tops of two mountains on Mt. Desert Island, Mt. Champlain and Mt. Cadillac, six or seven miles away, appeared to be half that distance.

"You're just in time," a crisp voice from a bent-over body wearing a farmer's hat said as Puss and I walked between a leaning black shed and the farmhouse.

"Captain Torrey?" I asked.

"One and exactly the same," he said, putting his fingers to the turned-down brim of his oval felt hat as I introduced him to Puss and Boots.

I asked him if he'd autograph the book about Swans Island I held in my hand, and he took the unlit cigar out of his mouth and smiled at me and the sun at the same time, showing his tobacco-stained teeth and his gleaming blue eyes, reaching for the book. He sat on a turned-on-end lobster crate that he rolled away from a pile of battered crates next to the side of his farmhouse, crossed his legs, turned the first two pages of the book, and began to write at the top of the printed dedication page which read "To Clyde Torrey."

As he wrote I ducked back to the car for my camera and then took his picture. To this day, I have that black and white photo which contrasts nicely the crooked and split vertical side-boards of his shed with the horizontal bottom of the lobster crate, one board un-nailed and flopping out on one end just behind his turned down rubber boots, and the dark spaces between his knuckle bones and the left sleeve of his faded, plaid workman's shirt crooking out from his dark and faded overalls. Clyde sat leaning against the base of the shed behind him where a long section of the once cedar-shingled side had been abandoned. After five minutes of writing, he handed me the book and waited for me to read the inscription.

"That's really nice," I said, "Thanks a lot."

"I need a driver for about a half hour," he said, smiling and looking half way between me and the sun again.

"I'm your man," I said.

"I'd be much obliged," he said, heading around the corner of the house. Puss and I followed him to an old four-door faded purple sedan parked on the grass. One headlight was missing, and the other hung from a wire. The back seat had been removed, replaced by an old Hudson car engine and a rusty anvil. A lobster crate had replaced the front seat.

During the next hour, Clyde attached a chain between an old plow and the ball of the trailer hitch on the back bumper of the sedan, and he walked behind the car as I drove, with Puss sitting on the lobster crate next to me. Three times we traced the rim of his half-grown garden in the field beyond his shed. He mumbled that he wanted to get the land turned over before fall so he could plow again in the spring.

We could see his old horse in another part of the meadow, and all my questions were answered when he told me that Sandy was a good horse but he couldn't pull the plow alone. Clyde's ox had died the previous winter and he needed to get another, but second-hand oxen were hard to come by on the island. Later, I found out that Clyde sometimes fell asleep in his car listening to night Red Sox games on the radio, and crawled out at sunrise.

Clyde was as generous as he was entrepreneurial in his friendships, as we experienced that first morning, and many more times over the years that followed, until his quick demise that soon followed the fire that burned down his farmhouse. This first friendship, however, was fresh in its summer brightness and its clean meadow salt air, and after our circular plowing, Puss and I rambled across the field to visit Sandy, the raspberry stallion, grazing head down undistractedly, in full and ignored view of the blue Atlantic. We could see the spire of the Atlantic Baptist church beyond the black farmhouse itself, the spruce forest hiding the campground owned and undeveloped by Clyde's nephew Mertic Morrison, and the impenetrable alders and swamp thickets on the other side of the road where the largest and oldest of the island deer herd kept their counsels. We left Sandy to his munching, and walked the rim of the meadow where we could look down at the half-tide rock beach glistening from the receding and rhythmic reach of the gentle incoming waves. We crossed between the rim and the small pond and looked down the boneyard airfield toward the distant Baptist Church, then turned and watched a yawl sail the mile-wide passageway between us and Placentia Island, then disappear to the southwest heading toward Black Point.

Clyde met us as we walked back through the meadow, this time with his cigar lit, and offered me a drink. Someone had given him a pint of scotch the day before, a rarity, and he thought a tip-full might keep the morning going in the right direction. He told us that land was available down along the Red Point shore and offered that we ought to take advantage of a good opportunity to take up neighborly residence. I told him we'd look into it, and

we said we'd meet again for sure, and left him to keep the summer morning
as it should be kept.

Chapter Seventy-Three

LATE IN THE FALL, Larry told me the following story.

In September he called Johnson Appleton on the phone and told him he
was going to San Francisco to find Eartha and the kids, and asked if Johnson
had heard anything he ought to know.

"They're back in Chico," Johnson said.

"What the hell," Larry said.

"Funny you called," Appleton said, "I was about to call you. They came
back three days ago. I've been trying to find out the story."

"I'm all ears. Did you?"

"Some of it. Orrin Oliver knows Bannister's lawyer, Art Mallory, who
doesn't know that Orrin's working for me. Bannister's wife filed for divorce
and he panicked. He knows she'll clean him out and he'd never get an even
break with Judge Carthage in Oroville because Carthage has known about
Bannister for years. He talked Eartha into coming back to Chico so he could
make a deal with his wife, plus he doesn't want your kids. He wants to keep
his wife happy and keep Eartha in San Francisco without your kids."

"That slimy prick."

"Let me handle this, Larry. If you come out here, you'll make it worse."

"I'm coming. Tell that fucking Bannister that I'm coming."

"Not smart, Larry. If you lay a finger on him, you'll lose everything."

"I'll think about it, but I'm coming."

Larry flew to Chico three days later and went directly to Bannister's office
at the bank, but he wasn't there. The receptionist on the other side of the room
from Bannister's secretary recognized Larry who saw the look between them
when he entered the room. Bannister's secretary said, "Mr. Bannister's out of
town, Mr. Bourke. He's gone on vacation. He won't be back for several weeks."
Larry knew that Johnson Appleton had told Oliver to leak to Bannister
through Mallory that Larry was coming, so Eartha must know also.

Larry played a hunch. He called Skip Garrison on the phone and told
him he was in town to see if he could get his kids back, and asked him for a
favor.

"Anything, buddy," Skip said. Larry asked him if his daughter Gina was
going to baby-sit for Eartha that night.

"By god, she is," Skip said. Eartha had called in the afternoon and said that she wanted to go to the movies with her girlfriend that evening and Gina was going over at 8:00 p.m.

"Thanks Skip. I don't know if I can work this but I'm in your debt."

"The hell you are buddy. Any time. I hope something works out for you."

Larry drove to Raley's drug store and bought an instamatic camera that fitted into his jacket pocket and went to the Oaks looking for Jaeckel but he wasn't there. Larry didn't want to see anyone else, and ate at a small restaurant called Fugio's on the corner of the Esplanade and 8th Street. While he was eating he thought it would be nice to see one of his student friends. He went to the Brazen Onager for a dark beer and didn't recognize anyone, and was relieved. He really didn't want to see anyone.

At 7:45 he drove to Mangrove and parked a hundred yards from Klingman's, where he could see Eartha coming down Third. Sure enough, at 8:10 he saw her in the rear view mirror, rounding the corner. She went into Klingman's for several minutes, then came out again and stood in front, waiting. At 8:15, she started walking toward the street. The cars in back of Larry blocked his view of the car she got into, but in a few seconds Bannister's Cadillac passed Larry going north on Mangrove. Larry kept his hand up to the side of his face until they passed.

He waited until Bannister was far enough ahead so he wouldn't realize he was being tailed, and Larry pulled out. Bannister took a left on 5th Avenue and drove to the Esplanade where he crossed and turned left, heading south. Larry stayed three or four cars behind, following on the Esplanade as it curved around the edge of the college and became Broadway, then down Broadway where Bannister turned right on 5th Street as the light turned. Larry had to wait for the light and lost sight of Bannister until he caught up at the railroad station on the corner of Nord and 5th. Two cars separated them as the light turned.

After the railroad tracks, 5th became Haun Lane. They passed two warehouses and a nursery. One of the cars turned right on Hickory and Larry purposely dropped further behind as Haun Lane became the Chico River Road. When it angled south, Bannister stayed to the right, cutting west on Morehead. The car in front of Larry stayed on the Chico River Road, and Larry dropped further back. Bannister speeded up, and soon Larry was two hundred yards behind him. They were in flat country, almond orchards on both sides of the road, spiny shadows in the early evening dark, darker because there was no moon.

Bannister went about a mile, slowed down, and seemed to turn left into the orchard. Larry slowed further, keeping his eyes on the approximate place where Bannister's car disappeared. He passed two entrances to a circular drive that led to a large house off the road on the edge of an almond orchard. Larry drove for a mile and turned around and drove back. He could see only straight ahead where the beams of his headlights illuminated the road. He drove a hundred yards past the circular drive, turned off his lights and pulled his car as far off the road as he thought safe without getting stuck.

He walked back and entered the first opening of the circular drive. It was a warm night and tree-peeper sounds stopped as he passed a brush thicket. One upstairs light shone in the big house. Bannister's car was nowhere in sight. Larry followed the circular drive through a large rose garden across from rows of almond trees and next to several parking spaces with logs on the ground to separate them. As the circular drive wound back towards the road, there was an open machine shed on the left and a parked tractor.

Leading off from the drive, an orchard road led into the darkness of the trees. Larry followed the road for fifty yards before he saw Bannister's parked car, a black shape in the middle of the orchard thirty yards ahead. Larry stepped between the almond trees and waited. His heart was pounding.

Larry knew it was an old orchard because the trunks of the trees were a foot in diameter. It was harvest season but this orchard was yet untouched, and ripe almonds in their jackets hung down from the branches. Larry's head brushed against them as he ducked through the orchard toward Bannister's parked Cadillac. Larry felt dizzy, then straightened, reaching above his head to make sure he didn't bump it on a low limb. Touching a long and thick arm of an almond tree, he grasped it to steady himself. The bark was prickly, iron rough.

Larry remembered swinging on apple boughs when he was a boy, and it occurred to him that these boughs would cut his hands.

In a few moments the dizziness went away and Larry moved again toward the dark shape of the car. When he got within ten yards, he waited and listened. The car windows were open and he could hear the low tones of their voices. He tried to make out their conversation but it was too muffled, and he waited. He didn't know what he was going to do. He remembered what Appleton said to him on the phone, but he was excited, thrilled in a strange way by the drama of the situation. He smelled smoke and he realized that Eartha was smoking. Bannister didn't smoke.

Soon he saw Eartha's arm stretch out the window, and a lighted cigarette butt traced an arc several feet from the car to the ground. Larry waited. The low monotone of the voices stopped. Larry waited another several minutes and moved closer, ducking down and approaching the long sedan from the rear. He put his hand lightly against the trunk of the car to steady himself as he squatted, and he felt the slight rocking movement of the car.

"Jesus," he said to himself, "they're fucking." He took several deep breaths and stood up and approached the open window on the driver's side of the car.

"Howdy," he said, leaning one arm on the door and looking in. Bannister and Eartha were coupling, Eartha on top with her chin buried against Bannister's shoulder. When Larry spoke, they wrenched together in one movement as Eartha screamed, and Bannister half-groaned and half-gurgled deep in his throat as he tried to get out from under Eartha. Eartha screamed again as they bumped against each other and Eartha was thrown against the steering wheel and then down on the floor. Bannister sensed he was in physical peril and struggled violently to separate himself from Eartha and get out of the car.

Larry, strangely calmed by the psychological violence of his own appearance, said, "You trying to call the cops or something, or do you just want to wake up the people in that house over there?"

Instantly, Eartha and Bannister stopped moving, Eartha's buttock and right leg on the floor to the right of the gear shift, her left knee crooked across Bannister's face, and Bannister underneath her leg, on his back across the seat, his legs toward Larry and his hand over his head frozen where he had been groping for the door handle.

"If you get out of the car, Bannister, I'll keelhaul your baby white ass raw against the side of one of these nice almond trees."

"Eartha baby, our road stops right in this orchard." As he spoke, Larry reached into his pocket, said "Cheese" and took a photograph, the flashbulb brightening the almost-naked bodies in the front seat as if the moon had risen on desperation itself. "I'd take another, but I only need one."

Tears of shame and fury shone in Eartha's eyes, and Bannister, who lost his thick glasses in the turmoil, blinked in terror.

Larry said, "Don't come home tonight, Eartha, or tomorrow, or the next day, or I'll print 2000 copies of this picture and distribute them on the streets of Chico. I'm taking the kids east and my lawyer will prepare the no-fault divorce with me in custody of the kids. Bye bye."

Larry walked back to his car and drove to his former home.

Chapter Seventy-Four

October, 1970

EARLY FALL IS THE best time on Swans Island. The light wind blows from the southwest, and the days are clear and gentle and quiet. One must know the island in the fall to understand what I mean by "gentle." By now, the summer people have drained their water pipes and gone back to their other worlds, the ferry schedule has been reduced, island men gather in the mornings around the Fisherman's Cooperative stove, the color of the island deer grazing backyard grass in late afternoon has changed from buff to dark brown, and on Saturday afternoon in the harbor, while casting a silver jig with a piece of salted pollack or herring on your hook, you can hear the Seabees or the radios on lobster boats moving back and forth to the floating flatcar at the wharf where they unload the day's haul.

Football players are playing out their lives on another planet called the mainland. The normal eleven-foot tide is pulled to twelve and thirteen feet by the gravity of the moon, and clammers dig two tides instead of one. Walking from the wharf to Russell Burns' boatyard, Harbor Island, which blocks all but the narrow channel to the southeast and the wider channel to the southwest, a half mile away, seems a few hundred yards away.

On our own last weekend, Puss and Semantha and I walked past the boatyard, waved to Russell and his son Rusty who were hauling the Davison's black-hulled sloop up the wooden runway, and continued past Normie Burns' wharf at the end of the harbor below the steep bank of blackberry briars, pale fuchsia lupin, and the last goldenrod of summer. Normie and his two sons moved lobsters from his boat into his own floating flatcar anchored a boat length from the end of his wharf. Normie was playing rock and roll tapes on his boat and he didn't hear me when I called to him. We walked up the steep hill leading to the lighthouse and found the blackberries growing on both sides of the road at the top of the hill. The berries were as big as my thumbnail, ebony black, shiny and juicy, full ripe so that they fell into our cupped hands as we coaxed the acorn-size, bunched globules from their stems. Our two-quart tin pails, formerly filled with California almonds, de-labeled and pierced on two sides at the top by an ice pick for a string to run through, hung from our necks. We stained our fingers reddish pink as we filled our pails to the brim, then pyramiding them higher, not wanting to leave a single one on the sun drenched bushes, and pushing the last few we could reach without stepping into the briars, into our mouths.

Several autumns before, during our first visit to the island when we met Captain Clyde Torrey and ploughed the rim of his garden, we had taken Clyde's advice and followed the road past Clyde's farmhouse, looking for the owner of any piece of shore property we might be able to buy. The road went by one old white farmhouse where the oil and stone became gravel, and led through a field to the edge of a spruce forest where a path led down through the trees. We parked the car and followed the path. It was a hot day in the sun but the spruce forest was cool, and in some places the ground was damp where the shore fog had settled during several late afternoons and evenings.

Soon, we could see the water through the trees, and we came out on the shoulder-edge of an arm of land leading on our left to Black Point, and on our right a blue stone beach leading to configurations of coastal granite which curved out of sight towards Red Point, jutting beyond the granite boulders into the blue passage between the Sister Islands and the Point. We stepped to the blue stone beach with walkway boards on the ridge leading to a white shoreline house seventy yards away. To our right, a small pond shimmered in the sun as two sea ducks exploded from the water. There were deer droppings all around us where deer came down through the trees to lap the salt from the tide rocks in the late afternoons. The shutters of the white house were closed, edged with yellow lichen. The only sound was the soft lapping of the half-tide waves at the bottom of the sloping beach.

"Daddy, what's the name of that ring you bought mummy before she died?"

"Sapphire."

"Daddy, this is a sapphire beach. There are zillions of blue stones. Can we buy that house?"

"Whoever owns it probably wants to keep it, but what a perfect place it is. Let's go further and see what else is here."

We walked to the house where a cemented stone wall in front traced the edge of a three foot dropoff to the blue stones leading down to the water. We walked through the grass, avoiding the black clumps of deer droppings, to the back of the house, and shaded our hands and looked in the windows. The interior resembled a doll's house, with nineteenth century furniture and wall bookcases full of books, and a calendar on the kitchen door, and two deer heads on the living room walls. Outside, moss grew on the cedar shingles on the north side of the lower roof.

A rowboat was overturned in the grass, and a second pond became visible as we walked beneath the lower branches of a maple tree and out onto the ridge of a sloping seawall of blue stones that separated the ocean from the second pond. At the end of the seawall, the shoreline became the granite coast of Maine, with almost-flat Brobdingnagian-size boulders of various geometrical shapes, allowing us to traverse the shoreline without walking through the heavy brush on higher ground.

Several hundred yards further we came to another rock beach, miniature in comparison to the previous one, and a small cement and brick fireplace snuggled against the shore and near a path that led up to the land. Looking up from the beach, we could see a small, new, gray clapboard house with new asphalt shingles. A gray-haired man was spreading long black strings of material from a wheelbarrow with a pitchfork. Puss and I walked up the path, and he saw us and said, "Good morning!"

James Gillespie, a semi-retired company president from Duxbury Massachusetts, introduced us to Red Point, and in the next half-hour became our advisor and confidante and friend for life. We met his aproned wife Elsie, a Scotswoman with a Cape Massachusetts accent and a wry, ironic pleasant manner, toured his house with its hand-made half-models and nineteenth century American sea paintings, its beach rock fireplace with its engraved quotation, "They that go down to the sea in ships, receive the blessing of the Lord," and the finest Scots hospitality anywhere in the world save Scotland itself. He told us that land was available down towards Red Point, but that the two lots between his land and the federally protected sea wall, might be coaxed away from Bill Banks, the owner, if we caught him in a good mood. James Gillespie's favorite phrase was "You better believe it," and he dotted his i's and punctuated his agreeable passions with conclusive and dismissive certainty.

Three days later, Larry and I bound our agreement with Bill Banks with a modest check, and within three months owned outright the two acres of shoreline between the Gillespies and the natural sea wall. The following summer we burned scores of brush piles left by loggers ten years before. Larry and Mona came up for two weeks in early July and for another week around Labor Day, and Puss and I and Semantha spent the summer in a tent on the land. Jimmy Gillespie monitored our progress with a daily visit, and we stopped in on Clyde several times a week for the fun of it on the way back from the store. He had become to us, if not the gatekeeper, then certainly our original key to our own Swans Island.

Now on this warm early fall day two years later, Puss and Semantha and I stopped with our blackberries and found Clyde behind his house, asleep in the front seat of his car, the World Series blaring forth in the clear island air on his car radio. His horse Sandy had died suddenly the week before, and he was making his last stand against the elements and the passage of time. He woke as I put my fingers to my mouth to quiet the girls, and his small explosion of exuberance greeted us as if he hadn't seen us for a year. We offered him a portion of our blackberries, which he declined with an impatient wave of his hand, and said he was having stomach troubles. I asked him if he had been able to eat anything that day and he said he had the formula and he was getting his insides back in order. I knew from a previous encounter that it meant he was drinking coffee with a half box of gelatin and a spoonful of Ipecac in it. He knew the Ipecac had opium in it and he said that it settled his stomach.

Semantha, innocent of Clyde's emotional but neutrally motivated outbursts, offered him a peanut butter sandwich left over from our blackberrying picnic lunch, and Clyde exploded with, "Gory sakes NO, if I ate a spoonful of peanut butter I'd be up 'sides father in ten minutes!" He meant in the cemetery on the Atlantic loop road. Semantha jumped an inch when he said it, but I squeezed her hand and winked at her and she recovered.

Clyde saw that he had shocked her and he smiled at her and said tenderly, "Thank you, missy dear," which he pronounced "Dee Ah," and patted her shoulder. Then he looked at me and said, "When you have a spare moment, I need a favor." I spent the next hour and a half on the roof of his house, laying two unrolled lengths of tarpaper on his roof and nailing it down under old boards laid parallel on the slope of the dilapidated roof.

Back at Red Point, we arrived to see Larry and Mona pouring cement into sono tubes that would become the underpinnings of their summer house. Larry's son Nicholas mushed and pushed his yellow and red plastic trucks into and around the sand pile next to our new well. We shared the cost of the well drilling, and hit water at 212 feet.

"Columbus never saw this part of America," Larry said, mixing cement and sand and water with a hoe in the wooden box trough.

"I'll bet the Vikings were here," Mona said. "This is Viking country."

A breeze had blown up, and a sailboat heading through the tide rip between the western Sister and Red Point was dipping and rising against the rip. We could hear the flap of the canvas sails as they snapped in the crosswind.

"When can we go out in the boat again, daddy?" Puss said. "You said there's good wind this time of year. Why did you have Mr. Burns drag it out of the water so soon?"

"Well, 'can' is correct. I have to be a better sailor. Mr. Gillespie is going to give me lessons next summer."

"May Semanth come?"

"If Mr. Gillespie is there, she may."

Puss and Semantha and I went back to my lot and I resumed nailing the two-by-eights across the six-by-sixes. Larry and I decided to build our summer houses side by side. Later, as we all sat eating our beans and hot dogs on the picnic table, we watched a deer come ashore and lay exhausted on the edge of the seawall. It had swum all the way from the nearer of the Sister Islands.

Chapter Seventy-Five

LARRY AND I TALKED about the past several times that year but never reached any conclusions because things were turning up along the way, and all we ever really needed was the privilege of new observations. Our own past attempts to change things had merely worked along the edges of events that reduced our flyspeck existence to a metaphor of small worlds whirling in a universe of universes.

We tried to give ourselves even chances for happiness by participating without regret in the fates that provide beginnings as well as closings. Finally, one August after two drizzly weeks of socked-in, foggy tent talk, we tired of the talk about our past lives, and neither of us, without an agreement, ever felt the need to use the word "friendship" again.

Eartha moved back east a year later and got a job teaching first grade in Lawrence, Massachusetts. Johnson Appleton wrote me that Bannister's wife didn't divorce him after all, and he was having an affair with a tall blonde from Red Bluff. The following year Eartha moved in with her bachelor brother in Durfee. She picked up Semantha and Nicholas every other weekend and for a month every summer. She was entitled to the whole summer but when she found out that they could spend a month with Puss and me on the island, she wanted them to have that.

I saw her once, a couple months after she returned from San Francisco, when she brought back the children one Sunday night in North Brookfield, and she was friendly and sadly exuberant. For some reason she made a point of telling me that she had quit smoking, maybe because she was battling a slight double chin, but she looked sturdy rather than chubby, and she was still beautiful. I never saw her again. Larry told me later that he felt unencumbered when he saw her, merely that, but that he would have asked her to come back if he hadn't met Mona.

Epilogue

1970

IN THE FALL, AFTER the California almonds are harvested, new buds form on the branches, but they do not grow until spring. In the meantime, the trees must be pruned and the cut branches swept into piles and hauled away to be burned. During the northern California winter, pots filled with fuel oil are lined between the rows for smudge fires that will protect, with the help of wind machines, the early buds from frost.

After the winter rains and the cool beginnings of spring, the tips of flower petals appear on the pointed, acorn-like buds. When the buds burst, the orchards are full of bees.

Up close, an almond blossom is pinkish white, deep pink in the center, five-petaled and slightly cup-like, each petal a squarish pentagonal cape narrowing to the center. The tiny center itself is pale green, and from it spreads an array of minuscule yellow-headed stamens. From a distance, the almond orchard in full bloom is queenly and dazzling, white upturned wedding petticoats.

One day in the early Western Massachusetts spring following the election of Richard Nixon to the presidency of the United States, the forsythia bloomed in our front yard. Puss asked if she could cut some branches to go with the pussy willows we had picked in the wetland on the other side of the road near our water well. When she came into the house holding the cut forsythia, she told me that she had been thinking for a long time about the almond blossoms in California.

"They're probably in bloom right now," I said.

"I know it," she said, and went into her room with the glossy white little girl's furniture, to do her homework.

When I asked her later if she was OK, she said she was.

"What about the almond blossoms?" I said.

"Nothing," she said, looking out the window at the stream of cars moving along Old Hatfield Road.

"Come on, tell me."

"When I think of them, they remind me of mummy, that's all."

"That's really all?"

It wasn't all, and we talked for a long time that afternoon. We decided that we would fly to California and bring Ceil back home. When I told Puss that she could decide when we would go, she thought about it for several days and said, "In the fall when they harvest the almonds. I never saw them do it. I saw the spring blossoms but I never saw the harvest. If we are going to get mummy and bring her home, I want to do it when all the almonds are ripe. I know I'll have to miss school. Is that OK?"

"It's OK."

We called Jaeckel and told him of our plans and he agreed to call us with a couple weeks notice sometime in late August or early September. I gave him Jimmy Gillespie's telephone number on Swans Island in case he called before Labor Day.

He called September eighth, and Puss and I flew to California in early

October. I had booked rooms at the Oaks but Jaeckel picked us up at the Chico airport and insisted we stay at his ranch out on Ord Ferry Road. The days were still warm and the almonds were ripe, and we stayed four days. John sat Puss in his lap as he drove the "knocking" truck, hammering the trunks of the trees. Long rectangular prongs in the shape of tuning forks vibrated the trees, showering the almonds to the ground. A mechanical sweeper, attached beneath the truck, swept the almonds aside into rows so they wouldn't be crushed by the wheels. Jaeckel let Puss drive the pickup machine that scooped up the almonds in their husks and blew away the leaves and dirt.

For those four days it rained almonds in Jaeckel's orchards, pattering the top of the vibrator's cabin like marbles bouncing in all directions. John let Puss control the mechanical bumper, and he smiled his toothy, beady-eyed smile as Puss engaged the base of the vibrating fork against the trees and the harvest was time-stopped and life itself raining from the sky, full in the autumn sun, fruit all over the ground, and a little girl was happy.

"Ruth liked the harvest, the best time of the year," John said one night after dinner as we walked along the dry creek bed that followed the edge of the orchard. As we walked, coveys of black and white California quail flushed from the dry overhanging vines. "She came to this valley from the wheat fields of the great bend in the Columbia River country." As we walked, John told me some of Ruth's story.

"Her mother was a Davenport and they raised wheat and hops there. Her father was a County Sligo Colleary and for three generations they ran cattle and raised fine horses. Ruth took me back there once and she made me drive first to the Grand Coulee Dam. South of the Grand Coulee the ferry crosses the Columbia and the road snakes through the bluffs onto the high plateau. Ahead lay Goldendale, Toppenish, Wapato and Yakima. The great escarpment of the Cascades lie to the west and to the east there are the irrigated farms wrested from the sage. On farther are the wheat fields.

"Her father and brothers grazed cattle from the Columbia along the Cascades to Canadian border country, through snowy winters, chopping ice to water the beasts during the deep frost and taking them high into the hills in summer. That was the land of the Yakima Indians, and Ruth grew up among them, picking blueberries on the high glades of the mountains in summer with members of that tribe.

"Ruth taught school at Enterprise on Walloma Lake in eastern Oregon's Blue Mountains, and later walked here in the peace marches, standing with Women for Peace. She was at Harry Truman's train stop here in the valley, in Gerber.

"She used to have a yard full of flowers. A few of the roses still bloom."

We had walked far along the creek, and Puss and I listened as John talked, head down, rapt in reminiscence. At a turn in the creek bed, John led us up a small incline beside a ditch cut through heavy brush on the side of the creek and we could see back through the long rows of almond trees. We were in an older part of the orchard west of John's younger trees, and the black trunks of the trees here were gnarled and scaly, and the overhead branches needed pruning.

"We'll do these in a couple weeks after we get the best crop in. I should have cut this section back but I haven't found the time these past few years. We knew Ruth was going to die and I somehow just let it go. Maybe I'll get to it one of these days." As we walked back to the house, a jackrabbit appeared thirty yards ahead, then burst in one leap across the row and disappeared in mid-flight.

"They haunt the place," John said. "I used to shoot them to keep my eye for deer season, but Ruth scolded me for it. I don't do it any more. There are better ways, I guess, to keep your eye peeled on moving things."

At the end of our visit, we decided to drive rather than fly, and began our journey home, riding long hours every day in the back seat behind the driver of the hearse. It took six days to cross the country, through Donner Pass, across the Nevada desert, the salt desert to Salt Lake City, the Old Oregon Trail as far as Kearney, Nebraska, route 30 to Chicago, then the turnpikes home. On the third day, we were driving by a stand of cottonwood trees along the North Platte River, and Puss asked me if we could plant an almond tree in the Sunderland graveyard where her mother would be buried. I explained that almond trees wouldn't survive the New England winters, but that hickory trees bore nuts every fall, and that if we beat the squirrels to them, we could dry them and eat them and they would be very sweet. We could plant a hickory tree.

"I like that, daddy," she said.

"We'll have to wait a few years for it to grow," I said, "quite a few."

"That's OK," she said, "Mummy will be waiting with us."

Late in the afternoon of the fourth day, we were driving along the old Lincoln highway in Illinois, and Puss said, "We're lucky to be alive, aren't we, daddy?"

"Yes, we are, honey, and I love you, and your mother loves you very much."

"I know. Thank you for bringing mummy home. Before we went back to Chico this time, I thought about her being alone, and sometimes I cried. I wanted her to come alive again and come to us, but I knew I was making up something that couldn't be true. Now it will always be all right, I know it. I don't even have to talk about it any more. I think I can grow up now without being sad, and I can think of California and not be sad either. I can remember

Mr. Jaeckel and me in the bump bump machine and the almonds coming down all around us, and how he was happy a little bit even though Mrs. Jaeckel died and he loved her very much. I know that you think of mummy a lot too, and maybe now that she will be with us, maybe you can be a little happy once in a while too."

And so we passed by Lake Erie and into New York, past the Finger Lakes and the Cherry Valley, and into Massachusetts. When we arrived in our little town on the afternoon of the sixth day, it was Indian summer, and the light was warm and soft. I remembered that someone reminded me once that the sunlight in the Connecticut Valley is the only light in the world that equals the light of Florence, Italy, and on that sixth day we entered that light and felt its warmth, and knew that we were home.